# DEATH AT WILL

## TAM MAY

**Death At Will**

*Adele Gossling Mysteries: Book 3*

**Tam May**

Published by Dreambook Press.



Click or visit:
https://www.tammayauthor.com

Cover Design © 2022 by Aries/100 Covers

ISBN: 9780998338583 (Print)
ISBN: 9780998338590 (ebook)

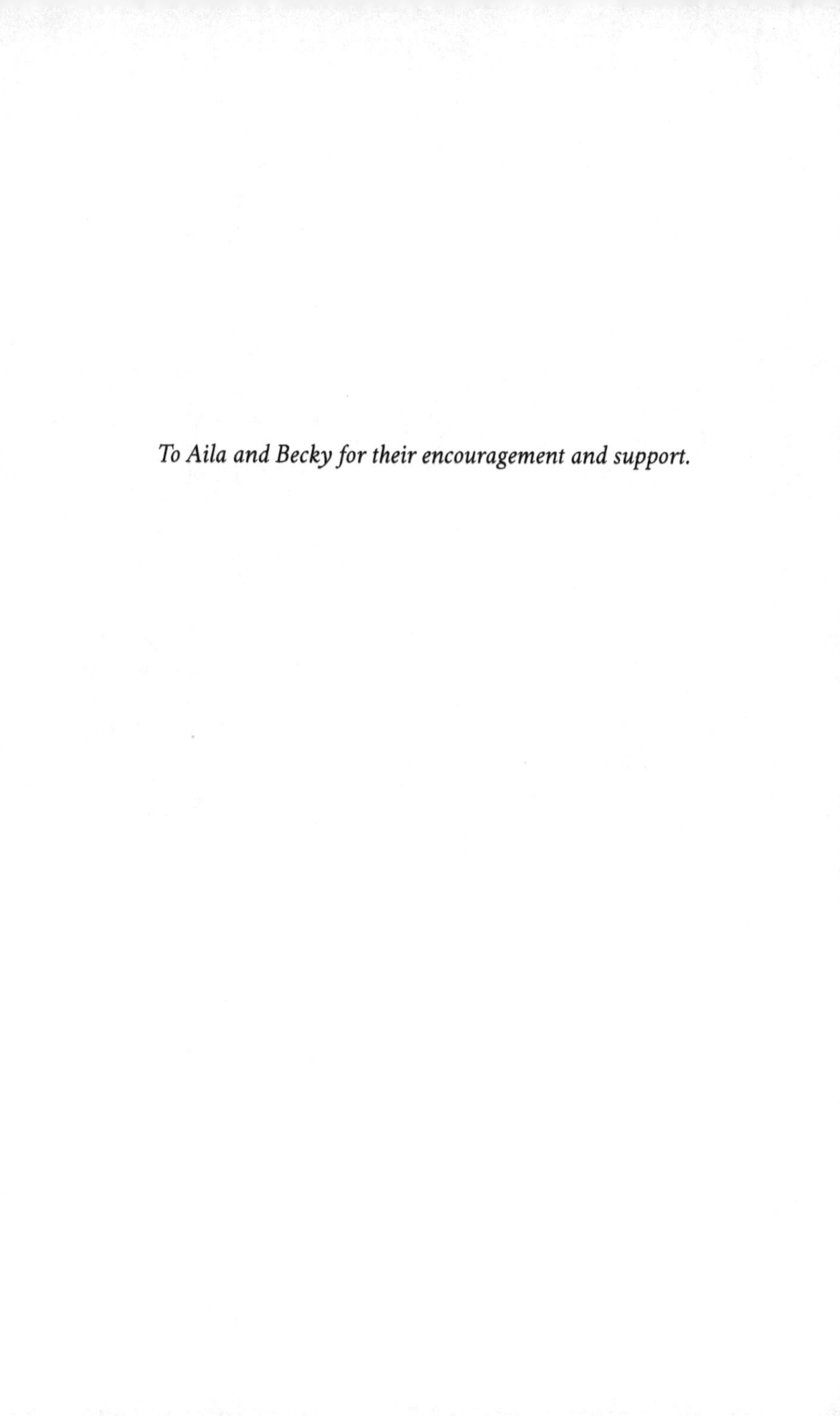

*To Aila and Becky for their encouragement and support.*

# CHAPTER 1

If you're interested in reading more early 20th century mysteries, my free offer at the end of this book is for you! So don't forget to check that out when you get to the end. Happy reading!

It was a blistering morning in late March during an election year, and Arrojo citizens were reeling from the visit from Theodore Roosevelt and Charles Fairbanks. When Missy Grace published an editorial about Mr. Roosevelt's ideas of fairness and conscience, Mrs. Faderman refuted it to whomever would listen at Raleigh's General Store, Ada's Millinery, and Dora's Tea Shop. In spite of their abhorrence of women's suffrage, Mrs. Faderman and her brood exercised their political opinions with the gusto of a beer garden on a Friday night.

The one place the ladies kept their opinions to themselves was Adele's Stationery. In the two years since Adele settled into country life, her progressive views had not changed though even Mrs. Faderman had to admit she didn't go "marching about with banners" or throw stones at the mayor's window. Because of this, people had adjusted to her outspoken ways and even her forward-thinking way of life, right down to her noisy Beaton Roundabout.

Mrs. Faderman's tight lips were sealed the days following Roosevelt's visit. Most shopkeepers on Bridge Street had removed the banners declaring "A safety's the score, Parker & Davis 1904!" from their windows as the town threw itself into preparations for the Easter holiday.

Adele was in her shop with her friend Nin Branch when the door creaked open and a lady stepped over the threshold. The woman was as smart and sporty in her appearance as any New Women that Adele knew in the city. Her gray suit hung in crisp folds against her shoulders and smooth across her waist, and her hair glossed bright red under the modest hat. Her picante face showed signs of one who would not shy away from a battle once she was pulled into it.

"Good afternoon," she said. "Mrs. Brown said you might help me."

"Mrs. Brown?"

"She means that old bloodhound Zephyr," Nin mumbled. She and the junk collector had a long-standing feud.

"Oh, Mrs. Brown!" Adele blinked. "I wouldn't think a young woman like you would know Zephyr."

She smiled. "Mrs. Brown and my grandmother were great friends."

"You live in Arrojo?" Adele asked.

"I do now," said the woman. "I grew up in Rosa Gris."

"I didn't think I'd ever seen you before," Adele said.

The woman held out her hand. "Rebecca Gold. You might be surprised to learn I know all about *you*, Miss Gossling."

"Indeed?" Adele straightened a display on an antique desk near the entrance to the shop.

"A lady detective," Miss Gold continued. "A rare thing in a town like this."

"Not so rare when you consider Adele is the deputy sheriff's sister," Nin said.

"Deputy Sheriff's sister or not, I'm not a detective," Adele insisted. "Perhaps I do occasionally interest myself in police business —"

"Don't apologize," said Miss Gold. "I rather think if more women would interest themselves in crime and punishment, we might all be better off."

"Your knowledge of crime is admirable," Adele said. "You were a secretary or a clerk?"

The young lady smiled. "I'm a lawyer, Miss Gossling."

"How delightful!" Adele took her arm. "There ought to be more lady lawyers just as there ought to be more lady detectives."

The woman laughed. "Perhaps we'll start a craze."

"Perhaps we will," Adele said. "Now, what can I do for you?"

The woman shifted her purse from one wrist to the other. "I have a client who wishes to draw up her will, and she's most particular about the materials. She gave me exact instructions." She handed Adele a short list.

Adele examined it. "The ink I have," she said. "As to the pens, I have the new Parker fountain pen, which is not quite what the lady asks for, but close enough."

"I should think Thea would fire me if I brought anything other than what she wrote," Miss Gold remarked. "She's — well, she's rather exacting."

Adele nodded. "As to the paper — well, I'm afraid I haven't any in stock. It's not the sort of thing Arrojo citizens use."

"A lady lawyer is little better than a persnickety cat, said the man," Nin mumbled.

Miss Gold whirled around, staring at her with almost frightened eyes. "Those are nearly the words my last employer used before I left!"

Nin slunk down with her hands close to the fire. Adele explained, "My friend sees and feels things no one else does."

"Branch," Miss Gold repeated. "Any relation to Atha Branch?"

This made Nin's face turn white. "My mother."

"My grandmother and your mother knew one another," said Miss Gold. "Granny had a great respect for her knowledge of herbs, though not many around here did."

The paleness turned a shade darker and Nin looked out the display window.

"I would be happy to order the paper for you," Adele said. "I've a shipment coming the day after tomorrow and I can add it to my order. Would that do?"

"That would be perfect." Miss Gold fumbled for coins in her purse. She was clearly disturbed at Nin's silence as she kept glancing at the dark woman whose silhouette created an angelic glare in the light. "Miss Branch, I'm terribly sorry if I said something —"

Nin gave a wan smile. "I oughtn't to be so sensitive about it anymore."

"No hard feelings, then?"

"Not in the least." Nin stuck out her hand, and, a little surprised, Miss Gold took it.

"May I offer recompense?" she asked.

"It's not necessary." Adele smiled. "It's compensation enough for us to be friends. Call us Adele and Miss Branch."

"Call me Anita," Nin chimed in. Adele glanced in surprise, as her friend hardly let anyone call her by her first name.

The woman smiled. "You're very kind. I was referring to refreshment. I lived in England for a time, and I got rather spoiled with the five o'clock tea. I noticed a delightful tea shop just across the street."

Adele pulled down the blind of the windows. "We were going to take some tea anyway."

"You may as well come with us," Nin said in her blunt, child-like way.

They trudged across the street and entered Dora's Tea Shop. The place smelled of leaves and vanilla, as Adele remembered of the tea shops she had gone to with her father as a child. The bright pink and cream decor soothed her as much as the tea. Every now and then, when someone opened the door, a whiff of scones or cream flew out into the street.

The tea loosened Rebecca's tongue as she told them of her journey back "home." "Granny was the only one who thought I could make something of myself as a lawyer," she said. "My parents were dead set against it. They wanted me to marry the son of a friend."

"That's always the way," Adele sympathized. "Marriage as the cure for womanly ambition." She tried not to sound bitter.

"One night, Granny slipped into my room with a bundle in her hands wrapped in old stockings. She untied them, and out spilled masses of coins. She'd saved them from the household money, slipping a penny here and a dime there into her pocket when Mama wasn't looking. They were meant for her burial but she insisted she'd rather see them spent on my lawyer's certification than gold trim for her coffin."

"A formidable woman," Nin remarked, spreading cherry preserves on a scone.

"Indeed she was," said Rebecca. "I didn't want the money, but she said she would tell Arnold — that was the young man — what I really thought of him in front of his parents if I didn't take it." She grinned. "Arnold's mother was one of those holy terrors one would rather avoid."

Adele smiled. "So you avoided the rampage and took the money."

"I went to Northwestern University to study law," she continued.

"Just like Mrs. Kepley." Adele nodded.

"I was determined to do right by Granny," she said. "I did better than most of the men in my class."

"Working three times harder and getting three times less the recognition," Nin growled.

"They could be quite brutal," Rebecca agreed. "Not that it disturbed me in the least. Granny taught me to stand up for myself." She sipped her tea. "I've been kicking boys in the knee since I was five years old."

Adele laughed.

"I managed to get a job as a legal assistant at Fox & Benton in Chicago."

Adele raised her eyebrow. "Rather prominent."

"How did you know that?" She stared at her. "You're right, of course. They are prominent, but only in Chicago."

"My father was a criminal lawyer in San Francisco," said Adele. A wave of pain went through her as it always did when she thought of Otis Gossling, now four years dead. "He had connections all over the country."

"They took on some rather bold clients." Rebecca poured herself another cup of tea while the waitress slid a plate of fresh strawberries onto the table, indicating they were a gift from Dora. "Businessmen who could rival Rockefeller in their arrogance and self-righteousness. One even put a knife in his rival's heart and thought it justified."

"Men behave like children when it comes to money," Nin snorted.

Rebecca laughed. "I almost think Mr. Fox and Mr. Benton would have jumped for joy if I had offered to take that client on."

"They eventually allowed you to take on clients?" Adele asked.

Rebecca's gray eyes turned stony. "Mr. Fox and Mr. Benton were contented to let me pour the coffee and file the paperwork. They thought I ought to be grateful to them for letting me sit in the back of the courtroom."

Adele nodded. "I've met many abled women in offices whose minds were withering away over the refuse and paper."

"Exactly," said the woman. "One morning when I came in, took the cover off my typewriter and folded it into a neat little square, I realized Granny's sacrifice — she died only a month before — would go to naught if I allowed myself to wither away any longer."

"So you came here to start your own practice?" Adele asked.

The woman nodded, her face pale. "I couldn't go back to Rosa Gris. Oh, I suppose I could have but — well, I preferred coming here."

"Let us be the first to welcome you to Arrojo," Adele said. "I know how alienating it can be to come to a small town like this where no one knows you. I was lucky enough to have a kind family make me feel welcome when I first came."

"They ought to have welcomed you," Nin said, "after what you did for their son."

Adele blushed. "That wasn't me, dear. That was the law taking its course."

The lawyer leaned her chin in her hand. "It seems you and I are on the same side."

"You fancy yourself an avenger of crime?" Adele asked, a twinkle in her eye.

"Perhaps I shall be one day," Rebecca said. "I imagine there's hardly more than an occasional theft or drunken brawl in a small place like this."

"We have our share of tragedies," Adele said.

Rebecca gathered her gloves and bag. "If my first client is something to go by, I don't anticipate much strife."

"The lady with the list?" Adele smiled.

The woman nodded. "Do you know the Marshes?"

Adele shook her head. "Not from Arrojo, I gather."

"They once lived here, but they built a mansion outside of Rosa Gris," said Rebecca. "They're quite prominent."

"A lucky thing to have them as your first clients, then," Nin said.

"I've known the Marshes since childhood," said the woman. "Not very well, of course. They weren't the sort of family to which one could get close."

"Moneyed people usually aren't," said Adele.

"Thea hired me," the woman continued. "She runs the family, you might say, with an iron hand."

"But she isn't very well," Adele guessed, "so she wants to put her affairs in order." Rebecca stared at her. "The exactness of the paper and the fountain pen gave it away. My father once told me people become most peculiar when they're attending to their death papers."

The door flew open and Mrs. Faderman marched in, her plumbed hat tipped to one side. Behind her, Mrs. Lynn scurried like a mouse, followed by Mrs. Cricket, Mrs. Abberton, and several other ladies from Arrojo's high society. Mrs. Faderman's eyes were gleaming, and her mouth twisted as if barely able to contain her rage. Adele exchanged a look with Nin, who was already leaning with her chin in the bridge of her hands with anticipation.

"Tell Miss Lesley we want to see her at once!" Mrs. Faderman ordered.

The young lady behind the cash register flinched. Dora stepped out a pair of swinging doors, wiping her hands on her apron. Though she was smaller and rounder than Mrs. Faderman, she looked impressively fierce. "May I help you, Mrs. Faderman?"

"On the contrary," said the woman, "we've come to help *you*."

Dora glanced around the shop, which was not very full at that hour. "I suggest we retire to my office to discuss any trouble —"

"Trouble?" the woman bellowed. "My dear, you'll have trouble unless you get rid of those!" Her long finger pointed at a row of tin boxes on the shelf. Their labels shone magnificently in the sunlight.

Dora looked puzzled. "The *aanand* teas? What's the matter with them?"

"Poison!" Mrs. Faderman spit the word out.

"Now, Irene, we can't be certain —" Mrs. Lynn ventured.

"Of course we're certain!" Mrs. Abberton flung her curled head back. "Mabel's as sick as a dog, is she not?"

"It could have been the cucumbers or the peaches —"

"Are you insinuating my peaches were rotten, Caroline?" This shrill demand came from Mrs. Cricket.

"Perhaps you should explain what all this is about, Mrs. Faderman," Dora said in a firm voice.

The woman folded her hands. "Belinda invited us all to tea to meet her cousin from Salt Lake City and served the red tea you recommended."

"She asked for a soothing tea," Dora interrupted.

"Perhaps she ought to have given her a mouth-shutting tea," Nin growled.

"Soothing!" Mrs. Faderman said. "Miss Lesley, less than half an hour later, Belinda's cousin, took to her bed with — well, it isn't very pretty."

"And why, pray, have you and the rest of the ladies not taken to your beds?" Dora raised her eyebrow. "I assume you drank the same tea?"

"That's right, Irene." Mrs. Lynn jumped forward. "We all drank the same tea."

"But we, Caroline, are from rugged Western stock." The woman's chest heaved like a robin's. "Mabel, I fear, is of a more delicate Eastern constitution." Mrs. Cricket hunched her shoulders as if ashamed of her relative.

"So because one person embarrassed you with her so-called 'delicate Eastern constitution,' you assume it was my tea?"

"I was *not* embarrassed!" the woman snarled. "I here because I'm very much concerned for the community."

"I'm sure you are," Dora said calmly.

"Who knows what these foreigners put in these overseas products?" Mrs. Faderman sniffed.

"I have it on good authority from my friend the teas are very pure," Dora insisted.

"Nevertheless, we insist you take them off the shelf and send them back to where they came from immediately."

"How extraordinary!" Rebecca declared.

"Mrs. Faderman is an extraordinary woman," Adele said.

"In her eyes, at least," Nin added.

"Perhaps Mrs. Cricket's cousin was expecting the watered-down leaves Mr. Raleigh sells," Dora declared, "or perhaps she has no taste for good, strong tea. Wouldn't surprise me in the least." The last was said under her breath.

"I'll thank you to be respectful, Miss Lesley," Mrs. Faderman snapped. "Remember your position."

"My position, ma'am, is to provide my customers with specialties they can't get elsewhere at the best value they can find," the woman said. "Commerce is rather sordid, I know, but necessary."

Mrs. Faderman winced.

"I would never give my customers anything I haven't sampled myself," Dora continued. "I've sampled every one of those teas and, as you can see, I'm hardly the worst for it." She put her hands on her hips. One could not deny, despite her small stature, her frame was muscular.

"Are you saying I'm a liar?" Mrs. Faderman narrowed her eyes.

"I am saying, ma'am, as the owner of this shop, I have a right to decide what I will and will not sell," Dora said. "If this woman did indeed get sick, I suggest you look at the remnants of her plate for evidence of overindulgence."

"Indeed?" Mrs. Faderman flared. "We shall see about that!" She walked out of the shop with the others trailing behind her.

The moment they were gone, a general buzz came from the few patrons who were left, smiles ricocheting around, as most were familiar with Mrs. Faderman and her outbursts.

"Does she huff and puff like that all the time?" Rebecca asked when they left the shop.

"Not all the time, but often enough to provide entertainment." Adele laughed.

"Dora was rather insistent those teas were all right," the lawyer said. "Still, I'm glad we ordered a domestic brand."

"It takes much to poison tea," Nin said with a knowing air.

Rebecca adjusted her hat against the wind. "Thea has a taste for exotic teas. I drank one of her blends once. The bitterness lingered on my tongue for days."

Adele laughed. "I can't imagine anyone serving poisoned tea to those ladies, though perhaps the thought might cross someone's mind."

"Let us hope not," Rebecca said. "You may find your detecting talents called upon again." She waved as she trudged down the street.

# CHAPTER 2

That night after dinner, as she and her brother Jackson were sitting in the parlor with a fire going, Adele told him about Rebecca Gold.

"A lawyer in Arrojo?" He lit his pipe. "I imagine she won't find much work here."

"You didn't think you would find much work here when you took on the job of deputy, did you?" Adele pointed out. "I don't see you and the sheriff sitting idle."

"Law and order is always necessary, Del," he said. "Even a country deputy has enough to preoccupy him."

"You seem to have more preoccupation in Rosa Gris than Arrojo lately," Adele remarked.

"Rosa Gris is growing," he said. "What with the new oil refinery outside of town. There are even rumors the Marsh Lumber Mill is going to be expanding soon."

"Marsh," Adele murmured. "Rebecca mentioned a Thea Marsh this afternoon." She played with her unfinished lacework. "Have you ever met the Marshes, Jack?"

"They would hardly be amiable to the police," he said. "There was some dispute one time between the lumberjacks and managers and the sheriff was called in, but Theodore Marsh settled things admirably."

"The favored son," Adele guessed.

Jackson looked at her over the curls of smoke from his pipe. "Did Miss Gold tell you that?"

"A mother who names her son after herself can only think of him as a saint."

Her brother laughed. "Only you would notice such trifles, Del."

"You never know, dear brother," she said in a cheerful voice. "It may not turn out to be such a trifle after all."

He snorted. "You see crime in every corner since you thrust yourself into the Blackstone case."

"I helped you with the Blackstone case," she corrected. "Even the sheriff said so."

"Hatfield is a very easy-minded man," he said. "He gives you too many liberties for my taste, and I've told him so."

"What did he say?"

"Wouldn't you like to know?" With a gleam in his eye, her brother took up the evening paper.

~~~~~

It took a week as well as several calls to the distributor to get the paper Rebecca ordered, as he was one of those men who never took a woman, even one running her own shop, seriously. Adele learned early on such men would only soften with time when they saw she was capable of perseverance and wily negotiation.

The paper arrived soon after lunch and she took advantage of the mild weather to close her shop and walk to Rebecca's office to deliver it herself. The alleyway was on the other side of the riverbed in the direction of where the more common elements of town began. Farther down was Quarry Lane which prominent Arrojo citizens regarded as little better than a lighter version of the Barbary Coast. Adele had been there once during the Black-
~~~~~

stone case.

But Adele's mind was not on crime that afternoon. She had received a telegram that morning from her and Jackson's favorite aunt in Santa Barbara inviting them down for the holiday, and she was thinking about how she would persuade Nin to join them.

She arrived at the office just as the lawyer was locking up, her parasol hung over her wrist and her hat skewed on her head.

"You look like you're in a hurry," Adele remarked.

"One doesn't keep Thea Marsh waiting," said Rebecca. "Even her daughter comes hurrying up the stairs when her mother calls."

"Then perhaps you can make Mrs. Marsh happy by giving her this." Adele unrolled the paper. "Is that to your liking?"

"More importantly, will it be to Thea's liking." Rebecca examined it. "I'm just on my way to the house now." She looked thoughtful. "You could come with me."

"And meet the iron hand?" Adele smiled.

"You could explain to her better than I about the paper," she said. "If she has questions."

"You anticipate she will?"

"She asks questions about everything." Rebecca looked tired.

Adele rolled up the paper and took her arm. "Two feisty ladies can placate a dragon better than one."

"She's not a dragon, really." Rebecca motioned her toward the hired wagon a little way down the street. "She knows what she wants and she's not shy about demanding it." She glanced at the clock in the window of the bank building. "And she demands everybody be on time."

"Then we'll dismiss the wagon and take my Beaton," Adele suggested. "It's only down the road."

Rebecca gave her a half-smile. "I heard about your automobile. You must frighten people here to death with it."

Adele couldn't help but smile as she remembered rumbling

down Bridge Street in the Beaton two years before while Arrojo citizens, including Mrs. Faderman and Mrs. Lynn, stared as if a herd of buffalo had just trampled through town.

Driving in the Beaton Roundabout on such a lovely day made both women feel even more at ease and they chatted about San Francisco. The route to the Marsh house was thankfully better paved than most roads leading into town and there was even the scent of honeysuckle dotting the narrow path leading up to the house.

It was indeed a large house, though not as large as the house of the Blackstones, her former neighbors. Its box style was plain but expansive and the gardens circled the drive. A man with a stoop appeared with a hoe. He greeted them in a cordial and reserved manner and offered to put the car away, but Adele preferred to park the Beaton herself.

She expected a tight-lipped servant to answer the door and keep them waiting in the hall while he saw if "the madame was in." But instead, a middle-aged woman led them into a large and cozy bedroom.

Adele could see why Rebecca was so nervous about the paper. Thea Marsh had all the regal countenance and posture of a queen, and her greeting to Adele when the lawyer introduced her oozed commandment. Her appearance was immaculate right down to the combs sweeping up her streaked dark hair and the wakefulness in her dark eyes. Adele guessed that, in her youth, Mrs. Marsh had been described as more handsome than pretty.

"My daughter reads me the newspaper so of course I have heard of your exploits," the woman said.

"Exploits?" Adele accepted the chair Rebecca offered.

A wary look appeared in the dark eyes. "You work with the police, don't you?"

"Sometimes," Adele said. "I take it you don't approve."

The woman looked at her diffidently. "Whether I or anyone

approves doesn't seem to matter much to young ladies like you and Rebecca these days, does it?"

"No, I can't say it does," Adele said softly.

"Perhaps that's the way it should be," Mrs. Marsh admitted.

"You must be glad Rebecca decided to set up her office in Arrojo," Adele said, "or you wouldn't have called upon her."

The woman smiled, but it was almost reluctant. "You're quite right, Miss Gossling. I confess, had my husband been alive, I should have followed his lead and hired a man. But then, I wouldn't have reason to hire anybody if he were alive."

"You mean he would have taken care of everything," Adele guessed.

"I mean he would have taken care of everything." She put emphasis on the last word.

"I often feel it's sometimes a lucky thing when women are left to take care of their own affairs," Adele said. "It forces us to admit we can handle things as well as they can. In some cases, we handle them even better."

Adele could feel Rebecca's alarmed stare, but Thea smiled, a genuine smile this time.

"I don't hold the same prejudices as my husband, Miss Gossling," the woman said. "Not when a woman must work to earn her keep, as, sadly, many do nowadays."

"My brother was just telling me last night how Rosa Gris has been growing the past few months." Adele nodded.

"Arrojo will be bigger in five years, mark my words."

"The Marshes know all about such things," Rebecca chimed in. "Their business is lumber, you know."

"Yes, I know."

"Theo — my son — just signed a contract with the housing development over near Barn Street," said Thea. "A hundred houses to start!"

"Those are residences, not businesses," Adele pointed out.

"That will come too, my dear," the woman assured her. "Theo said it will come, and if Theo said it, it will happen."

Adele saw her guess about Theodore Marsh being the favored son had been right. "As my father used to say, ma'am, from your mouth to God's ears."

The woman looked at her sharply. "A rather blasphemous statement."

"My father was a lawyer, and he never minced words."

Mrs. Marsh sighed, adjusting the blanket. "Men say what they like, don't they?"

"And rarely phrase what they say delicately," Adele added.

The woman rewarded her with another genuine smile. "That remark earns you a cup of very special tea, Miss Gossling. I see you brought my paper." She indicated the roll under Adele's arm.

Mrs. Marsh examined it as an expert would, even putting on a pair of pince-nez to look at it more closely. Adele pressed her hands together to stop them from trembling.

"It's fine paper, Thea," Rebecca said in a hopeful tone.

Mrs. Marsh rolled it up and handed it to Rebecca. "Miss Gossling's shop has an excellent reputation, even here in Rosa Gris. It's why I sent you there."

Adele blushed. "Thank you for the compliment, ma'am." She caught Rebecca's relieved expression from the corner of her eye.

Mrs. Marsh rang the bell. "Ella, some tea, please. I think the *shaanti* blend will do."

Rebecca hid a wince and Adele guessed it was one of the bitter teas her friend told her about.

"Now there's a business I'd like to see," Mrs. Marsh remarked as the middle-aged woman departed. "A shop with blends from all over the world."

"Dora Lesley has a fine tea shop," Rebecca pointed out. "We were there not long ago."

"Tea shop!" The woman scoffed. "More of a cake shop. I asked Theo to tell her she ought to bring in more teas from the Orient."

"She took your advice," Adele said. "She now has Indian teas on her shelves."

"Yes, I know." Mrs. Marsh sounded almost triumphant. "Theo brought me several to try."

"I hear they're quite good," Rebecca ventured.

"They're all right," said the woman. "Mona thinks they're as good the teas in Bengal but I completely disagree."

"Oh, you've been to India?" Adele asked.

The woman looked at her with an air of knowing. "I've had teas from every country in the world, Miss Gossling. I know a superior tea when I taste one."

"Yes, of course." Adele backed down.

"Mona and her husband lived in India for many years," Rebecca supplied.

The tray was brought in. Adele studied the bright green tea, its scent sour and floral.

"I'm sorry my friend Anita Branch isn't here," Adele said. "She's an herbal expert."

"Yes, I've heard of Miss Branch and her healing gifts," said the woman. From the stodgy tone in her voice, Adele guessed she didn't think much of what she had heard.

"She's really very knowledgeable," Rebecca defended, as if sensing Adele's annoyance.

"I don't doubt it." The servant left, and Mrs. Marsh said in a hearty voice, "My teas will put a spark in your veins."

The sour scent overpowered the room as she poured, making Adele's stomach tighten.

"There's a ritual to tea, you know," Mrs. Marsh said. "The English know it and so do people in the East."

"What is your ritual?" Adele asked.

"Tea at ten, tea at five, and tea before bed," she dictated. "Always strong." She looked dreamy for a moment. "Theo gets me all my teas. I've taught him all about them."

"He's such a thoughtful man," Rebecca said.

Adele glanced at her. The tone was wistful and light.

"No sugar, and no drinking it piping hot," Mrs. Marsh continued as she set three cups aside. "That's where the English and I differ. You must wait until it can go down the throat soothingly like water. And always leave a little bit at the bottom. An offering to the earth, so they say."

They waited in silence, taking their cue from Mrs. Marsh.

Adele took a sip with a little trepidation. The aroma seeped into her throat and the taste was pleasant and bold.

She sensed Mrs. Marsh's sparkling eyes on her, expecting approval. "It's very soothing," she murmured.

The woman smiled and sat back with the look of a satisfied cat. "One can travel all over the world in just a cup of tea."

"I'm sure you've seen more of the world than that," Adele said, smiling.

The woman's face sagged. "You're wrong, my dear. My husband had rather limiting beliefs about one's horizons."

"He wasn't a traveler?" Adele asked.

The woman grimaced. "I thank you for putting it so delicately. My daughter calls it narrow-minded."

"He was always dedicated to his business pursuits," Rebecca said by way of apology.

"He could have left the mill in Theo's hands at any time, and he knew it." Mrs. Marsh's voice was bitter. "He simply didn't like the idea of being with people who didn't know him. One has no control over strangers." She closed her eyes. "Sometimes I regret this heart of mine prevents me from traveling. Anywhere, mind you, that's the fun of it. I suppose it's silly for a seventy-eight-year-old woman to be talking that way."

"Not in the least," Adele said kindly. "These days, boats and trains accommodate people with all sorts of health conditions."

The woman opened her eyes and smiled at Adele. "Perhaps, but heart trouble is not one of those conditions that fares well at sea."

"Nonsense, Thea," Rebecca protested. "You were speaking only yesterday of going to the salt baths after the holidays."

"Speaking is not doing, dear," said the woman. "I fear I should see my last glimpse of the sea if I did that."

"I have no doubt you'll not only visit the sea, but some of the far-off lands you've always wanted," Rebecca said in a reassuring voice.

The woman took her hand and smiled. "You're a dear, Rebecca. Out of all Mona's friends, you were always the one I liked the best."

"I wasn't exactly Mona's friend," Rebecca reminded her softly.

"Sometimes I envy Mona," Mrs. Marsh said. "She got to see India at least."

"I don't fancy she enjoyed it much," the lawyer remarked. "She hardly talks about it."

"On the contrary, dear," said the woman. "She enjoyed it immensely in spite of all her troubles." A gray look crossed her face. "I never understood why they went."

"It was for William's work," Rebecca said.

The woman laughed. "You're a simple soul, Rebecca. William could have had his position at the mill any time he wanted after he married Mona. No, there were other reasons why they insisted on going." She gave her a meaningful look.

"I imagine they were fascinated by the culture," Adele said. "I visited Turkey once, and it was quite eye-opening."

"Her eyes were opened all right," said Mrs. Marsh in a troubled voice. "She used to read books on exotic places like that. Gregory used to say, 'One would think she's looking for her soul.' He thought it most improper." Her eyes sparkled. "But then, Gregory could be rather one-sided about such things."

Rebecca didn't hide her smile.

"He would have thought it improper for them to live to India," Adele guessed.

"He thought it improper for *her* to live in India," Mrs. Marsh corrected," or anywhere but here, really." The woman leaned back against the pillows.

Two women entered the room. One looked to be in her forties and had the same dark eyes and wavy hair as Mrs. Marsh, whom Adele guessed was the Mona in question. The other was a pert blond with a rabbity face.

Mrs. Marsh's daughter greeted Rebecca with an air kiss above each cheek. "Ella just told me you were here."

"Miss Gossling, Mrs. Bridge and Miss Peeler." Both women nodded.

"We didn't want to disturb your walk, dear," said her mother, accepting the same kind of air kiss.

Mrs. Bridge settled herself on a stool, leaving Miss Peeler to perch at the edge of the bed. "My, but you've become a frequent visitor as of late."

"Rebecca is taking care of my affairs, dear," said the woman.

Adele observed Mrs. Bridge's eyes slid toward the rolled-up sheet on Rebecca's lap. "Affairs?"

"Nothing you need worry about," her mother said quickly.

"I suppose you mean your will, Mother?" There was a strain in her voice.

Ignoring this, Mrs. Marsh said, "Miss Gossling owns a stationery shop in Arrojo. I've had Rebecca buy a few things and her stock is most superior and quite unlike the flimsy merchandise we see in the shops here."

Mrs. Bridge's voice came out like a melodic bird. "I must visit it one day, then." She turned to Adele. "I've heard you're quite independent-minded."

"I've discovered that for myself," Mrs. Marsh intervened.

"And you approve?"

"Why wouldn't I?" Her mother asked in a sharp voice.

"You surprise me, Mother." The woman's eyes arched. "You surprise me about a lot of things lately."

"Your mother doesn't approve, Mrs. Bridge," Adele said. "But as she rightly pointed out, whether she does or not has no bearing on ladies like me."

"Bravo, Miss Gossling!" Mrs. Bridge clapped her hands. "You'd better get used to it, Mother. With the direction the country is going, we'll be seeing more women like Miss Gossling."

Miss Peeler spoke for the first time. "Forrest says Mr. Roosevelt is a good man."

"You're always telling us what Forrest said," Mrs. Bridge snapped. "I'd like to know what *you* say for a change."

The girl sniffed. "If Forrest likes him, why shouldn't I?"

"Nice or not, he might be our next president," Mrs. Marsh said.

"We'll see some much-needed changes in this country if he is," Rebecca said. "I've been told there's an entire movement to beautify the cities now."

"Indeed there is," Adele said. "I know from friends in San Francisco."

"And maybe women will get the vote if he's in office," Mrs. Bridge added.

"Heaven forbid!" Mrs. Marsh growled.

"And yet, here you are, speaking with a lawyer and getting your papers in order," Mrs. Bridge pointed out. "Don't you think that's rather hypocritical?"

"I do so out of necessity, not liberation," her mother snapped.

"Yes, but Theo could easily take care of all that, couldn't he?" Mona asked.

"He can't make my will, can he?" Mrs. Marsh motioned the maid to set the two new cups on the tray.

Adele was amused to see Miss Peeler shrink back. "No thank you, ma'am. I only came to see if you needed anything from the general store. I'm meeting Forrest for lunch, and we'll be passing by there."

"No thank you, dear." Mrs. Marsh looked at her with affection. "You're always looking out for me."

The young woman smiled but Adele caught the arch look in Mona's eyes.

She saw her excuse to leave and rose. "I'm afraid I must be getting back to my shop."

"I'm happy you had tea with me." The woman smiled. "You're clearly a level-headed young lady, and I like sensible girls."

"Miss Gossling is hardly a girl, Mother," Mrs. Bridge observed. "Though she is quite young. Young and already running her own business." A tinge of envy crept in her voice.

"I must earn my living, Mrs. Bridge," Adele said. "Shall I drive you back, Rebecca?"

The lawyer looked expectedly at her client.

"Yes, I won't need you anymore today." The woman said.

Rebecca put a handful of papers in her case. "I'll have an answer for you on these tomorrow." She slipped the rolled paper under her arm. "And I'll have this ready for your signature. Do you want me to bring the witnesses?"

"I fancy Mother can find her own witnesses," Mrs. Bridge said.

"Mona's quite right, dear," said Mrs. Marsh, wiping her forehead with her handkerchief. "I want to enjoy the holidays this year. Who knows if it will be my last?"

"Nonsense," Rebecca scoffed.

"Mother, you have become morbid lately." Mrs. Bridge shifted the blanket closer to her mother's chest. "Is that why you're making your will? Because you don't think you'll see another Easter?"

"That's my business, Mona." The tone was like steel.

"Fingers in every pie," Adele heard Mrs. Bridge murmur, "even those not baked yet."

Her mother held out her hand to Adele. "Come again, won't you? I'm afraid I'm mostly confined to this room, my heart being what it is. Sometimes I do go out to the yard, though. It's very pleasant there in the spring."

Adele smiled. "I'm happy to have met you."

"Yes, please do come and see us sometime," Mrs. Bridge echoed.

"I'd like to speak with you about your stay in India," Adele said.

All at once, the dullness in the woman's eyes faded into a fierce spark. "I shall be glad to tell you all about it. India's a fascinating place, but only if you know it from the native's perspective."

"You know I prefer not to hear about it, dear," Mrs. Marsh winced.

"You're always going on about how Father never let you travel," her daughter replied. "Hearing about it is almost as good as being there, isn't it?"

"Not when you speak of it, Mona." Mrs. Marsh's voice was firm. "I would be obliged if you would cease to discuss it."

"Not everything can be silenced at your will, Mother." The melodic tone of her daughter's voice had a harsh edge.

"I have the right to decide what will and will not be discussed in my own house, Mona."

The woman pressed her hand to her forehead. "Of course, Mother. Of course."

The silence that followed made Adele feel stiff. Catching Rebecca's arm, they both bid the Marshes goodbye and escaped.

# CHAPTER 3

The week before the holiday was filled with last-minute arrangements, and Adele putting her shop in order before she, Jackson, and Nin packed themselves off to Santa Barbara. She breathed a sigh of relief when at last she locked the door and pulled down the shades of Adele's Stationery.

They had three days of complete ease with their Aunt Belle in her house in Santa Barbara left to her by a generous but phlegmatic husband. They returned on Monday. Jackson was out of humor, grumbling how he had spent the entire holiday listening to their aunt reminisce of when she and their father were children.

"One would think Father was a cherub, the way she talks," he growled.

"No one would ever say he was, not even he himself," Adele insisted. "Papa was as human as you and I."

Her brother gave her a look. "I'm surprised to hear you, of all people, say so."

"I may have been close to Papa, Jack," she said. "But I wasn't completely blind."

"No man is a cherub, Mr. Gossling," Nin added, "not even if he has shiny cheeks and a bow and arrow."

"I assure you, Miss Branch, I have neither rosy cheeks nor a bow and arrow!" he snapped.

Adele coaxed Jackson into playing chess with them, and she and her brother were surprised to find Nin astute at the game. Jackson's foul mood left him and he seemed almost glad to lose to a woman. He was still congratulating her when the train pulled into the Arrojo station.

Tomas met them in the wagon, his face lighting up when he saw how rested they looked. The man worried worse than a mother hen, rubbing his hands and clicking his tongue all the time.

She and Jackson saw Nin to her flat and then rode home. Adele hadn't realized how much she missed Caliber Street until the wagon turned into the little fork where Mr. and Mrs. Bellingson's house stood with its strange peach-colored mailbox.

Jackson asked Tomas and Ruth about their holiday and received animated stories in return. Their five children gathered to offer their salutations, and Adele disbursed the small gifts she had brought back with her.

"It's rather nice to be greeted by smiling young faces," Jackson admitted as they finished lunch.

"Mr. and Mrs. Blanch weren't very tolerant of children," Adele agreed. The Blanches had taken care of their house in San Francisco.

"One can't compare the proprieties of the city to the practices of the country," her brother said.

"I didn't think your Chicago experiences would make you such a snob, Jack."

A grim look appeared on her brother's face. "I believe in everything in its place, dear sister."

Adele snorted. "No wonder Mrs. Faderman keeps inviting you to her dinners. You're like two peas in a pod."

"Mrs. Faderman's interest in me is more about my status as a bachelor," Jackson said with a wince.

Adele laughed. Tomas entered, followed by Sheriff Hatfield.

"I thought your worldly relations would keep you for at least one more day," Adele greeted him.

"We were called back yesterday, much to Ma's relief." There was a cross look on his face. Adele realized long ago the Hatfield relations never put him in the best frame of mind.

"Police business?" Jackson was immediately alert.

The sheriff accepted the cup of coffee Ruth handed him, but when she pointed to the largest chair in the room to fit his six-foot frame, he remained standing. "Not exactly."

"That sounds mysterious," Adele said.

"I received word Mrs. Theodora Marsh died on Saturday night."

Adele sat up. "That's impossible! I spoke to her only a week ago."

"Nevertheless," said Hatfield. "The poor woman is dead."

"But is it even our jurisdiction?" Jackson asked. "They don't live in town."

"The Marsh house is between here and Rosa Gris, so it's as much ours as theirs," he said. "The Rosa Gris sheriff was all too happy to let us look into it."

"But you implied it might not be police business," Adele pointed out.

The sheriff set the cup down on the table. "Dr. Brody is positive she died of heart failure."

"Who's Dr. Brody?"

"A Rosa Gris doctor." Hatfield shrugged. "Apparently, he has quite a reputation with the affluent of that town."

"I'm not surprised," Adele said. "Mrs. Marsh seemed to take her social position to heart as much as Mrs. Faderman."

"Then it isn't murder," Jackson said.

"Apparently, she had a bad heart for several years," Hatfield said.

"Yes, she told me," Adele said.

"And yet, you're not satisfied." Jackson watched him.

"It was very sudden," he said. "Overnight, really. I'm always uneasy about overnight deaths."

"Heart failure can happen at any moment," Jackson said.

"True, true." He tapped his cup with his spoon.

"What else does Dr. Brody say?" Adele asked.

"Mrs. Marsh was found at about seven o'clock this morning by her maid and her nurse."

"And the time of death?" Jackson asked.

"Dr. Brody says approximately eight or nine hours."

"So she died around ten or eleven o'clock the night before," Adele said.

"No one suspected anything was wrong?" Jackson asked.

Hatfield shook his head. "Nobody saw or heard anything. Everyone retired early. Mrs. Marsh had a strict rule about 'early to bed, early to rise.'"

"And Mrs. Marsh was one to insist everyone follow her rules," Adele said. "Whether it suited them or not."

"How do you know that?" Her brother eyed her.

"She ruled the roost, as they say, and never let others forget it," Adele said.

"I've heard she could be rather a tyrant," Hatfield said dryly.

"Well, if there's no crime involved, we're out of it." Jackson said.

"That's what we need to find out," Hatfield said.

~~~~~

When Adele arrived on Bridge Street to open her shop, it seemed as if only half the town were present. Raleigh's was open as usual, and Mrs. Raleigh, cleaning the windows, waved to her. The "CLOSED" sign hung on the doorknob of Dora's Tea Shop, but Adele could see figures moving about behind the long
~~~~~

windows. Other places that usually bustled in the mornings like the bakery and the butchery were silent.

Nin came in as soon as she opened and, without a word, put the kettle on.

"You're a dear." Adele smiled.

"One must take care of one's friends," Nin said, rather shyly.

Adele unfolded *The Arrojo Courier* and searched through the pages. She found what she was looking for:

*Theodora Marsh, who was once one of Arrojo's prominent citizens, died yesterday of heart failure. She enjoyed a family holiday and went to bed in good spirits. The morning found her lifeless body oddly wrapped in a blanket. Gregory and Theodora Marsh left Arrojo some time ago to start Marsh & Sons Lumber Mill outside of Rosa Gris and built Marsh Manor as one of the largest houses in our area. Mrs. Marsh is survived by her eldest son, Theodore Marsh, her daughter, Mrs. William Bridge, and her younger son, Forrest Marsh.*

She handed the paper to Nin. "You saw this?"

"You know I never read papers." Her friend sniffed.

"I'm sorry for Rebecca," Adele said. "Perhaps it was just as well Mrs. Marsh insisted on settling her affairs."

She began tidying up the shop, which had become a little dusty over the holiday. As she swept, the bell rang. Rebecca stood in the doorway, her face and eyes ragged.

"I'm so glad you're back!" she burst out.

Nin sat her down and put a cup of tea in her hands.

"You've heard about Thea's death?" the woman asked.

Adele nodded. "The sheriff told us this morning."

"She must have known, since she asked you to make out her will," Nin added.

"But she didn't expect she would need it for years," Rebecca insisted. "In spite of what she said, she didn't think for a moment this would be her last Easter."

"Her doctor said it was heart failure, didn't he?" Adele pointed out.

"Yes," said Rebecca quietly, "that's what he said."

Adele studied her. The woman's neck and shoulders were stiff. She held the teacup still with both hands as if afraid it would drop. "You don't believe him?"

"It isn't that," Rebecca said.

"And yet —" Nin hinted.

She pressed the rim of the cup to her chin. "It's impossible, I tell you!"

"That she died of heart failure?" Adele asked.

"She had heart trouble, yes," Rebecca said, "but not bad enough to kill her all of a sudden like that. Even Dr. Brody admits it was unexpected."

"And yet, he was certain she died of heart failure," Adele said.

"But it can't be!" Rebecca put the cup down on the counter. "She was in such fine spirits last night, almost as fine as she was at Easter."

"How do you know?" Nin asked.

"I stayed at the Marsh Mansion over the holiday," She looked down at her hands. "I had nowhere else to go and Theo asked me to come."

"Go on." Adele leaned against the counter.

"She got out of bed before lunch. That was a rarity for her, so she must have been feeling up to it. Isn't that right?" She looked helpless.

"It would seem so," Adele admitted.

"She couldn't stop complimenting Ella on her fine cooking at dinner," Rebecca said. "Her appetite was voracious — well, compared to her usual. She even said she didn't think she'd eaten so much since her husband died."

"She was in a good mood, then," Adele said.

"After dinner, we played charades and cards and laughed so much! I don't think I've ever seen the family laughing together like that."

"The holidays bring out togetherness," Adele said softly.

"She was happy." Rebecca's eyes filled with tears. "Happier than I can remember."

Nin sat on the floor in front of her. "You were very fond of her, weren't you?"

"Yes, in a way," Rebecca said. "I didn't always agree with the way she treated people. But she was fair and kind to me."

"They say sometimes people who are about to die have a reawakening before the end," Adele said gently.

"No, it wasn't that," Rebecca insisted. "I told you, things just aren't right."

"In what way?" Adele sat down.

"Thea's room, for one."

"What about it?"

"Ella came to me, you see, after she and Nurse Pegg discovered the body."

"The housekeeper and nurse?" Adele asked.

"The poor things must have been frightened to death," Nin remarked.

"Ella was. Nurse Pegg, I believe, has seen death before, and she's not the sort to fly into hysterics."

I would imagine not, given her profession," Adele said.

"Nurse Pegg wouldn't allow any of us in the room. She told us to call Dr. Brody and remained there on guard until the doctor came."

"Very sensible thing to do." Adele nodded.

"Theo asked Dr. Brody if I could come in since I was Thea's lawyer."

Adele refilled her cup with tea and pushed it into her hands. "What makes you think Mrs. Marsh's death was more than heart failure?"

"I've nothing I can really put my finger on," Rebecca admitted. "Call it women's intuition."

"There's nothing the matter with women's intuition," Nin insisted, "except men belittle it because they don't have it."

Rebecca smiled for the first time. "The room was — off."

"In what way?" Adele asked.

"That's just it," said the lawyer. "I don't quite know how to explain it. It was messy, of course, though not more than any usual person would mess a room before bedtime."

"But for Thea Marsh, it was unusual," Adele guessed.

"Yes," Rebecca agreed. "That's it, I guess. And there was the teacup."

"The teacup?"

"You remember what Thea told you," Rebecca said. "Tea before bed. She always had it. She usually set the cup on the bedside table so she wouldn't knock it down when she got up. It wasn't there this morning."

"Maybe she didn't have her tea last night," Nin suggested.

"She had it," Rebecca insisted. "Ella said Theo brought it up to her as he usually did."

"And the maid — what's her name?"

"You mean Polly, the parlor maid?"

Adele nodded. "Polly didn't take it away?"

"That's what Mona suggested," Rebecca sighed, "but she couldn't have taken it away without seeing the dead body of her mistress, could she? Ella screamed loud enough to wake her husband downstairs. Imagine what poor Polly would have done if she had found the body."

"Screamed loud enough to wake the dead, most likely," Nin said dryly.

"I asked her, of course. She swore she hadn't entered the room since yesterday afternoon." Rebecca twisted a ring on her finger. "I tried to tell Dr. Brody, but he was anxious to have the whole matter settled for the family's sake. He's already issued the death certificate."

"Already?" Adele was surprised.

Rebecca nodded. "I tried to get him to wait, but he said there was no need to upset the family." Her hands shook. "Poor Theo!"

"I imagine they were close," Adele remarked.

Rebecca glanced at her. "Yes, he was very fond of her. Perhaps the only person in the family who was."

"What does he think of his mother's death?" Adele asked.

Rebecca looked down at the teacup still in her hands as if suddenly remembering it. She drank it down as if it were whisky. "He believes the doctor, of course, but he's willing to indulge me."

"Indulge you?"

"My uneasy feeling," Rebecca said. "I asked him to lock the door to Thea's room and not let anyone in."

"To maintain evidence," Nin murmured.

"If there is any," the woman said. "I've seen several criminal cases. The lawyers are always adamant the crime scene — if indeed that's what it was — remain untouched and untrodden."

"Quite right," Adele agreed.

"I'm afraid I caused some strife within the family, though," she admitted.

"Why is that?"

"We were having breakfast this morning, and Ella came in and said she wanted to clean up, now that —" she gulped, "— Thea's body had been taken to the morgue. Theo told her the door was to remain locked and only I have the key and can give the order to unlock it."

"I imagine that didn't go over well with the family," Adele said.

Rebecca looked sheepish. "Mona insisted it was absurd to think there was any reason to keep the room locked. Forrest agreed with her, though that hardly matters, as he agrees with her on everything."

"She may be right," Nin pointed out.

"She might," Rebecca said. "I just want to be sure."

"Sure it wasn't murder?" Adele asked.

Rebecca fidgeted in her chair. "Perhaps I'm making something out of nothing."

Adele laid her hand on the woman's shoulder. "You really ought to tell the police, Rebecca."

The woman looked horrified. "They would laugh at me."

"Not Hatfield," Adele insisted. "He takes everything seriously."

"A missing teacup might be important," Nin added. "It might be evidence."

Rebecca shook her head. "I don't want them involved until we're sure."

"We?" Nin raised her eyebrow.

"That's why I've come." She turned to Adele. "I've heard about you from people in town."

"Yes, I'm sure the gossips were very eager to tell all about me to a newcomer," Adele said warily.

"Missy told me told me how you solved the murder of Lucy Blackstone and that schoolteacher's death," Rebecca said.

Adele felt her face turn red. "I didn't solve anything. I merely followed a few feelings of my own, and drew some conclusions, and then handed it to the police to do with what they wished."

"Exactly!" Rebecca jumped up. "Come with me to the mansion and look at that room. If we find anything that might pass for evidence, I'll gladly go to the police with the rest."

Adele paced back and forth, her hands behind her back. She could hear her brother saying, "It's best you keep your nose out of police business from now on." She didn't doubt he was right. The townspeople looked at her as if she were going to expose them as they passed her shop, and some had refused to enter since the Millie Gibb case. And yet, the idea that Thea Marsh, a woman she had liked, could be dead from anything but what Dr. Brody had said perked her curiosity.

"I'll make a bargain with you," she said. "Let my brother come with us, and if we find nothing, no harm done. If we find something, he can inform the sheriff in his official capacity."

"But why?"

"If there is something, our having gone through the room, no matter how careful we are, might have vital consequences," she explained.

"It would be tampering with the crime scene," Nin chimed in.

"But we don't even know if there is a crime scene!" Rebecca said.

"If you want us to find out," Adele said, "we must do it with some authority behind us. I won't go without it." Her tone ended on a mulish note.

Rebecca was quiet for a moment. "Your brother will be discreet?"

"He always is," Nin assured her. "But how do we get him here without arousing the sheriff's suspicions?"

"Leave that to me." Adele put on her hat.

She crossed the street to Rutledge Bakery, which had just opened. Scents of bread and cake made her almost giddy. As she anticipated, three of the girls from the Wrigley School were dawdling over the counter while Mrs. Rutledge stood with a paper bag in her hand, ready to snap up any treat they desired.

"Good morning, ladies," Adele said.

In the two years since she had met them, the girls had grown to be almost ladies. Beatrice, her strawberry blond head glittering in the sun, was nearly thirteen, and the two other girls, Sandra and Fanny, were both a year older.

Their delight mirrored girls half their age as they scurried around her.

"Have you some secret mission for us?" Sandra asked, her dark eyes alighted.

"In a way, yes." Adele tried not to smile. "Make your purchases and meet me outside."

She did not have long to wait, as the girls shot out of the door a few moments later, each swinging a small paper bag in her hand.

"Well?" Beatrice looked at her expectedly.

"I've a small but very important task for you," she said. "One of you could manage it easily."

"Which one?" The girls leaned forward eagerly.

Adele put her hand on Fanny's shoulder. "I'd like Fanny to do it."

Fanny beamed while the other girls sulked.

"You'll accompany her, though," Adele added, which made the two girls perk up once more. "You all know what my brother looks like?"

"Yes, indeed!" Sandra said, two red flags appearing on her cheeks. Adele couldn't help but recall the way some of the girls, now that they were nearing marriage age, had been eyeing Jackson's tall, elegant figure. His handsomeness had always been enough to turn any young lady's head.

She turned to Fanny. "I'd like you to get him away from the station on some excuse. I need you to speak to him privately, but I don't want the sheriff or anyone else knowing about it."

"I can manage that all right," Fanny said with an air of confidence.

"Give him a message," said Adele. "Tell him to come to his sister's shop at once. It's very important he come alone and the sheriff know nothing about it. Is that clear?"

"How intriguing!" Beatrice said with a sparkle in her eye. "You've trapped a murderer, and you want him to arrest the fellow?"

"Don't be silly, Bea," Sandra snapped. "There's been no murder, so how can there be a murderer?"

"Just because the paper hasn't said anything doesn't mean there hasn't been one, bum it," Beatrice growled.

Adele smiled. "It's about time you stopped saying 'bum it,' dear. It's not becoming to a lady."

"You told us a lady may say what she likes," the girl pointed out.

"Indeed she may," said Adele, "but only if she does it in a lady-like way so as to fool people into thinking she's speaking politely." The girls burst out laughing. "On your way, all of you." She gave them each some coins and they ran off.

"I didn't know you took an interest in children, Adele," Rebecca remarked when she returned.

"The girls at the Wrigley School aren't really children anymore," she said. "I trust them with little errands. They'll bring Jack here in a few moments, and the sheriff will be none the wiser."

True to her word, her brother sauntered into the shop, the silver deputy sheriff's badge shining in the sunlight. "All right, Del, why the hush-hush?"

"Does the sheriff know you're here?"

"I told him I was going to the Bush farm to check on that stolen horse," he said, amused. "Those girls of yours insist you have a murderer locked in your storeroom."

Adele laughed. "I'm afraid they let their imaginations run away with them. No, no murderer, Jack."

"Not yet," Nin said.

"Are we playing guessing games now, Miss Branch?" he asked in a stiff tone.

"I never guess, Mr. Gossling," she answered. "I take evil and death in any way it comes."

He crossed his arms, looking at his sister. "Well?"

She told him all Rebecca had said as the woman sat silently with her hands in her lap. It was as if Jackson's badge made her nervous again.

He looked at Rebecca. "It would be better, Miss Gold, if you would tell the sheriff about your suspicions, just as my sister suggested."

"I promised Theo I wouldn't," she insisted. "I promised him there wouldn't be any scandal."

"But if his mother didn't die of natural causes —"

"I didn't say that wasn't true!" she insisted. "I merely said I had a feeling about it."

He sighed. "I understand your trepidation. But there's a procedure to these things, you know."

"Fiddlesticks!" Nin burst out. "Don't you believe in helping a friend?" Rebecca gave her a grateful look.

"When there's no crime involved, I'm the first to help anybody," Jackson's tone was crusty. "But if there is a crime—"

Adele took his arm. "We need your professional and astute eye, Jack. If there is nothing in it, then there's nothing in it. If there is something, Rebecca will convince the family to go through the proper channels."

"They won't have much of a choice," he remarked.

"Then you have no reason to object to looking around, do you?" She insisted.

"I have no objection as long as there is a method to it," he insisted. "One simply can't go bursting into a room with a magnifying glass hollering 'murder afoot!'"

"Don't tell me the Anspaches never entered a room without permission." She eyed him.

He looked away and she was sorry she had spoken. But then he said, "I suppose it can't do any harm to look around as long as the family consents, and we're very careful. But *only* if we have their full consent, Del."

"That you have, Deputy," Rebecca said in a relieved tone.

"*And* I have your promise if there is anything in the least suspicious, you go to the sheriff."

"You have my promise." She bowed.

Adele gave her brother a peck on the cheek.

~~~~~

The Marsh housekeeper regarded Jackson with trepidation when she saw his badge, but when Rebecca told her he had come to help, she softened and led them upstairs to Mrs. Marsh's room.
~~~~~

"She and her husband were fond of Thea," Rebecca remarked after the woman left. "I don't believe they would object if they knew the real reason." She fiddled with the lock.

"You looked relieved when she told us the family was out," Adele observed.

Rebecca's hand paused on the door handle. "I told you how they reacted when they discovered Theo gave me the key to this room."

"And you promised there wouldn't be any scandal," Adele said.

"I promised Theo."

There was silence for a moment, and then Jackson took charge. "Shall we go in and see what we can find?"

The room was indeed a mess. Cinders were scattered on the carpet, and several pieces of small furniture were shifted around with one small table knocked over. In another corner, a large lacquered vase lay on its side.

Jackson examined it. "The carpet here is wet, but where are the flowers?"

"Daisies," Nin murmured.

Jackson glanced at her.

"We found them in the wastepaper basket. I suppose they must have been removed," Rebecca said. "They were daisies." She glanced at Nin.

"Someone was careless with the fire," Jackson remarked, glancing at the cinders.

Adele studied the cupboard against the wall. Its contents were clearly of an oriental nature. "I see Thea indulged her love of the exotic with *objects d'art*," she said. "That's rather attractive." She pointed to a bronze figure of a dancing woman.

Rebecca smiled. "Mona brought that back from Bombay."

"A fussy room," Nin observed.

"Yes, she was as fussy about her room as she was about her life," Rebecca lamented. "That's why it struck me as odd the room should be so out of order."

"It looks as if she might have been stumbling around in the dark." Jackson glanced over the room. "With the furniture moved like this and the vase tipped over."

"She never got out of bed at night. Even her tea was served here." Rebecca motioned toward a small night table.

Jackson examined it carefully. A small round tray sat on the table.

"She always had her tea served just before bed?" Adele asked.

Rebecca nodded. "Theo made it and sometimes brought it up."

"I see what you mean about the cup missing," he said. "There's even a spot here where the saucer left some spilled tea."

Adele exchanged glances with Rebecca. "Yes," the lawyer said. "That was one of the things that was off to me. Thea was always very immaculate."

"Could it have been the maid who spilled the tea when she took the cup away?"

"She swears she never entered the room after lunch, Jack," Adele said.

"But what about after Dr. Brody removed the body?"

"Impossible," Rebecca said. "I told you, Theo gave me the key and told everyone to keep away from the room until I allowed it."

"The cup must be in here somewhere." Adele peered through the glass doors of the cupboard, and then moved on to the bureau, opening the top drawer.

"Del!"

"Rebecca gave us permission to search the room," Adele pointed out. She looked at the woman.

"Naturally you may search," her friend answered. "I think we have sufficient reason to believe something is amiss now."

"Because a cup and saucer are gone?" Jackson asked. "She may have broken them and thrown them away."

"But I told you, she was most careful!"

"Accidents do happen, Miss Gold," he said gently.

Adele closed the bureau drawer. "Someone might have hidden them."

"For what reason?" Jackson asked.

"For evil reasons, dear brother." Adele opened the next drawer carefully. There were handkerchiefs and other linens inside. She saw one corner was unfurled and absently straightened it. Her hand touched something hard, and she folded back what looked like a shawl.

"Jack!"

Her brother peered over her shoulder. Embedded in what looked like a tablecloth was a small cup with painted daisies and a saucer to match.

"I knew it!" Rebecca's eyes were wide.

"Don't jump to conclusions," Jackson said in a calm voice. "It might have been there for some time."

"With that pool of tea at the bottom?" Adele asked. "Thea told us she always leaves a small bit of tea as an offering to the earth that gave it to us."

She could see her brother was trying not to smile. As Adele reached for the cup, he pulled her hand back. "Just in case —" He took the cup and saucer carefully.

"Isn't it strange there should be such a dark stain at the bottom of the cup?" Adele asked.

"What kind of tea was Mrs. Marsh drinking the night before she died?" asked Jackson.

"A green tea," Rebecca answered. "With cardamon and ginger. Theo bought it for her from Mrs. Lesley's shop. One of those Indian teas."

Jackson turned to Nin. "Would such herbs leave a dark stain at the bottom of the cup?"

"If not prepared properly," she remarked.

"There's your answer then." He looked knowingly at his sister.

"But a dark violet stain?" Adele asked.

"Those herbs aren't violet," Nin insisted.

"I suppose you have an explanation for that?"

He was silent for a moment. "No. No, I haven't." He started to reach a finger inside the cup.

A scream came from Nin, "Don't touch it!"

"Miss Branch, are you all right?" Rebecca stared at her.

"Don't touch it!"

"Really, Miss Branch," Jackson sniffed.

Adele put her arm around her friend's shoulders. She looked pale and stared at the teacup as if a snake were coiled in it.

# CHAPTER 4

*J*ust then, Mrs. Bridge appeared in the doorway. "What are you doing?" Her voice cut like a razor through the black veil. Behind her lingered both her brothers, her husband, and Miss Peeler.

Rebecca stepped forward. "I asked Miss Gossling and Deputy Sheriff Gossling to come."

"You mean you came in here without permission?" the younger Mr. Marsh, who had an almost transparent look with shocking blond hair and pale features, growled.

"Deputy sheriff?" His brother stepped into the room, a head taller than everyone else with a reedy figure and large eyes.

"I'm not here officially, sir." Jackson assumed what Adele called the "lawman pose" with his feet a little apart and his back straight. "That is, I wasn't until now."

Mrs. Bridge's shrill voice sounded like a whistle gone astray. "How dare you invade my mother's room!"

"Theo gave me leave to do as I thought best, Mona," Rebecca said in a sharp voice.

"That's true, I did," Mr. Marsh admitted. "But I must say, Becca, I hardly expected you to bring the police."

"I told you, sir, I didn't come here initially in the name of the law," Jackson said. "My sister asked me to look into this matter unofficially."

"What matter?" Forrest Marsh asked. "Our mother died of heart failure."

"So I understand, sir," Jackson said. "But I also understood there may have been some — extenuating circumstances associated with your mother's death."

"Extenuating circumstances?" Theo Marsh looked a little pink. "I really don't —"

"You saw it too, Mona," Rebecca pointed out. "You saw there was something wrong, just as I did."

The woman pulled her coat around her shoulders. "I never said any such thing."

"That's not true!" Rebecca insisted.

"My sister would never question the verdict of a medical man," Forrest Marsh said. Adele noticed the darkened look in Miss Peeler's eyes.

"Thank you, dearest." His sister put her hand on his shoulder. "Everything will be all right, don't worry." She looked steadily at Jackson. "Since you put it so bluntly, Deputy, have you found any 'extenuating circumstances'?"

"We found this." He held up the cup.

"You said yourself it was missing." Theo Marsh turned to his sister.

"Where did you find it?" the woman asked.

Adele could tell her brother was a little embarrassed so she supplied the answer. "I found it in one of the bureau drawers under some linen."

"You went through Mother's things?" She turned away, a handkerchief slipping underneath the veil.

Another man with a wave of red hair and a bushy mustache stepped beside her. "Don't upset yourself, dear." He put his hand on her shoulder but Adele noted she quickly slipped away, leaning against the wall.

"I went through them," Adele admitted. "I have no legal obligations like my brother has."

"How very clever," Mrs. Bridge seethed, "when one has a sister along who can violate a citizen's rights."

If Jackson felt the insult, he was admirably collected about it. "Can any of you identify this as the cup your mother drank from the night before she was found?"

Mrs. Bridge let out a sob. Her younger brother put his arm around her shoulders. The eldest Marsh stared at it. "That's the cup I brought up to Mother, yes. It was part of a tea service she liked."

"Can you account for the appearance of the cup, sir?" Jackson asked.

"Appearance?"

"The dark purple stain at the bottom?"

"It's tea, isn't it?"

Nin spoke up for the first time, her voice throaty. "It isn't tea. Don't touch it!"

Mrs. Bridge gave her an arch look. "And you are —"

"Anita Branch is a friend of my sister's," Jackson said. "She is also a specialist in herbs."

The woman peeled back the veil as if to get a closer look at Nin. Adele could see her eyes were bright. Then they darkened as she lowered the veil again. "I know something of herbs myself, Deputy. The stain you speak of is tea."

"Mother adored strange blends," Theo added. "She once had a Sumatran blend that left a light blue powder. We never discovered what it was." He smiled at the memory.

"What does it matter what it is?" his brother demanded. "Mother died of heart failure."

"It might matter a great deal," Jackson said in a quiet voice. "You realize this is an abnormality?"

"Abnormality?" Mr. Bridge blinked.

"The cup and saucer hidden in the bureau drawer —"

"There must be a perfectly logical explanation for that," Mrs. Bridge interrupted. "That fool Polly, or Ella —"

"Polly swears she wasn't in this room from yesterday afternoon," Rebecca said.

"Polly swears!" Mrs. Bridge snorted.

"And Ella couldn't have done it," her older brother said thoughtfully. "Nurse Pegg was with her when they found Mother, and no one was in the room since I left her last night."

"Can you be sure of that, sir?" Jackson asked.

The man looked confused. "Well, no, I can't be sure of anything, of course."

Jackson set the cup down carefully on the bureau. "Given the circumstances, I'm afraid I must take this to the sheriff."

"The sheriff!" Forrest stared at him.

"It will be all right, dearest." Mrs. Bridge pressed his hand. Adele could see from the side of the veil, the woman's face was equally stricken. "Just exactly what do you think happened, Deputy?"

Jackson turned to Theo Marsh. "I assume you're head of the family, sir?"

"Yes." The man's face fell. "Yes, I suppose I am."

"I must inform you this room is to remain under lock and key for the time being. I shall send one of our men to guard it."

"Is that really necessary?" Mr. Bridge asked.

"I'm afraid so, sir," said Jackson. "Until we know what happened in this room, we can't take any chances —" He cleared his throat.

"You can't take any chances of anybody tampering with what might be evidence in a crime," Mrs. Bridge finished.

"That's absurd!" the younger Mr. Marsh burst out.

His sister lifted her veil. Her countenance was calm. "Dr.

Brody signed the certificate. He's entirely satisfied our mother died of heart failure."

"No one said she didn't, Mrs. Bridge," Jackson insisted.

"As you seem to be in your official capacity now," Mrs. Bridge continued, "is there anything else we should be prepared for?"

Jackson looked down at the daisy pattern on the carpet, and Adele knew he was searching for words. "Well, as a matter of fact, ma'am, I ought to mention —"

"Don't mince words, Deputy," Mrs. Marsh said. "If there is something we should know, say it."

"If there is just cause, the Rosa Gris coroner may ask for an autopsy on your mother."

"Autopsy!" Miss Peeler screeched.

"You mean they would have to dig up her body?" The younger Mr. Marsh looked as if he were going to be ill.

Mrs. Bridge again pressed his shoulder. "They need our permission for that, and we simply won't give it."

"I'm afraid you'll have to, ma'am," Jackson said. "If there is evidence your mother may have died from of anything but natural causes."

"The police seem to make assumptions about everything when their suspicions are aroused," Mrs. Bridge said. "Even meddling in a family's grief if it suits them."

"Mona —" her husband began.

"We did get permission from a representative of your family." He gave Rebecca a meaningful look.

"Representative!"

"I was Thea's lawyer, Mona." Rebecca glared at her. "Theo retained me as the family lawyer, and he's head of the family now."

This clearly stung Mrs. Bridge, and she turned, pressing her hand against the door frame.

"Becca's right, Mona," Mr. Marsh said. "In a way, I'm glad you came, Deputy. It will clear the whole matter for us." He took Rebecca's hand. "I'm glad you brought them in, Becca."

The lawyer blushed.

"You're acting very sensibly, sir," Jackson said. "I'll send an assistant deputy out here at once."

"We will do as you say, sir." Mr. Marsh turned to Rebecca. "Perhaps you ought to lock the door after you and keep the key, Becca. It might be safer."

"Safer?" Mr. Bridge asked with a snort. "Why, do you think we killed Mother?"

"No one has established there was any killing, sir," Jackson reminded him as he herded them outside.

~~~~~

Jackson asked Rebecca to accompany them to the police station. "I think the sheriff will want to hear the details from you directly," he said. "Since you were the first to suspect."

They reached the station at the noon hour. There were a few assistant deputies there, their desks laid out like miniature picnics. Crinkling paper echoed throughout the room as Assistant Deputy Edison and two others grappled with sandwiches, soup and coffee. Sheriff Hatfield joined this quiet reverie at his own desk, significantly larger to fit his generous frame, with the entire surface cleared for the feast Rowena, the Hatfield housekeeper, always prepared for him. He rose, pulled the napkin he had tucked inside his shirt collar out with a little embarrassment, and bowed to the ladies.

"We didn't mean to disturb your lunch, Sheriff." Adele leaned against her parasol.

"It's always a pleasure to see you, Adele." His face looked rosier as she sat down.

Jackson began at once. "It seems the Marsh case may not be as open and shut as we thought."

Hatfield's eyebrows jumped. "I wasn't aware there was a Marsh case."
~~~~~

"There is now, sir," Jackson said sheepishly.

"We've just come from there," Adele said.

"From where?"

"Thea Marsh's room," Nin answered. "We searched it."

He gave Jackson a sharp look.

"It was at my invitation." Rebecca stepped forward.

"And you are?"

"Rebecca Gold." Her voice became clearer. "I was Mrs. Marsh's attorney. I'm also the family attorney."

"I see." Hatfield's stern countenance eased. "Perhaps you'd better explain what this is about, Miss Gold."

Rebecca supplied the information. "Adele insisted we ask her brother to come with us, unofficially, of course."

"Very wise." The sheriff nodded his approval. "Despite having permission from the family, I needn't tell you tampering with a possible crime scene is very serious business."

"We weren't tampering," Nin insisted. "We were searching."

"So you've stated, Miss Branch," he said. "What exactly were you searching for, if I may ask?"

"Anything out of the ordinary," Adele said, "and we found it." She glanced at Jackson.

He placed the cup and saucer on the desk. "Mrs. Marsh always had a cup of strong tea before she went to bed. We found this hidden in a bureau drawer under some linens."

"You've verified it was hers?"

"Naturally, sir," Jackson said.

"Hidden, you said? I agree it's rather odd," the sheriff mused.

"Odder still is what we found in the cup," Jackson said. "You'll note the stain, Sheriff. Miss Branch advised us not to touch it. She had a reaction." He cleared his throat.

"I reacted to evil vibrations," she murmured.

Hatfield studied it, though he kept his distance. "Adele, may I trouble you for that glass of yours?"

Adele eased the magnifying glass with a goldleaf trim from

around her neck where she carried it on a chain. She handed it to the sheriff.

"Can you tell what it is, Sheriff?" Rebecca asked. "The stain, I mean."

"It might be anything, Miss Gold," he said.

"Anything that is cause for concern?" Adele eyed him.

"If my deputy sheriff believes so, and your friend had a bad reaction, I would imagine it might." Jackson gave a half-smile, and Nin hunched her shoulders. "It can't hurt to take it to Dr. Rhodes and have him analyze it."

"If he agrees," Jackson mumbled.

"He'll agree because I'll tell him there is cause for suspicion," Hatfield said in a firm voice.

"He won't take your word for it, sir," his deputy pointed out.

"Especially when he hears Mrs. Marsh's own doctor already signed the death certificate," Adele remarked.

"Death certificate!" Hatfield jumped up. "I wasn't aware it had gone that far."

"Indeed," said Rebecca.

He plucked his hat from the stand behind him. "I've had only a few dealings with Dr. Brody but I've always found him to be a sensible man."

"You're going to ask him to amend the death certificate?" Jackson looked surprised.

"It's the only way we can get Rhodes to examine the teacup," said Hatfield. "And the family to agree to an autopsy if there is a need."

"Jack brought up that possibility," Adele said. "The family was none too keen about it."

"They may not have a choice," Hatfield said grimly.

"That's what I told them, sir," Jackson said.

"Surely, the idea of serving justice would be convincing enough for Dr. Rhodes?" Rebecca asked.

Nin snorted. "Nothing short of the barrel of a gun would convince that man!"

"Our county medical examiner is a thorough man, but not always very cooperative," Hatfield said. "Nor is he much a man of action unless one encourages him."

"You mean forces him," Adele said.

"Shall I accompany you?" Rebecca asked.

"I would appreciate it if you would," he said. "As you represent the dead woman."

"Adele was the one who found the cup," Nin pointed out.

"Adele shall come also," he said. "Unless she has business to attend to."

"They can wait," Adele said.

They saw Nin to her shop and Jackson to Brent Drugstore's lunch counter for his midday meal. Rebecca asked to stop by her office and promised to meet them at Dr. Brody's. Adele and Hatfield proceeded to the clinic near Quarry Lane, where the doctor was known to spend the lunch hour tending to people in the poorer neighborhoods of town.

"So the family isn't keen on having their mother's body examined, eh?" Hatfield remarked.

"I can hardly blame them," Adele said.

"I saw them in town this morning," he said. "They hardly seemed inconsolable."

"I didn't think they're especially mourning their mother's death either." Adele raised her parasol as the sun had begun to seep through her veil. "With the exception of the eldest Marsh, that is."

"The favored son?" Hatfield grinned.

"Head of the family now," Adele sighed. "To his relief, perhaps."

"I don't know about that," Hatfield said. "A man who's been molly-coddled all his life can either be devastated or liberated by the coddler's death."

The lawyer was waiting for them outside. They walked into a small room smoky with dust from ill-fitted windows and three long benches of waiting people.

Sheriff Hatfield showed her his badge. "Please let Dr. Brody know we must see him immediately."

The woman scraped her chair back. "Is this about a patient?"

"You could say that," he said. "A Mrs. Theodora Marsh."

"Oh!" The woman looked even more startled and scurried toward the gray doors at the far side of the room.

"It's clear she's read the papers," Adele remarked.

"I fancy Dr. Brody won't be very pleasant about this." Rebecca sounded nervous.

"Police business is rarely pleasant, Miss Gold," said the sheriff. "As Adele has had ample opportunity to realize."

"Indeed." She took the woman's arm. "The sheriff always does his duty, Rebecca." The man gave her a modest smile.

Dr. Brody was a rather stark man with thinning hair and horn-rimmed glasses. He had a pleasant countenance and the kind of soothing smile one would expect of a doctor. He greeted them in a quiet tone, motioning toward two chairs for the ladies.

"My nurse said you want to see me regarding the Thea Marsh death." He glanced at Rebecca. "I had some idea you were a little anxious the other day, my dear."

"You're quite sure your patient died of heart failure?" Sheriff Hatfield asked, sliding out a notepad.

"Quite sure, Sheriff," he said.

"You said yourself her heart was improving," Rebecca pointed out.

"I'm afraid you misunderstood me," he said. "A heart condition doesn't really improve. It sometimes goes into a sort of sleep. Even then there's no telling when it might suddenly wake up." He gave a small smile. "Hearts are rather unpredictable." For some reason, this made her blush.

"You believe it was her heart condition that brought on the attack," Hatfield said.

"It's difficult in most cases to be sure of an exact cause of death unless one does an autopsy."

"That's precisely why we're here." Hatfield took out the teacup. "Do you know much about toxins, sir?"

"Toxins? You mean poisons?"

"You don't sound very surprised at the question," Adele observed.

"I wouldn't go as far as that," he insisted, "but when a medical man hears the word 'toxins,' that's generally what we think of."

"Do you know much about them, sir?" the sheriff persisted.

"I have no lab, of course, but in my profession, Sheriff, one knows something about such things," he said.

"Then perhaps you can give us an opinion." He handed him the cup. "Careful! We've been told by an authority that the substance in it might be lethal."

"Lethal?" The man looked confused.

"An herbalist friend of mine told us," Adele said.

"Oh, I see." The man eyed it. "It looks like some sort of organic matter, but I'm no expert in such things."

"Thea drank from that cup the night before she died," Rebecca said. "I saw it sitting on her nightstand."

"And the cup was found hidden in a bureau drawer," Adele added. "A rather strange place to put it, don't you think?"

"Unless a maid was being lazy," Dr. Brody said with a little smile.

"We've determined she wasn't," Rebecca said.

The doctor pulled a magnifying glass that looked much stronger than the one Adele carried from his bag. The reflection made his dull brown eye a massive stone as he examined the interior of the cup. The pleasant expression on his face turned into concern.

"I think I understand why you came to me." He handed Hatfield the cup.

"Miss Gold told me you signed a death certificate attributing Mrs. Marsh's death to natural causes," Hatfield said.

"I had reason to believe it was at the time," said Dr. Brody.

"I don't question your decision, sir," Hatfield said with a bow of respect. "However, if we are to follow up this new evidence, we must have that certificate rescinded."

The man nodded. "I understand, Sheriff."

"I have no authority to require it," continued the sheriff, "as I'm coroner of Arrojo county, but Rosa Gris is not my jurisdiction. However, if I were to take it to the Rosa Gris coroner, it would carry a lot of weight."

"Thea Marsh was both a friend and a patient, Sheriff. I want to do all I can." The man rose and scribbled something down on piece of paper. "I would be much obliged if you would hand this to my nurse, and you'll have your amended certificate this afternoon."

"You're very cooperative, sir," Hatfield said with a vigorous shake of his hand.

"I'm well aware some of my colleagues believe in hindering police investigations rather than helping them," he said in an ironic tone. Adele hid her smile, knowing he was referring to Dr. Rhodes.

As they left the office, Rebecca asked in an anxious tone, "What about the autopsy, Sheriff?"

"Dr. Rhodes will need to decide if one is necessary," said Hatfield. "There will have to be an inquest now, since Dr. Brody's initial death certificate may be incorrect."

"Then we will almost certainly need permission from the family to exhume the body," Rebecca surmised.

Hatfield eyed her. "Adele told me the family objected to the idea."

The lawyer pressed her hands together. "They didn't take it well."

"They would naturally be abhorrent if they thought their mother died of natural causes," said Sheriff Hatfield. "I'm sure they'll see reason if we find it might be otherwise."

"Yes," Rebecca said. "Theo's very reasonable."

Adele pitched her parasol over her head. "Well, what next?"

"I'll go back to the station and wait for the certificate," said Hatfield. "And then, it's off to the lion's den." He grimaced.

"Surely Dr. Rhodes won't object to examining the teacup now that Dr. Brody admits there is cause for alarm," Rebecca said.

"You don't know Dr. Rhodes," Adele said warily. "He'll probably argue it's unnecessary."

"Probably," said the sheriff, "but I've dealt with him enough these past three years to convince him otherwise."

"I would relish seeing the expression on his face when you hand him the death certificate with 'suspicious circumstances' on it." Adele grinned.

"Dr. Brody, I'm sure, will be much more delicate." Hatfield cocked his hat. "That's my headache."

He walked the ladies to Bridge Street and bid them a polite goodbye. Adele watched him sauntering down the street, cocking his hat to passersby, even those who were less than fond of the police.

# CHAPTER 5

$\mathcal{A}$dele was busy for most of the day. Several of the more affluent citizens came to buy holiday stationery for their Christmas correspondence even though it was still eight months away. They spent a lot of time extracting her opinion on this or that color or paper, whether red ink was appropriate or gaudy, and what seal should they use for the envelopes. She gave her advice as freely as she gave her opinion.

She came home with sore feet from a new pair of shoes she bought in Santa Barbara. Dinner that night was a quiet affair, as even Jackson seemed preoccupied.

"Dr. Rhodes give you any trouble?" Adele asked.

Jackson snorted. "Doesn't he always?"

"You went with the sheriff to the lion's den, then." Adele smiled.

"Dr. Brody came with us too," he said.

"He's a very decent doctor," she agreed. "Perhaps we ought to frequent him more."

Tomas, who had just brought in another plate of potatoes, looked at her with alarm and withdrew.

"I suppose Hatfield was hoping some of that studiousness would rub off on Dr. Rhodes," Jackson said ruefully.

"And did Dr. Brody's presence help?"

He gave her a wary look. "I can't understand why Rhodes has to be so ornery!"

"He thinks quite highly of himself," Adele said. "But he can't ignore the evidence."

"He was riled by the idea of having to stay late in his office to analyze the teacup," said Jackson. "Hatfield saved him from that."

"Oh?" Adele raised an eyebrow.

"He suggested Martin do the tests."

"You mean Dr. Rhodes actually consented to allow his assistant to take the reins?" Adele mused.

"You can't deny he tries to throw everything at Martin," Jackson said. "Not that Martin had an objections. Since he was involved in the Lucy Blackstone case, he's been as bitten by the detection bug as you, dear sister."

"I was not bitten by any bug, Jack," she said stiffly. "A woman was found dead in my gazebo. What was I supposed to do?"

"Sit back like a good girl and let the police handle it," he said.

She threw a cushion at him.

"Hatfield suggested Rhodes look over the findings in the morning, and, if he approved, naturally, he would request the autopsy and perform it himself."

"Naturally," Adele growled. "So he can take the credit for all of it. The man is insufferable."

"But thorough, especially if he finds something," Jackson pointed out. "We need a man like that, Del. We're lawmen in one of the smallest counties in this area. We already have too many strikes against us."

Adele took her needlework in her lap, but she remained thinking for a moment. "Jack, what do you think Martin will find?"

He shrugged. "Hard to tell."

"Dr. Brody seemed sure there was something in what Nin said about it being an evil substance."

"It might not be," he said. "It might be quite innocuous. You said yourself Mrs. Marsh liked exotic herbal tea. It might be something to cause no more than a stomachache."

"And if it isn't?" Adele asked.

"Then," he said slowly, "it's a matter for the police."

"And the family," she added. "I don't know how they will take it if it turns out there was poison in her cup."

"Poison is much easier to detect once one has matched it to the body," he said. "You remember the Millie Gibb case."

She shuddered as she thought of how Millie had looked when they found her slumped over a book in her room.

Jackson leaned back with his pipe. "Science is a wonderful thing for the law."

"But not always reliable," she reminded him.

"You sound like your mystical friend," he said.

"Nin's herbs and feelings are no figure of fun, Jack," she insisted. "They've been around much longer than Dr. Rhode's laboratory. I expect they shall last longer too."

He laughed and did not deny it.

~~~~~

A few days later, the inquest regarding Thea Marsh's death was held. Although the Rosa Gris police were glad to give Hatfield the case from their end, the coroner of that county held fast to his authority, so the inquest was held in the Rosa Gris city hall. Rebecca begged Adele and Nin to attend with her. "I can't face it alone," she admitted. "The thought that Thea might have really been poisoned —"

"We don't know anything yet," Adele reminded her.

"Dr. Rhodes wouldn't even tell the sheriff," Nin snapped.

"Martin must have found something," Adele agreed. "But it isn't necessarily proof of poison."

They took Adele's Beaton to Rosa Gris. The town was about
~~~~~

twenty minutes away, but the road was rocky, and while Adele drove with skill, both Nin and Rebecca grabbed the car handles every time the car jumped.

When they reached Rosa Gris, the air was clean of the red dust that so permeated Arrojo, replaced by a duller packed brown mud. The town was more developed and larger because branches of larger companies from Sacramento and San Francisco had established offices there. There were rumors corrupt officials maneuvered the boom fifty-odd years ago, and, as a result, it had more of a reputation than Arrojo.

But today, Adele felt as if she were on Bridge Street again. Though the Marshes had lived in Rosa Gris for some time, many Arrojo citizens had known them in their earlier days, and Arrojo, once it had adopted a citizen, never forgot him or her. It was no surprise that, at the meeting hall, Adele observed crowds of Arrojo citizens lingering outside. The more exclusive Rosa Gris people glanced at them as they hurried past, no more than mildly interested in the goings on.

"Theo!" Rebecca waved her handkerchief above the crowded heads. Theo Marsh waved back, looking ill at ease in a crisp mourning suit as he stood with the rest of the family. He tried to smile but did not approach.

"How trying it must be for him," Adele said sympathetically. "To be in mourning and have to tolerate this."

"Not if his mother was killed," Nin said. "I should think he would want to know." She shifted her hat to one side.

"Perhaps it's better not to know," Rebecca murmured.

Adele stared at her. "I wouldn't expect to hear those words from a lawyer."

Rebecca gave her a rueful smile. "You forget, my expertise is wills and legal documents, not crime and murder."

"I'm sorry." Adele pressed her hand. "I grew up with the idea that justice served is the true calling of any lawyer."

"Your father must have been a very admirable man."

"He was admired by all who knew him." And yet, as Adele said this, she was aware her father hadn't been admired by his own son.

Skirts rustled behind them, and she turned to see Mrs. Faderman with the rest of the ladies, squinting through her pince-nez at the Marsh family. As she lowered her head, she met Adele's eyes. Her lips were a tight, straight line. "Really, Miss Gossling, I find it incredible you should be here."

"Why is that, Mrs. Faderman?"

"Well, it's hardly appropriate." Her eyes swept over the other two ladies. "Such sordid matters."

"You don't seem to have a problem with your daughter being here," Nin remarked, glancing past her to where Vanessa Faderman stood chattering with a few of the younger generation.

"Vanessa is in town seeing the milliners about her trousseau," said the mother stoically. "She just happened to stop by."

"Congratulations on her engagement," Adele put in.

"It must be a great relief to you," Nin murmured, as although Vanessa's countenance was pleasant, she lacked the pleasant character to accompany it.

Adele hid her smile as she introduced Rebecca. "Miss Gold is the family lawyer," she said.

Mrs. Faderman eyed her. "I heard you just returned to the fold, Miss Gold."

"The fold?"

"You were raised in this area, were you not?"

"Yes, ma'am," she said. "In this town, in fact."

"It's always good when our young people return to the fold." The woman nodded with approval. "It continues to build the foundations on those we've already laid."

"I have no family left in this area," Rebecca murmured.

"It hardly matters, my dear," Mrs. Faderman assured her. "The foundations are still there."

"I hope you'll forgive Miss Gossling and Miss Branch," the lawyer said. "They're here to offer their support on my request."

"I'm sure it will all prove to be a mistake," said the woman reassuringly. "Mrs. Marsh was not the sort of woman who would get herself killed."

"Poor Mrs. Marsh was rather ill, after all," Mrs. Lynn, who joined them, put in, her tone sad.

"But she was getting better," Nin said.

"Age does not make people get better, Miss Branch." Mrs. Faderman held up a finger. "If anything, it makes people get worse."

"It makes them less tolerable, at any rate," Nin growled.

A man appeared on the steps and shook a cow bell so vigorously it echoed down the street.

Mrs. Lynn glanced at the Marshes. "The family looks so troubled, don't they, Irene?"

"Naturally," said the woman. "It's troubling to have one's dirty linen aired in public."

Rebecca stiffened. "The Marshes have no dirty linen, Mrs. Faderman. They're most respectable."

"Well, you know the old saying, Miss Gold." The woman sniffed. "'There's no smoke without fire.'"

"Like the last time," Mrs. Lynn murmured. "Like the last time."

"What are you babbling about, Caroline?" Mrs. Faderman looked at her through her pince-nez.

"Oh, well, I —"

The man who rang the bell did so again, this time with vigor. Adele, Nin, and Rebecca followed the herd into the meeting house, a large room with benches that still had splinters in them. Rebecca left them to take her place alongside the Marshes at the front of the room. Adele and Nin squeezed in together on a bench in the back. Adele spotted her brother and Sheriff Hatfield in the corner with some of the other city officials, including Martin and Dr. Rhodes. Dr. Brody was with them.

The inquest was conducted in a hurried fashion at first. The Rosa Gris coroner, Mr. Elms, looked almost like a child behind the large table, but his bushy eyebrows and sideburns gave him a severe appearance. In contrast to his rather small stature, his voice carried through to the back of the room.

The family gave its account of the events of the night their mother died, and it seemed almost as if the coroner was hardly interested. Dr. Brody and Rebecca were more elaborate. Dr. Brody explained his initial diagnosis and his decision to reverse it.

"You have reason to believe this stain found at the bottom of the cup from which Mrs. Marsh drank contains something other than tea?" the coroner asked.

"I have little knowledge of organic substances," he responded. "But it was suspicious enough to warrant testing. Had the cup not been hidden in such a peculiar way, we would have found it in the room earlier, and I would not have been so hasty in signing the death certificate." The last was said in a defensive tone.

"I'm sure you did your best under the circumstances," the coroner reassured him.

Dr. Rhodes was then called.

"You were asked, Doctor, to examine the contents of the dark stain in the deceased's teacup in your lab?"

"I was."

"And what did you find?"

"The dark stain was a syrup of some sort."

"Synthetic or organic?"

"Organic, of course."

"Can you be more specific?" asked the coroner.

Dr. Rhodes long face shortened with a twisted smile. "Like Dr. Brody, I'm not a botanist, sir."

"What, then, could you determine?"

"The substance contains atropine and scopolamine."

"And what are these, Dr. Rhodes?"

He gave another twisted smile. "Lethal poisons."

There was a soft gasp from the Marsh family.

"In other words, evidence of these poisons would point to some organic substance containing them added to the tea?'

"I don't know."

"Could the tea blend itself contain such substances by mistake?" the coroner inquired. "I understand Mrs. Marsh was fond of exotic blends."

"I can't say," the doctor growled. "That's the work of the police."

Adele heard Sheriff Hatfield clear his throat sharply.

"But you can say the poisons found in the cup caused Mrs. Marsh's death?" the coroner went on.

"I did not say so, sir."

This time, there was a more audible gasp from more members of the family.

"You told me these substances are quite lethal," the coroner remarked.

"In a lethal dose, yes. But it's impossible to tell how much was in the tea based on the stains alone."

"Naturally, if the poor woman ingested them —" the coroner murmured.

"She did indeed ingest them," Dr. Rhodes said. "Of that I am sure."

A buzz filled the room, and the coroner held his hand up for silence. "Please explain, Doctor."

"After we found the atropine and scopolamine in the cup, it was necessary to obtain a release to exhume the body," he said. "The family agreed rather reluctantly." He shot the Marshes a damning look. Adele saw Mrs. Bridge grit her teeth in defiance.

"There was atropine and scopolamine found in the body?"

"Yes," said the doctor.

A short piercing scream sounded from the Marsh family, and

Adele saw Mr. Bridge and Theo Marsh bending toward Mrs. Bridge, who was doubled over.

"Has she fainted?" Nin whispered.

After some murmuring, the woman sat upright on the bench, clutching a glass of water. It was clear both her husband and brother were trying to convince her to leave the room, but Mrs. Bridge shook her head. She handed the glass back to her husband and sat composed, her hands in her lap, looking expectedly at the coroner.

"If I may proceed without further delay." Dr. Rhodes was clearly unimpressed by such reactions.

"By all means," said the coroner dryly. "Dr. Brody stated Mrs. Marsh died of heart failure. May we conclude the poisonous substances found in her body were what caused her heart to fail?"

Dr. Rhodes remained quiet for a moment as if he were waiting for the tension in the room to build. He said slowly, "Mrs. Marsh did not die of heart failure."

A small cry rose from the Marsh family but Mrs. Bridge's figure was immobile. Adele realized it had come from the younger son, as she watched Miss Peeler put her arm around him.

"Mrs. Marsh died of respiratory failure," the doctor continued.

"Impossible!"

This exclamation came from Theo Marsh as he grasped the edge of his chair with both hands.

Dr. Rhodes gave him one of his infamous seething looks. "The symptoms are very clear to any experienced medical doctor, sir."

Adele was glad Dr. Brody had left the room, as she felt indignation rise in her chest at the implications.

"Can you explain, Doctor Rhodes, the difference between heart failure and respiratory failure?" the coroner asked.

"I should think it was rather obvious," he sniffed. "The heart fails in the one while the lungs fail in the other."

"If the signs are so obvious, as you said earlier," Mr. Elms said, "why do you think Dr. Brody attributed Mrs. Marsh's death to heart failure?"

Dr. Rhodes' tone was surprisingly kind. "There was no reason for Dr. Brody to think otherwise. He did not witness the actual death and, as Mrs. Marsh was known to have heart trouble for some time, it's natural he would rule her death heart failure barring an autopsy. I might have done the same thing if I were in his place."

"I shouldn't have thought he would be so generous toward a colleague caught in a mistake," Adele whispered to Nin.

"One can afford to be generous when one is in the right," her friend snorted.

A small sob rose in the room and Adele saw Mrs. Bridge bend her head down, slipping the black handkerchief underneath her veil. Her husband put his hands on her shoulders. She didn't draw away from him as she had that day at the house.

"One more question, Doctor. Can you confirm the time of death?"

The doctor leaned his head back, entwining his fingers. "I was told Dr. Brody arrived when the body was about eight or nine hours dead. That was at around seven a.m., so I imagine it would have been around ten or eleven o'clock the previous night."

The coroner dismissed Dr. Rhodes and, in a few moments, the gavel came down with the ruling of "death by person or persons unknown."

The small room exploded in a sea of voices and pounding feet. Rebecca made her way toward them. "I'll go back to town later," she said. "I think the family needs me." She glanced back with a worried look.

"At least there's no more uncertainty," Adele said gently. "The police can do their duty now."

"It's horrible!" Nin shivered.

"Murder is rarely pretty, dear," Adele said gently.

"The pretty can be deadly," Nin agreed. The way she held on to Adele's hand and her glowing eyes told her this was not an idle comment but coming from a deeper place.

They met Jackson and the sheriff outside. Hatfield put on his hat with resolve. "Well, Jackson, it looks as if we're on the scent again."

"It's unfortunate we weren't called in sooner," said her brother, rather gloomily. "No doubt there is evidence that no longer exists in Mrs. Marsh's room after so many days."

"It's lucky Rebecca had the foresight to keep the door locked," Adele said.

"A very forward-thinking woman," Hatfield agreed. "That law office in San Francisco missed a very skilled lawyer."

"It serves them right," Nin growled.

"And now?" Adele looked expectedly at the sheriff.

He buttoned his coat. "Come, Jackson. We've a crime scene to look at. We can do that with some thoroughness now, since the family can no longer object."

"I'm sure that won't keep them from trying," Jackson said in a rueful tone.

"And I'll go back to making my living," Adele said with a smile.

"It might do you good to get your mind away from this ugly affair," Jackson agreed.

"Even the pretty can be deadly," Adele said, echoing her friend.

# CHAPTER 6

As Adele expected, the magpie gossips were hard at work when she returned to Arrojo. People gathered on the street to engage in conversations about the inquest before going about their business. A pocket of ladies, headed by Mrs. Faderman, talked in hushed tones near Raleigh's store. She snuck behind Nin's shop and slipped inside her own to avoid Mrs. Faderman's incessant questions.

Zephyr Brown lingered just outside, her child's wagon parked on the pavement. She opened the door and motioned her in. "I'm glad to see you."

"Just come back from Rosa Gris, I reckon." Zephyr jerked her head in the direction of Raleigh's. "Storm in a teacup, I say. No pun intended, seeing as it was the teacup that did it." She chuckled.

"It was murder," Adele sighed.

"Ain't no one said so," she insisted. "'Death by person or persons unknown' don't always mean murder."

"I can't see it that way, Zephyr," Adele said. She reached under the counter and pulled out the ball of twine, as the woman collected all kinds of throw-away objects and sold them for a living.

Zephyr cocked her head, her blond hair gleaming. "Suppose a bunch of people are in the woods shooting ducks and one of them hits another? That ain't murder, but death by person or persons unknown. Until they find the person and know him, that is." She cackled with laughter.

"Mrs. Marsh wasn't out shooting ducks," Adele said dryly.

"Never can tell about those old biddies," said the woman. "They got the strength to roll a wagon out of a ditch when it suits them."

"Mrs. Marsh was certainly that type," Adele admitted.

The woman secured the twine to her wagon. "Them type of ladies like to make themselves queen of their castle."

"You knew her?" Adele was surprised.

The woman grinned. "I knew Thea Marsh way back when. Knew her husband too. Big man with little ideas, if you know what I mean."

Adele leaned against the counter. "I'm afraid I don't."

"Ideas about what everyone was supposed to be in life," said Zephyr.

"You knew him?"

"Knew some of the lumberjacks that worked for him," she said. "Mr. Marsh was as finicky as they come. Employee was no better than a servant in his eyes. I reckon the ladies of the house felt the same way."

"How can you tell?" Adele asked.

"No reason why Thea Marsh would be so keen on being queen of her own castle once he died unless she were quieted while he was alive," Zephyr pointed out. "That daughter of hers is the same way, I guarantee it."

"Only a very backward-thinking man would raise a daughter like that," Adele agreed.

Zephyr laughed. "Good he ain't alive to see what the ladies like you have up their sleeves."

"And the two sons?" Adele asked. "I'm surprised they didn't turn out to be tyrants like him."

"Why, no, girl, ain't you ever seen the chain of command work in one of them rich families?" Zephyr snorted.

"I think I see what you mean," Adele said slowly. "The father dominates the wife and daughter and the daughters turn on the sons and make them weak."

"Exactly!" the woman said triumphantly.

"By all accounts, then, murder should stay within the family," Adele said.

The woman studied her. "Why, what do you mean, my girl?"

"When volatile emotions stay hidden in the family for so long, someone is bound to explode," Adele said. "Murder might be one way."

The woman shrugged. "I ain't got no head for that new head shrinking business they're talking about, Mr. Freud and all of them. All I know is what I see."

Adele laughed and saluted Zephyr as the woman left the shop.

~~~~~

Dusk set in early and by the time Adele closed the shutters of her shop, gauzy orange and purple clouds lined the sky. She had to admit the times of day were prettier in the country where there were no tall buildings to block out the beauty of nature falling over them. She walked slowly toward the police station, sometimes stopping to look back at the rainbow of colors.

The sheriff and her brother were hard at work but she noticed Edison looking out the window with a daydreaming gaze. "Enjoying the view, Mr. Edison?" She tapped the edge of his desk as she passed.

The young man, who seemed perpetually startled, leapt from his chair and bowed.
~~~~~

"Edison!" The stern shout came from the interview room. "To your work, lad!"

Edison bent over the typewriter, pecking away at it with two fingers.

She found a startling sight in the interview room. The long table was completely filled with odds and ends spread out all over the place. Sheriff Hatfield sat in one chair while Jackson sat opposite him, as if they were both surveying the items and trying to make sense of them.

"I see your box of question marks is filled tonight, Sheriff," she remarked as she settled in a chair.

"The Marshes allowed us into their mother's room without a murmur," Jackson explained. "We were able to do a thorough search."

She eyed the items on the table. "There were still plenty of clues left for you to find."

"A rather motley crew of clues," he agreed.

"Luckily your friend locked the door," Hatfield said. "Otherwise, that meticulous housekeeper would have insisted on giving it a thorough cleaning and probably would have had everything swept away. There would have been no clues left for us to find." He added with a snort, "Not that the Marshes were very appreciative."

"They'll understand when they see every morsel you found will help bring you closer to who killed their mother," Adele assured him.

"Now it's up to us to make sense of them," Jackson lamented.

"I see you found the teapot." She glanced at a small teapot with the same rose pattern as the cup and saucer she had found.

"Hidden in the back of the cupboard," Jackson said. "I'm surprised we didn't find it before."

"Perhaps it wasn't there before," Hatfield suggested.

"I don't see how anyone could have gotten into that room, sir," said his deputy. "Miss Gold is the only one who has the key now."

"We can't know that, Jack," Adele said. "Maybe someone had another key made or even came in through the window. I noticed one of the windows was unlocked."

"With a ladder, I suppose," said her brother in a doubtful voice. "Hardly possible without being seen."

"Nonetheless, I did see a rather tall ladder near the shed when we passed by," the sheriff said.

"The teapot will go to Dr. Rhodes," said Jackson. "Though we didn't find any dark stain inside like we did with the cup."

"It seems odd if someone were trying to poison Mrs. Marsh, they would put this poisonous syrup in her tea but not her teapot," Adele observed.

"That's one question mark we have to answer," Hatfield said.

Adele caught sight of a sheet of unfolded paper revealing the cinders they had found near the bed and fireplace. "Do you think these are important, Sheriff?"

The man shrugged. "Everything is important when murder is involved, Adele. You know that."

"Especially because there were hardly any cinders inside the fireplace," Jackson said. "We'll need to ask Mrs. Stern if she lit a fire that night."

"You didn't interview anyone?" Adele stared.

"The family refused to let us," Jackson said, somewhat annoyed. "They don't seem to understand this is a murder investigation."

"They're still in shock, Jack," Adele said. "Imagine if the doctor told us Papa died of heart failure but then we found out it was something else entirely, and his death wasn't natural."

"Adele is right." Hatfield rose, leaning against the wall. "You know it does no good to force these things, Deputy. People give quick answers that aren't always truthful just to get it over with when they're questioned before they're ready."

"I suppose you're right, sir," Jackson grumbled.

"I see you took the vase too." Adele reached her hand toward it.

"Careful!" her brother snapped. "There might be fingerprints."

She bent down, examining it. "The pattern is rather busy."

"A gift from her daughter, I imagine," said Jackson. "I've seen things like that on display pottery from India in Chicago."

"Mrs. Marsh was the sort to find practical uses even for the finest art," Adele said. "Practicality before beauty."

"Why do you say that?" asked the sheriff.

"The water stains on the rug," Adele said. "The vase was used as a vase and not as an ornament."

"Someone emptied out the vase," said Jackson. "We found those underneath the bureau." He pointed to several daisies, now dry and wilted, in the corner of the table.

"She had flowers in the room, and someone either didn't like them or needed the vase for another purpose," Adele said.

"Your imagination is running away with you, Del," her brother said. "A more likely explanation is Mrs. Marsh herself knocked over the vase by mistake and spilled the water, then threw away the flowers."

"Under the bureau?" Sheriff Hatfield eyed him. "I agree with Adele. Those flowers were thrown aside in haste."

"Haste seems to be the mood," Jackson said. "Cinders spread out, water stains on the rug, a hidden cup and saucer."

"And yet," said Hatfield, "*that* was rather plainly in view." He nodded toward a fountain pen nib that sat like a large bug with one golden eye. "Perhaps Adele can tell us something about it."

Adele peered at it with her magnifying glass. "Not the kind sold at Raleigh's for sure."

"I haven't seen one like it in your shop either, Del," Jackson said.

"That's because the wholesaler is out of stock and has been for some time," Adele said. "A new design from Sethwell's. They call it the spoon nib."

"Eh?" Hatfield leaned forward.

"Notice how slim and curved it is," she said.

The sheriff took the nib in hand and turned it around. "Slim and curved like a spoon." A slow smile spread on his face. "How clever of you, Adele."

She felt her cheeks grow hot. "It wasn't my idea, Sheriff. Credit Mr. George W. Hughes of England. His was the original spoon-tip nib."

"It must be popular if the wholesaler is out of stock," Jackson remarked.

"For good reason," she said. "The point is fine and smooth and it writes beautifully. And being new, I find it difficult to believe Mrs. Marsh would be using it, much less carelessly leave one on the floor."

"From all I've heard, Mrs. Marsh was hardly a woman to leave anything carelessly about, whether she used it or not," Hatfield agreed. "So the question now is, to whom does it belong?"

"Perhaps to Miss Gold," Jackson suggested. "Del said she often conducted her business in that room. Lawyers use fountain pens, don't they?"

"This was not the sort of pen I saw in Rebecca's hand when I visited the Marshes," Adele said.

"A lawyer can use more than one sort of pen," Jackson argued.

"We'll be sure to ask her when we interview her," said Hatfield.

"When will that be?" Adele asked.

"We'll try tomorrow morning," said the sheriff.

"We ought to at least be able to speak with the men," Jackson said.

"And the women?" Adele asked.

Jackson looked a little disturbed. "Mrs. Bridge was rather hysterical when they got her home, or so we were told. Dr. Brody had to give her a sedative."

"Mrs. Bridge didn't strike me as the kind to need sedation for long," Adele said. "In fact, I'm surprised she needed it at all."

"She's hard as nails, I'll wager," Sheriff Hatfield agreed.

"Like her mother," Adele said with a small smile. "Zephyr and I had a chat about it just this morning."

"What could that vagabond know about the Marshes?" Jackson scoffed.

"She has a legitimate business in town, Jack," Adele insisted. "And she knows and observes people more than you think."

"What did the affable Mrs. Brown have to say about the family?" Hatfield asked.

"Nothing that would interest the police," Adele said. "Though enough to make me think Mr. Bridge's offhand remark about one of the family being involved might not be so off-hand after all."

"Really, Del." Jackson sniffed. "Just because the last few cases of murder involved the family doesn't mean this one does."

"There is no evidence to prove any of them were involved," the sheriff agreed. "In fact, there isn't really evidence to prove it wasn't Mrs. Marsh herself who put that poison in her own cup."

"I'm not so sure the family will be amenable to that suggestion," Jackson remarked. "It might even set Mrs. Bridge off in hysterics again."

"And Forrest Marsh's fiancée?" Adele asked.

"I didn't get the impression she was the hysterical type," said Jackson. "But then, I imagine she wasn't much involved with Mrs. Marsh."

"Yet," the sheriff corrected. "I was told she and Mr. Marsh just got engaged."

Adele took the parasol in hand, twisting it around. "You won't have an easy time getting much out of them, I imagine."

The sheriff led them outside the room. "That's why I'd like you to be there when we interview the family and servants. They know you better than they know us."

"I'm happy to help all I can," she said.

He looked rather flustered with his dark, wide eyes. "You've always helped us with interviews in the past, Adele. I'm grateful, you know."

"Yes, Sheriff, I know." She smiled. "Though I rather think Jack finds it inappropriate."

"He's not in charge of these investigations," said Hatfield.

"I'm sure to get a mouthful from Mrs. Faderman and her brood," she added.

"They're not in charge either." His voice became firmer. "As long as I hold this badge, I'll do things my way. Within the limits of the law, of course."

"I've always admired your independent thinking, Sheriff," Adele said in a warm voice.

This seemed to startle him and he suddenly turned around and shouted, "Edison!"

The young man stopped typing.

"Put the evidence back in the box." Hatfield pointed to the interview room. "And mind you wear gloves and be very careful."

"Certainly, Sheriff," said the young man, scurrying inside.

"I've just asked your sister to come with us tomorrow to the Marshes," Hatfield said as Jackson gathered his coat and gentlemanly attire.

"And Nin too," Adele chimed in.

The sheriff looked uncomfortable. "I hadn't thought —"

"She did tip us off to the fact that the stain in the cup was dangerous," Jackson reminded him.

"I think you ought to let her in Mrs. Marsh's room, now that it's been cleared of evidence, and see if she senses anything peculiar," Adele said. The silence of the two men agitated her. "Her gift shouldn't be wasted, Sheriff."

"My only concern is for the family," said Hatfield. "They're less than thrilled about the practical side of this investigation. If they thought we were bringing in a spiritual guide —"

"Nin is hardly that," Adele insisted.

"I imagine she would be horrified at the idea of helping the police with her — feelings." Jackson let the last word drop with such a sarcastic tone that even Edison, who was passing by with the box, chuckled.

"And yet, that's precisely what she does," Adele said. "Just when the police need it most." She gave Hatfield a meaningful look.

"You know I never have an objection to help when I can get it," he said. "As long as the help stays in its place."

"Has it ever not?" she asked.

Hatfield tipped his hat as she and Jackson headed in the direction of Caliber Street.

# CHAPTER 7

She and Nin met Jackson and Hatfield outside the Marsh house the next morning. Mrs. Stern let them into the house, the expression on her face fitting her name. "The family is just finishing breakfast," she said.

"We won't disturb them," Sheriff Hatfield said. "Is there a room we can use for our interviews?"

"You mean interrogation," the woman said under her breath. "The parlor or the study?"

"The parlor will do," said Jackson. The woman's attitude gave his posture and voice a stiff angle. "Let the family know we wish to question them in the parlor after they're finished. My sister and Miss Branch wish to see Mrs. Marsh's room and then they'll join us."

"Has Miss Gold arrived?" asked Sheriff Hatfield.

The woman held out her hands for the men's hats. Jackson gave her his, along with his cane and gloves, which made her sniff. Hatfield held on to his.

"Miss Gold is breakfasting with the family," said the woman.

"Have her join us after she's through," said the sheriff. As they headed for the parlor, he gave her a meaningful look. "We're only here to do our duty, ma'am. We'll disturb the family as little as possible."

This somewhat softened Mrs. Stern's countenance, though the lines around her mouth stood out as she watched the two men disappear through the double doors.

It was clear Mrs. Stern and the maid wasted no time tidying up after the police had gone. Everything in Mrs. Marsh's room was so clear of dust and debris that it looked as if the room hadn't been slept in for a long time. The furniture was in its place and the bed tightly made up. The carpet underneath the small table was gone which, Adele guessed, the police had taken because of the water stains.

Adele remained in the doorway, watching her friend. Nin closed her eyes and held her hands together as she circled the room, each step deliberate and slow. Adele had seen several times how Nin's auras could sometimes produce a violent reaction, and she felt nervous as she watched her friend's face grow pale.

But when Nin spoke, her voice was calm. "Deception," she said. "Like a ribbon of air tying a bow around the room."

"Do you know who is deceiving who?" Adele asked.

The woman shook her head. "There's closeness. A tying of flesh."

"Family ties," Adele murmured.

"Misdirection too," said Nin, "like a sign pointing toward the opposite road."

"Go on," Adele said.

Nin leaned her head forward and sniffed like a dog on a scent. "I smell —" she held her stomach with both hands, "something faint, but sickly, like a melting flower."

"One of Mrs. Marsh's teas?" Adele suggested.

Her friend opened her eyes and lurched out of the room, leaning against the wall. The color came back to her face and she dropped her hands from her stomach. She gave a small laugh. "I was feeling ill for a moment."

"It's all right, dear." Adele took her arm. "You don't know what the sickly scent was?"

"I've never encountered it before," she said.

"Was it some kind of herb?" Adele asked. "Not, for example, a perfume?"

"No, no!" Nin insisted. "It comes from a shadowy place in nature."

"Thank you." Adele hugged her shoulders.

Her friend looked at her. "Perhaps you're right, Adele. I've no right to refuse calling on the auras if the cause is worthy."

They went downstairs, Nin's step more assured and her color was rosy. They settled in a corner near the window. Nin opened it all the way to let in the sunlight. Adele told Hatfield of their experience while Jackson scribbled on his pad.

"Well done, Miss Branch," the sheriff said. "We are most grateful."

"I doubt a scientist could have done better," Jackson admitted, looking down at his notes.

"He would have done worse," Nin snapped.

"I imagine you're right, Miss Branch," he said with a small laugh.

The doors opened and Rebecca hurried in. "Mona is out of her state," she reported. "I've explained everything. I think the family will be more cooperative now, Sheriff."

"It's lucky we have a lawyer on our side," Hatfield grinned. "It hasn't always been the case."

Rebecca accepted the overstuffed chair Jackson indicated. "I'm told you wanted to speak to me first."

"We thought you could give us some insights."

"Insights?"

"About the family," Hatfield said.

Rebecca leaned forward. "I'll do what I can, Sheriff."

"Can you tell us a bit more about Mrs. Marsh's state of mind before she died?" the sheriff asked.

"As I told Adele, Thea was in the best of spirits."

"How was she over the holiday?" asked Adele.

Rebecca smiled. "She was glad to have everyone around her."

"I thought the family all live here," Jackson said.

Rebecca nodded. "Mona and her husband took up residence when they returned from India."

"And Theo?" Adele asked. "May I refer to the family by their first names? I feel as if I know them."

"I don't think they would mind." The lawyer glanced at the mantelpiece. "I doubt Theo ever had ideas of living anywhere but here. He once told me his mother would die if he left her."

"But his younger brother didn't feel the same way?" Hatfield raised an eyebrow.

"I believe there was some talk about his leaving once he and Stephanie wed."

"Was?" Adele asked.

"Still is, I imagine." Rebecca gave a grim smile. "I know Stephanie would like nothing more than to get Forrest away from his sister."

"She does seem rather attentive to her younger brother," Jackson remarked. "But, then, older siblings often become protective of younger ones." He threw Adele an affectionate look.

"Sometimes to the younger one's detriment," Adele couldn't help but add.

"So they've all lived at home for quite some time," Hatfield concluded. "I assume, then, they got along well with their mother."

The woman pressed her hands together in a triangle, her face growing a little uncertain.

"She demanded of them, and they sometimes pushed back," Adele guessed.

"You don't know that for a fact, Del," Jackson pointed out.

"But I do," Rebecca said. "Adele is right, though the family would think you put it a little brutally."

"Sometimes brutal words are the only true ones," Nin insisted.

"Well put, Miss Branch," the sheriff said. "You've known the family for some time, I understand."

"Our house was next to theirs," said Rebecca. "Before Gregory had his big success, that is. Even then they weren't, well, like any other family."

"How do you mean?" Jackson asked.

"Well, it's difficult to explain."

"Please try," he said. "The character of the victim and her family is important to us."

"When I was a child, I remember Thea as a very different person."

"How different?" Adele asked.

"More —" Rebecca paused as if fishing for the right word. "Silent. Complacent, even."

"I think I see," Adele nodded, remembering Zephyr's words: *No reason why Thea Marsh would be so keen on being queen of her own castle unless she were quieted while her husband was alive.*

"Gregory expected certain behaviors from everyone in the family," Rebecca echoed her thoughts. " And Thea made sure he got it."

"What sort of behaviors?" Jackson asked.

"He arranged everyone's life," said Rebecca. "Theo was to run the business, and Forrest was to help him. Mona was to marry a man worthy of the family name. They would produce Marsh heirs to take over the business and house for future generations."

"A pig lording over his sty," Nin growled.

"Thea hadn't much chance — well, I suppose to be herself," Rebecca continued. "Not with him, at least. With the children, it was different."

"You mean she was a domineering mother?" Adele asked.

"Del, don't put words into Miss Gold's mouth," Jackson said.

But Rebecca was nodding. "Oh, I suppose she took her strong character as far as it would go," she said. "Especially with Theo."

"Queen of her little corner in the castle," Adele murmured, feeling her anger rise.

"Those were different times," Jackson reminded her.

"Not so different," she snapped. "We're only speaking thirty-odd years ago."

"It's quite true, Deputy," said Rebecca. "So many of my friends had mothers who were already speaking out against injustices even when they could do little about them. Thea always kept silent."

"Thirty years ago," the sheriff added.

"Yes, thirty years ago," said Rebecca. "I suppose when Gregory died, she felt safe enough to be herself."

"And it wasn't always an agreeable self," Nin guessed.

"Very well said, Miss Branch." Jackson glanced up from his writing pad. Nin blushed and turned to the window.

"How did her family take to this new voice?" Hatfield asked.

"Theo had no qualms," said Rebecca. "He was — well, he was the favorite, I suppose you could say. He never took advantage of his position, though." The last was added with fierce defense.

"And what about Forrest and Mona?" Adele asked.

"Forrest was always lacking ambition," said Rebecca. "He never went against doing anything he was told, especially by the women in his family."

"Including Mona?"

Rebecca gave Adele a wry smile. "You know how mothers and daughters are."

"Not really," Adele said slowly. "Our mother died when I was barely five years old."

Silence lingered in the room for a moment, and Adele felt Nin take her hand.

"She didn't get along with Mrs. Marsh as well as her brother did," Jackson supplied quickly.

"Mona — I don't know quite how to say it." Rebecca sighed.

"It's as if some tiger spirit gets hold of her sometimes, and she shows her claws. But then she quiets down again."

"I rather thought her more of a donkey," Adele remarked. "Stubborn and self-preserved."

The sheriff laughed. "I'm rather a donkey myself, so I can appreciate that." His tone turned serious. "I understand from Adele that Mrs. Marsh took you on because she wanted to arrange her affairs, including drawing up her will."

"Yes, Sheriff," she said. "Her will and a few other legal documents related to the business and family holdings."

"Do you know why Mrs. Marsh wanted to draw up her will just at this time?" Jackson asked. "Was it because of her heart trouble?"

The lawyer pondered this a moment. "She never really explained why. I suspected, though, it had something to do with Forrest getting married."

"Eh?" The sheriff blinked.

"She once remarked there was hope of 'little Marshes' the day Stephanie came to stay here. She seemed to have 'little Marshes' on her mind." She grimaced. "She even said she thought Theo might get married one day and there would be proper 'little Marshes.'"

"She didn't think of her younger son's future children as proper 'little Marshes'?" Nin raised her eyebrows.

"She was old-fashioned, Miss Branch. To her, heirs come from the eldest son," Rebecca said.

"So she was thinking about future generations?" Adele asked. "I suppose I can see how that would make a woman like Thea want to make a will."

The sheriff nodded in agreement. "Miss Gold, perhaps I haven't the right to ask, but as I'm a donkey," he grinned, "what are the terms of Mrs. Marsh's will?"

"I'm not sure I know what you mean?"

"Who inherits what?" Jackson asked.

"Oh." She sank in the chair. "You'll appreciate I'm not at liberty to speak of the will unless the family consents. I prefer to remain silent until the family knows the contents. It's their right to know first, after all."

"I understand." The man nodded. "I wouldn't give anything away either if I were in your shoes, murder investigation or no murder investigation."

"It's not a question of giving anything away," she said, a little annoyed. "It's a matter of professional ethics, which I take very seriously."

"Indeed, indeed," said the sheriff. "But you do realize the terms of the will may give us a clue as to who could have killed your employer."

The blood drained from Rebecca's face. "You mean you think one of the family did this awful thing?"

"We must start somewhere," Hatfield murmured.

"And that somewhere is the family." She sat very still. "Adele assured me you were a fair man, Sheriff. It seems a little presumptuous."

"This is now a murder investigation, Miss Gold." Sheriff Hatfield's pleasant countenance grew hard. "I follow the evidence wherever it leads, even if it upsets those close to the victim."

"What makes you think someone on the outside didn't do it?" Rebecca asked. "Gregory wasn't always — delicate in business. I'm sure he incurred many enemies. As his widow, Thea might have inherited that wrath."

"It's not unheard of," Jackson admitted.

"If Mr. Marsh incurred the wrath of a former associate or rival, that person would more likely have gone for the sons rather than the widow," Hatfield said. "Maybe even the son-in-law, depending on how deeply involved he is with the family business."

"Perhaps you're right." Rebecca sighed.

"Did Mrs. Marsh mention having any enemies, either hers or

her husband's?" asked the sheriff. "Anyone who might have threatened her?"

"I'm sure she would have told me if she had," Rebecca said. "Theo would have told me."

"How would he know?" Adele asked.

"They told one another everything."

Beside her, Nin sniffed.

"One more question, Miss Gold." The sheriff produced a paper packet from his pocket and unfolded it, laying it on the coffee table. "Do you recognize this?"

Rebecca looked at the fountain pen nib. "I don't recall it."

"It was found near Mrs. Marsh's bed in her room," he said. "As you did business with her, we thought it might be yours."

"No, Sheriff," she said.

"Can you identify it, then?"

"If you're asking if it was hers, the answer is no," said Rebecca.

"How can you be sure?" asked Jackson.

"Thea was, as I told you, a proper lady in her manners and habits," said Rebecca. "She used gold tips, not silver." Her face grew dark. "Is it important?"

"We shall see," said Hatfield. "We'd like to see Mr. and Mrs. Stern next, and then we'll speak with the family."

Rebecca rose. "Should I be present when you speak with them?"

"I don't think that's necessary," said the sheriff. "Unless they wish it, since you're their lawyer."

"I was really more Thea's lawyer," she said ruefully.

"But not in the face of a criminal investigation," Jackson pointed out.

"That's true," she admitted. "I really couldn't do much anyway. I think Theo's keeping me on more for sentiment."

"Or because he needs you as a friend," Adele said, smiling.

"And you're sweet on him," Nin said in her candid way.

Rebecca gave her a sharp look as she left the room.

# CHAPTER 8

Mrs. Stern's face held the same sour expression as she came in with her husband. She nodded to the ladies and sat like a scarecrow on the couch, her knees knitted together and her hands balled in her lap.

"How long have you been working for the Marshes?" Hatfield asked.

"Going on fifty-three years now," said Mr. Stern. "When Mr. and Mrs. Marsh got married."

"And you do a little bit of everything," Adele said, smiling.

"Mr. Marsh didn't like a lot of people fussing about the house," said Mr. Stern. "He hired us because we could do everything. I act as the butler and do the gardening and any odd job that needs a man. My wife is housekeeper and cook. We've only Polly, the one maid, to help us."

"And Polly doesn't add up to much, the breezy girl," Mrs. Stern added with a growl.

"You do a lovely job taking care of this place," Adele said warmly.

"I'm sure it's a challenge," Jackson added. "We had five people running our house, and there were only three of us."

"It wasn't so bad, sir." Mr. Stern was beginning to warm up. "The family is always most considerate. Mrs. Marsh insisted they not tax us more than they have to."

A groan came from Mrs. Stern, and she held her handkerchief to her eyes.

"You liked her very much." Adele wandered over to the couch and sat near the woman.

"She was a fair mistress always," said the woman with a sniff.

"We don't want to distress you," said Hatfield. "But we need to know a little more about the night Mrs. Marsh passed on."

"Killed! Why don't you say it?" the woman screeched. "She was killed and you think one of the family did it!"

"Please, Ella," her husband begged.

"They have their faults, but not one of them would ever think of murder," she choked.

"The sheriff never said any such thing," her husband pointed out.

"We're trying to get information, ma'am," said Jackson. "As you were the first to find her, you could help us a great deal."

"Yes," said the woman. "Yes, I want to help." She took a deep breath, and her posture became like a knife again. "I apologize, Sheriff. Ask me what you like."

"Who brought Mrs. Marsh her tea that night?" Hatfield asked.

"Mr. Theo did," she said.

"He always did that?"

"The night tea, Sheriff," Adele said. "I remember Thea telling me that. He chose a special tea and always brought it up. Isn't that right?" She glanced at Mrs. Stern, who nodded.

"I always brought up the others," said the woman.

"Others?"

"Mrs. Marsh believed in tea in the morning, tea in the afternoon, and tea before bed," Adele remarked.

"She was most particular," said Mrs. Stern. "Polly always spills things when she goes up those stairs."

"Did you make her bedtime tea for her that night?" Jackson asked.

Her features sharpened. "I did not! Mr. Theo made it for her."

"Part of the ritual," Adele mumbled.

"I see." The sheriff looked thoughtful.

"He never put anything in it!" the housekeeper snapped. "Water and tea, that's all."

"We're not accusing him of anything, ma'am," Sheriff Hatfield said. "We're only trying to get information." The woman calmed down, nodding. "When did Mr. Theo bring her the tea?"

"About eight o'clock," she said. "Mrs. Marsh took to her room ever since she had that accident a year ago."

"She fell down those stairs late one night," Mr. Stern added. "Gave her quite a fright."

"She was already in bed when you entered the room?" Adele asked.

"Yes, miss," said the woman. "They ate early, about six. The others retired to the parlor for coffee, but she went straight to her room."

"She was tired from her argument," Nin said softly.

The woman stared at her. "Argument, miss?"

Nin glanced at the window without answering.

"Did you see her before she went to bed?" asked Hatfield.

"Of course I did." The woman sniffed. "I always ask the mistress if she needs anything before bed."

"And did she?"

"She asked me to close the curtains," she said. "They put in streetlights on the road last year, and the mistress said it made the room too bright for her to sleep at night."

"What time was this, Mrs. Stern?" Jackson asked.

"About ten o'clock, I should say."

"Then you would have been one of the last to see her alive," he said softly. "The doctor said she died between eleven and midnight."

"Oh, Deputy!" The woman began to sob. This time, Nin, whose misanthropic moods were always broken by sympathy, put her arms around the woman's shoulders like an affectionate child. Mr. Stern looked shocked, but his wife seemed either not to notice or to care. She was soothed in a few moments.

"Was there anything strange in your mistress's behavior or in the way she looked?" Hatfield inquired.

"She was a little agitated," Mrs. Stern admitted. "I thought it was just the sort of mood one gets after the holidays, you know. But maybe she did have some argument that afternoon." She shot Nin a look.

"With whom do you think she had an argument?" Hatfield asked.

The woman sniffed. "It's not my place to guess, Sheriff."

Adele patted the woman's hand. "But your guess would probably be better than anyone else's," said Adele. "It's clear you have insights, Mrs. Stern, or you wouldn't agree so readily with my friend about there being an argument. It might prove important."

Her husband leaned forward. "As my wife said, it isn't our place to speculate."

"We're not gossips, sir," Jackson said firmly. "We're here to do a duty by your mistress."

The woman hesitated a few moments more, then said, "I think it might have been Mrs. Bridge."

"Did they often argue?"

"I wouldn't quite say that," the woman said. "Mrs. Bridge was very careful."

"That's an interesting remark, Mrs. Stern," Adele said. "What do you mean, 'careful'?"

The woman blushed. "I didn't mean anything special by it, miss. But, well, Mrs. Bridge says things sometimes that can be taken the wrong way."

"Insinuations," Nin put in.

"If you say so, miss." The woman sniffed. "I don't know any

fancy words. But Mrs. Bridge is a good woman and she tried hard not to upset her mother."

"What do you think they could have been arguing about?" The sheriff held up his hand as Mr. Stern opened his mouth. "I know, it's not your place to speculate. But it would help us a great deal."

"Mrs. Bridge had her own ideas about running the house," said Mrs. Stern. "Only last week she and the mistress were arguing about buying Polly one of those new electric irons. Mrs. Marsh was afraid she would burn the house down. Knowing Polly, she probably would." The last was said with a snort.

"So you think Mrs. Marsh was upset because of some squabble over domestic affairs?" Jackson asked.

Mrs. Stern shot him a look. "Such matters might be trifling to you, Deputy, but they can be quite irritating to the lady of the house."

"Of course," Jackson assured her.

"Had Mrs. Marsh already drunk the tea when you came in?" asked Hatfield

"No, sir. The service was still sitting on the night table."

"Had she already poured it into the cup?" Jackson asked.

"No, sir," said Mrs. Stern. "Mr. Theo just set it on the table, pot and all."

Both lawmen looked at one another. "He brought it in at eight and you saw her at ten but she still hadn't had her nightly tea?" asked Hatfield.

"Oh, but that's nothing unusual, sir," Mr. Stern jumped in.

"She always said herbs needed to steep, and she never drank the tea until it was almost cooled down," Mrs. Stern said.

"Never piping hot," Adele echoed.

"That's right, miss." Tears filled the housekeeper's eyes again. "She said it was better for the body that way. Cleansing, you know."

"There, there." Her husband patted her shoulders.

"She must have drunk it soon after you left the room," Adele said.

"You mean it was sitting there — poisoned — all the time?" The woman let out a screech.

"You weren't to know, Mrs. Stern," the sheriff said kindly.

"Where did Mrs. Marsh usually leave the cup in the morning?" asked Jackson.

"Why, on that night table, of course."

"But it wasn't there when you discovered her in the morning, was it?" Hatfield asked.

The woman looked confused for a moment. "Why, no, it wasn't!" She struggled to speak. "I suppose Polly must have taken it away."

"She didn't," Adele said. "Miss Gold asked her."

"Well, Polly doesn't always remember what she does and doesn't do." The woman rolled her eyes.

"Could Polly have hidden the cup?" asked Adele.

"Hidden, miss?" The woman stared at her.

"We found the cup and saucer hidden among some linens in the bureau drawer."

The shock on the woman's face was replaced by anger. "That woman! The nerve!"

"Polly?" Jackson asked.

"No, Nurse Pegg," said Mrs. Stern.

"You think she hid the cup and saucer?" The sheriff looked surprised.

"You just suggested it was that scatterbrained maid," Nin said.

Mrs. Stern gave her a stoic look. "Polly may be scatterbrained, miss, but she's a good girl. Besides, she wouldn't dare."

"No, I don't suppose she would with you around," Nin growled.

"Why would Nurse Pegg hide them?" Adele asked.

The woman shrugged. "She has strange notions, that woman. Heard she once worked in an insane asylum." A tone of self-righteousness crept into her voice. "She might have done it just to see if she could get me or Polly into a fix. She's always prowling about, moving and hiding things."

"She's hidden things before," Mr. Stern offered. "There are people who can't help doing such things, can they?"

"You ask her!" Mrs. Stern insisted.

"We shall." Adele could see Hatfield was trying to hide his smile as he went on in a serious tone, "Did you leave her alone after you closed the curtains?"

"Yes, sir," she said.

"And no one came in while you were there?"

"Mr. Theo came in just as I was leaving," she said.

"He always came in to say goodnight," Mr. Stern added. "Always very responsible, that young man."

"How long did he usually stay?"

"I'm sure I can't say," said Mrs. Stern. "When I left, she was telling him a story about how she and his father met." She sobbed, "He always listened to her stories. None of the others did."

"There, there," her husband murmured, again touching her shoulders.

"So, really, Mr. Marsh was the last to see his mother alive," Jackson said.

This brought on a deeper sob from Mrs. Stern, and Nin went to her again. Hatfield glared at his deputy, and Adele knew he was giving him a silent reprimand. Her brother was thorough about his job but sometimes at the cost of sensitivity.

"One last question," said the sheriff when Mrs. Stern had once more calmed down. "Did either of you see or hear anything unusual that night?"

They were both silent for a moment. Mrs. Stern shook her head, her face still half buried in her handkerchief. Mr. Stern's brows came together. "Well —"

"Yes?"

"Oh, it was nothing," he insisted. "A rustle in the bushes outside my window."

"Where is your room?"

"First floor in the back, sir," he said. "But it was mighty windy that night."

"Do you always hear such noise on a windy night?" Jackson asked.

The man hunched his shoulders. "No, sir. Not always. Least ways, I don't always notice."

"He sleeps like a log," Mrs. Stern put in.

"Then it must have been enough to wake you," Adele said.

"Well, miss, now that you mention it," he said, "it was more than a rustling. Like someone was settling in for the night."

"Did you get up to see who it might be?" Jackson asked.

"No, sir," he said. "I supposed it to be a stray dog. We get them often around here."

"And you, Mrs. Stern?" Jackson turned to her. "Did you hear or see anything?"

"I fell right to sleep," she insisted. "I always do, what with so much on my shoulders in the daytime."

"Yes, of course," said the sheriff with a kind smile. "I'm sure the family appreciate your hard work."

Mrs. Stern's tight face indicated she thought they did not.

~~~~~

The interview with Polly, the maid, was short and uneventful. The young woman, though kind-hearted, really was, as Nin had put it, a "scatterbrain." She seemed too bewildered to do more than keep repeating the last she had seen of Mrs. Marsh was when she changed the sheets in the bedroom that afternoon.

"What about dinner?" Adele asked. As with most of the younger ladies, Hatfield had let her take the reins for questioning Polly.

"Dinner, miss?"

"You helped serve the dinner, didn't you?" Nin prompted.
~~~~~

"Oh, I forgot about that, miss." The girl giggled. "Get so used to things around here."

"You saw Mrs. Marsh then," Adele said.

"Well, not to speak to, miss," said the girl.

"How did she seem to you?" Adele leaned forward.

"Why, just as usual," said the girl. Adele suspected Polly hardly knew what Thea's usual was.

"When did you go to bed, Polly?" she asked.

"About ten-thirty, miss," she said. "What with the dishes and all —" The girl sighed.

"Was anybody else awake when you went to bed?" she asked.

"No, indeed, miss. Ain't no one awake when I go to bed. I'm the last, you see." She looked down at her hands.

"You work long hours, don't you, Polly?" Adele asked kindly.

"Mrs. Stern don't like being awake after ten," she said. "She leaves me the dishes and all the cleaning."

"Thank you, Polly." Adele glanced at Hatfield, who nodded with approval.

The girl rose. But she dawdled a bit, playing with the edge of her apron. "Miss?"

"Yes, Polly?"

"You asked if anybody else was awake. I think Mrs. Marsh was."

"Eh?" The sheriff leaned forward.

"That is, sort of awake in her sleep," said the girl shyly.

"What are you talking about?" Jackson's voice was a little harsher.

Adele gave him a look. "You mean she was dreaming?"

"I think so, miss," said the girl. "I went by her door, you see. And I heard her mumbling."

"You didn't hear what she said, did you?" Jackson eyed her.

The girl stiffened. "I ain't one for listening at doors."

"Of course not," Adele said in a soothing tone. "But you thought she was dreaming."

"Well, it had to be a dream, miss," said the girl. "Ain't no one there to talk to so late at night, is there?"

"And this was at about ten-thirty?" the sheriff asked.

The girl nodded.

"Thank you, Polly." Adele pressed her hand. "That's very valuable to us."

The girl grinned. As she left the room, she ran into Nurse Pegg. Adele caught the frightened look on the girl's face as she pressed against the door to let the nurse through. Nurse Pegg had the sort of quiet look one expected from a nurse as well as the faded hair and eyes of a middle-aged woman who spent much of her life taking care of others. Adele immediately felt sorry for her.

She motioned Nurse Pegg toward one of the chairs and sat on the couch facing her. "It's good of you to stay on even though your work is done," she began.

"I always do once my patient dies," she said, her tone wistful. "Always here to help tie up the loose ends."

"You're very responsible." Adele nodded in approval.

"I see a job is done," she insisted. "Unlike *some* people who think I don't know my duty."

"You mean the Sterns?" Nin now sat cross-legged on the rug, as was her habit.

The woman stared. "Young lady, it's very unsanitary to sit on the floor like that."

"I'm not sitting on the floor," Nin protested. "I'm sitting on the rug."

"Even worse," said the nurse. "Those cleaners are notoriously bad at picking up dust. And germs stick to dust."

"Is it the new cleaners or the lady who manages the cleaning you don't trust?" Adele watched her.

"You're mistaken, Miss —"

"Gossling."

"Oh, yes, the detective lady." Adele tried not to wince. "You're mistaken, Miss Gossling. It's Mrs. Stern who doesn't trust me. I imagine she'll all but try to accuse me of having something to do with poor Mrs. Marsh's murder."

"She did suggest you hid the teacup in the bureau drawer," Adele admitted.

"What?" The woman jumped. "Why, that fiend!"

"Can you enlighten us as to why she might have said such a thing?" Jackson asked.

"I've no idea, I'm sure." The woman sniffed. "I suppose it's because Mrs. Marsh asked me to do things for her that she's always done. Servants can be quite territorial."

"But you do sometimes hide things," Adele prompted gently.

Nurse Pegg folded her hands in her lap. "Only for good reason. One day she came in and found me hiding a bag of licorice in one of the drawers." Adele glanced at the sheriff. "Mrs. Bridge brought them from the confectioners — oh, she was just trying to be kind — but, well, the doctor advised Mrs. Marsh to let go of sweets. She had a fancy for them, you see, almost like a child. And they weren't good for her."

"Why did you choose the bureau?" asked Jackson.

The woman blinked. "Well, I could turn around when Thea wasn't looking and put it in there." She eyed him. "But I didn't put that cup there. More likely *she* did it!"

"She?"

"Mrs. Stern."

"And why would she do that?"

"Because she put something terrible in it she didn't want anybody to know about."

"Mr. Marsh made her the teas," Nin reminded her.

"But Mrs. Stern was in the kitchen," the woman pointed out. "It would be easy for her to put something in it when no one was looking."

"The Sterns seem fond of their mistress," Hatfield remarked. "I shouldn't think they would want to do away with her."

"Mrs. Marsh was quite demanding," said the nurse.

"So are many mistresses," Jackson pointed out. "A seasoned housekeeper such as Mrs. Stern would be used to that."

The nurse shrugged. "There are rumors she and her husband will get a nice nest egg when the will is read."

"I don't think you really believe what you're saying, Nurse Pegg." Adele eyed her.

The woman sighed. "You're right, Miss Gossling. I don't believe it for a moment."

"We don't believe for a moment you put that teacup in the drawer," Adele assured her. "You took very good care of Mrs. Marsh. That much is clear."

"And if you had really wanted to kill your charge, you could have done it in many other ways more fitting to your position," Nin added.

Nurse Pegg gave her a seething look. "I've taken care of some of the most prominent citizens in Sacramento."

"Yes, certainly," Adele said. "You also gave her medicines the doctor prescribed?"

"Only a sleeping draught," she said.

The sheriff leaned forward. "But Mrs. Marsh had a heart condition, did she not?"

"That's not quite true, Sheriff." She held up one finger as if she were giving a lesson. "Some heart conditions need medicines and some don't. One must simply be careful."

"And Mrs. Marsh was careful?" Adele asked.

"As careful as a high-spirited woman could be," said Nurse Pegg.

"And a demanding one," Nin said ruefully.

The nurse shifted. "Young lady, I really would feel much more comfortable if you sat in a chair."

Adele gave her friend a look, and Nin rose, settling on the couch beside her.

"That's better." The woman smiled. "Yes, Mrs. Marsh sometimes took chloral hydrate when she couldn't sleep."

"What form?" asked the sheriff.

She gave him a strange look. "Liquid."

This made both lawmen sit up.

"Does it leave a dark stain?" asked Jackson.

"Of course not," said the nurse. "Not that I've seen, anyway."

"The doctor gave this to her?" asked Adele.

"Yes, but she took a very small dose," said Nurse Pegg.

"Every night?"

"Oh, no. Once, twice a week perhaps." The woman seemed to understand. "But she hadn't taken it for at least three weeks."

"Can you account for the dark stain in the teacup, then?" Jackson asked.

"I could hardly comment on that," said the woman with a sniff. "That's a police matter."

"We understood you and Mrs. Stern found Mrs. Marsh," Adele said.

"We did," she said. "We met on the stairs and went up together — Mrs. Stern to give her breakfast and I to see how she had passed the night."

"You saw Mrs. Marsh in her bed," Adele prompted. "Did you examine her?"

"Only for a moment," said Nurse Pegg. "When I saw she was dead, I told Mrs. Stern to call the police and barred the door."

"It was clear from a glance Mrs. Marsh was dead?" Sheriff Hatfield asked.

"Oh, yes," said Nurse Pegg. Her face grew a little white. "Her position and her countenance — well, they were rather distinct."

"So you must have known Mrs. Marsh didn't die of heart failure," Jackson said. "You would know the signs."

"I didn't get a chance to do more than glance," the nurse protested. "I didn't want to touch anything."

"That was very sensible of you," Adele said.

Nurse Pegg looked at the sheriff. "If there is nothing else, I should like to go."

"Will you be taking a new position so soon?" Jackson asked kindly.

"I've some things to see to here, and Miss Gold has informed me I must stay for the reading of the will," she said. "I always do my duty." This last was said with finality as she left the room.

# CHAPTER 9

When Theodore Marsh walked into the parlor, it was clear the man was suffering. His tall frame sagged, and his shoulders rounded. The robust blond hair looked stringy and his face haggard and blue from paleness. He seemed to have a hard time keeping his eyes open.

"You look as if you haven't been getting much sleep," Adele remarked.

Nin scurried forth with a glass of brandy that seemed to come out of nowhere and sat a little away from the man, her sparkling eyes soft with sympathy.

"I'm afraid I'm not a very strong person," he admitted. "It's all this — it's this —" His tongue seemed to fail him, and he slumped back.

"We know it isn't easy for you, sir," Hatfield said. "And we wouldn't be here if it weren't necessary."

"I realize that, Sheriff," he said. "I want to help you. I want to know who did this awful thing." He turned away and held his hand to his face. There was a respectful silence in the room as they all waited until he turned to them, fully composed. "Please feel free to ask me anything you wish."

"We would like to know about your movements the night before your mother —"

"You can say it for what it is," said Theo. "Died. Killed, perhaps."

"You were here, sir?" Jackson prompted.

"Yes, but not for dinner. I came home late."

"Oh?"

"We're negotiating a rather lucrative business deal," said Theo. Despite his grief, there was a note of pride in his voice. "The largest venture we've ever had. And there was a lot to do so I was forced to work on a holiday weekend."

"I assume your brother was working late too?" Hatfield asked.

The man gave a rueful smile. "Forrest has never been as interested in the business as my father wanted him to be. His job is more along the lines of an errand boy."

"You don't trust him," Nin observed.

"It isn't that, Miss Branch," said the man firmly. "He's simply not very, well, high-reaching when it comes to business."

"How late did you stay at the office?" asked Jackson.

"Oh, quite late," he said. "But not too late. I always come home before eight o'clock. Mother —" His voice caught and he turned again with his hand to his face, commanding silence as he recovered. "Mother would get restless if I wasn't there to say goodnight to her."

"That seems unfair to you," Jackson said quietly. "Obligating you to tuck her in, as it were."

"It wasn't like that, Deputy," said Theo. "She always said she slept better when I was there to make her bedtime tea."

"Which you did," said Hatfield.

"Yes, sir. The same as I did every night."

"And you took it up to her room, the same as you did every night," Adele said.

"Yes." He blinked. "It was sort of a habit."

"She told me about her tea rituals," Adele said softly.

"And how was your mother's mood when you took her the tea?" asked Hatfield.

"Uplifted, I would say."

Hatfield's head shot up. "We understood from Mrs. Stern your mother was rather agitated."

The man blinked. "If she was, I certainly didn't notice it."

"Mrs. Stern seemed to think your mother had some kind of argument with your sister earlier that day," Jackson said.

"She might have," the man said in a cautious tone. "I did see Mona go into her room after lunch. But they often bickered about one thing or another." He gave a rueful smile. "Mona can be quarrelsome when she chooses."

"Perhaps she was in a better mood because you brought her the tea," Adele suggested.

He gave a vague smile. "I brought her flowers too."

"Daisies?" Adele glanced at the sheriff.

"They were her favorite," he said. "She said they were cheerful and simple. One ought to have something cheerful and simple when life becomes so complicated." The far-off tone made Adele think he was quoting Thea.

"So the flowers in your mother's room were from you," said Hatfield.

He nodded. "I filled the vase myself and arranged them."

"How long did you stay?" The sheriff leaned back.

"Not long," he said. "I arranged the flowers and we had a little chat as we always do. I don't — I never kept her up too late."

"What did you talk about?" asked Jackson.

"Business, mostly," he said. "She always liked to know what was going on with the mill."

"She took an interest in it?" asked Hatfield.

"I wouldn't say an interest, sir," said Theo. "More a curiosity."

"Was anyone else working with you in the office that night?" Hatfield asked.

He shook his head. "I often work in the mill alone. I find it difficult to get much done in the daytime. So much noise and bustle going on and the saws working."

"Yes, quite so," Hatfield agreed.

"You didn't ask your secretary to remain with you?" Adele asked.

"No, Miss Gossling, I don't subject the female workers to any rules I don't expect the male workers to follow," he said. "My father had that policy, though I imagine his reasons for not demanding the secretaries stay on past their usual hour was more financial than humane." This last was said with some bitterness.

"It's kind of you to keep that policy for the right reasons," Adele smiled.

He bowed.

"After you said good night to your mother, what did you do?" asked Hatfield.

"I went straight to bed, naturally."

"You saw no one else before you went to bed?"

"Well, no." The man looked confused. "Not really, that is. I heard the Sterns downstairs going to their rooms." He cocked his head. "Come to think of it, it was rather quiet in the house."

"Everyone was in bed already," Nin suggested.

"No, not that sort of quiet, Miss Branch. As if everyone was out."

"And that was unusual?" asked Jackson.

"Quite unusual," he said. "I mean — for everyone to be out of the house together like that."

"Did Mrs. Marsh comment upon it when you spoke to her?"

"No, I don't think Mother noticed," he said. "Her room is quite insulated, Deputy. She didn't hear much of what went on beyond it."

"Getting back to the tea you made your mother that night," the sheriff continued, "We were told you were the one who brought the tea in the evening."

"Most of the time," he said. "She was quite fussy about it. Once

Mona brought her some Chinese tea from San Francisco and it made her quite ill."

"Was the tea you gave her that night a new blend or one already in the house?"

"A new blend," he said. "I'd gone to that little shop in Arrojo at lunchtime, the one with the pink tables."

"Dora's Tea Shop," Adele said.

"Yes, that's it. I'd heard she received some teas from the Orient, and I wanted to take a look. I wanted something special for Mother." His eyes wrinkled as if he were trying to keep the tears from falling.

"And you bought it," said Jackson.

"Yes. A red tea. I don't know what the name of it is. It had other things in it, of course. The tin is in the Indian language, so I don't know what exactly." He leaned forward. "Perhaps Miss Leslie can tell you."

"You prepared it yourself, didn't you?" Nin asked.

"I always do, Miss Branch." He glanced at her. "Mrs. Stern is the best of women, but she has no respect for Mother's teas, you see. Mother always told me you have to let them sit and then press the leaves through the mesh —" His voice caught, and he was silent again.

"Respect for the goodness of the herbs," Nin murmured.

"Yes! You understand. You know something about herbs, I've been told."

Nin's face grew grave as she turned toward the wall.

"All you talked about with your mother was business?" asked Hatfield.

The man stiffened. "What else would we talk about, Sheriff?"

"We're not asking you to reveal family secrets, sir," Jackson said, equally stiff. "But sometimes what a victim says or how she behaves matters in an investigation."

"Victim," Theo murmured, his face contorted with grief. "Yes, she was a victim, wasn't she? But of whom? And why?" This came out as the cry of a child, and rather than turn his head and cover his face with his hand, he shut his eyes, letting the tears flow.

Jackson's tone softened. "We'll find out, Mr. Marsh. That's our job."

"Yes," Theo said. "Yes, of course it is. I apologize for my outburst. I've heard only good things about the Arrojo police." Hatfield and Jackson looked relieved. "No, we didn't just talk about business. We talked about the family too."

"Mrs. Stern told us Thea was reminiscing." Adele smiled.

"Yes, she had been doing that quite often lately." He sighed.

"Why do you think she was reminiscing, sir?" Hatfield asked.

The man shrugged. "Perhaps she was missing Father now that time was passing."

"You don't believe that." Nin narrowed her eyes.

Theo jolted in his seat but then settled in and mumbled, "Father could be rather unpleasant at times."

"Tyrannical might be a better word, from what we've heard," Jackson suggested in a gentle tone.

"He wasn't very tolerant of women unless they stayed in their place." Both Adele and Nin grunted. He gave them a sheepish smile. "It never sat well with him that both my mother and sister showed an interest in the lumber business."

"Did they?" Adele asked.

"Oh, only in a mild sense," he said. "Mona did ask a lot of questions about it at one time. But she got over it."

"I'm sure she had no choice," Adele said dryly.

"You said you talked about the family?" Jackson prompted.

"Well, yes," the man admitted. "We talked about my brother."

"Your mother was concerned about his upcoming marriage?" Adele asked.

"She liked Stephanie," he said. "But, well, Stephanie doesn't like this house."

"And she wants Forrest to leave it," Adele said softly.

"Mother liked having all of us here," said Theo. "I suppose

most parents do when they grow older. She wasn't keen on the idea of Stephanie and Forrest moving to Los Angeles."

Adele leaned her head sideways. "Your mother certainly knew what she wanted, didn't she?"

"I wish I could make you understand," he said with a sigh. "She always had a strong will. I suppose Father, with all his good intentions, suppressed that with his expectations. And when he died, it — well, it came pouring out." He sat up. "But a woman doesn't get killed because she has a strong will!"

"Let us hope not," said Sheriff Hatfield dryly. "I've a delicate question, Mr. Marsh. Have you any idea about the terms of your mother's will?"

The man looked dazed. "Becca would know about that, Sheriff."

"Miss Gold is standing by her ethics," Jackson said. "She won't reveal the contents of the will without your permission."

"Of course she would say that." Theo smiled. "Becca is a good girl. She always was."

"She's more than a girl, Mr. Marsh." Adele eyed him. "She's a woman."

"Or haven't you noticed?" Nin put in.

"Do we have your permission?" Jackson asked.

The dazed look lingered as silence filled the parlor. Then Theo jerked his head. "What? No, that's none of your business!"

"It might be very pertinent, sir," Hatfield said. "And if you've nothing to hide —"

"Sheriff, you and your deputy have probed into our affairs for the last several hours. You should know none of us has anything to hide." The man's lips drew in a thin line. "Mother was very private with her affairs. The will was her affair."

"It's now your affair, sir," Jackson said. "You're head of the family."

"The will is hers, and I will not expose it to the prying eyes of the police before we've even had a chance to know what's in it," Theo said firmly. "You see my point of view, I hope?"

"Yes, sir, I see your point of view," Hatfield said. "I think that's all for now, Mr. Marsh." The man stood up. "Oh, by the way," he pointed to the fountain pen nib on the table, "is that yours?"

It took a while for the man to scrutinize it before he handed it back to the sheriff. "No, sir."

"You weren't sure, though," Jackson observed.

"Only because it looks like the sort of thing we might have around the office," he admitted. "But, no, I haven't seen it before." He squinted. "Rather an odd shape."

"Spoon tip," Adele said.

"Oh, how clever!" He seemed almost delighted. "I like such things, you know. My father always said a man's business tools were as important as a man's business."

"I couldn't agree more," Adele said with a small smile.

After he left, Jackson leaned back. "Well, that went as expected."

"What do you mean, Jack?" Adele asked.

"I was expecting a milksop," he said. "One of those men who hangs on to his mother's apron strings and remains a bachelor all his life. That's what we got all right."

"Your perception of people is very narrow for a policeman, Mr. Gossling," Nin snarled.

"I go from my experiences, Miss Branch," he retorted. "My experiences with all sorts of men far exceeds yours, I gather."

To this, she narrowed her eyes.

"I can't help but agree with Jackson," Sheriff Hatfield said. "I watched many such men try to find the courage their mothers had taken away from them, doing the most dangerous duties at sea."

"You blame the mothers?" Adele raised her eyebrows.

"Perhaps I have no right to speak," he said. "I could easily be one of these 'hanging on his mother's apron strings,' and Ma can be very strong-willed at times."

"But she never took away your courage," Adele said kindly. The man gave her a gracious nod and played with his watch chain.

"Nevertheless, he had some interesting insights about his mother and father," Jackson pointed out.

"It wouldn't have taken much to guess them," Adele said. "I've met countless older women who were freed from the shackles of their husbands' expectations only by his death."

"Perhaps so," Jackson said. "But 'pouring out' her strong will on her family —"

"Like lava pouring out of a volcano," Nin remarked.

"An apt description, Miss Branch." Jackson nodded.

"Sheriff, how long ago did Mr. Marsh die?" Adele leaned forward.

Hatfield glanced at Jackson, who flipped through his notebook. "Twenty-two years now."

"Forrest seems hardly older than that," Nin remarked.

"Actually, he's older than you think, Miss Branch," said Jackson. "He was thirteen when his father died."

"That's a lot of time for children to get used to an entirely different mother," Adele remarked.

"Perhaps one of them never got used to it," Nin said.

"A mother taking the reins of the family is hardly a motive for murder, Miss Branch," Jackson said.

"I never said it was," Nin snapped. "But a domineering woman can be one of the most volatile species on earth."

Sheriff Hatfield nodded. "What about this business with the will?"

"Yes, funny how he suddenly found his courage when we asked his permission to know the contents," Jackson remarked.

"He wants to be loyal to his mother," Adele pointed out. "It makes an interesting question, though. Why have his back up about this one thing?"

"Maybe he's afraid this one thing will incriminate somebody," Hatfield suggested.

"And it's not very difficult to guess who that somebody is," Nin added.

"He was the closest to his mother," Jackson said.

"You mean he was her favorite," Adele corrected. "It's not the same thing, Jack."

"Even the favorite can turn to hate," Nin chimed in.

The remark was left hanging in the silence.

he Bridges opened the parlor doors tentatively and, after Sheriff Hatfield motioned for them to enter, almost crept in. Adele was surprised to see Mona completely subdued. She had removed the heavily veiled hat so her face shown worn and faded with streaks of tears. The corner of her husband's eye rose into a small knot and remained there the entire interview.

"I hope you're feeling better, Mrs. Bridge," Adele said kindly.

"Thank you," said the woman. Her voice was low and calm.

"This has been ghastly for all of us," Mr. Bridge said. "I'm sure it's a misunderstanding."

"You still think your mother-in-law died of natural causes?" The sheriff cocked his head.

"This whole poison business." His tone became grizzled. "Anybody could have mistaken it for, well, something else."

"Some of those teas were medicinal," Mona chimed in. "One never knows how someone will react. What might be healing to one person is toxic to another."

"That's a very good point, dear." Mr. Bridge took her hand.

"Please, may we get this over with?" She looked expectantly at the sheriff.

"We're going through some routine questions," Hatfield began, "looking at the evening of the twenty-sixth."

Mona ventured, "We went to see a play that night at the Rosa Gris Theater, didn't we, William?"

"Yes, certainly, certainly," her husband said. "I've a poor memory for dates." He gave a small laugh.

"What play?" Jackson asked.

"Must you speak as if we're under suspicion?" Mona turned away.

"Perhaps in a way we are, dear," said her husband. "The play was *A Midsummer Night's Dream*."

"A rather long one," Hatfield remarked. Adele hid her surprise. She would hardly have thought the sheriff, with his adventurous life, would know the length of a Shakespearian play.

Mr. Bridge smiled ruefully. "Three hours and forty minutes, to be exact."

"The play began at eight o'clock," Mona recalled.

"And you stayed at the theater the entire time?" asked Jackson.

Mona gave him a wry look. "Have you ever attended a play, Deputy?"

"I have indeed," he said. "Many times I've slipped out before the end with my pipe when the play was boring."

"But always discreetly and politely," Adele confirmed with a small smile.

"One does not 'slip out' of Shakespeare," Mona said in a tight voice.

"'Though she be but little, she is fierce,'" Nin quoted. They looked at her in surprise, and she hunched her shoulders, looking out the window.

"You stayed in your seats the entire three hours and forty minutes?" Hatfield asked.

"I did," Mr. Bridge said. "I'm not much for socializing during intermissions. My wife likes me to come with her to these sorts of things, so —"

Adele noticed the stinging look Mona gave him.

"You never moved from your place in all that time?" Jackson eyed him.

The man shifted in the chair. "My wife will attest to that, Deputy. I was exactly in the same place when you left, wasn't I, dear?" His sandy mustache peaked with anticipation.

"Indeed you were in your place," she said shortly, "when I came back."

"Back from where?" asked the sheriff.

"I went out after the first act," she said. "I needed some fresh air. Those theaters can get rather stuffy."

"Where did you go?"

"Where everybody else goes." She glared at Hatfield. "Really, Sheriff, this is too much!"

"We're only doing our duty, ma'am," said Hatfield in his quiet way. "We're interested in finding out who caused your mother's death."

"No one 'caused' it," she insisted. "It was an accident. It must have been."

"One does not put poisoned syrup in a teacup by accident, dear," said her husband in a low voice.

"Mother herself could have done it," she challenged. "That sleeping draught the doctor gave her —"

"We've asked Nurse Pegg about that, Mrs. Bridge," Adele said, "She told us your mother hadn't touched it for at least three weeks."

"Nurse Pegg wasn't with Mother all the time." The evenness in her voice turned to shrillness.

"If Nurse Pegg says Thea didn't take it, I'm sure she knows," her husband said in an absent tone.

Adele had been watching Mona. The woman's fox-like face gathered like one to whom a thought had occurred that she was determined to dismiss from her mind. Nin leaned forward and whispered, "She thinks someone else killed her mother."

"I don't think that's what your wife meant, sir," Adele said slowly.

"Eh?" The sheriff looked at Mona.

The woman sat very still. "I've heard you've a bee in your bonnet about this sort of thing, Miss Gossling."

"What sort of thing?" Jackson asked.

"Crime," she said shortly. "I've heard you hang on to the idea crime is always involved when someone dies."

"I don't know where you heard that, Mrs. Bridge, but it isn't true." Adele felt her bones grow cold.

"As it happens, ma'am, it's us who hang on to that idea," Jackson said in a curt tone.

"We have no choice but to investigate that possibility," Hatfield added, his voice firm.

"I think you're hanging on to the same idea, Mrs. Bridge," Adele said. "I don't believe you think for a moment your mother accidentally killed herself. Do you?" She gave her a bold look.

"It seems your sister is a mind reader, Deputy," Mona said. "She seems to think she knows what's in my thoughts."

"I'm the one who suggested it to her," Nin spoke up, "except I don't read minds. I feel auras and mists coming from people."

"And you felt it from me." Mona's shoulders sagged. "I've heard you're a clairvoyant, Miss Branch, and a very good one."

"Then it's true?" Hatfield peered at her.

The woman buried her face in her gloved hand, nodding.

"If you suspect someone, perhaps you'd better tell us." Adele was starting to grow annoyed. "If that person is innocent, he or she has nothing to fear."

"I can't," she said.

"Dear, you're not making any sense." Her husband gave them an apologetic look. "My wife — sometimes, when things get too much for her —"

"Yes, yes, it's too much!" the woman sobbed.

"We don't want to distress you," Hatfield said in a gentle tone.

"Please, dear." William took her hand. "The police can't do their duty unless we tell them all we know."

"You're right, of course." She drew back, her voice heavy, "It isn't that I 'suspect' anyone. But there are things —"

"I think you'd better tell us about these things," Jackson said.

"Will, you said something about poisonous syrup in Mother's tea." Mona turned to her husband.

The man blushed. "I was only repeating what I read in the newspaper."

"Was it poisoned syrup?" She looked anxiously at the sheriff.

"We think it was some form of liquid, yes," said Hatfield. "We found no traces of any powder."

"Then I think there is something the police should know about my brother."

"Which brother?" asked Jackson.

"Theo, of course."

"Why 'of course'?"

"Forrest never had a diabolical thought in his head," she declared. "He's an angel."

"He and my wife have always been close," William explained.

"We had to form alliances," she lamented.

"Alliances?" Adele asked.

"My mother adored Theo, as I'm sure you guessed," said Mona. "My father was always at the mill. Forrest and I were left to ourselves. One can't live without alliances, can one?"

"No, one can't," Adele said, thinking warmly of her brother.

"What about Mr. Marsh, Mrs. Bridge?" Jackson leaned forward.

"He has a friend," said Mona. "His name is Lom Brethren. I think you ought to have a chat with Lom."

"What has Lom got to do with anything?" William sounded irritated for the first time.

"Lom is a chemist," she reminded him. "He does experiments on plants and things at the university laboratory."

"What are you implying, Mrs. Bridge?" the sheriff asked.

"He knows about poisonous plants and herbs," said Mona. "We had quite an interesting conversation once about the plumbago indica. I saw it quite often in the forests of India. He seemed fascinated by its toxic powers."

"Mona, this is absurd!" William thundered. "You can't think your brother would —"

"I heard them talking in the garden only a week before — it happened." She shuddered.

"What were they talking about?" asked Jackson.

"That I can't say," she said. "But a few days later, Lom sent around a package. I caught a glimpse of it. It seemed like black water in a small bottle."

"Black water?" Hatfield's eyebrows jumped.

"It was very dark," she said.

"This is all nonsense," William grumbled. "Perhaps it was a burglar. We were all out that night, and the servants' quarters are at the other end of the house. That silly girl, Polly, often forgets to lock the French windows. Anybody could have gotten in."

"Why would a burglar be carrying around poison or want to put it in your mother's tea?" Jackson asked. "There was no evidence of burglary at all."

"Still, it might have been someone from the outside," he insisted.

"Is there anyone you can think of who might have had reason to poison your mother?" asked Hatfield.

Mona looked surprised. "She barely left this house."

"In the last few years," he corrected. "Grudges can hold for decades."

"I don't think Mother ever had a grudge against anybody." Mona folded her handkerchief in half. "She was too agreeable with people outside of the family."

"And inside the family?" Adele eyed her.

"Families are not always agreeable toward one another, are they?" The woman eyed her back.

"Your father, I'm sure, made enemies?" Jackson inquired.

"You mean in business?" William asked. "I imagine so."

"You're not sure?" Hatfield looked at him. "You work at the mill, I was told?"

"I was manager of the Highland Cotton Company in India for years, Sheriff," he said. "I took the position at Marsh Lumber only when we came back."

"If it isn't too impertinent to ask," Jackson said, "Why did you come back?"

Adele could tell they both were uncomfortable with the question, though Mona answered readily enough. "Theo wrote me to say Mother was starting to have heart trouble. As the daughter in the family, it was only right for me to come back and take care of her."

"And your brothers?" Hatfield asked. "I understand they both live in the house as well."

"That was their decision," Mona said.

Hatfield glanced at William. "You gave up a lucrative position in India. You hold no resentment?"

"I gained an equally lucrative position at the mill," William insisted. "I've nothing to complain about."

"Neither of you sound very bitter about giving up your life abroad to come back to this house," Jackson observed.

"There's no reason, Deputy," Mona said. "It's simply the way things were."

"I always intended to come back to California," William said.

"I would like to have stayed."

The firmness of Mona's response surprised even her husband. "You never told me that, dear," he said.

"It was all so fascinating," Mona said. "The life and the people."

"I see you have as much regard for the exotic as your mother," Hatfield remarked.

"My mother and I were alike in many ways," she said softly.

"It couldn't have been easy," the sheriff said. "I know. My mother needs care, and it isn't always easy for me."

Mona's slim figure shot up like an arrow. "What has my brother has been telling you?"

"Telling us?"

"About me," she said. "He thinks Mother was a burden on me and that I'm jealous of him."

"Are you?" Nin peered at her.

Mona smiled as one did to a child. "What would I have to be jealous about?"

"I think you can answer that question better than we can, ma'am," the sheriff said.

"I accept things as they are and as they must be," Mona said. "When William told me we were going to India because he had a job there, I accepted it, even though I'd never been out of this town. Didn't I, dear?" She took her husband's hand.

William nodded. "You took to the place better than I did. Never a complaint like many of the other wives." A flash of affection appeared in his eyes.

"You were taught to accept things as they are," Adele said softly.

"Yes, I was," Mona said. "Is there anything else you'd like to know, Sheriff?"

Hatfield picked up the fountain nib. "Does this look familiar to either of you?"

William examined it, shaking his head. "I don't recall ever seeing it."

"Not in the Marsh Lumber offices, sir?" Jackson questioned.

"I'm not in the offices very much, Deputy," he said.

Jackson blinked. "I thought you were a manager."

"More a foreman, really." He sounded a little distracted. "I like to be on the floor with the men, you see. I'm not one who finds an office much comfort."

"I can understand that," Jackson said. "I prefer to be out and about myself."

"I shall make certain to send you with Edison more, then," Sheriff Hatfield said in a rueful tone. Jackson hid his smile.

"Do you recognize it, Mrs. Bridge?" Adele asked.

"I haven't much to do with such things." She said. "But I should think it was the sort of thing Theo or Forrest would use."

"It's elegant-looking," her husband admitted. "Perhaps it belongs to one of the secretaries."

"It certainly is a woman's tool," Adele prompted. "Are you sure you never used something like this for your correspondences, Mrs. Bridge?"

"I don't write correspondences, Miss Gossling," she said. "Mother insisted on doing that herself. And I — I haven't any friends to write to." She looked down at her hands.

"Writing can be a nuisance, even to friends," Nin declared.

Mona smiled. "Thank you for saying that, Miss Branch. Perhaps you and I shall become good friends without writing to one another."

Nin smiled at her. But when the Marshes had left, she burst out, "Not jealous, my eye! She's as jealous as a luna wolf!"

"And as harmful as one when provoked, I should think," Adele added.

"I thought suffragists were about female solidarity," Jackson said dryly.

"One can be critical of anyone when their behavior warrants it, Jack," Adele said. "I agree with Nin. She's jealous of Theo. Probably of Forrest too."

"I can't say I blame her," Hatfield crossed his legs. "Life can be very difficult for the only daughter in the house."

"I don't think the son-in-law has it any easier," Jackson said. "I didn't get the impression Mr. Bridge was too happy with his token position at the mill."

"The question is, would he kill to gain a better one?" Hatfield inquired.

"I don't imagine he has much say in anything that goes on in the mill," Jackson remarked, "or that this would change with Mrs. Marsh's death. What do you make of this business with the chemist friend, Sheriff?"

"It's worth looking into," said Hatfield. "We can't be sure until we know what the will says, of course, but I'm banking on the idea that Mr. Theodore Marsh will most benefit by it."

"He's the only one who really loved his mother," Adele pointed out.

The last two members of the family came in for their interview. Adele mused how Stephanie seemed at ease in the mourning dress, as if Thea were her own mother.

"I admire you being such a comfort to your fiancé and his family, Miss Peeler."

"Stephanie is a great comfort to all of us," Forrest agreed, giving his fiancée an affectionate look.

"Even though Mrs. Bridge doesn't like her," Nin said in her blunt way.

Jackson gave her a sharp look. "That's hardly for you to say, Miss Branch."

"Mona can be a little severe," Forrest admitted, "but she's as fond of Stephanie as we all are."

"Is that how you feel, Miss Peeler?" Adele asked.

"Forrest loves me. That's all that matters." She insisted.

"Perhaps Mona was a little hard on Stephanie when she first came," he admitted.

"Why is that, sir?" asked the sheriff.

Stephanie answered. "My father worked in the shipyards of San Francisco, and my mother took in extra washing. My sisters and I had to work since we were sixteen."

"My sister worked with many young ladies like yourself, Miss Peeler," Jackson said. "In fact, she's done so since she was eighteen. Several times she took on the work of a woman when the woman was ill so she wouldn't lose her job."

Miss Peeler said softly, "How very kind of you, Miss Gossling."

"I admire your candidness," Adele said in an equally kind tone. "I'm sure Mrs. Marsh did too."

"Yes, Thea liked me." Stephanie glanced at her fiancé for approval and he nodded.

"How long have you been engaged?" Hatfield asked.

Forrest slipped his hand into hers. "About a year."

"And when do you plan on marrying?"

"We don't know yet," said Forrest. "This ghastly business with Mother —" A troubled look appeared on his face. "You'll find out what really happened, won't you, Sheriff?"

"That's why we're here, sir," Hatfield said with resolve. "We're asking everyone to tell us what they were doing the night before your mother was found dead."

"We went rowing, didn't we, dearest?" Stephanie looked at him.

He nodded. "I left work early and met Stephanie at Pringles."

"At about what time did you leave?" asked Jackson.

"Six o'clock, I should say," he said. "I wanted to go home and change first, and look in on Mother."

"Oh?" Hatfield raised his head.

"I often looked in on her in the evenings to make sure she was all right."

"Forrest was very attentive toward his mother," Stephanie shot out.

"When did you look in, sir?" Hatfield asked.

"Quite early," he said. "Just before I left, actually."

"How was she feeling when you went up to her?" Jackson asked.

"Oh, subdued," he said.

"Was her tea beside her?"

He shook his head "But it wouldn't have been, Deputy. She usually took her tea before bedtime."

"What did you and she talk about?" Hatfield asked.

The man blinked. "We talked about nothing. I popped my head in, asked how she was, she said she was fine and wished us a good time and that was that."

"You didn't talk about the mill?" asked Hatfield. "We understood your mother had a keen interest in it."

"She left matters in Theo's hands," said the young man. "I had very little to do with it except when my signature was necessary on some document."

"Did you resent that, sir?" Jackson gave him an even look.

"Not really." Forrest shrugged. "I was a boy when Father died and left it in Theo's hands. I suppose it's natural he should run things as he sees fit."

"You didn't want to come work there," Adele said softly.

"Whether I wanted to or not, Miss Gossling, was beside the question," said Forrest candidly. "It was expected of me."

"They didn't leave you much room, did they?" Nin remarked, not without sympathy.

Forrest gave a small laugh. "I often call myself the forgotten child."

"All that will change, darling," Stephanie soothed. "You'll get another job when we move to the city."

"We understand you will both be leaving Arrojo when you marry," Hatfield said.

Stephanie smiled but there was a noticeable silence as Forrest's face grew grave. "I don't know what will happen now."

The smile disappeared from his fiancée's face.

"When did you get to Pringle's?" The sheriff changed the subject.

"About a quarter to six."

"That ought to be easy to check," Jackson glanced at the sheriff.

"I'm sure the waiter will remember us," he said. "We go there quite often."

"I like elegant places," Stephanie put in.

"I'm sure you do," Nin mumbled.

"Then we went to Shift's to rent a boat," he said.

"He ought to remember us too," Stephanie put in.

"I'm not sure he will." Forrest turned a little red. "The whiskey bottle on the table in his shack was half empty."

"For Mr. Shift, that would still render him sober enough to give witness," Jackson remarked.

"How long did you row?" asked Hatfield.

"Not long," he said. "An hour, perhaps. We ended up near the mill and we took a walk, then rowed back."

"It was a lovely night," Stephanie said. "We were out quite late."

"How late?" Jackson asked.

Forrest sniffed. "I don't have a watch, Deputy. Theo took my father's when he died."

"Took it or was given it?" Adele raised her eyebrow.

"What does it matter?" The man shrugged.

"I was only thinking your mother might have given it to him," Adele said.

"You're right, of course," said Forrest. "Mother gave it to him. But only after he asked for it."

"And he always got what he asked for from your mother," Jackson guessed.

"He was the eldest," said the man simply.

"Many mothers consider their youngest son the angelic child," Jackson remarked.

Forrest gave a crooked grin. "Not in our family, Deputy. Mona used to say it was us — her and I — against them — Mother and Theo."

"You don't really believe that." Adele eyed him.

"No, I suppose I don't," said the young man. "I can see why Mother preferred Theo."

"That's very big of you," Nin mumbled.

"I'm not very athletic, as you an see." He was indeed quite pale and thin. "I inherited Mother's troublesome heart. I used to call it a 'talking heart' when I was a child."

"So you couldn't be very active in sports and activities," Jackson said. His handsome face grew softer with sympathy.

"Theo played football when he was in college," he said. "He might have done something with it but for the family business."

"I'm sure you have other talents, Mr. Marsh," Adele said kindly.

"Oh, he does!" Stephanie leaned forward. "He's good with numbers. I've told him he ought to go to school and learn accounting or bookkeeping."

"Mona says it would only confuse me."

"Mona says!" Stephanie's cheerful countenance was broken by a vicious look.

"You and your sister are very close, aren't you?" Adele asked.

"We always have been." He nodded. "More so after Father died."

"And you don't like it." She looked at Stephanie. She felt her brother's hand press her arm.

"I only wish —" The young woman bit her lip.

"Wish what, dear?" Forrest looked at her.

"Nothing."

"You're a very likable man, Mr. Marsh," Adele said.

"I've found it's best in life to be agreeable." His tone was a little defensive.

"It wasn't an insult, sir," Jackson said. "My sister admires people whose natures are less combative than hers." He was rewarded with an arch look from his sister.

"And I admire her for her spunk." Forrest smiled. "Stephanie is plucky too. Women with courage awe me."

"Including your mother and your sister?" Jackson asked.

"I wouldn't say Mother had pluck," he said. "She had — strength." He looked down at the carpet.

"But Mona?" Adele prompted.

"Mona was never one to let go of an injustice if she thought someone had been unjust to her," said Forrest. "I suppose that's plucky."

"Did she feel your mother was unjust to her?" Adele asked.

"Not my mother, no," he said. "My father."

"Oh?" Hatfield looked up.

"That's why she said it was her and I against Theo and Mother," said Forrest.

"A rather interesting family," Jackson remarked after the couple had left.

"The sins of the father," Nin quoted.

"The sins of the mother too," Adele added warily.

# CHAPTER 11

*A* few days later, the morning greeted Adele with a blistering wind that created a thin film of red from the flying dust. It pressed against the windows as she and Jackson had breakfast in the dining room, forgoing their usual spot on the veranda in favor of a less sand-swept meal.

Tomas came forward with a silver tray of mail, which he set down in front of Jackson. Her brother sorted through the mail, handing his sister those addressed to her. He picked up a letter with the unmistakable black border of mourning. "Well, well."

Adele peered at the card he had taken out of the envelope. "I hope *we* haven't been invited to a funeral."

"No," he said briefly. "A will reading."

She stared at him.

He held up the card and read, "'The Marshes request the presence of Mr. Jackson Gossling and Miss Adele Gossling to the reading of the will belonging to their recently departed mother, Theodora Marsh.'"

Adele dropped the letter sent by her San Francisco friend Elsie on the floor. "I thought will readings were only for those who benefit."

"Maybe Mrs. Marsh had more regard for the local police than we thought," Jackson mused.

"This isn't funny, Jack." She threw her napkin down on the table. "I'm going to call Rebecca and see what this is about."

But the young lawyer was as surprised as they were. "I can't imagine why they would do such a thing," she said. "You're both strangers. Thea never even met your brother."

"Theo didn't tell you they were going to do it?" Adele asked.

"Not a word," said Rebecca.

"I wonder which one of them sent the card," Adele murmured when she had hung up. "It's not signed, is it?"

Jackson shook his head. "Perhaps it's a whimsy of grief."

"The family only knows you in your professional capacity," she pointed out, "and yet, the card is addressed to Mr. Jackson Gossling and not Deputy Sheriff Gossling?"

"Someone took pains to make sure it was clear this was a personal invitation." Her brother gathered his gentlemanly paraphernalia from the hallway.

"They didn't want you to bring the sheriff with you," Adele surmised. "Jack, do you think it's proper for us to go?"

Her brother shrugged. "The information might prove very useful. In any investigation, one must walk through every door that opens."

The Marsh house still had the air of graveness as the day before, but even Mrs. Stern seemed more at ease, as if the police's questions had cleared the air so they could all mourn in peace. Adele noticed the startled looks on Forrest and Stephanie's faces when she and Jackson entered the parlor, and even William froze with his whisky in hand.

Mona was clearly taken aback but quickly recovered. "I'm afraid this isn't a good time to make inquiries, Deputy," she said politely. "Perhaps you can come back later this evening."

"I'm not here as a policeman, Mrs. Bridge," said Jackson.

"Oh?"

"We thought you invited us," Adele said, handing her the card.

The woman's face turned pale as she read it. "I don't understand."

"I invited the Gosslings," Theo said, his expression as worn as his tone.

"Invited!" Forrest gasped. "This is a family affair."

"The police wanted to know about the will," Theo said in a stiff tone. "I thought having Mr. Gossling here would save us having to explain."

"I think it's very sensible," Mona said unexpectedly.

"Sensible?" Forrest stared at his sister.

"It will be all over town this afternoon anyway," she pointed out. "The gossips will undoubtedly make a lively story of it. If there are witnesses to verify the truth, we won't be bothered with their prying questions. And who better than the deputy sheriff?"

"I thought you would see it that way, Mona." Theo seated himself next to Rebecca, toying with the edge of the tablecloth.

She took Adele's arm and led her to a chair outside the table where the family gathered. "I know you and your brother are on our side."

"We're all on the side of justice," said Jackson in a calm voice.

"How do we know you're not here as the sheriff's spy?" Forrest asked in a dry tone.

"No one is spying on you, sir," Jackson said. "We're all trying to get at the truth of who did this awful thing to your mother."

The young man nodded, hanging his head.

As they settled in, Adele observed the people gathered in the room. There were clearly legacies for the servants, as they were all there, even Polly the housemaid, who sat so straight Adele thought she was going to shoot up to the ceiling at any moment. Nurse Pegg was there too, dressed in gray but looking more impatient than solemn. The family itself looked like a strange combination of dread and anticipation.

Rebecca cleared her throat and began. The will was short and to the point. Mr. Harold and Ella Stern received a small legacy, which caused them both to react with relief, as if they hadn't been sure they would be left much of anything. Nurse Pegg, who had provided "excellent care, though in a sometimes brutal manner that was no doubt necessary" had possession of the Homer painting hanging in Thea's room.

"She must have admired it more than once," Adele murmured to Jackson.

And, indeed, Nurse Pegg looked satisfied as she leaned back with a small smile.

Rebecca continued reading with some trepidation, "To Miss Rebecca Gold, whose friendship and insights proved invaluable to me, I stipulate she shall remain the family lawyer until she decides to withdraw on her own accord or give up her profession in lieu of a higher calling brought on by the married state."

"Higher calling!" Adele growled.

"If she did, she wouldn't be the first to do so, Del," her brother pointed out.

"The woman is still trying to control people's lives from the grave," Adele hissed.

Rebecca's voice shook as she continued with the reading. The will concerned the family now, and both Gosslings leaned forward to listen.

Forrest Marsh, the youngest child of Gregory and Theodora Marsh, was to receive one hundred shares of the Marsh Lumber Mill and remain employed in its management for the remainder of his life. He was granted a share in the house, and if he chose to leave it, he would forfeit both his share in the house and his position at the mill. A snarling sound came from Stephanie's lips, and she took his hand in both of hers. Forrest remained as retired and unmoved as when the police had questioned him the day before.

"She hardly looks happy." Adele nodded toward his fiancée.

"His mother secured his loyalty by giving him a generous

inheritance and then threatening to take it away if he should try to be independent of it," Jackson agreed.

As if the same thought were going through her mind, Mona leaned toward her younger brother and, with a soft voice, said, "Don't worry, darling. It's all for the best."

The Bridges came next. Mona and her husband were left the house and the servants. Adele watched the family carefully. Both Theo and Forrest had no reaction to this, and she imagined the house had been somewhat of a prison for two men educated to see the domestic space as a necessary evil to a man's life. Mona pursed her lips and crumpled her black handkerchief into a ball. William looked out the window, his chin a little high. Adele followed his gaze and realized he was staring at the hills beyond the house. His dark eyes grew lighter with a far-away look.

"I don't think he wants to stay," Adele whispered.

"Perhaps he's dreaming of going back to India," her brother replied.

Rebecca read the following: "To William Bridge I also leave one hundred shares of Marsh Lumber Mill with confidence he will use them in the best interests of the company of which he has become a vital part."

A gasp came into the room, and Adele realized it was Mona. She put her handkerchief to her mouth as if she were trying to hide her shock.

"Well, well," Jackson said. "It won't make his fortune, but he did quite well for a son-in-law."

"I don't think his wife is happy," Adele said. "Look at her face, Jack. She looks as if she's about to claw him."

A buzz wrapped around the room as Adele realized Rebecca stopped talking. She was shifting papers, but her brows were anxiously drawn. The people sitting at the table also seemed to gather more into themselves, their shoulders raised and heads turned.

"To my beloved son Theodore Marsh," Rebecca read, "I leave

the remaining stock his father willed me upon his death. I also leave him to run Marsh Lumber Mill as he sees fit with confidence he will continue to build the empire his father created for his children and grandchildren and their grandchildren. I cherish his common sense and practicality and trust him implicitly in all things."

Breaths drew and heads fell back. Only Theo remained immobile, staring straight ahead, his hands folded in front of him.

"He's just become a very wealthy man," Jackson remarked.

"He hardly looks as if he relishes it," Adele replied.

Rebecca took a drink of water and spoke in a grave tone, "Should any one of the shareholders — Theodore Marsh, Forrest Marsh, or William Bridge — decide to leave the company, he shall forfeit his shares to be divided amongst the remaining shareholders. Should one of them expire, the company shall be run by the surviving shareholders to do with as they see fit."

"Well!" This exclamation came from Forrest, and Stephanie gave a little cry.

Rebecca's hand covered Theo's but only for a moment. She rose. "That's all there is."

Mona jumped up. "Ella bring the coffee, please. And sherry and more brandy. I think we could all use it."

"Right away, ma'am," said the woman, teetering out. Adele expected her to grumble, but neither she nor her husband looked put out that Mona was now mistress of the house.

Rebecca leaned over Theo's shoulder. "Are you all right?"

"Of course he's all right!" Mona snapped. "He's the patriarch of this family. He's got to be all right."

"I can't see how that matters," Forrest said as he played with a brass globe.

"Oh, but it does, my dear," said Mona. "*He's* head of the family. *He* makes the decisions."

"You've taken your place in this house well enough, dear," William said with a note of melancholy.

"Why shouldn't I?" Mona demanded. "Mother always trusted me with domestic affairs. It's the one thing she did trust me with."

"Please," Theo finally spoke, raising his head. Adele saw his eyes were damp. "Let's not quarrel."

"Of course we won't quarrel." Mona's lips curved as if she were trying to smile. "Have we ever?"

"Not in front of strangers, anyway." Forrest glanced at Jackson and Adele.

"I don't consider the Gosslings strangers anymore," Mona said. "They may even call us by our first names to our faces, now that they've seen our dirty linen."

"I wouldn't call the reading of a will dirty linen, Mrs. Bridge," Jackson said softly.

"Call me Mona, please," she said with a shrill laugh. "We're all on intimate terms."

"I'm for being honest," Stephanie piped up. "I can't see there were any real surprises. We all knew — well, it was obvious."

"Yes, it's all quite obvious, isn't it?" Mona remarked. "Big brother gets the lot, and younger siblings get the crumbs."

"One hundred shares are hardly crumbs, dear," William mumbled.

"Yes, but you don't get them if you leave, William, dear." Mona's self-satisfied tone struck Adele.

"I think it was very decent of Thea," William said slowly. "I'm not family, after all."

Forrest lay his hand on his brother-in-law's shoulder. "You're as much family as any of us, Will."

"Mother had a right to do what she liked," Theo said in a weak voice. Rebecca put a glass of brandy in his hands but he didn't drink from it.

"You mean Mother had the right to do what *you* liked," Mona corrected.

Theo's face looked as tight as a drum. "What the devil do you mean?"

"Mona, this isn't like you," her husband said softly.

The woman stood near the fireplace, her gaze following Rebecca as the lawyer put the last of her papers in her bag. "I never thought of it before, but it's rather convenient when a childhood friend becomes the executor of the family will," she remarked.

Rebecca shut the bag. "Your mother was my friend, but she had no hold on me."

"Not Mother, no," Mona agreed. "But Theo — that's a different matter, isn't it?"

The lawyer glared at her. "I don't know what you mean."

"You left that firm in San Francisco not long after Theo told us he'd been to the city and ran into you, didn't you?"

"I left some months after that meeting, yes," Rebecca said in a strained voice. "What of it?"

"Did you ask her to be Mother's lawyer, Theo?" Mona turned to her brother. "Is that why she came back?"

"Mrs. Bridge." Jackson stepped forward. "If you are trying to make some accusation, I wish you would make it."

"I don't accuse anybody of anything, I'm sure." The woman gave a small laugh as she drank her sherry. "I'm curious from a legal standpoint, though."

"Legal standpoint?" Forrest blinked.

"Rebecca refused to tell the police what was in the will," Mona pointed out. "Theo said so, didn't you, Theo?"

"Yes, I did." Rebecca held the bag to her chest. "I would never betray the confidence of a client."

"You're very selective to whom you betray that confidence," the woman continued.

"Mona, please stop this." Theo pressed his hands to his forehead. "I've never heard you talk like this."

"You're the one acting strangely," she insisted. "For a man who just inherited a fortune, I should think you would be happy or at least relieved."

"Our mother is dead!" her brother growled.

"Precisely."

The man regained some of his composure and swallowed the brandy. "Don't make this sordid, Mona."

"I should imagine you weren't at all surprised," Mona persisted. "That's why you have no reaction."

Theo looked down at his hands as if they were foreign to him. "Perhaps I shouldn't be, but I am. I didn't think —"

"You didn't think!" His sister sneered.

"Oh, for God's sake!" William growled.

"It's not for God's sake, my dear, but for ours that I say this," she said. "When someone isn't surprised he's inherited a fortune, it's because he already knew. Wouldn't you say so, Deputy?"

"We all *knew*," Forrest said. "Let's not beat around the bush, Mona."

"I believe your sister is trying to say your brother knew because someone told him," Adele said quietly.

"Del, stay out of it," her brother hissed.

"Very clever of you, Miss Gossling." Mona glanced at her. "And who better to know about such things than the lawyer who drew up the will?"

Rebecca threw her bag down on the table. "You know I don't like guessing games, Mona."

"I thought lawyers were masters of evasion," Mona said. "I'll speak plainly, if you like. I overheard you telling Theo about the will."

"That's not true!" Theo jumped up. "I never knew a word of what was in the will, nor did I care!"

"You can afford not to care," Mona said. "But you did know."

"And when did this alleged conversation take place?" Jackson asked quietly.

"Not long after your sister's first visit," said Mona. "I happened to be passing by the library and heard their voices."

"You were spying, you mean!" Rebecca snapped. "You were always rather good at that, Mona. Slipping into corners where you weren't wanted."

"Whether wanted or not, I heard," Mona insisted.

"What exactly did you hear?" Jackson asked.

Forrest glared at him. "Are you acting in your official capacity, Deputy?"

"I am, sir," Jackson said with a sniff. "It's my duty."

"Your duty to encourage nonsense?" William eyed him.

"The deputy knows I'm not talking nonsense, William," said his wife. "I know what I heard. I heard Rebecca making a list for Theo of what he would get."

"I was going over a list of assets, yes," Rebecca said. "Because your mother asked me to. She wanted to make sure nothing would be left to chance. You know her memory wasn't good."

"And you told him then what he would inherit!" Mona insisted.

"Rebecca said nothing of the kind," her brother insisted. "We went over the list without even mentioning the will."

"You could have taken a good guess," Forrest said quietly.

"Nothing was further from my mind," Theo said.

"And if your brother did know about the will?" Jackson asked. "What then, Mrs. Bridge?"

"What then, indeed?" Mona screeched.

Theo's composure left him completely, and he collapsed in a chair. Adele watched as the young lawyer's face turned pale as she went to him and put her arm around his shoulders. "I think it's best we leave now, Theo."

The man seemed bewildered for a moment. He rose, accepting her hand,

and they walked out of the room.

# CHAPTER 12

*A*dele accompanied her brother the next morning to the police station on her way to the shop. Twin chestnut horses stood fidgeting in front of a familiar wagon.

"Dr. Rhodes is here," she remarked.

"Probably to give his full report about the autopsy." Jackson nodded. "Lucky we heard most of it at the inquest so it's just a matter of paperwork now."

And, indeed, Dr. Rhodes was sitting in the best chair in the station with a cup of coffee freshly made for him with Edison's shaking hands. He eyed it as if it were turpentine, then nodded at Jackson and gave Adele his usual sniff.

Hatfield leaned back in his chair. "Your friend Miss Grace must have a spy working for her," he said, amused. "I needn't ask about the contents of the will." He threw the *Arrojo Courier* down on the desk with the headline MARSH WILL READ! THEODORE MARSH GETS THE LOT!

"I saw that this morning," Jackson said.

"It must have made your breakfast quite indigestible," Dr. Rhodes said. "Women ought not to be allowed in the newspaper business."

Adele stiffened. "Nor any business, Mr. Rhodes?"

"Just as you say Miss Gossling," the man grumbled.

"Missy is only doing her job," Adele defended. She scanned the article. "And her spy gave her the facts. If her brothers were running the paper, they would publish the insinuations too." She gave Dr. Rhodes a meaningful look.

"Were there insinuations?" Hatfield leaned forward.

Adele nodded. "Mrs. Bridge had some interesting things to tell us yesterday."

"Things we might want to look into, sir," Jackson said.

The sheriff folded his hands. "Do *you* think they're worth looking into, Jackson?"

His deputy shrugged. "It's your investigation, sir."

The sheriff gave a grunt. Adele knew he had been trying to get Jackson to take more initiative in their police work since he accepted the job as deputy sheriff two years before.

"What did Mrs. Bridge's insinuations amount to?" Hatfield asked.

Adele took a seat on the edge of his desk. "Her brother killed their mother, or had something to do with the killing."

"She never said that, Del," Jackson said quickly.

"Naturally not," said Adele. "A woman like her would never say such things outright. She's been taught well."

"Perhaps you ought to take a few lessons, Miss Gossling," Dr. Rhodes mumbled.

She glared at him. "I was taught to speak my mind, Doctor. I'm not ashamed of it."

"What did she say, then?" Hatfield looked at his deputy.

"She claimed Theo knew the contents of the will before the reading," said Jackson.

"I imagine it was no surprise to any of them, given he was the favored son," the sheriff remarked.

"Mrs. Bridge went further than that, sir," said Jackson. "She claims she heard Rebecca showing him the will a few days before their mother's death."

"Perhaps she did," said Hatfield. "Rather innocently. I don't think there's any doubt she is, as our clairvoyant friend would say, 'sweet on him.'"

"A woman doesn't conspire to commit murder even if she is sweet on a man," Adele insisted. "Not a professional woman like Rebecca."

"I heard of a case where a woman doctor poisoned the mother of a man she loved without his knowing it so he could get the inheritance that much sooner," Dr. Rhodes said, sipping his coffee.

"I'm sure you have," Adele said evenly, "in the pulp magazines."

He set the cup down. "I don't read such filth, Miss Gossling."

"No, you just speak it occasionally," she mumbled. Luckily, the doctor was too preoccupied with his papers to hear.

"You use the word 'claimed.'" The sheriff looked at Jackson with a shrewd eye. "You don't believe what she says?"

"She was rather erratic, sir," said Jackson.

"You mean enraged," Adele said. "Clearly, her own inheritance wasn't enough for her."

"I don't think that's true, Del," Jackson insisted. "The house and the servants and her husband's stock in the company are a feather in any woman's cap."

"A rather nice prize for the man," Dr. Rhodes sneered.

"But hardly worth killing for, if that's what you mean," Adele said.

"That is not my business, Miss Gossling," the doctor retorted.

"I assume Miss Gold was there when Mrs. Bridge made this insinuation?" Sheriff Hatfield asked. "What did she have to say?"

"She admitted she spoke to Theo about his mother's assets, but only to verify them." Jackson took his place behind his desk.

"Mrs. Marsh asked her to make sure everything was accounted for, as she was apt to be forgetful."

"Very logical." Hatfield nodded.

"A little too logical, if you ask me," said Dr. Rhodes.

"It's lucky nobody asked you, then," Adele snapped.

"Whether it was sour grapes or not," the sheriff said, "I don't think we can discount what Mrs. Bridge has told us so far, including that bit about Mr. Brethren."

"Lom Brethren?" Dr. Rhodes inquired.

"You know the man?" Hatfield eyed him.

"Somewhat," said the doctor. "He attended a few of my lectures at the University of California in San Francisco. So he's now a chemist? Well, well. What exactly did Mrs. Bridge say about him?"

After Hatfield had briefly informed him, Adele couldn't resist. "Do you think he would be the type to give poison to a friend, Dr. Rhodes?"

The doctor gave her a seething look. "Your imagination is running away with you, Miss Gossling. Professional men don't do such things."

"And Mr. Brethren is a professional as far as you know?"

The man nodded. "He struck me as a little misguided, perhaps, with this interest of his in plants and organic matter. But there was nothing that would point toward shilly-shallying. No doubt Mrs. Bridge was exaggerating."

"Or her imagination was running away with her." Adele smirked.

"I think it's worth questioning him now more than ever, sir," Jackson said. "He may be able to tell us something about this black water Mrs. Bridge mentioned."

Dr. Rhodes brought his hand down on the wooden desk. "Black water! What nonsense!"

"You needn't get so hot-headed about it." Adele glared.

"Maybe it didn't come from Mr. Brethren," Jackson suggested. "Maybe it was some medicine Dr. Brody sent."

"If he did, it was witch-doctoring," Dr. Rhodes snarled. "The Merck Manual, no doubt. I thought better of Dr. Brody."

"Whether it was witch-doctoring or not, there was a package," Adele insisted. "I spoke with Mrs. Stern, and she confirms it. And there was a dark stain in Thea's teacup."

"And so you conclude they were one and the same?" Dr. Rhodes asked.

"Don't you?" Adele challenged.

"That, Miss Gossling, is a problem for the police to solve. Not me, and certainly not *you*." The last was said with emphasis as the doctor rose. "I find your enthusiasm for such gruesome detail most disturbing. I'm surprised you didn't lurk around the laboratory window when we did the autopsy. Come to think of it, I can't be sure you didn't."

Jackson was on his feet. "Your insults toward my sister are intolerable, Dr. Rhodes. I suggest you apologize."

The doctor looked at the young man, whose face was stiff with rage and his tall frame muscular enough to challenge a gunman. Adele couldn't help but think how puny the doctor looked with his somewhat portly figure and a few inches shorter, his hair grayed at the edges.

Dr. Rhodes cleared his throat. "I apologize, Miss Gossling. Whatever else you New Women are, you do have common sense."

"I thank you for giving us some credit," Adele snapped.

The doctor left, and Edison burst out, "You ought to have given him a blinker, sir."

"That would be in bad taste, Assistant Deputy," Jackson said.

"Bad taste or not," said Sheriff Hatfield, "I would have done it myself if he refused to apologize."

"It's very comforting to know so many men in this town are ready to defend my honor," she said with a smile, kissing her brother's cheek. "But I'll thank you both to remember that I could have given him a blinker myself without hesitation, had the occasion called for it."

Edison and the other assistant deputies snickered.

"Nevertheless, we can't deny he made his point," Hatfield said. "We can't assume the dark stain in the cup was the same as this black water, or even the package Mrs. Stern saw contained this vial of black water at all."

"But if it did," Adele said, "what was this black water Mona saw and how did it get into Thea's teacup?"

"How indeed," Hatfield murmured. "Question marks, question marks."

~~~~~

Adele was thinking of those question marks as she left the police station and walked slowly down Bridge Street. The air was warm and dry but for once not sandy.

Mrs. Taylor, the owner of Taylor's Boarding House, stepped out of Ada's Millinery with a large round box, pushing Adele's shoulder as she passed.

"Oh, terribly sorry, dear!" the woman exclaimed, fluffing up the ruffle on the sleeve of Adele's jacket.

Adele smiled. She had gotten to know Mrs. Taylor well from the previous year. The woman had appreciated her help and discretion in solving the Millie Gibb case, which had happened right on Mrs. Taylor's doorstep.

The woman glanced down the street. "It's most painful, isn't it?"

"I'm not sure I follow you." But Adele knew she was talking about the Marsh murder.

"The poor family," said the woman. "I know what it's like to have a crime committed right in your own house." She braced herself. "And now, there is sure to be squabbling in the family because of that will."
~~~~~

"So the gossip has started already," Adele said dryly. "I ought to have known."

"I hear things, but I don't spread them around. We've plenty of magpies to do that for us in this town, don't we?" Her eyes cast down the road again.

Adele followed her gaze and saw what she meant. When she first came to town, she heard with incredulousness about Mrs. Faderman's movable tea parties that were as much about gossip as tea. Until she saw one for herself, she thought them just a fancy. Now every time an unpleasant incident occurred, the ladies were out with their lace dresses and high hats, coiffures tightly pinned to withstand the town's wind and dust, sauntering up and down the street with teacups in one hand and angel food cake in the other.

"Shameful, I call it!" the woman growled. "Why, what would anyone visiting from the city think of us?"

"They would think we were eccentric," Adele mused, "and charming, I expect. They wouldn't be at all shocked, Mrs. Taylor, I promise."

"Well, you would know, wouldn't you, dear?" The woman shifted the box to her other hand and nodded her goodbye.

Adele felt a pinch on the back of her neck. In the two odd years she had been in Arrojo, even those as friendly as Mrs. Taylor still thought of her as a city girl!

Nin was standing in front of her shop when Adele approached. Without a word, she handed her the morning edition of the *Arrojo Courier*. Adele wrinkled her nose.

"I wonder if Missy really does have a spy," she mumbled as she unlocked the door to her shop. "I can't imagine how she got the news so fast."

"This came straight from the family," Nin said as she stepped inside the cool place.

Adele stared at her. "The Marshes told her?"

Nin nodded as she set the kettle on the burner.

"Theo, no doubt," she said.

Nin nodded again. "Aren't you going to read the story?"

Adele sniffed. "I had enough of that will yesterday."

"Did William Bridge really point a pistol at Theo Marsh?" Nin's eyes widened. In spite of her usual placid attitude, she liked hearing the gossip as much as Mrs. Faderman liked giving it.

Adele lifted the blinds. "Missy didn't write that, did she?"

"Certainly not," said Nin. "I heard Mrs. Cricket say it."

Adele rolled her eyes. "For the most part, it was a civilized reading."

"Good morning, Miss Gossling!" Adele winced at the raspy voice she knew well as Mrs. Faderman peered through the open doorway. "Won't you and Miss Branch join us?"

"Rather early for tea, don't you think?" Nin remarked.

"They say morning tea is better than morning coffee," Mrs. Faderman insisted. "Mrs. Theodora Marsh certainly thought so."

Adele knew she was trying to get her to talk about what she knew from her relationship with the police. The question marks came into her mind, and, as Mrs. Faderman and her brood often let slip more information than they wheedled out of her. She took Nin's arm and said, "We'd be delighted."

She heard Nin wince, and her eyes trailing to the kettle letting out its steam. Her friend complained more than once the growling remarks always spoiled her tea, but she knew Adele had her reasons when she decided to join them and followed obediently.

A small table was set against a fence between two shops where Mrs. Faderman's maid oversaw the refreshments. Mrs. Faderman handed a cup to each of them. "I suppose you know all about this Marsh business, Miss Gossling."

"She was invited to the reading," Nin said.

"Most peculiar," Mrs. Faderman said. "But then, the family has always been peculiar."

"What do you mean?" Adele asked.

Mrs. Lynn approached to take another cup of tea. She hunched her shoulders in her modest way. "Oh, they aren't peculiar, Irene. Just —" She shuddered.

"Evil," Nin supplied.

"Really, Miss Branch," Mrs. Faderman said. "Saying such a thing about people you don't even know!"

Mrs. Lynn lowered her voice to almost a whisper. "I don't like to use such words."

"You once knew them very well, didn't you, Caroline?" Mrs. Faderman asked.

"Did you, Mrs. Lynn?" Adele looked at her.

"Well, yes," said the woman. "They lived just down the street from us. Then I suppose the house became too small for them." She sighed. "It was a lovely house with a garden full of wisterias."

"Yes, yes," Mrs. Faderman said. "I believe you were talking about the Marsh family being evil?"

"Not evil exactly." Mrs. Lynn put another lump of sugar in her tea. "Mean, perhaps."

"There didn't seem to be much love between them," Adele admitted.

"Yes, they were mean to one another," she said. "They were perfectly charming to us. But — well, we sometimes heard voices raised, if you know what I mean."

"Whose voices?" Adele leaned against the table.

"The men's," she said. "Gregory — that was the father, you know — had one of those ringing voices that made every word sound like a command."

"He was rather much," Mrs. Abberton, who had joined the party, now stated, her curls bobbing in the sun. "He belonged to the Elks, same as Albert. Always tried to tell the council what to do."

"He must have been a beast," Nin remarked.

"I always find it such a shame when the children — well, they learn from their parents, don't they?"

"I'm sure Theodore Marsh couldn't wait to take both his father's and mother's place," Mrs. Abberton snickered.

"That's just it, dear," said Mrs. Faderman. "Perhaps he couldn't wait. For the mother, at least."

"I take it you think he had something to do with her untimely death?" Adele raised an eyebrow.

Mrs. Faderman gave her a shrewd look. "Are the police following that line of inquiry?"

"How should we know what line of inquiry they're following?" Nin challenged.

"Or does someone else believe Mr. Marsh may be involved?" The woman's eyes became shrewder.

"I'm sure you would know more about that than we would," Adele said in an airy tone.

"Unlike you, Miss Gossling, I don't involve myself in police matters," the woman snapped.

Adele tried not to flinch. "Mr. Marsh is a very nice man."

"Nice men still commit murder," Mrs. Abberton declared.

"I meant he isn't the sort of man who would kill his own mother just for money," Adele insisted.

"It would be too simple," Nin chimed in.

"For once I agree with you, Miss Branch," Mrs. Faderman said. "Still waters run deep and all that."

"Simple or not, murder is murder!" Mrs. Abberton pounded the table as if to make her point.

"He used to play with John and Stephen," Mrs. Lynn lamented. "He always let them make up the rules of the game because they were younger, and he never minded when they changed their minds."

"How very self-sacrificing for a boy," Nin remarked.

"Self-sacrificing my eye!" Mrs. Abberton said, clearly taking advantage of the attention now on her rather than Mrs. Faderman. "He was waiting his chance, you can be sure."

"Really, Hester." Mrs. Faderman sniffed.

"You can't deny Theodora Marsh had him well under her thumb," the woman said.

"I detest that sort of woman," Mrs. Faderman said. "Husband dies, and it's as if she's put on the trousers."

"Some women wear the trousers even when their husbands are alive," Nin said, looking at her with an innocent expression. It was well known Mr. Faderman did not let out a peep until his wife gave him permission.

"Tyranny is rather like a disease, isn't it?" Mrs. Lynn lamented. "It moves down from person to person."

"That's very profound, Mrs. Lynn," Adele said. "Now that Thea is dead, I wonder to whom it will go."

"The daughter, I say," Mrs. Abberton said.

"What would you know about it?" Nin challenged.

The woman strolled to the other side of the street where some of the ladies gathered outside Moffitt Jewelry, admiring a sapphire tiara in the window.

"Perhaps she knows more than you think, Miss Branch," Mrs. Cricket now joined in, swiping a cucumber sandwich from the table. "Perhaps we all do."

"What do you mean?" Adele asked.

Mrs. Faderman gave her a tilted smile. "I'm sure you would find the story to your liking, Miss Gossling."

"Why is that?"

"Mona Bridge once had an interest in joining her brothers at the Marsh Lumber Mill."

"You mean she wanted to be a lumberjack?" Nin leaned against the table.

"Don't do that, dear." Mrs. Faderman brushed crumbs stuck to Nin's free-flowing dress as if she were dusting off dirt.

"Don't be vulgar, Miss Branch," Mrs. Cricket snapped.

"She wanted to run it with them?" Adele prompted.

Mrs. Cricket wrinkled her nose. "Most unbecoming to a young lady."

"It was her upbringing, I expect," Adele said. "When one is put in a pressure chamber, one is apt to explode."

"I don't know I should call it an explosion." Mrs. Cricket sniffed.

"Mona never so much as raised her voice," Mrs. Lynn said.

"Why didn't she join them?" Adele asked.

Mrs. Cricket put her hand on her hip. "Perhaps we ought to tell her, Irene. It would be a good lesson for young ladies with revolutionary ideas."

"Adele isn't a revolutionary," Nin snapped. "She's just a businesswoman."

The woman leaned forward confidentially. "Mr. Marsh — Mr. Gregory Marsh — had just died. *That* will was read and proved quite unsatisfactory to some, at least."

"What was wrong with it?" Nin asked.

"There was nothing wrong with it, Miss Bridge." Mrs. Cricket sniffed a strange-looking morsel from the serving platter, then took a nibble before eating the entire thing in a few bites.

"I think I can guess," Adele said. "The will kept the men and the women in the family in their place."

"And rightly so, I should think." Mrs. Abberton now rejoined them. "Young ladies ought not to go sticking their noses into dirty places."

"Houses have dirt too," Adele said dryly. "Dirtier than offices."

"There's dirt, and there's dirt, Miss Gossling." The woman narrowed her eyes.

"Wills are always about who gets what, and rarely are they satisfying," Mrs. Lynn said.

"Exactly, Caroline!" Mrs. Cricket brushed the crumbs from her gloved hands. "Gregory left the house to his wife, and the young lady was nineteen with no marriage prospects so, naturally, she was expected to help her run it."

"Mona was nineteen?" Adele asked.

"And unmarried," the woman emphasized. "She had no business thinking about managing a lumber mill."

"Helping to manage it," Nin corrected.

"Hence the lesson, Miss Branch," said the woman. "A young lady, not at all bad-looking though lacking in vivacity, with plenty of money — her father saw to that — had better things to do with her time."

"Such as search the marriage market." Adele eyed her.

"Such as search the marriage market," Mrs. Abberton said with a note of pride. "Mona Marsh was quite sought after in her day."

"But she was seeking something else?"

"Yes, and heaven knows who or what put it into her head," said Mrs. Cricket. "I'll never forget what she said at Renee's engagement party. Don't you remember, dear?" She turned to a fair-haired woman, whose stoutness did not hide her former beauty, sitting in one of the chairs in front of the green grocer's.

Mrs. Renee Leighton nodded. "Could have knocked me over with a feather."

"And in rather poor taste," added Mrs. Abberton. "Her father not yet cold in his grave!"

In spite of her abhorrence for the weak, sweet tea, Adele poured herself and Nin another cup. "What happened?"

"She announced she was going to take her place at the mill," Mrs. Lynn piped up.

"Take her place!" snorted Mrs. Cricket. "The arrogant way she spoke, you would have thought her father left it to her instead of her brothers!"

"Forrest told us he was very young when his father died," Adele said.

Mrs. Abberton nodded. "Oh, he was just a child, but expectations still stand."

"Yes," Adele said with a sigh, "they do." She couldn't help but remember how her own father wanted Jackson to follow in his footsteps with the law firm, though her brother had never shown an interest in that direction.

"Mona was certainly premature with that," Mrs. Cricket said. "The will hadn't been read yet, but she assumed she would get her share of the mill. Heaven knows why."

"If a young boy got his share, why shouldn't she get hers?" Nin insisted.

"Because she's a woman, Miss Branch," said Mrs. Abberton.

"Poor William," Mrs. Lynn mused.

"William Bridge?" Adele turned to her.

The small woman nodded. "He was rather taken by her. Many young men were, of course. She was so pretty and — well, alive."

"She was as wet as a jellyfish, Caroline," Mrs. Cricket snorted.

"No, no, it wasn't that," said the woman. "She wasn't chatty like so many young ladies were in those days. She was just — alive."

"Ambitious, you mean," Adele said gently.

"She ought to have put her ambitions in another place," Mrs. Abberton declared. "And she did soon enough, I can tell you."

"After the reading of the will, you mean," Adele guessed.

"Marsh Lumber went to her brothers," Mrs. Abberton said. "Her mother had controlling stock, of course. But she was content to let her precious boy run things."

"She kept plenty of control, though," Mrs. Cricket chimed in.

"And Mona received nothing." Nin gritted her teeth. "Typical."

"She received a dowry, Miss Bridge," Mrs. Abberton, said. "That's hardly nothing."

"A generous sum too," said Mrs. Cricket. "She ought to have been grateful. Instead, she — well, she —"

"Yes?" Both Adele and Nin leaned forward.

"It's not quite for young ladies' ears," she finished.

"You said it would be a lesson to us," Nin pointed out.

"I've changed my mind." Without another word, the woman

wandered toward Mrs. Faderman standing at the other side of the table.

The rest of the ladies seemed content to take their cue and dispersed, and Mrs. Faderman's maid came to collect the cups. Adele took her friend's hand.

"If they won't tell us," she said in a low voice, "we'll find out for ourselves."

# CHAPTER 13

*A*dele lingered over the breakfast table the next morning, thinking of the gossips.

Her brother cleared his throat rather wildly and realized he had been doing so for some time. "Am I distracted?" She gave a small laugh.

"You would have jumped at my invitation to join us at the Marsh Lumber Mill if you hadn't been," he said dryly.

"Is the mill back in business already?" Adele asked. "I thought, with Thea's death —"

"The death of one's mother is hardly a reason to stop business, Del," he said gently.

"It all depends on how one feels about one's mother," Adele murmured. "Or one's father." She remembered the conversation the day before.

"What has the father to do with it?" Jackson put down his paper.

"I don't know." Adele spread butter and jam on the last slice of toast. "I only feel it's important."

"Del, if you're thinking about the Marshes, Gregory Marsh died twenty-two years ago," Jackson reminded her.

"He's still a subject of gossip."

"You mean the subject of that tea party?" Jackson asked. "I saw them from the station yesterday. Hatfield is seriously considering putting a stop to it. Loitering or disturbing the peace or something."

"They certainly disturbed my peace," she admitted.

"Did they gossip about the Marsh will?" he asked. "That was to be expected."

"It went a little further than that."

He laid down the *Arrojo Courier,* waiting.

"Let's say they were anxious to rattle a few family skeletons," Adele said with a glint in her eye.

"They can rattle them all they wish," he said. "If it has nothing to do with Thea's death, it will get them nowhere."

"Don't play the proper policeman with me, Jack." She leaned forward. "You're dying to know what they said."

"All right, so I'm dying to know." He shook the paper open.

"I'll be delighted to enlighten you, dear brother." She told him about the tea party.

His handsome face showed annoyance. "Now I will encourage Hatfield to put a stop to their chatter!"

"They were only echoing what was on Hatfield's mind yesterday, and yours too," she pointed out.

"Which was?"

"There might be a case against Theo."

"I don't think Hatfield thought any such thing, Del," he insisted. "We're merely looking for a place to start."

"I think you ought to start twenty-two years ago," Adele declared. "You know more than anyone how the past can rot the roots of the family tree, Jack."

He did not answer but finished his coffee in silence. She felt the heaviness of his brooding even in the light morning air and pressed his hand. "I'm sorry, dear."

"I realize you believe you have the right to a piece of the

investigative pie," he said stiffly. "Rebecca did call you in for help. But now that we've firmly established it as a police matter, I suggest you let the police handle it."

"Then why did you just invite me to go with you to the mill?" she challenged.

He threw down the paper. "I didn't invite you. Hatfield did!"

"You're beginning with the family," she guessed.

"Partly." Jackson rose, setting the chair neatly under the table.

"You're beginning with the head of the family," she corrected.

"The current head of the family, yes," he said.

She leaned her chin on her hand. "Why?"

"I told you, we have to start somewhere."

"Come on, Jack." She eyed him. "There's more to it than that."

"Hatfield sent me to question Mr. Brethren yesterday," he said.

"If Theo was involved, I hardly think you would get much out of him," Adele said. "He's Theo's friend, after all."

"He's also a scientist, Del," said Jackson as they made their way to the front entrance to gather their things.

They set out on foot to the station, treading slowly for Jackson to carefully maneuver out of the way of debris in the road so as not to spoil his shiny boots.

"What facts did he bring to light that make you want to question Theo?" she continued.

"He hasn't seen Theo for some weeks," Jackson said. "He's been away working on a project in Los Angeles, or so he says."

"So he says?" She stopped walking. "You don't believe him, then?"

Her brother was silent, pressing the walking stick against the red dust, which he usually avoided. "I've had enough experience with the Anspaches to know when someone is lying."

"The guilty look on his face?" she teased.

"You know I don't go by feelings like your friend," he snapped. "He couldn't show me receipts from hotels and restaurants."

"That's not unusual, is it?" Adele asked.

"It wasn't only that," he said. "While he was rifling through papers, I happened to catch sight of a report signed by him. It was dated five days before Thea's death."

"So you think he wasn't out of town when he said he was?" she asked slowly.

"It would stand to reason," he said. "And then there's Mr. McClure."

"Mr. McClure?"

"His partner at the lab." Jackson grimaced. "A rather odd sort of fellow. Brethren said he could verify he was out of the lab when he said he was. Mr. McClure verified all right, but his memory seems to have been a little hazy."

"You believe he was lying too?"

"I told you, Del," he said evenly, "I know when someone is lying."

"What does Hatfield say about it?"

"He's more interested right now in what Theo has to say," Jackson said.

At the station, they found a wagon polished like a chariot with two horses lingering outside. Hatfield leaned against the post, smiling. "I hope you won't be too uncomfortable, Adele," he said in a tentative voice.

"After that rattletrap my sister insists on keeping, I'm sure this will be as cushioned as a Pullman," Jackson remarked as he helped her into the back seat.

"Only if the road isn't bumpy," she teased.

"Even if it is, I can assure you a smooth ride," Hatfield said as he climbed into the driver's seat. "I once headed the Wells stagecoach from Sacramento to Los Angeles after the driver was wounded by highwaymen."

"I shall feel safe in your care, Sheriff," Adele said kindly.

His cheeks became like red apples as he hastily shook the reins.

Marsh Lumber Mill was an impressive building situated amongst a parting of California black oak. A group of lumberjacks were having coffee outside and smoking cigarettes. They glanced appreciatively at Adele as she dismounted the wagon. She threw them a cautious smile as she unfolded her parasol. Jackson made as if to adjust his deputy sheriff badge. The men took the hint and turned away.

Theo ushered them into his office, finding the most comfortable chair he could for Adele and sending for coffee.

"You have an impressive establishment here, sir," Hatfield said as he glanced out the windows.

Theo seemed pleased. "I'd be happy to show you around, Sheriff, if you care to see it. My father had three experts advise him about how it should be built. He wanted everything to be perfect."

"I imagine he was quite an exacting man," Adele said.

Theo glanced at her. "He had his standards, Miss Gossling, as does any successful man of business."

"He wasn't a successful business man *yet*," Jackson said tactfully.

"He knew he would be, Deputy," Theo said. "Men like my father know what they're capable of and know how to get it."

The coffee arrived, and the secretary, Miss McMillian, served them with admirable efficiency.

"You don't seem to have many people working for you," Adele remarked as the woman went out, closing the door behind her.

"My father never believed in much hired help," he said, "at home or in business."

"And you've kept things the same." Hatfield leaned forward.

Theo smiled. "Father trusted me to run the mill. And Forrest, of course, when he came of age."

"You said your brother was more in the line of emptying the refuse," Jackson said dryly.

"I've no doubt in my brother's capabilities as a businessman,"

Theo insisted. "It's only his lack of ambition that's held him back."

"Perhaps his ambition lies in other directions," Adele suggested.

"You're no doubt referring to Stephanie," said the man. "I believe she has plans for him once they marry. I'm grateful for that. I want my brother to be happy now that —" He stopped his hand curling into a fist around the pencil.

"Now that your mother is no longer here to run your lives," Adele finished.

"Del!"

"I was going to say, Miss Gossling, now that he's going to be married," said the man evenly. "Perhaps you'd better ask me what you've come to ask me, Sheriff, though I think I can guess."

Sheriff Hatfield rubbed the rim of his hat as he sometimes did when he had an uncomfortable duty to perform. "I understand your sister made several statements —"

"Accusations, you mean," Theo said quickly.

"Call it what you like," said the sheriff. "Deputy Gossling had to tell me, of course."

"Naturally," said the man, undaunted.

"We're here to get your perspective on those statements," Hatfield continued.

"It's good to see the police don't take such things at face value," said Theo.

"Your sister claims you saw the will, or knew its contents before your mother died," Jackson began.

"Yes, some conversation Rebecca and I were supposed to have had." He grimaced. "It never took place, Sheriff. Rebecca swore to that."

"You went over a list of assets, I understand?" Hatfield asked.

"Purely business," said Theo. "Mother wanted me to confirm what she had in her records. There was no mention of the will when we spoke." His gaze wandered. "I suppose I can see how

Mona might jump to conclusions if she heard only a small part of our conversation."

"You're very forgiving, Mr. Marsh," Adele said.

"Why shouldn't I be, Miss Gossling?" He turned to her.

"Why indeed?" Jackson asked. "One might suggest you can afford to be forgiving now."

"I don't like what you're suggesting, Deputy." The man glared at him.

"You can't deny you weren't the least surprised when the will was read."

Theo rose and, with his hands stuffed in his pockets, strolled to the window, looking out at the puffs of smoke among the tall trees. "You mistook my grief for reticence, Deputy."

"I don't think so, sir." Jackson's voice was firm. "I've had a lot of experience with taking things beyond face value."

There was silence in the room as a bird sang its song in a tree outside.

"Did you know what was in the will?" the sheriff asked.

"I knew she wanted to get her legal affairs in order," he said. "Her heart was giving out on her. That's the way she put it. And I suppose — well, people begin to think of practical matters when they think — they believe —" A groan escaped him.

"Thea was admirably practical for a woman who did whatever her husband told her without argument," Adele said mildly.

Theo's lips were crooked. "I sometimes believed she was more practical than my father."

"And being practical, she would have told someone what she was planning to do," Adele said. "She would have told someone she trusted. She trusted you the most, didn't she?"

He returned to the chair. "You're very clever, Miss Gossling. All right. Yes, I had an inkling about the contents of the will. Mother asked me to witness it."

"Did she?" Hatfield glanced at Jackson.

"She called me into her room one day," said Theo. "She said

she had an important paper she needed me to sign. She often asked me to do such things, so I thought nothing of it. But when I began to read it — well, it was quite clear what it was. I refused then and there and left the room."

"That was very honorable of you," Jackson said.

"I wasn't thinking of honor," he insisted. "I didn't think it would be fair. If I signed it, Mona and Forrest would think — well, you saw what happened after the reading." He shuddered.

"You may not have signed it, sir," Jackson said squarely. "But from your own admittance, you read it."

"Only a part of it." He sat up, his eyes darkening. "Why should it matter if I did?"

"I've met men who, knowing good fortune awaited them, tried to speed up the process," Jackson mumbled.

"That's absurd!" Theo said. "I refused to sign the will so I wouldn't know its contents. As I said, I felt it wouldn't be fair to my brother and sister."

"Nor did you want to incur their wrath, I imagine," Hatfield remarked.

"You already had an enviable position in your mother's good graces," Adele added softly.

Theo was silent for a time. "Yes, I suppose I can't deny that. Mother — it wasn't right for her to have a favorite. I've no idea even why she chose me."

"You were the eldest," Jackson remarked.

"Perhaps," Theo said in a cautious tone. "But I paid my dues for it."

"A devoted mother can sometimes be a burden." Hatfield nodded. Adele was startled at the sincere tone in his voice, as she knew how devoted he was to his own mother.

"Someone said to me the other day that tyranny is like a disease," Adele lamented.

"A very accurate remark," Theo said.

"Yes, considering it came from a woman whom many think rather fluttery." Adele couldn't help but smile. "Mrs. Lynn."

"Oh, yes," the man said in a flat tone. "Rebecca told me the ladies were out gossiping yesterday. Some strange tea ritual, is that it?"

"Their movable tea party," Adele said.

"I'm rather surprised you would listen to that sort of talk, Miss Gossling." Theo eyed her.

"Sometimes there are dregs of truth in the loose tongues of women, Mr. Marsh," she said.

"Yes, I suppose I can't blame you." He sighed. "That is, after all, why I invited you and your brother to the reading of Mother's will. I wanted someone reliable who would know the facts."

Adele sat on the edge of the chair. "The ladies spoke of your sister's past ambitions."

"Del —" Her brother began, but a sign from Hatfield silenced him.

The man grimaced. "I've heard you approve of rebellious women, Miss Gossling."

"I find them a trifle annoying myself," Jackson said dryly. Adele shot him a look.

"Do you think it's wrong for a woman to have ambitions, Mr. Marsh?" She cocked her head.

"Not when there is valid reason," he said. "Or when the woman is sensible about them. But Mona — well, her ambitions were unnatural."

Adele heard a door slam nearby and guessed Forrest Marsh had returned to his office.

"I find your use of the word 'unnatural' interesting," she said.

"So do I," said the sheriff. "Do you mind explaining?"

"I don't want to criticize my sister," Theo said. "She hasn't had it easy. Mona — well, I suppose you could say she has a will of her own, but she wasn't always encouraged to express it."

"Just like your mother," Adele murmured.

"Yes," he said, "just like Mother."

"What has that to do with these unnatural ambitions?" Jackson asked.

"She took to strange ideas," he said. "Like those Bombay natives and their rituals."

"You mean when she lived abroad?"

"Yes, Sheriff," he said. "After she and William went to India, I came out to see them."

"When was this?" Hatfield asked.

"Oh, about five or six years afterward. It was all very strange." He shivered.

"You mean different," Adele corrected.

"No, more than that," he said. "Oh, it was fascinating. But Mona had changed."

"In what way?" Adele leaned forward.

"She just wasn't the same girl." He pressed his hands together. "More apathetic, I suppose you could say. Before that, she would always be thinking something, you see." He gave a far-away smile. "We were very close when we were children. Father wasn't so harsh on her then."

"Girls have freedom when they're very young," Adele said wistfully.

"She spoke as if she didn't really care what she said," he continued, "as if nothing mattered to her anymore."

"Perhaps something was troubling her," Jackson suggested.

"The climate was certainly oppressive," he admitted. "Like living inside of a hothouse. But she didn't seem to mind that."

"Her interests," Jackson prompted. "You said something about natives and rituals."

"She and William lived in a fairly good part of the city," Theo said. "But Mona used to accompany him to the plantation, which was more in the forests. There were aboriginal people living there."

"Primitive people?" Hatfield asked.

He shook his head. "She insisted these people were quite civilized."

"They had their rituals?" asked Adele.

"Mona told me they knew all about the plant and animal life," he said. "She confided in me once she would sneak out of the house and join them in their explorations. I went out for a walk with her once, and she seemed to know every tree, plant, and flower there." He leaned forward. "She showed me a book with information she was collecting on all these specimens. She was like a scientist waiting to make a great discovery."

"And you consider that unnatural ambition?" Adele inquired.

"It was the way she spoke about it, Miss Gossling," he said. "I can't really explain it."

"It sounds as if she and your friend Lom Brethren have much in common," Jackson remarked.

Theo shrugged. "Lom is interested in in plants because of their medicinal qualities. He wants to help mankind."

"Speaking of Mr. Brethren —" Jackson began.

"I was wondering when you would get around to that," Theo said. "I have nothing to hide, Deputy. I did see Lom, just as Mona said."

There was silence for a moment, and Adele observed the sharp look between sheriff and deputy.

Theo said in a nervous tone, "It was entirely innocent, I assure you."

"Poisons are not innocent, sir," Jackson said.

"Perhaps not for people," said Theo. "But they're quite effective on dangerous pests like raccoons."

"Raccoons?" The sheriff stared at him.

"I take rather an interest in the gardens around the house, Sheriff," Theo said. "They've always been a hobby of mine."

"I noticed they were quite beautiful," Adele remarked.

The man smiled, a genuine smile for the first time that afternoon. "I do the planning and Harold does the work."

"And Mr. Stern told you there were raccoons in the garden," Jackson guessed.

"You've no idea how nasty the creatures can be, Deputy," he said. "You have to get rid of them as quickly as possible, or they will ruin your garden."

"When was this, sir?" Hatfield asked.

"Oh, a few weeks or so before the holiday."

"When did you consult Mr. Brethren about it?"

"A week or so before —" He covered his mouth and face as he had done at the reading of the will. When he spoke, his voice was choked. "Before my mother died."

"Why did you wait so long?" Jackson asked.

"I beg your pardon?" The man blinked, clearly caught in memory.

"Why did you wait a week to consult Mr. Brethren when Mr. Stern spoke to you about the raccoons earlier?" the deputy asked. "You said yourself one must act quickly with raccoons."

"I was preoccupied with the mill," said Theo. "We were in the midst of an important contract. I was working fourteen-hour days." He sat up. "You're welcome to ask the Sterns if you don't believe me. I asked them to make an early breakfast for me and a late supper."

"We believe you, sir," Hatfield said. "Can you tell us about the conversation you had with Mr. Brethren?"

"Lom came over for a drink," he began.

"On your invitation?" asked Adele.

"No, he showed up on his own," said Theo. "He'd been in Southern California that week on a pet project of his."

"Well, at least he didn't entirely lie to us about that," Sheriff Hatfield mumbled to Jackson.

"Lie?" Theo sat up. "Lom is as honest as a monk."

"I've known a monk or two who were less than honest, sir," Jackson said with a grimace.

"Go on," Hatfield said.

"We were out in the garden looking at the parrot tulips. They were just starting to bloom."

"And you didn't want them ruined," Adele guessed.

He gave her a short smile. "That's what reminded me of the raccoons."

"And what did he recommend?" asked Hatfield.

"Atropia belladonna," said Theo.

"That's quite a name to remember," Jackson eyed him.

"I told you, Deputy, I have an interest in plant life."

"And yet, you consider your sister's interest to be unnatural ambition," Adele said dryly.

"That's entirely different, Miss Gossling," he insisted. "My interest is in beauty, not exoticism."

"There is hardly beauty in the belladonna plant, or so I've been told," Jackson said.

Theo laced his fingers again. Adele could see they were so tightly woven, his knuckles were red. "Its fruit is rather pretty, like dark violet cherries."

"Pretty but deadly," Sheriff Hatfield said sternly.

"Yes, indeed," said Theo.

"Did he give you the belladonna?" asked Jackson.

"We were speaking more of nature, not pharmaceuticals," Theo insisted. "My idea was to plant the belladonna in the corner of the garden, and let the creatures find it."

Adele shivered. "That's rather morbid."

"But effective," Theo said.

"And did you?" asked Jackson.

Theo shook his head. "I forgot about it with the holiday and Mother —"

"Yes, of course," said the sheriff as he rose. "Thank you for your cooperation, sir."

"I want to help catch who did this, Sheriff," said Theo firmly.

Adele lingered for a moment, pressing her hand on the door handle. "Mr. Marsh, may I ask you a personal question?"

"Really, Del," Jackson hissed.

Theo seemed equally reluctant to speak. "You may ask anything you wish, Miss Gossling, but I can't guarantee I'll answer."

"Fair enough," Adele said. "I've been told your sister was once interested in being a part of your family's lumber mill."

"You've been told," Jackson snorted. "What my sister means is she heard it from the gossips."

"All right, yes," Adele said. "I was curious."

"I don't see what it has to do with my mother's death."

"Probably nothing," Sheriff Hatfield said. "Nonetheless, I'm rather curious myself."

Theo turned his chair a little away from the light of the window, making his countenance more shadowy. "My sister had whims when she was younger."

"And that was one of them?" Jackson guessed.

"We never thought it came from her, really," Theo said. "Mona wasn't brought up to think about such things."

"You mean she wasn't brought up to think a lady could be a businesswoman," Adele said.

"If you care to put it that way, Miss Gossling."

"You said 'we' didn't think it came from her," Sheriff Hatfield said. "Do you mind explaining that?"

"Mother and I," he said. "It's a rather common story, I should think. A man wishes to marry a woman whose family owns a prosperous business. It's only nature he should want to be a part of it. As a son-in-law, that is."

"And the son-in-law in question is William Bridge," Jackson said.

"In this case, yes."

"You and your mother had objections?"

"William is a good sort," said Theo, "but he hadn't proven himself to be a good businessman."

The sheriff eyed him.

"His father inherited a tailor's establishment. Been in the family for generations, that sort of thing. William ran it to the ground within two years of his father's death."

"I see what you mean." Jackson coughed. "And yet, he's now working in the mill.

"That was Mother's idea," he said. "She thought if we gave him a position when he and Mona came back from India, it would help them feel settled."

"She liked to keep her family close at hand," Adele said shrewdly.

He gave her a meaningful look. "William had solid managerial experience under his belt by then, Miss Gossling."

"How did your brother feel about that?" Hatfield asked.

"Forrest was twenty-three at the time," said Theo. "He didn't have much say in business matters."

"Your mother gave them to you unconditionally," Adele guessed.

"Not unconditionally, Miss Gossling," he said in a low voice. "Never unconditionally."

Adele picked up a statue on the shelf, turning it around in her hands. "Your mother liked William, didn't she?"

"She liked his solidity," said Theo. "We both did. Mona — well, she can be a little hysterical at times. William knew how to calm her. And he was serious about business, at least when he came back from India."

"His solidity earned him a rather nice share of Marsh Lumber Mill," Jackson remarked.

Theo regarded him with a pained look. "I suppose you think I resent that, Deputy. Nothing pleased me more than to hear she left those shares to him and to Forrest. They've both helped improve the mill since they started working here."

"As I said before, sir," Jackson said, "you're a very fair man."

Adele placed the statue back on the shelf, feeling a slight soreness in her hands from its heaviness. She suddenly saw an ornate wooden box with the lid half off. She could see sharp little spears inside, and she realized what they were.

"You have a sentiment for pens, Mr. Marsh?" she asked, fingering the edge of the box.

Theo smiled. "Your inquisitiveness suits you, Miss Gossling, from what I've heard."

"I prefer to call it what it is," Jackson growled. "Nosiness."

Sheriff Hatfield leaned forward, his height allowing him to see over her shoulder.

A hand reached over and snatched the box. Theo shut the lid and held it in his lap. "I'm afraid the explanation behind it is rather less romantic than Miss Gossling supposes."

"Oh?"

"Or perhaps I should say superstitious," he mused. "Each of these nibs represents a very important contract my father signed for the company. He believed it was good luck to keep them."

"You must believe it too," Jackson remarked.

Theo shrugged. "Business was everything to my father. He said it ought to be the first thing a man thinks of when he wakes up in the morning and the last thing he thinks of before he goes to bed at night."

"Yes, that's just the sort of thing a father would tell his son," said Jackson.

"He never put business above family, Deputy," the man said sternly. "I don't want to give you the wrong impression."

"Are they all there now?" asked the sheriff.

"All?"

"The ones he used for his contracts."

The man blinked. "I don't know, I'm sure. I never counted them."

Hatfield produced the fountain pen nib they had found in Thea's room from his pocket. "Then you wouldn't know if one was lost."

"As I said the first time you showed it to me," said Theo, "I've never seen it before in my life."

"It would be a simple thing to check," Jackson said. "I'm sure you have records of all your contracts. Compare the number of nibs in the box to the number of contracts and see if they match."

"It wouldn't be as simple as you suppose, Deputy," Theo snapped. "Have you any idea how many contracts we've signed since the mill opened?"

"You have records, nonetheless," Jackson argued.

"Is it really so important?" The man eyed him.

"Considering it was found near your mother's body, sir," said the sheriff, "we find it most important."

The man leaned forward, examining the nib. "Spoon tip, you called it? One of the clerks did convince me to try something similar, now that I recall."

The sheriff eyed him. "Why didn't you mention the fact when we asked you about it before?"

"I was distraught," Theo insisted. "I wasn't thinking properly. The name triggered my memory." He examined the tip again. "The one I bought wasn't as fine as this."

"Where is that tip, sir?" Jackson asked.

The man gave a chuckle. "I really can't say. It didn't appeal to me, so I gave it to my secretary. I believe she may have given it to a nephew of hers. She often gives things to him. Poor fellow just started a clerkship and hasn't much money."

"You've no objection to us speaking with your stationer to confirm this, then?"

For the first time, Theo looked rattled. His face showed a shade paler, and his lips were uneven. "Surely, you can't think —"

"You can't deny it's rather oddly shaped," said Jackson. "My sister is an expert on such things. She tells us it's not widely available."

"But, really! It could belong to anybody."

"True," the sheriff admitted. "All the same, we would be pleased to know where you buy your fountain pens, sir."

"Since it's not from my shop." Adele couldn't help but feel a little put off.

Theo bowed with a gallant gesture. "It shall be in the future," he promised. "But I still don't see what right —"

"You claim you've never seen it," Hatfield said patiently. "If it isn't yours, you should have no objection to our knowing who your stationer is."

"The shop, Sheriff, is Josiah Brown & Sons Stationers in San Francisco," said Theo. "It was my father's favorite place for business stationery."

Hatfield glanced at Jackson who nodded to indicate he had written down the name. Adele watched as Theo closed the box and put it back on the shelf, his hands a little unsteady.

# CHAPTER 14

Though Jackson tried to persuade Adele to let them take her home, she insisted she had a few good hours of work left in the day. They reluctantly dropped her off at Adele's Stationery. The moment she stepped inside, Nin appeared, brushing her wild hair from her face and shaking spots of black powder from her skirt, letting a mulch scent into the air.

"Sage," she said apologetically. "Cleansing, but not very pleasant."

"Better than ink," Adele remarked as she gave a rueful glance at a row of empty bottles and the large bottle of red ink she had left on the counter the night before.

"I'll help you," her friend volunteered.

Adele smiled. "If you start to fill those bottles, Nin dear, the police will think you just stabbed ten people and let the blood run all over your dress."

"Perhaps I'm not very tidy," Nin admitted.

Adele squeezed her shoulders. "My father used to say one may hide many truths under tidiness." She stared at the stack of blotters, remembering how clean the one on Theo's desk had been. "I wonder what truth Mr. Theo Marsh might be hiding under his tidiness."

"He does seem rather fastidious," Nin agreed.

"He has a tidy explanation for everything," Adele said.

She gave Nin a brief account of their interview with Theo. Her friend listened carefully as she perched on the edge of the counter, her light blue skirt rising with the sweeps of wind that passed through the open doorway, causing some passers-by to eye her with dismay or sniff at her careless nature.

When Adele finished, her friend looked at her with her cat-like eyes. "Do you think he did it?"

"Do you?" Adele looked at her steadily.

"If you mean, do the auras come alive when you speak of him," said her friend sharply, "you know I'm not a conjurer. They have a will of their own."

"Yes, I'm sorry," Adele said. "I don't like to think of a devoted son killing his mother."

"Many devoted sons have done just that," Nin pointed out. "If one is to believe the sensational stories in the newspapers."

"Some are true and some aren't," Adele said.

"I don't think Rebecca would be very appreciative of your suspicions," Nin remarked.

"I didn't say I have suspicions," Adele said. "I'm only trying to find answers to the sheriff's question marks."

"Like the vial of black water?" Nin shivered. "And the fountain pen?"

"A lost fountain pen," Adele corrected. "Part of one anyway." Her eyes wandered to the shelf where she kept the fountain pen supplies. "One Mr. Marsh now admits he might have seen before."

"Such things get lost all the time," Nin pointed out. "I can't recall how many pens and pencils I've misplaced."

"If it were only misplaced," Adele said, "someone would have claimed it a long time ago."

"It may not be important," Nin said. "There are certainly thousands like it everywhere."

"It's not a typical fountain pen, dear," said Adele. She slipped several boxes of clean nibs from the shelf and lined them up on the table. "And even then, they're not all the same."

They were all indeed different even if to a slight degree. Some had sharper points and some were curved while others were flat.

"I never knew there was such variety in a simple fountain pen," Nin admitted.

"It's not your business to know." Adele fingered the tips. "If only I could have gotten a closer look at that box!"

"What would it prove if you had?" her friend asked.

"If there are nibs in the box like the one we found," she said, "it might mean he knows something he isn't telling us."

"Is there no chance of his showing it to you?" Nin asked.

Adele shook her head. "He was rather annoyed I found it in the first place."

"He did say it was a superstition for his father to keep them," Nin said. "It's been my experience any simple belief becomes sacred amongst families."

"Theo didn't strike me as superstitious," Adele said.

"That doesn't mean he isn't respectful of someone else's superstition," Nin pointed out. "Especially if it proved true. The mill is quite prosperous, isn't it?"

"Owing more to business savvy than silly beliefs," Adele remarked.

Her friend looked hurt. "They're not always silly, Adele. Beliefs can hold power over people's minds, as much power as calls from the earth."

Adele put her arm around the woman's shoulders. "I know, dear. I'm sorry."

"You sounded almost like your brother just now," said Nin in a sulky tone.

"He's not as cynical as he was a few years ago," Adele said.

"Though I can't say you've made a believer out of him when it comes to intangible evidence."

"My evidence is tangible to me," said her friend in a stubborn tone.

A flurry of colored pinafores appeared on the street, and Adele caught sight of Beatrice, Rachel, and Sandra from the Wrigley School outside of Hyde's Confectionery, each carrying a brown paper bag in her hand. She heard Nin say, "Aren't they a little old for candy?"

"You're never too old for candy," Adele lamented.

"You oughtn't to send them anywhere on a job for you," her friend remarked. "They might leave powdered sugar all over the place, and people in town already suspect you're up to no good with them. Even Mrs. Wrigley."

As Nin spoke, the cloud in Adele's mind began to clear. "A job like borrowing a box of nibs."

She grabbed her friend's hand and pulled her out of the shop, clomping over puddles of mud from a spilled water bucket earlier that day. Nin, less conscientious, stepped into them so the hem of her dress lined with mud.

"Good afternoon, ladies," Adele said.

They turned around with pleased looks on their faces. Mrs. Wrigley and others in town still insisted on referring to them as girls even though they would be putting up their hair in another few years.

"Good afternoon, Adele." Beatrice curtsied, then slipped her bag into her pocket as if ashamed to be caught with such childish delights.

"Going back to school, of course," Adele guessed.

"After sneaking past the napping teacher on guard, no doubt," Nin murmured.

"Nothing of the sort, Miss Branch," said Rachel with a lofty air. "Mrs. Wrigley always encourages us to take a constitutional."

"In the heat of the afternoon?" Nin challenged.

"Oh, my skin is so delicate!" Sandra fretted over the veil on her hat, holding it close around her chin.

"Don't be so squeamish, Sandy," Beatrice snapped.

"You must get back to school as soon as possible," Adele said, taking Nin's arm. "Shall we accompany you?"

Beatrice, her green eyes letting off sparks of ginger that went with her strawberry blond hair, said slyly, "You've something for us. I knew it! The Marsh case?" She lowered her voice.

A trio of women passed by them, and Adele recognized the crow-like face of Vanessa Faderman, who, in two years, had grown enough like her mother to be alarming. The young lady glanced at Adele with a stern look, and her eyes slid toward Beatrice's eager face. Adele pulled herself up and stared back at her. Beatrice, with her keen eyes, took the hint.

"It's very kind of you to see us back to school, Miss Gossling," she said in a surprisingly elegant tone.

"Yes, very kind," Sandra chimed in, and Rachel, as if to emphasize there was only goodness in the exchange, took out her rosary.

They soon departed from the main vein of Bridge Street, and Beatrice began again, "It *is* about the Marsh case, isn't it?"

"In a manner of speaking," Adele said.

"We can't be as inconspicuous as we were when we were children, you know," Rachel said in a cautious tone.

Adele pressed Nin's arm to keep her from making a retort about how young ladies oughtn't to be so pretentiousness about their age. "I realize that. You'll soon usurp Vanessa Faderman and her brood as the belles to watch for."

"Oh, we've already done that," Sandra said in an airy tone. "At least, Agnes, Fanny, and I have. Fanny's mother said she might even let her come out next year."

"At age fifteen?" Nin growled.

"She already started putting up her hair earlier this year," Sandra protested.

"I suppose our generation is simply more mature than yours," Beatrice snarled.

Nin narrowed her eyes but said nothing.

"I don't want you to pick up information," said Adele. "I must ask you to be a little wilier this time."

All three threw off their lofty shells and leaned in with eager faces.

"I need you to take something for me."

"Take!" Rachel clutched her rosary. "You mean steal?"

"Well, borrow," Adele said.

"That's downright criminal," Sandra declared.

"Oh, bum it, where is your sense of adventure?" Beatrice scowled. "Go on, Adele."

"It's rather a little thing, nothing valuable," Adele assured them. "Of no importance, really."

"How disappointing." Rachel's face fell.

"Well, I wasn't going to suggest you be felonious, dear," Adele said dryly.

"What is it you want us to steal?" Beatrice asked.

"Borrow," Adele corrected. "A fountain pen nib."

"Is that all?" Sandra's face relaxed. "Why, we could find a nib in one of the teachers' desks in a second."

"I think Adele means she wants us to take it from someone in the Marsh family," Beatrice said.

"You have the intelligence of a criminal mind," Nin said sweetly. The young woman glared at her.

"Actually, yes," Adele admitted. "Mr. Theodore Marsh."

"Did he do it?" Rachel's eyes widened.

"We don't know," Nin said. "That's why we need the nib."

"He wrote that will himself and signed it with the pen you want us to steal!" Beatrice snapped her fingers. "Oh, what deviousness!"

"Bea, dear, don't let your imagination run away with you,"

Adele said. "A friend of mine drew up the will and witnessed the signatures."

"No tomfoolery there," Nin said.

"Then how could the nib of a fountain pen be important?" Sandra asked.

"I don't know," Adele admitted. "That's what I want to find out."

"And you need the said nib to know." Beatrice nodded.

"A nib," said Adele. "There's a box — a very special box — in Mr. Marsh's office." She described carefully what the box looked like and where it was located. "It's simply a matter of obtaining one or two," she finished.

Beatrice slid her feet along the dirt road, making a scraping noise as she had when she was younger. Her face showed a far-off look. She spoke slowly, "The Saint Cecelia Fund."

"The what?" Sandra stared at her.

"The Saint Cecelia Fund," Beatrice repeated. "For the Catholic girls' school in Newark Mrs. Wrigley told us about." She sighed. "Poor girls."

The other two girls gave Adele a look that told her they had no idea what Beatrice was talking about. "What about the Saint Cecelia Fund?" she asked.

"It's Easter, you know," said Beatrice. "They've no money to buy Easter baskets for the sisters, poor souls. Miss Banting is going there for the holiday, you see."

Nin, who had been watching the young lady closely, now said in a sly tone, "What a liar you are."

"No, it's true Miss Banting said she was going to Newark for the holidays," Rachel chimed in.

"We simply must build a collection for those poor girls," Beatrice said. "We'll start with Mr. Raleigh and Mr. Hyde. They're always generous over the holidays."

"With the business you give Mr. Hyde, I shouldn't wonder," Nin mumbled.

"And then we can go to the industrial center outside of town," Beatrice continued, her hands behind her back. "Plenty of God-fearing workers there who will give a penny."

"Oughtn't we ask the managers first?" Sandra asked, picking up the spirit of the tale. "They've so much more, and we don't want to deprive the workers of their Easter goose."

"Naturally," said Beatrice. "And we must go right away before they close for the day. Mrs. Wrigley is bound to compliment us on our charitable work."

"Especially since you shall use my wagon and driver," Adele said with a grin.

"That's very kind of you, Adele," Rachel said.

"Anything to oblige young ladies with charity in their hearts," Adele said.

Beatrice gave her a smile that reminded her of the fox in the henhouse of a fairy tale book her father used to read to her when she was a child.

~~~~~

Adele stayed late in her shop, anticipating the girls would return with the wagon. Nin, after admitting some disgust at the way Beatrice had used charity as an excuse for theft, had gone back to her place. At five o'clock, Adele heard her shut the shutters of her shop and knew she had climbed the stairs to her flat above and would be closing all the curtains and remaining there until morning. A few young men came into the stationery store and bought gifts for their college friends, but the afternoon was a quiet one.

When dusk settled in the sky, she at last heard the pounding wagon wheels with the slight creak of the loose side of the seat. The wagon stopped outside her shop, and the three young ladies, along with Carolyn, still mousy at Beatrice's side even at age thirteen, muddled down, rejecting Tomas's outstretched hand. They flounced into the shop with a little too much air and too much
~~~~~

perfume, as they had all taken great care to dress in their street clothes, complete with feted hats and parasols.

"I hope you didn't make a menace of yourselves," Adele said crossly.

"We were as obedient as little lambs," Sandra insisted.

"I highly doubt that." Adele smiled. "But judging from your beaming faces, you got what you wanted?"

"We got what *you* wanted," Beatrice said evenly.

Carolyn, who was without doubt the most timid of the group, extracted three fountain pen nibs that looked like the ones Adele had seen in Theo's box.

"Very good." Adele nodded with approval.

"That Mr. Marsh is an awful stuffed worm," Beatrice declared. "Wanted to know absolutely everything about the fund and the Saint Cecelia school."

"And I'm sure you supplied him with great detail," Adele remarked. "Most of it untrue."

"I don't lie, Adele," Beatrice declared. "I'm going to be a writer when I leave school. Writers are allowed to tell stories."

"She made Mr. Marsh believe every word of it," Rachel said, not without a little pride.

"She was very convincing," Sandra added. "She even had me believing it."

Adele laughed and turned to Carolyn. "And you were elected head thief?"

Carolyn, whose plain face was already too red from its unfortunate color, turned almost purple.

"I shouldn't have said that." Adele patted her shoulder.

"Borrowed, remember." Beatrice insisted.

"It wasn't very difficult," Carolyn said. "Not once I saw exactly where the box was."

"We gave her explicit instructions," Beatrice said. "We kept Mr. Marsh occupied and blocked his view while Carolyn slipped the nibs into her glove. Wasn't that clever?"

"Too clever," Adele said. "But your propensity for cleverness is my fault, not yours." She felt a stab of guilt as she thought of how her brother would reprimand her for her tactics with what he called "innocent young girls."

She opened the cash register and gave each young lady several dollars. Where nickels had sufficed a few years ago, now the young ladies used their money for magazines and new hats. They squealed with delight and bid her a fond farewell as they raised their parasols outside the doorway.

Carolyn lingered for a few moments. "Won't they be angry at you, Adele? The police, I mean."

"They often are," Adele said, "but they recognize a just cause when they see one."

But it seemed as if this time there might be more than a few snippy remarks from Jackson, for when she reached the police station and laid the nibs on Hatfield's desk, her brother exploded with anger, throwing at her more than his share of reprimands.

"What's done is done," Hatfield said with a shrug. "I suppose we can think of some excuse as to how we got them if they prove to be important."

"You're taking a rather glib attitude, Sheriff," Jackson said in a rough tone.

Hatfield's shoulders stiffened. "It isn't like you to question my judgment, Deputy."

"Jack would never do that, Sheriff," Adele said quickly. "I don't intend for you to take the blame. I'm perfectly willing to go to Mr. Marsh myself and tell him."

"And what will you tell him, though I shudder to ask?" Jackson growled.

She reluctantly gave him an account of the Wrigley girls' deception.

Even Hatfield's mouth was set. "This is quite serious, Adele. It's one thing for you to put your hand in, but quite another to persuade school girls to do so."

"They're not school girls anymore," Adele insisted. "One of them will be coming out next year."

"Nonetheless," he said, "listening at corners and gathering information is one thing. Stealing is quite another."

"Borrowing," Adele murmured.

"It's beyond reprehensible, Del!" her brother thundered.

"I told you I accept the consequences," Adele insisted. "As long as we have them, don't you think it's worth looking at them?"

"I don't know that it's legal for us to do so," Hatfield said slowly.

"Perhaps not for you," Adele said. "But I've no legal bounds as a citizen, do I?" She looked at Edison, who was sitting hunched behind his desk. "Mr. Edison, will you please bring us the evidence from the Marsh case?"

The young man looked at the sheriff expectedly. Jackson too, his hands in his pocket, looked to his superior. Hatfield swung back a little on the tilting chair, his pleasant face tight. Finally, he said, "You heard the lady, Edison. Bring the evidence from the files, if you please."

As Edison teetered off to the tiny file room in the corner of the station, Jackson mumbled, "I fail to see how you can justify your behavior, Del."

"Perhaps I have more fearlessness than you, Jack," she said. "It seems you lost your courage somewhere on the train between Arrojo and Chicago."

Her brother narrowed his eyes in answer and stalked out of the station.

"That was highly unjust," said Hatfield in a quiet tone.

"I'll apologize to him tonight." Adele sat down with a seething glare.

"I don't deny your brother is more conservative than I when it comes to procedure," the sheriff said. "But considering my ways are as slipshod as the sea, I credit him for keeping me in this position in the last year."

Adele stared at him. "What do you mean?"

"It's no secret the city council is less than pleased with my, shall we say, unique style of policing?" Hatfield gave a wry smile. "I've had several rather stern letters about it."

"What nonsense!" Adele exploded. "I heard the last sheriff couldn't find a silver pin in a bale of hay while you've solved several serious cases efficiently."

He looked down at his desk, his hands flat on the surface. "I thank you for your confidence in me, Adele. But I can't agree with you about Sheriff Nealy. He was a cautious man who knew when to light the fire under the toes of the council."

"I'm sorry," Adele said. "I forgot you worked with him for a time."

They were silent for a few moments, and Edison clamped toward them with a box labeled THEODORA MARSH CASE in hand.

"Don't rattle it so, lad." Hatfield's confidential tone was gone and his hearty manner rumbled through the small station as he opened the box and took out the fountain pen nib, now properly enclosed in an envelope with a careful label on it.

As Adele laid the three nibs on the table neatly next to it, a creak sounded from the station door and Jackson returned. His face was still dark, but Adele knew he had probably taken a stroll down the street, yanked some leaves off a tree, as he had when his temper got the better of him as a child, and was now calm and rational.

"We were wrong," was the first thing he said.

Adele knew what he meant. The three nibs were nothing like the one they had found. They were wider, their points dulled from use, and the ink dry at the tip but otherwise the rest of the nib was clean, as if they had only been used once.

"No spoon tip among them," Adele admitted.

"That proves nothing," Hatfield insisted. "These might have

been used by Gregory Marsh a long time ago. I recognize the older style."

"Their style isn't the only factor, Sheriff," Adele said. "Remember what I told you during the Blackstone case about people's writing habits?"

He blinked, clearly at a loss, but Jackson said, "You said people get attached to certain writing tools until they become as indistinguishable as their handwriting."

"You've always had a good memory, Jack," she said kindly and he gave her a small smile, indicating forgiveness.

"In other words, you believe Mr. Marsh would use the same fountain pens for every occasion," the sheriff said.

"Just as one uses the same inkwells," Adele said.

"I think we ought to check with Josiah Brown & Sons," Jackson said.

"We will, of course, question the stationer," said Hatfield.

"I wonder who left the nib," Adele lamented. "And, more importantly, why it was left."

"Why?" her brother echoed. "Accident, of course. Criminals are careless. One can hardly think of what is falling out of one's pockets when one is committing a crime." Edison, who had gone back to his typewriter, snickered.

"I don't think it was carelessness, Jack," she said.

"Del's ideas." Jackson grinned at Hatfield.

"It was too conspicuous," Adele said. "Right by the bed, wasn't it?"

"In plain sight," the sheriff agreed.

"Where the police were sure to step on it," Adele said. "Rather convenient for a killer to be that careless."

"Have you any ideas as to that, Adele?" Hatfield swiveled in his chair to face her.

"One might call it incriminating evidence," she said.

"Oh, really, Del!" her brother snarled.

"If it was left there to incriminate Theo Marsh," Hatfield said. "It seems pointless, as it's an easy thing to check."

"Even the cleverest criminals can't be clever to the last detail," Adele said. "You told me that, Sheriff."

"A fountain pen nib is hardly evidence anyway." Jackson shrugged. "We've bigger fish to fry."

"Perhaps." Hatfield leaned back in his chair, his fingers poised in a V, his eyes distant. "I can't help but feel Adele is right. One way or the other, this is a family affair."

"If it had been the father who was killed, it might be different," Jackson agreed. "Women's deaths are often more personal than men's. It's difficult to believe anyone from Gregory's past would suddenly decide to reap vengeance on her twenty years later."

"And yet, the past is always a shadow of the present, isn't it?" Adele murmured.

# CHAPTER 15

The next morning showed a brilliant blue sky and only one or two clouds. Adele had promised the day before to take Nin to breakfast so they sat in Dora's Tea Shop at a table near the window while the morning went by at a leisurely pace.

"It's a shame Dora didn't ask you to advise her on some of her blends," Adele remarked as she poured herself another cup of the flowery tea she and Nin had ordered.

"Who says she didn't?" Nin asked. Her friend stared at her. "It was a long time ago. Not long after Mama died. She thought I needed the money."

"Why did you refuse?" Adele asked.

"I didn't want to see anyone then."

Adele nodded sympathetically. "I was almost thankful for the mourning rituals imposed upon Jack and me when Papa died. I didn't have to make any excuses not to see people."

"It wasn't that," Nin said shyly. "They all thought — you know what they all thought of me and of Mama. I didn't want any more accusations about witchery."

"As if you would ever poison anyone," Adele sniffed. "You're so passionate about healing."

"They don't know that," Nin said. "They don't think that. At least, they didn't, until you came to town."

Adele smiled. "I'm glad I've straightened out your reputation, dear."

The bells crashed against the door frame as it burst open. Dora, tending to her books at a quiet table in the corner, growled at the newcomer. Rebecca Gold's face twisted with agitation, her head bare and her blouse unbuttoned at the top as if she were interrupted before she had finished dressing.

"Adele, you've got to stop them!"

"Will you please quiet down!" Dora hissed, glancing at some out-of-town customers fidgeting in their chairs.

Adele led Rebecca to their table, motioning to the waitress to bring her a cup of tea. "It won't do to make a scene, dear."

"I wasn't trying to." Rebecca drank the tea down like water.

"Now," Adele said as the young woman breathed easier, "stop who from doing what?"

"Your brother."

"Jack?"

"He's arrested Theo!"

Adele glanced at Nin. "Arrested him for what?"

"For Thea's murder, of course!" The woman's voice rose to a shrill tone. "It's absurd!"

"Why would Jack arrest Theo?" Adele asked.

"They found something," said Rebecca.

"How do you know?"

"Mona called me," she said. "Damn, why didn't she call me right when it happened?"

Dora again shot a growl in her direction.

"You're the family lawyer, so you ought to have been told right away," Nin agreed.

"I'm Theo's lawyer," she said sternly.

There was silence as the out-of-town customers finished their tea. The cash register echoed in the tea shop as the creaking door left a mark of bells in the air. Dora rose and before going to the counter gave Adele a meaningful look.

"He may just want to question him," Adele pointed out. "The arrest is only a formality."

"No, no, it's more than that," said Rebecca. "I'm sure of it."

"What exactly did Mona tell you?"

"The police insisted on searching Theo's room."

"That's not unusual," Nin said. "They always want to search everywhere."

"Mona said they were looking for something specific," Rebecca said. "They were very hush hush about it."

"The black water," Nin whispered to Adele.

"Mona said the police found something in Theo's room," Rebecca said. "She didn't know what, but that's why they arrested Theo."

"You're the family lawyer," Nin said firmly. "Why don't you go down to the station and ask?"

Rebecca's agitation eased. "Of course! I can do that, can't I?"

"Not only can you do it," Adele said. "It's your duty to do it."

The lawyer rose, adjusting the pins in her hair and buttoned her blouse. "I didn't even put my hat or coat on," she said with a small laugh. "Mona's phone call caught me off guard."

"We shall accompany you while you finish dressing." Adele motioned to Nin. "You want to be properly dressed like the family lawyer ought to be when we go down to the station."

"Yes, of course." Rebecca's voice grew more assured. "Theo would want me there. He needs me there."

The front door flew open again. Dora gritted her teeth. Mrs. Faderman sauntered in with Mrs. Lynn and some of the other ladies. To Adele's surprise, Assistant Deputy Edison and Assistant Deputy Dooland came in last, hovering a little in the back.

"Don't dawdle, Mr. Edison!" Mrs. Faderman snapped.

"Assistant Deputy Edison, ma'am," the young man said with a

sheepish smile. His companion let out a guffaw but a glare from Mrs. Faderman made him slink against the doorway.

"You have your duty, Mr. Edison." Mrs. Faderman folded her hands, her closed parasol tapping her ankle.

Edison cleared his throat a few times and then, straightening to his full average height, he approached the counter. "Are you Mrs. Dora Leslie?"

"You know she is, young man!" Mrs. Abberton said in her hoarse tone.

Edison cleared his throat a few more times. "Ma'am, there's been a charge brought forward by a Mrs. Irene Faderman regarding some of your wares."

"This is a tea shop, my boy," Dora said. "You had better be more specific." It was clear to Adele she was trying to be serious but was having a hard time keeping the amusement out of her face.

"Ma'am, I regret to inform you —"

"Regret!" Mrs. Faderman growled.

"I'm obliged to inform you I have a court order to seize —" he looked down at the piece of paper in his hand, his eyes squinting — "samples of those Indian teas."

"Samples? What for?" Dora glared at him.

"On suspicion of possible harmful substances."

"Harmful?" Dora eyed him. "You'll have to explain yourself, Assistant Deputy."

"Don't vacillate, Mr. Edison," Mrs. Faderman insisted. "Tell the woman straight out."

"Lethal substances, ma'am," said the young man.

"You mean poisons!" For the first time, Dora looked alarmed. "Nonsense!"

"Nonsense or not, ma'am, we've a court order," said the young man.

"Tell her what else is in the order, Mr. Edison," Mrs. Faderman prompted like a teacher to a shy school child.

"I was coming to that, ma'am. One thing at a time, the sheriff always says." The assistant deputy stiffened a little.

Mrs. Faderman leaned over the counter. "Miss Leslie, I suggest you ask everybody to leave."

"But there is no everybody," Nin said. "There's only us and we were about to leave anyway."

Mrs. Faderman glanced at her, then looked at Dora again. "The order also states you're to close down this establishment until the court is fully satisfied there are no other harmful substances lying about your shop."

"Poppycock!" Dora exploded. "There has never been anyone who walked out of my shop less than satisfied with what I serve. I've had praises from European chefs who came especially to sample my angel food cake and raisin tarts."

"I've no objection to what comes out of the kitchen, Miss Leslie," Mrs. Faderman said. "It's only what comes out of the tins." She cast an accusing eye at the row of Indian teas.

"Then you admit this is your special ax to grind," Dora said shrewdly. "You're trying to blame your guest's overindulgence on my teas."

"I'm doing no such thing!" Mrs. Faderman glared. "My concern is for the community."

"Mrs. Faderman should have been a lawyer," Rebecca whispered.

The woman eyed her through her pince-nez. Her gaze ran down Rebecca's hatless and coatless figure, stopping at the boots slipped on haphazardly but not properly buttoned. Rebecca blushed.

"That's as may be, ma'am, but the order stands." Edison now stood with his feet a little apart and his face determined, placing the paper with smeared type on the counter in front of Dora.

Dora made a show of reading through it. She gave Edison a vehement look that made even Adele cringe. "The sheriff sent you?"

The young assistant deputy hung his head.

"And will the sheriff compensate me for the business I'll lose while my shop is closed?"

"You'll have to speak to him about that, ma'am," said Edison.

"If you wanted to stay in business, you ought to have been more careful about your stock, Miss Leslie." Mrs. Abberton sniffed.

Dora put the order down. "Did the sheriff happen to tell you how long I was to be out of business?"

"Just until the samples are analyzed, ma'am." Edison gave Dooland an authoritative look and the young man slipped behind the counter.

Dora gave a sign to the waitress, who stood in front of the tea canisters. "How long will that take?"

"I don't rightly know, ma'am," the young man admitted. "Dr. Rhodes will be doing the analysis."

"Then I can expect to wait until kingdom come," Dora declared.

"Oh, not that long, ma'am," said Edison. "I'm sure the sheriff will put a rush on it."

"Dr. Rhodes will take all the time he needs," Mrs. Faderman insisted. "There may be lives at stake if even one of those teas is poisonous. You shall have to tell everyone who bought them to bring them back."

"Fortunately for you, Mrs. Faderman, that is a very small number of people." Dora slammed the drawer to the cash register. "The most lucrative customer I had is already dead."

"You mean Thea?" Rebecca burst out.

"Yes, I was referring to Mrs. Marsh." Dora looked at her. "But I very much doubt my teas had anything to do with the poor woman's death."

"But can we be sure?" Mrs. Faderman asked.

Dora's face grew almost dangerous. "Are you making accusations, Mrs. Faderman?"

"Irene would never accuse anyone of anything," Mrs. Lynn said in her mousy voice.

"No, she just influences the police to get court orders," said Dora in a dry voice. "All right, Deputy Assistant. You may tell the sheriff he'll receive my full cooperation." She gave the waitress another sign and the woman stepped aside. Dooland straightened his jacket and began collecting the canisters.

Dora ambled over to them. "It seems I'm being forced to shut down. It's a good thing you finished anyway." She smiled at Adele. "Shall I wrap up the rest of the scones to take with you? Unless you want to take those to your lab to make sure they aren't poisonous?" She gave Edison a meaningful glare.

"We've orders to take just the teas ma'am," said the assistant deputy in a confused tone.

Adele's gaze fixed on Assistant Deputy Dooland, who had a surprisingly delicate hand as he collected the tins in a box the waitress had shoved at him. "I wonder —"

"We must hurry," Rebecca said. "We don't want Theo to be held longer than he has to."

Mrs. Faderman turned from the doorway. "Theodore Marsh, you mean?"

"None of your business," Nin snapped.

The woman was anything but put out. "The police are leaning rather heavily on the family, aren't they?"

"I don't wish to be rude," Adele said swiftly, "but Nin is right, Mrs. Faderman. It really isn't any of your business."

"Prying old woman!" Nin growled as they stepped out to the busy sidewalk.

Adele took her arm. "I think I've an idea of how we might show Theo had nothing to do with his mother's death."

"Then you don't believe he did it?" Rebecca's eyes lit up. "I knew I could trust you!"

"It might prove otherwise," Adele cautioned.

"I'm willing to take that chance," the lawyer insisted.

"You remember when we examined Theo's room and Nin said there was something evil in the leaves we found?"

"Indeed." Nin shivered.

"Teas can contain leaves and berries that aren't suitable for humans, can't they?"

"You mean those teas?" Rebecca glanced back at the tea shop.

"Any gardening enthusiast knows plants can shed noxious spells under innocent-looking shrubs," Adele said. "I remember Mrs. Woods who lived on our street had half the San Francisco police at her door because she was given a lovely flower as a gift and had no idea it was wolfsbane."

"I shouldn't wonder," Nin said dryly.

"A woman who already has heart trouble might succumb to some strange herb someone else wouldn't react to," Adele pointed out.

"I see what you mean," Rebecca murmured.

"We would know more if we could get the tea tested," said Adele.

Rebecca was silent for a few moments as they stood in front of her office. "You mean if you did, it might prove Theo was innocent because the poison that killed Thea was in the tea itself."

"It's a chance," said Adele. "You're sure you have no idea what made you react so, Nin?"

"I don't know every plant and flower in the world," Nin said in a sulky tone.

"You knew enough to know it was bad," Adele said gently. "Perhaps it's time for science to do the rest."

"Science!" Nin sniffed.

The first thing the three ladies saw when they entered the police station was Theo sitting in the jail cell against the wall of the office with his hands covering his face. Rebecca strode to him and spoke in a hushed tone.

"It was rather devious of you, Jack," Adele snarled as she caught hold of her brother's arm.

"Devious?"

"Not to tell me you were planning to arrest Theo."

"You're not privileged to all police business, Del," Jackson said.

"You know Rebecca is my friend." She dropped into a chair.

"I can't see how Miss Gold has anything to do with it."

"She's his lawyer," Nin insisted.

Sheriff Hatfield leaned back in his chair. "I was wondering when you would arrive to ask questions."

"I'm not asking questions," Adele said. "Theo's lawyer is. Or is *she* not privileged to know police business when it pertains to her client?" She glared at her brother.

Jackson put his fountain pen down. "The sheriff told me last night we had enough to bring Theo in. I didn't tell you because I was afraid you would interfere."

"Interfere!"

"You must admit, Adele, you don't exactly have a record for keeping out of the way when it comes to criminal matters," Sheriff Hatfield said.

"Only when there is a question!" Adele insisted. "As there was with Richard Tanning."

"You think there is a question with Mr. Marsh?" the sheriff asked.

"That would depend," Adele said, "on what you're charging him with and the evidence you have against him."

Hatfield tapped his finger against the desk, making a hollow sound. Edison, who was arranging specimens from the tea canisters in small glass dishes, jumped.

"You're not going to tell me?" Adele could feel her anger rise. "I thought you had respect for my instincts."

"Instincts, yes," Jackson said. "Meddling is something else."

"We never meddle," Nin growled.

"I didn't say *you* did, Miss Branch," Jackson said. "I'm well aware my sister drags you into this with her ideas or hunches or whatever she calls them." He gave Adele a meaningful look. "I had no obligation to tell you anything, Del."

"But you've an obligation to me." Rebecca spoke in a clear tone. "I'm representing Theo, and I insist on knowing the details."

"That's certainly your right, Miss Gold," said Jackson.

The sheriff rose. "Edison! Make the ladies coffee."

"They just had tea at Dora's Tea Shop, sir," Edison said.

"I didn't ask for your report, lad," Hatfield snapped. "We shall be here for a while, so the ladies will need coffee."

In his usual mild manner, he waited until the coffee was served, making all three women, even Nin, sit at the table in the interview room. He then laid the facts before them.

"I suppose you know we paid Mr. Brethren another visit," he began.

"Theo told me." Rebecca nodded.

"We knew he lied, so we could hardly let that go," said the sheriff. "I can't say I blame him. Young men protect their male friends as a point of honor."

"I don't believe Lom would deliberately withhold anything," Rebecca said stiffly. "He probably didn't realize it would be so important."

"If he didn't think it important, he would have told us he saw Theo a few days before his mother died," said Hatfield. "As it happens, he admitted he lied and for good reason."

"I know the reason." Rebecca glanced at the jail cell.

"Then you know Theo lied as well," said the sheriff, "when he told us he forgot to put a fatal plant in his garden."

"I don't follow you, Sheriff," Adele said.

"Mr. Brethren gave his friend a little more than gardening advice," Hatfield said. "He gave him a poisonous substance. That was the black water Mona saw. It was an extract from the belladonna fruit."

"That hardly proves anything," Adele insisted.

"We searched Mr. Marsh's room this morning." The sheriff reached into the evidence box and extracted a small paper bag. "We found this in a pigeon hole in Mr. Marsh's desk."

An audible gasp came from Nin as she folded up on her usual position on the floor like a swan hiding its face between its wings.

"Dr. Rhodes tested it?" Adele asked sharply.

Hatfield nodded. "He confirmed it's entirely possible a small amount would have caused Mrs. Marsh's death."

There was silence for a moment. Rebecca said, "Sheriff, will you please allow Theo out of the cell for a few moments? I'd like to ask him some questions."

"That's your privilege," said Hatfield, motioning toward Jackson. "He's been very cooperative. I doubt he'll try to run away."

"Why should he run away when he's guilty of nothing?" Rebecca snarled. "He's an honorable man, Sheriff."

"I know, Miss Gold," Hatfield said.

Jackson led Theo to the interview room. The man looked ruffled, though it was clear his inbred composure had taken hold, and he seated himself with an admirable combination of dignity and humility.

"Theo," said Rebecca, her voice soft, "the sheriff told us what they found in your room."

"What did they find?" Theo asked, dazed. "I don't understand any of this."

"The vial your friend sent you, sir," said the sheriff. "We told you about it."

"Oh, yes, yes." The man's eyes closed.

"Why didn't you tell us Mr. Brethren sent you belladonna when we spoke to you before, Mr. Marsh?" Jackson asked.

"I don't know what it was doing in my room!"

"Please, sir," Hatfield said. "Your sister told us you received a package from Mr. Brethren."

"Oh, that. Yes, I remember now. He did send me something in a small glass jar."

The sheriff produced the vial from the paper bag. "This glass jar?"

Theo shrank from it. "I don't know!"

"Why didn't you tell us?" Jackson asked again.

"I was so flustered, I forgot. I swear I did!"

"You forget you were given poison during a murder investigation?" Hatfield raised his eyebrows.

"Did you ask your friend to lie for you and forget that too?" Jackson asked.

"Jack!" Adele shot him a look.

"I suppose Lom lied because he saw my fate well before I did." Theo buried his face in his hands.

"There is no fate, Theo," Rebecca said. "We'll clear the whole matter up in no time."

"You're a treasure, Becca." He grasped her hand. The lawyer gave a quick smile, her face turning red.

"If you forgot about the vial, as you claim, why was it so carefully hidden away?" Jackson asked.

"I don't know," Theo lamented. "I distinctly remember throwing it away."

"You forget you had it in the first place but remember throwing it away?" Jackson asked with a small smile.

Sheriff Hatfield glared at him. "May I remind you, Deputy, we do not use Anspach vigilante methods in this police station?"

Jackson shifted his weight from side to side, and Adele was almost glad the sheriff's quiet tone had an effect. "I apologize, Mr. Marsh."

"I suppose I can't blame you for being suspicious, Deputy," Theo said. "It does sound all muddled."

"Maybe Dr. Rhodes can prove Thea Marsh died of belladonna poisoning," Nin said, "but can he prove the belladonna extract you found in Mr. Marsh's room was the same one that killed her?"

"A very good point, Miss Branch," Jackson said.

"Unfortunately, the stain in the teacup is rather damaged," the sheriff admitted. "Dr. Rhodes is in doubt whether he can match it to the substance in the vial."

Rebecca rose. "Then you've really no case, have you?"

"I never hang my hat on only one piece of evidence, Miss Gold," said the sheriff without looking up.

She sat down again. "As I'm the counsel for the defense, you realize you have an obligation to tell me everything, Sheriff."

"Counsel for the defense," Theo murmured. "So I'm to go to trial!"

"That's for the district attorney to decide," said the sheriff. "The vial is strong evidence. There's this as well." He pointed to the fountain pen nib in the evidence box.

"I thought we were through with that, Sheriff," Adele said. "It didn't compare to Mr. Marsh's others."

"Others?" Theo looked confused.

"My sister decided to do a little detecting of her own," Jackson said. "She had some of the nibs in that box of yours examined against this one."

"How in the world —"

"It's better you didn't know," said Adele.

"Adele was only trying to help, Theo," said Rebecca.

"I suppose I ought to have thrown that box away years ago," the man lamented.

"Superstitions of the father weigh heavily on the son," Nin murmured. He looked at her with startled eyes.

"It's true this one doesn't match those in the box," said Sheriff Hatfield. "But we spoke with Mr. Brown of Josiah Brown & Sons Stationers, and he confirmed Mr. Marsh buys all his stationery there."

"Theo told us that himself," Adele pointed out.

"He also confirmed," Jackson put in, "that nibs very much like this one have been ordered by the Marsh Lumber Mill."

An expression of terror whitened Theo's face. "Do you think I killed my mother and wiped it completely out of my mind?" His hand reached to grasp Rebecca's wrist.

"Of course not." Rebecca held his hand tightly. "You couldn't hurt a fly, Theo."

"Mr. Marsh was willing to hurt an animal more substantial than a fly, Miss Gold," Jackson reminded her. "A raccoon, to be exact."

"He wouldn't have hurt them," Nin said quietly. Adele knew from the momentary distant glance of her cat eyes this was a flash of one of her visions.

"Thank you, Miss Branch." Rebecca looked at her gratefully.

Theo was silent, though a slight gasp came from his lips. He rose, his face composed once more. "I'd like to go back to the cell now."

When Jackson had taken him out of the room, Rebecca glared at the sheriff. "You know there's only a slim chance of getting a trial based on the evidence you've got, Sheriff."

"I'm not the one doing the convicting, Miss Gold." Adele could see he was trying to control his temper. "I only gather the evidence for the district attorney."

"It's still flimsy," Adele said quietly.

The sheriff played with the edge of the fountain pen, then put it back in the box.

Rebecca gathered her things. "I intend to speak to the judge and get the whole thing thrown out as soon as possible."

"That's your privilege," said Hatfield. "I never interfere with the doings of lawyers."

"Sheriff Hatfield is always very fair, whatever direction the case goes, Rebecca," Adele said. "He's not one of your corrupted officials."

"He won't plant evidence where there is none," Nin agreed.

"Thank you, Adele." Hatfield gave her a gracious smile. "And you too, Miss Branch." Here, the smile was a little wary.

"I never said I thought Sheriff Hatfield was corrupt," Rebecca insisted. "But sheriffs can be a little too anxious to pursue a quick solution to a crime."

"Indeed some can, miss." He gave her a sweeping bow. The gesture angered her, and she stalked out of the station with Adele and Nin at her heels. Adele threw the sheriff an apologetic glance as she let the door close behind her.

Rebecca's cheeks were flushed with an uneven look on her face.

"That wasn't very cordial, you know," Adele remarked.

"If he weren't so cocksure —" she snarled.

"He's anything but," Nin said.

The anger drained from Rebecca's face. "I'm sorry. I'm used to dealing with city police. They care only for a conviction, not the truth."

"Sheriff Hatfield is no city lawman," Adele assured her.

"But he needs evidence Theo had nothing to do with his mother's death," Rebecca said. "That much is clear."

"And you expect to get it?" Adele eyed her.

"No." Rebecca took her by the shoulders. "I expect *you* to get it."

Adele said quietly, "I'm a businesswoman, Rebecca."

"I'll hire you as a detective, if you prefer," said the woman in a stubborn tone. "Consider yourself working for me as any private detective would."

"Heaven forbid!" Nin murmured.

"You heard what my brother said," Adele pointed out. "They don't like me interfering."

"I have a right to hire any private detective I like," Rebecca insisted, "to find evidence my client is innocent if I believe him so."

Adele studied the young woman's face. She saw there was more than a long-standing infatuation driving her. She regarded Adele with begging blue eyes. She was determined to get the client she believed innocent out of the jaws of justice. Adele had to admit the evidence Hatfield offered was the paltriest she had ever seen him present.

"What do you want me to do?" she asked.

Rebecca squeezed her hand. "We both know the sheriff has enough to bring Theo to trial, and it's entirely possible he would be convicted if the district attorney is smart enough to twist the most damning evidence in his favor."

"The vial of belladonna and the pen nib," Nin said.

"You want me to find something to refute that evidence?" Adele raised her eyebrows.

"You know the law," Rebecca said. "It isn't necessary to prove who did it. It's only necessary to convince a jury there is a shadow of a doubt as to whether the one on trial is guilty."

"I see," Adele said.

"I know you feel as I do," said Rebecca. Her voice was picking up strength. "It's too neat and tidy."

"Poke holes in the queen's pie?" Nin gave a small smile.

"Something like that," Rebecca said with a serious face.

"If anyone can do it, Adele can." Her friend took her arm.

Adele held her parasol with both hands and looked down at the ground, its usual powdery red dirt showing the imprint of a hundred shoes. "And if I discover the evidence is damning after all?"

"You won't," Rebecca said with finality.

# CHAPTER 17

*A*dele and Nin watched Rebecca go into her office. Her figure was stiff like a wooden statue, and her gait showed the intensity of her feelings.

"Heaven help the blindness of a woman in love," Nin muttered.

"I don't think it's only love, dear," Adele said. "I think the sheriff reminded her she was a lawyer, and lawyers have a job to do."

"If Rebecca is right, it won't come to that," Adele said.

"No, it won't come to that."

Adele glanced at her. "One of your feelings?"

"The tones from the Generous Ones are all skewed in this case," said Nin, a disturbed look on her face. "When there's poison involved, Sister Earth is displeased, and the signals are vague."

"I wish they were clear," Adele murmured.

"I'm sure your doubtful brother doesn't," Nin remarked.

They walked a little, Adele's mind wandering as people hurried past them.

"Where do we begin?" Nin asked.

"With a theory."

"What theory?"

"Thea was killed by poison but not the one found in the vial."

"What other one could there be?"

"I think we should pay Dora a call," Adele said. "We ought to console her in her troubled times."

"She's in no trouble," Nin insisted. "It's all nonsense."

"We'll offer her comfort all the same," Adele said, "with a soothing cup of tea."

Although Dora bought the two-story building where she set up her tea shop, she refused to live on the second floor, insisting it would only force her to work more hours than she was willing. She had taken a small house on a quiet street a few blocks up from Caliber Lane. Her house was not as wide as Adele's, but it had a pleasant garden where Dora grew roses and gardenias. As they went through the gate, Adele could smell the sweet flowers.

They tried knocking on the door, and, with no answer, they went out to the back. Dora, completely covered in an old cotton dress and large-brimmed hat, was weeding a patch near the fence.

Adele could tell by her jerking movements the woman was still angry. Dora could not hold back for very long, and when she saw them, she immediately burst out, "That toad of a woman!"

"At least you've an opportunity to spend some time tending your roses," Adele said gently.

"She had no right to interfere with my business!"

"You ought to spread more manure," Nin said in her blunt way, staring at the gardenia shrub.

"Just because she has to save face when her guest gets sick." Dora snapped off the thick gloves.

"For some women, society is everything," Adele said.

"Thank goodness some of us are more useful in life," Dora growled.

"There will be more of us useful in the future," Adele

promised. "Even society women will find their usefulness beyond being their rich husbands' ornaments."

"And in the meantime, my business, and possibly my reputation suffers."

Adele put her arm around her shoulders. "They'll find nothing, and it will all be over in a few days."

Dora pouted. "I've a shipment coming in from England tomorrow."

"I shall speak to Edison about coming by to help you unload it," Adele said. "It's the least he can do after that ridiculous warrant."

Dora gave a loud sigh. "I don't blame the poor boy. Not with Mrs. Faderman practically holding a pistol to his head!"

"She may find herself in an unpleasant situation one of these days," Nin remarked.

"I hope that's one of your prophecies, Miss Branch." Dora glanced at her.

"More of a hope at the moment," Nin said.

They all laughed, and Dora, clearly calmed, said, "Come inside, and I shall serve you the best coffee you've ever tasted. Sometimes I get mighty tired of tea."

"About teas," Adele said as they went inside the quaint kitchen, "you're quite fond of those Indian teas, aren't you?"

"I never sell my customers anything I don't drink myself," Dora said. "You know that."

"Then you have some at your disposal?" Adele glanced around the small kitchen.

"I have most of them tucked away in the pantry," Dora said. "They're my personal stock, and damned if the police are going to get them."

Adele sat down at the table, and Nin took her usual position on the floor. "You don't happen to have that red tea blend in your pantry, do you?"

Dora shot her a look from the stove. "What are you up to?"

"Perhaps proving a man innocent," Adele said.

Dora grinned and leaned into the pantry, which was hardly more than a small cupboard. She pulled out a green box. "Mr. Marsh bought several from me, but I believe this is the one you want. You do want the one he bought the day before they found his mother dead, don't you?"

"I believe we are of one mind," Adele said.

"I've no wish to help the police just now, heaven knows," Dora said. "I imagine they have the poor man locked up. If this will free him, what better revenge on their foul assumption than to carry poison in my shop?"

"If there is indeed no poison in your shop," Adele said softly.

"Don't tell me you believe it!"

"There is no poison in your shop," Nin declared. "They only took them because no one understands the power of Sister Earth and her gifts."

"Her gifts can be enemies too," Adele reminded her. "The belladonna, for instance."

"It's only in the way people use them," Nin insisted.

"And sometimes, not only her gifts but her enemies can save lives," Adele said quietly.

"What in heaven's name do you mean by that?" Dora stared at her, the coffee pot in her hand.

"Theo always made his mother's tea," Adele said.

"I don't see your point."

"She was poisoned by something in her tea."

"Oh, yes, I read something like that in the newspaper." Dora put her hands on her hips. "You think my tea did it?"

"There may be something in the blend that, given Thea's poor health, might have accidentally caused her death," Adele said carefully. "If that's the case, Theo couldn't have killed her."

"Not intentionally," Nin added.

"It would be accidental," Adele insisted. "That's a very different thing than murder."

"I must say, that gives me an entirely new perspective on those teas," Dora said. "I never cared much for the Marsh family, but Mr. Marsh was always a gentleman."

"Then you'll help us?" Adele pressed her hand.

"If it might help prove a man innocent of murder, I suppose I'll have to," Dora said. "Though I don't much like the idea of Mrs. Faderman possibly being right."

"But she wouldn't be right," Nin pointed out. "If there is something that accidentally caused Thea's death, it could have just as easily accidentally caused her guest to get sick."

Dora's mood lightened. "In that case, you can have anything you wish."

Adele slid the canister of tea at Nin. "Dear, we need your expertise. Can you tell us what herbs are in it?"

She wished Jackson could see Nin, as her examination of the tea was as thorough as his of a murder scene. She sniffed it, poured it in the palm of her hand to examine every leaf, and spread it on the table, hunching over the pile with closed eyes.

"Cardamon, ginger, anise, I think. And pepper," she said at last.

"Pepper?" Dora wrinkled her nose.

"It brings out the other spices," Nin explained.

Adele grasped her shoulder. "Remember when we were in Thea's room, and you smelled a sickly floral scent?"

"I didn't really smell it," Nin admitted. "I felt it. It filled me like a mist."

"Is it in this tea?"

"I don't know," Nin admitted. "I don't always smell a scent when I feel it that strongly."

Adele sank in a chair.

"What's all this about sickly floral scents?" Dora asked. "It sounds like Mrs. Faderman's perfume." After Adele explained, the woman said, "You think that sickly scent might have been this poison that killed Thea?"

"If Nin reacted so strongly, it was important," Adele said.

Dora gave a half-smile. "I'm sure Dr. Rhodes could give you a very scientific lecture as to why Miss Branch reacted as she did."

"Dr. Rhodes is a leech," Nin said brutally.

Dora laughed and bowed. "I couldn't agree with you more. If he finds anything in my teas, I shall eat my hat, false cherries and all." She threw a glance at the hat hanging from the peg in the hallway.

Adele smiled and gathered the tea. "I won't be asking Dr. Rhodes for any help. But someone else could help us."

"Mr. Brethren?" Nin eyed her.

"He has some knowledge of herbs and plants," Adele said. "He wants to help his friend, or he wouldn't have lied to the police." She glanced at Dora. "May we take a sample of this with us?"

"Take the entire canister," Dora said.

~~~~~

Nin refused to ride in the Beaton Roundabout, so they took the wagon. To Adele's surprise, Nin insisted on driving. Her haphazard rein on the horses made Adele shudder at first, but she saw the woman had a real rapport with the animals, hardly using the whip to steer their way down the road into Rosa Gris, where the university stood in a cluster of gray buildings. They found the laboratory at the edge of the campus, illuminated by more electric lights than Adele had seen on the street.

Lom Brethren was the opposite of Theo. He was chunky and had pale hair and eyes. A clean beard masked his face, though Adele could see worry in his eyes.

"I behaved stupidly, Miss Gossling," he admitted after Adele introduced them.

"Call me Adele," she said kindly. "I'm a friend of the family now."

He bowed. "It's my fault Theo was arrested."

"It was no one's fault," Adele insisted. "It's where the evidence led the police."
~~~~~

"They always have to arrest *someone*," Nin said. "Otherwise, they don't get elected again."

Adele shot her friend a look. "I don't think Sheriff Hatfield had that in mind when he took Theo in." She accepted the hard stool Lom offered her. "Still, it was unwise of you to lie to the police."

"I realize that now," he said. "I thought it was harmless since I know Theo had nothing to do with his mother's death. He was devoted to her."

"And he resented her control over him," Adele said softly.

"Well, what grown man wouldn't?" Lom challenged. "I don't think Theo even realized she was doing it. He wanted to get married once, you know."

"Did he?" Adele stared at him.

"To a woman who came to assist us in the lab some years ago," he said. "Thea thought she was too unfeminine."

"Too much like his mother," Nin remarked.

"I suppose so," said Lom. "It's all a grave mistake. Theo only wanted to get rid of the raccoons."

"We're trying to disprove some of the evidence the police have on Theo," Adele began. "We thought you could help us."

"I'll do anything I can, of course." The young man laid down the tongs in his hand. "It's better we go to my office. I'm afraid the laboratory is disturbing your friend."

Nin had barricaded herself behind a few chairs, laying them on their sides so as to make an enclosure. Adele could see the distress whitening her face. She helped her friend out of the box of chairs and followed Lom into a narrow but cheerful office where Nin immediately opened the window.

"My friend is a woman of the earth," Adele explained. "She prefers the outdoors."

"Then we shall go to the courtyard," said Lom, smiling. "It's a little chilly, but if you prefer it —" He looked questioningly at Nin.

"I do." Her voice was a little uneven.

They found a pleasant spot in the sun.

"What is it I can help you with?" he asked.

"Tell us about what you gave Theo for the raccoons." Adele settled onto the grass, smiling inwardly at what her brother would say if he saw her.

"McCabe would know more about that than I would," he said.

"McCabe?"

"Dr. McCabe," he said. "He works with me." He gave her a crooked smile. "He's rather eccentric. But he's out at the moment."

"Tell us what you can," Adele said.

"Atropa belladonna isn't exactly something people want to know about."

"We're not people," Nin said. "We're trying to find out about a murder."

"What are its effects if taken too much?" Adele asked.

He peered at her. "Are you sure you want to know? It isn't pretty."

"We're not shrinking violets," Adele insisted.

"Any number of unpleasant things, really. Rapid pulse, difficulty breathing, swelling, dry throat, delirium, convulsions." He spoke in the monotone of a doctor explaining a terminal illness to a patient. He was so matter-of-fact that Adele, imagining Thea's last night, shivered.

"I warned you it wasn't pleasant," he said.

"It's barbaric!" Nin growled.

"Yes, I suppose there's a more humane way of getting rid of the raccoons," Lom admitted.

"Not to mention a woman," Adele said dryly. "How much of it is needed to kill someone?"

"Very little," he said. "I don't know exactly. McCabe would know."

"What a gruesome man," Nin remarked.

"Are the leaves as poisonous as the fruit?" Adele asked.

"Indeed," said the chemist. "Even one leaf can be fatal." He eyed her. "What are you getting at, Miss Gossling?"

"Tea," said Adele. "Belladonna isn't just a poison, is it?"

"You mean the name." Lom smiled. "'Beautiful woman' in Italian."

"Women used it to beautify themselves?" Adele asked.

"McCabe told me they sometimes reddened their cheeks or widened their eyes," he said.

"The absurdity of beauty!" Nin growled.

"You can talk, Miss Branch, because you clearly have no need of such artificial means." The man cast his eye at her, admiring her cat-like grace and stunning features. Nin glared back at him.

"What about medicinal uses?" Adele asked. "I've heard of belladonna plasters."

"For pain and neuralgia, yes," he said. "I don't say I approve of such things, but perhaps it's better to use what nature gives us than what comes from the lab. That's why I work with organic matter."

"Very admirable," Adele said.

"I think I'm beginning to understand your questions." Lom's expression grew excited. "If Theo's mother accidentally took too much of something that contained belladonna, he couldn't have had anything to do with her death. He's innocent!"

"Could you detect whether there is belladonna in the stained teacup found the morning after Thea's murder?" She looked at Lom. "Dr. Rhodes couldn't, but your lab is more equipped for such things."

"It's possible, though I can't promise," he said. "I would have to get hold of it, of course."

"The police still have it."

"Adele, you wouldn't!" Nin stared at her. "You know how the sheriff feels about evidence leaving the station."

"Mr. Brethren, how much do you know about leaves?"

The young man was taken aback. He took a pipe out of his pocket and, with a nod from the ladies, lit it. "Well, my landlady has a few ferns in the house," he said, amused.

"I mean the properties of leaves," Adele said.

"She means if they're poisonous or not," Nin added.

"I should think that's more your line than mine, Miss Branch, from what I've heard about you." He looked at her steadily.

Nin shrugged and played with her hair.

"Can you test their properties even if you don't know what the leaves are?" Adele persisted.

"Sometimes yes, sometimes no," he said. "I can certainly try. I assume there's a plant you're interested in having tested?"

She produced the tea from her purse. "I'm interested in this tea blend."

"Tea?" He squinted at the plain box.

"The tea Thea drank that night," Adele said.

"But don't the police have it?"

"This is a new container," she said. "A tea shop in Arrojo sold it to him. That shop is now closed under suspicions that the entire line of teas might be dangerous."

"I think I see," he said as he took the packet.

"Tea blends are sometimes mysterious," Adele remarked.

"They are indeed," Lom agreed. "What can heal one person can harm another."

"How long will it take before you know?" Adele asked him.

"I must run tests, of course," he said. "But bear in mind, Adele, tests won't necessarily reveal anything. Science isn't perfect."

Adele couldn't help but notice her friend's cat-like smile.

# CHAPTER 18

Adele asked Nin to meet her at the train station the next morning. Ruth rose before sunrise and did some of the cooking in her own house rather than the main house so the scent wouldn't reach Jackson. Before Adele left, she handed her the bacon sandwiches and pound cake in a basket. Tomas, half-asleep, clicked his tongue and shook his head, knowing she was up to something, but his wife gave him a meaningful look that made him retreat back into the bedroom of their cabin. Being careful not to awaken her brother, Adele left the house.

She arrived at the police station, knowing Edison would be there alone. The young man looked more alert than usual. He greeted her with flustered attention, offering her coffee several times.

"I really can't stay, Mr. Edison." She placed the basket carefully on the table. "I'm on my way to the train station."

"Oh, a trip, miss?" He sounded almost disappointed.

Adele smiled. "I'm going to see some friends in the city."

"I'd like to visit San Francisco one day," he said in a wistful tone.

"You've never been?" He shook his head. She felt genuinely

sorry for the young man. "The next time you have a day off, tell me, and I'll arrange a grand time for you. I've several male friends who would be happy to show you the city."

"Well, miss, I didn't — I wasn't thinking —"

She couldn't help but laugh at his flushed face. "Don't worry, Mr. Edison, it will all be perfectly respectable." She pushed the basket toward him. "I made you lunch. I know how hard the sheriff has been working you."

"Kind of you, miss." His eyes shone. "You're always so generous to us 'round here. Those sugar cookies you brought last week were the sensation of the station." He blushed.

She laughed. "I'm glad you all liked them, but the credit goes to Ruth."

"She's a fine cook, miss."

"Mr. Edison." She now put on a worried expression. "You could help me a great deal."

"You mean you want to take evidence out of the station?" He stiffened.

Adele laughed. "You're too clever for me. Yes, that's what I mean."

"The sheriff would be awfully angry with you," he reminded her. "Like those other times."

"But this time is different," Adele insisted. "Miss Gold, Mr. Marsh's attorney, asked me to work on her behalf."

"Oh!"

"I'm very serious, Mr. Edison." Here, she couldn't be more sincere. "Do you really believe Mr. Theo Marsh killed his mother?"

"Well, I don't know, miss." He blinked. "Hard to believe any son would kill his mother. Why, even thinking of such a thing makes my stomach turn."

"Exactly!" Adele said. "It's unthinkable. And Miss Gold asked me to prove it. Lawyers have access to evidence, you know."

"Well, if you put it that way." He relaxed somewhat. "What is it you want, Miss Gossling?"

"I want the teacup Mrs. Marsh used the night she was killed."

"Oh, dear!" the man burst out.

"There's a chance the tea may have had poisonous leaves," she said. "It was one of Dora's."

"Well, then, it wouldn't be anybody's fault if she died that way, would it?" The young man looked relieved. "I mean, if the tea were poisoned already."

Adele hid the smile on her face at the thought of how Dora would rip him apart if she heard. "That's what I want to prove, Mr. Edison. I've someone who will examine them for me. No tampering with evidence, I assure you," she added quickly.

"Is that why you're going to the city?"

"I'm going to the city to see Mr. Josiah Brown of Josiah Brown & Sons Stationers," she said.

"Oh, a professional visit?" He looked interested.

"Yes, a professional visit," she said quickly. "You're always so sweet to me, Mr. Edison. I wonder if you can help me with one more thing."

"Yes, Miss Gossling?"

"The nib."

"The nib?"

"The fountain pen nib they found in Mrs. Marsh's room," she said. "I'm interested in selling them in my shop, and I'd like to show it to Mr. Brown so he can advise me where to get hold of it since it's so rare."

"Well, it hardly seems decent," he mumbled. "Doing business with evidence from a murder case."

"I know it sounds shoddy," she pondered, "but I've got to earn my living, Mr. Edison. Just like you had to earn yours when you closed down Mrs. Lesley's shop."

He hesitated. "What if the sheriff should ask for the evidence?"

"I'll take full responsibility," she insisted.

He sighed and brought her the cup and fountain pen nib, both of which she wrapped carefully in a scarf and placed in her bag.

"There's one more thing, Mr. Edison," she ventured. "Mrs. Lesley has a shipment coming in today, and she requested you help her unload it. I think, given the trouble the police caused her, it would be a nice gesture."

"Oh, indeed, miss!" he said. "I feel terrible about what the sheriff did, really I do. Closing her shop that way."

"I'm sure the sheriff will find a way to compensate her," Adele said with a smile. "He's a kind and fair man."

"Indeed he is, miss," said the young man. "Best lawman in the Far West, they say."

Adele turned at the doorway. "Really?"

"Well, some say it," said the young man with a blush.

"I agree with you." She smiled.

Nin was waiting for her at the station. She looked ready for the holiday in a rose dress with green trim and ribbons. Adele suspected for a long time Nin's abhorrence for womanly fashions was more a front, and at least some of her generous inheritance was spent at Ada's Millinery in town.

"You look lovely, dear," she said. She was always taken aback by her friend's intense beauty. Her loveliness attracted many an admiring stare, which Nin returned with a much less favorable impression.

"You said we were paying a call," said Nin.

"I'm sure you found it all very mysterious." Adele pushed the money for the tickets to San Francisco at the clerk in the window.

"I've ceased to question your ideas, Adele." Her friend smiled.

"The only idea I have is to keep my promise to Rebecca," she said. "Refuting the evidence seems like the best way."

"I assume you have the evidence?" Nin asked.

Adele nodded as she thanked two men who vacated the bench on the platform to let them sit. "I saw Edison this morning."

"And made his eyes pop, no doubt," said her friend. "I wondered why you chose to wear dark purple. It's very becoming."

"You make me sound devious," Adele said.

"You do sometimes employ less than savory means to get what you want." Her friend eyed her. "But it's the way of women as long as men treat us as they do."

Adele took her arm. "Things are changing, dear. We won't have to be devious much longer."

"I doubt that." Her friend sniffed.

"I had Tomas run the teacup down to Mr. Brethren," Adele said. "He's a dear man but he's taken too much liking to Jackson's prim ways."

"You mean sanctimonious ways." Nin sniffed. "Your brother is as tightly laced as a priest."

"Papa used to say his morals will be his downfall," Adele said softly.

The train to San Francisco pulled into the station, and they climbed on.

"What have we to do in the city?" Nin asked.

Adele produced the fountain pen nib from her bag. "We're going to find out the truth about this."

"I thought your brother already found out the truth."

"He spoke to the father, Josiah Brown," Adele said. "I want us to speak to the sons also. They may know more. They often do." She studied the nib. "Perhaps they can tell us all about this little gem."

"Looks rather like a pointed finger, doesn't it?" Nin remarked.

"Hopefully not an accusatory one." Adele glanced out the window.

"Because no one will claim it?" Nin asked. "You forget, Adele, a fountain pen might be unique to you, but to others, it's simply something to write with."

"That's as may be," Adele said. "But its connection to a crime makes it something more than a writing tool."

"Perhaps it isn't connected at all," Nin insisted. "It was a careless accident that has nothing to do with the crime."

Adele shook her head. "I agree with Rebecca. It's all too neat and clean. The vial found in Theo's room when he says he threw it away, and this pen nib found near the body. I believe someone left it there deliberately. The question is, who and why."

It was another hour before they arrived at Josiah Brown & Sons Stationers. The shop proved to be what Adele expected. Located in a pale enclave of Union Street where the shops grew more exclusive the farther they pulled away from Union Square, it was small, polished, and, unlike her own shop, which always had the scent of its wares, made one feel as if one were walking into a hospital room as one entered. Everything was under glass, paper and wooden stands untouchable. Three clerks, whom Adele assumed were the Brown sons, stood with their hands behind their backs. They did not look eager to come forward when the two ladies entered.

"They look like stuffed birds," Nin whispered.

"Let's hope they're magpies worse than Mrs. Faderman," Adele whispered back.

The young men feasted their eyes on Nin and shuffled toward her, stumbling over one another's tongues to offer aid.

"We wish to speak to Mr. Josiah Brown." Adele took over with authority.

This made them lethargic once more, and as two of the clerks shuffled back to their places behind the displays, the third lingered. He looked older and more circumspect than the other two. "Mr. Brown does not normally see people in the morning, madame."

"Miss," Adele corrected. "I'm sure he'll see us. It's a matter of some urgency."

"A matter of murder," Nin broke in.

This gave the man's crow-like face a startled expression. "Murder?"

"My friend has a colorful imagination," Adele said quickly. "I have genuine business to conduct with Mr. Brown. I'm a stationer, you see."

The man finally showed some signs of life. "If you'll wait one moment." He rolled toward the back of the shop.

"Money talks, I see," Adele remarked as she cast a glance around the shop. "Mr. Brown seems the type to value pretentiousness over utility."

"Or prettiness," Nin added, wrinkling her nose at a row of ugly brass paperweights sitting against the wall.

"One must be inspired to write," Adele agreed. "Otherwise, one ends up with rather boring correspondences."

Nin laughed just as the man returned. "This way, ladies."

He led them through the narrow shop where the light grew dimmer and the merchandise heavier. A wooden stairway creaked as they climbed to the upper floor, where the man knocked tentatively on a door at the end of the short hallway. A hoarse "Enter!" sounded from within.

The man turned to them. "Your names?"

Adele, determined to meet this cold reception on equal terms, handed him her business card. The man made them wait in the hallway with the unswept dust and dirt. There was some shuffling behind the closed door, and he came out.

"Mr. Brown will see you now for five minutes," he said. "He's very busy."

Adele narrowed her eyes. "So are we."

The man's eyebrows jumped a little, clearly unaccustomed to a woman striking back. He opened the door, cleared his throat and signaled for them to go in.

Mr. Josiah Brown was, after such a presentation, as unimpressive as Adele imagined he would be. He sat slumped in the chair that did not flatter his stout figure, his balding head shining from the pale light. His mustache and beard were clearly an attempt to look threatening, as they were far too long for his small face. The hoarse tone sounded damp close up.

"Miss Gossling?" He looked from one to the other.

"I am Adele Gossling," she said.

"Aren't you going to ask us to sit down?" Nin growled.

"So sorry," the man mumbled as he nodded toward two uncomfortable chairs. Adele expected her friend to sit down on the floor, but, to her surprise, she took one of the chairs with regal posture.

"The name Gossling sounds familiar to me," he said.

"You spoke with my brother, Deputy Sheriff Gossling, of the Arrojo police," she said.

"Oh, yes," the man grumbled. "Most persistent man. Well, what can I do for you?"

"You saw my card, sir," she said. "I'm here on business."

"You wish to purchase some wares for your shop?" The man leaned back. "I often get small town shops coming to me. We do have the best selection." The vain attempt at modesty made her want to laugh.

"And you have many of the best customers, I'm told," said Adele. "Even from the small towns."

"I like to think so." He gave a half smile, showing uneven teeth.

"It was one such customer I wanted to ask you about," she said. "Mr. Theodore Marsh."

The name made the man sit up. "You realize customer information is confidential."

"I realize that," she said. "I also realize merchants are often more open about their lucrative patrons unless they have reason not to be. Do you?" She eyed him.

Mr. Brown's lips pursed as he sat up straighter. "Indeed not!"

"Then you wouldn't mind telling me if you recognize this." She took out the pen nib and laid it on the desk.

The man barely looked at it. "Certainly I recognize it. It's one of ours made especially for us. The Brown Spoon Tip, we call it."

"Rather assuming to name it after yourself," Nin remarked with a sly smile.

The man blinked at her as if the thought had never occurred to him. "You wish to purchase a box, Miss Gossling?"

"I might," said Adele shortly, "though I doubt Mr. Marsh would abandon his patronage in your shop to give it to a small, local place."

"I'm afraid you can't expect him to do that," said Mr. Brown. "There's a tradition, you see. Mr. Marsh's father and grandfather were my patrons." He was clearly proud of this.

"Let us hope future generations have more common sense," Nin growled.

"Really, I don't see —"

"A man like you, I expect, would be rather, shall we say, sensitive to his shop's reputation?"

"Every shop owner is, Miss Gossling," he sniffed, "but we respect family traditions."

"Even when the family has the shadow of doom over it?" Nin asked.

Mr. Brown's eyes gathered under his heavy brows. "Look here, what is this all about?"

Adele was silent for a moment, contemplating what to tell this pompous little man. She decided to hit him with the truth as bluntly as her friend would. "Murder, Mr. Brown."

"Murder!" The man stared into space as he sat back.

"Someone killed Theodora Marsh," Nin said.

"That does put a different light on things." The man took out his handkerchief and wiped his face.

"I've been asked by the family lawyer to find out certain information," said Adele.

The man seemed to take this with more dignity than Adele gave him credit for. "A lady detective? How perfectly charming."

"You mean perfectly alarming," Nin snarled.

Adele tried not to laugh. "Mr. Marsh bought all his stationery from you?"

"A matter of tradition, as I said." The man bowed his head.

"And I'm sure very justified," Adele complimented. "He bought fountain pens from you as well?"

"We have the best quality." The man took a box from the shelf, making some ceremony of opening it and removing the tissue paper. "Genuine silver, no leaking."

Adele couldn't help but admit he was justified in his pomposity regarding his wares. "They are impressive, Mr. Brown."

"We have them made especially for us," said the man, warming up. "It might be worth your while, assuming you have enough wealthy patrons to buy them." His eyebrows rose.

"There are plenty of high society people who come into her shop," Nin said.

"I might take you up on that, Mr. Brown," Adele said. "But for now, I'm interested in someone else who might have bought them. Mr. Marsh, for instance. Can you tell us when he last bought this?" She glanced down at the nib. "It's fairly new, I see. There are no scratches or ink residue on it."

"I see you know your business, Miss Gossling," the man said, as if he were reluctant to admit it. "I'm afraid I can't answer your question. My time is mostly spent here in my office. I rarely go out to the floor nowadays."

Adele gave Nin a knowing look. "I imagined that was the case."

"It's more suitable for the owner to be engaged elsewhere, don't you agree?"

She gave him a wary look. "I'm a sole proprietor, and I prefer to deal with my customers firsthand."

He sniffed. "Well, for a small establishment, I can understand."

"Perhaps one of your sons can answer our question," Nin said.

"Sons?" The man folded his hands.

"Out there." She motioned toward the door.

The man's look became sheepish. "Oh, I see. I have no sons."

"But your shop is Josiah Brown & Sons," Adele pointed out.

"A family establishment has more respect than a sole proprietor, Miss Gossling," he said in a pompous tone. "It's a shame women can't benefit in the same way."

"No, it would look rather silly if I named my shop Adele Gossling & Daughters, wouldn't it?" Adele said dryly. "Especially as I'm not married and have no wish to be in the near future."

This clearly insulted Mr. Brown's vision of how the world worked, as his mustache leaned to one side. "That is unfortunate."

"I think it's very sensible," Nin snapped.

"May we ask the clerks, then, whether they recently sold anything to Mr. Marsh?" asked Adele, picking up the parasol she had leaned against the desk. "It's very important."

"That won't be necessary." He rose. "I shall call them."

He pressed a button near his desk and, in a few moments, the three filed in, lining up against the wall like soldiers with their arms at their sides.

"Miss Gossling is inquiring about Mr. Theodore Marsh," the man said. "She would like to know when he was last here and what he purchased."

There was a dead silence for a few moments as each clerk seemed to be trying to remember who Theodore Marsh was. She slipped a photograph of Theo she had taken from the evidence box her brother had used to make his inquiries. "This is Mr. Marsh."

"There is no need for that, Miss Gossling. They are quite

familiar with our regular customers. Aren't you?" He gave each a menacing look as if it were more a threat than a question.

They nodded in unison.

"Well?" He tapped the end of his pencil on the desk. "We're waiting."

One of the clerks, whom Adele took for hardly more than sixteen or seventeen stepped forward. "I sold him some ink wells, sir."

"When?" Mr. Brown pronounced the word with impatience.

"A few months ago at least," he said.

"When?" his employer repeated.

"Aug — no September, sir," he said.

"Don't you have a sales book?" Nin ogled him with her cat eyes.

"Sometimes I forget —"

"That is not sufficient, Mr. Mani," the man roared. "How many times have I told you —"

"I'm sorry, sir," the young man murmured. "I was alone, and it got busy —"

Adele gave Mr. Brown a quick nod, which quieted him. She smiled at the young man. "Mr. Mani? I'm sure Mr. Brown's customers appreciate your attentiveness."

"Indeed, I hope so, miss!" the young man burst out. The other young man, who looked only a few years older, guffawed while the older clerk glared at him.

"I'm sure you can tell us about that sale to Mr. Marsh," Adele continued.

"Well, miss." He cocked one eyebrow. "Mr. Marsh was in a hurry, as I recall. He doesn't come to the city often. Had some meeting or other, and he ran out of ink just before. Joked there was hardly any point in going to a meeting with no ink." He grinned, but a severe look from his employer made his face grave once more. "So he bought two bottles of Sanford black ink, it was."

"Yes, I know the brand," Adele said. "I sell such fineries to my clients too." She glanced at Mr. Brown in a meaningful way. "Did Mr. Marsh buy anything else?"

"The new mechanical pencils." Here, Mr. Mani's voice swelled with pride. "They just came in, and I was the first one to sell them." This earned a glare from his fellow clerks.

"That was most enterprising of you," Adele said. "Anything else?"

"No, miss," he said. "I tried to get him to buy one of the lionhead paperweights, but he called it rather gaudy."

"And quite right too," Nin mumbled, as she and Adele had seen that same lionhead paperweight on the shelf.

"He didn't buy any fountain pens?" Adele asked.

"No, miss."

"Nor fountain pen nibs like this?" She held up the nib.

The young man scrutinized the nib for what seemed like a long time.

"Don't dawdle, Mr. Mani," Mr. Brown said briskly. "Answer the lady's question."

"Not him, miss," said the young man.

Adele stiffened. "But someone else bought them?"

"The lady bought them for him."

She and Nin exchanged looks. "Can you describe the lady, Mr. Mani?"

"She was his wife."

"His wife!" Now even Mr. Brown became interested. "Impossible, Mr. Mani!"

Adele peered at him. "Are you sure she said she was his wife?"

"Quite so, miss," he said. "She distinctly said her husband, Mr. Marsh, had sent her to buy some of those nibs, as she was in town shopping, and he couldn't get away."

"Mr. Theodore Marsh has a wife," Mr. Brown murmured. "Well, well."

Adele leaned back with her hands folded. "I've never seen Mr. Marsh's wife. I'm curious as to what she looks like."

"Ladies are always curious about one another, aren't they?" the young man said with a chuckle. Mr. Brown reprimanded him with a glare. "Well, miss, it's difficult to describe her, you see, as she was wearing a large green hat with a veil."

"Was she tall, short, thin, fat?" Nin asked. "Speak up, boy."

"She was rather tall, I should say, for a lady, that is," said Mr. Mani, squinting a little. "Rather stiff-shouldered. Well-dressed. Blond hair."

"Blond hair?" Adele asked.

"Yellow-blond hair, I should call it," Mr. Mani said. "Used to see 'em on the clowns who came in with the circus when I was a kid."

"That will do, Mr. Mani," his employer snapped. "You may go."

Adele rose, signaling Nin. "Thank you, Mr. Brown. You've been most helpful."

"Perhaps you want ten, or even five?" He pushed the box of nibs toward her. "Just a trial, of course, to see if your high society customers take to it."

Adele smiled. "Yes, I think I'll do that. Thank you, Mr. Brown."

The street was now busy with the lunchtime crowd. Adele slipped the small packet of nibs in her purse.

"Odious little man," Nin snarled. "Sons indeed!"

"Odious but useful," Adele said. "So Theodore Marsh's wife bought him the nibs."

"He has no wife," Nin declared.

Adele took her arm. "That's what makes it so fascinating, dear."

"The woman he was once engaged to?" Nin suggested.

"If she had come back into his life, I'm sure we would have heard about it," said Adele. "The woman was known to the family, after all."

"A mistress, then?"

"I can't see Theo keeping a mistress with yellow hair."

"Heaven only knows what a straight-laced businessman like him would keep for his own pleasures." Nin shuddered.

"A tall, stiff-shouldered woman wearing a large green hat with blond hair," Adele mused. "Nothing brings out yellow more than green."

"I don't follow," Nin said.

"It was just a thought." Adele shielded her eyes with her gloved hand. "There must be a cab somewhere."

As she spoke, a hansom slid to the curb. Before she could reach for the door handle, it popped open, and a man with the pose of a crane and sandy brown hair emerged from the narrow space.

"Adele!" He took his hat off with one hand while grasping hers in the other.

"Hello, John." She glanced at Nin. "You remember my friend Miss Branch?"

"I remember you," Nin said in a cold voice.

"Two years ago, wasn't it?" He bowed. "In all that time you never sent me more than a Christmas card."

"Nor did I ever send you that telegram about coming back to the city." Adele eyed him. "For once your prediction was wrong, John."

"It wasn't a prediction, my dear," he said in a sincere tone, "only hope."

The lump of defiance in Adele's chest eased. John looked worn, and a few lines made their way around his eyes.

"I'm very glad to run into you," he said. "Now I don't have to eat alone."

"Oh?"

"It's lunchtime, isn't it?" he prompted.

Adele consulted her watch. "So it is."

He smiled. "I would be pleased if you both joined me."

"We have a train to catch." Adele kept her hand on the doorknob of the cab.

John gently took it and closed the door, signaling to the driver, who sped away. "That's what you said the last time. This time I won't take 'no' for an answer."

"You always were too persistent," Adele remarked.

"And you were always too obstinate," he said with a laugh. "A rather adorable quality, I always thought."

"Do you find an obstinate mule adorable too?" Nin asked in an innocent voice.

He avoided her gaze. "You wouldn't refuse an old friend a second time, would you?"

"Are we old friends, John?" Adele asked.

"Always," he breathed. "We may not be engaged, but we'll always be friends. Just as I was your father's friend until the end." He said the last in a delicate tone.

"Yes, that you were," Adele admitted. "I can't deny I miss the veal cutlets at the *Fior d'Italia*."

"Then you shall have them." He held his arm out to Nin. "May I?"

Nin's almond eyes regarded him with trepidation, but Adele gave her a nod, and she lightly tucked her hand in his arm.

The entrance to the restaurant was crowded with people, but one swipe of his hand earned them a choice table in the corner. The soft clink of silverware and china eased Nin's tight face as she looked around with curiosity.

"Your time in the country has done you good," John observed after they ordered. "Your color is back."

"My color?" Her hand flew to her face.

"They say country air brings a flush to a young lady's cheeks."

She bit her lip. "I don't find that sort of talk appealing, John. Didn't I hear a rumor about you and Nora Higgins getting engaged this spring?"

"Nora and I are good friends," he insisted. "Just as you and I are good friends."

"I'm surprised." Adele folded her hands. "Nora is as passionate about reform as I am. We worked at the Tenderloin Settlement House together."

"You think I disapprove of reform," he said.

"Well, don't you?" Nin eyed him.

"Indeed not, Miss Branch," he said. "I approve of good deeds from compassionate ladies."

"Reform isn't a good deed, John," said Adele. "It's necessary, and every woman and man's right in this country."

"I couldn't agree more," he said in a sweeping way.

"This is the first I'm hearing of it," Adele said dryly.

"That was my fault." He ventured to take her hand, but only for a moment. "I'm afraid my lawyer's need for objectivity bled into my personal life."

Adele stared at him as the first course was put in front of them. Its earthy scent filled the small space around them.

"You ought to eat your soup before it gets cold," Nin said.

"I'm afraid I've given your friend a shock, Miss Branch," he said, amused. "I actually admitted wrongdoing. Adele once accused me of being too saintly for my own good."

"In your own mind only," she said. "But I am surprised you would say such a thing."

"We see things more as we ought when we grow older, Adele," he said in a mild tone.

"Indeed we do," she said softly.

"I suppose that's why your brother is living in the country with you," he said, "or did you miss something of home?"

"I have a life in Arrojo, John," she insisted. "It might seem paltry to you, in this grand city with your grand cases before the court. I read about your defense of Cecilia Davis last year. Quite a coup for Russel, Rand & Bellows."

"I thought you would approve," he said. "Nicholas Davis was just the sort of tyrant you would want to stab with a dagger."

"He paid for his tyranny with his life," Adele said. "Perhaps all tyrants pay with their lives for those they hurt the most."

"That's rather too philosophical for such a bright day." He glanced out the window.

Adele leaned forward. "What would you say about a son who kills his tyrannical mother?"

"I thought we were trying to prove he didn't kill her," Nin said.

"Not another case you're involved in." John sighed. "I thought you were through with that."

"The man's lawyer is a friend of mine," Adele said.

"And you do anything for a friend." He smiled. "I know."

"You didn't answer the question." Nin played with a sugar cube.

"I think a son has no more business killing his mother than a wife has killing her husband, tyrant or not," he declared. "There are less lethal ways of dealing with a tyrant."

"Perhaps you're right," said Adele.

"You think the man didn't do it?" In spite of his debonair air, John showed a lawyer's interest.

"I wasn't sure before," Adele admitted. "Now I'm sure."

"He isn't the type," Nin agreed.

"No one thought Mrs. Davis was the type either," said John. "A rather phlegmatic woman, even reticent. Always behaved as if others knew best."

"It's precisely those women who are the most dangerous," Adele said. "I'm sure if you looked at the criminal case studies, you would find most of the women who killed their husbands were reticent."

"I see you still hold that unsavory fascination with crime." He picked up his dessert spoon.

"Why shouldn't she?" Nin insisted. "She's helped solve a few."

"With your insights, dear," Adele said, pressing her hand. Her friend smiled and turned away.

"I shudder to think," John remarked. "As I recall, you tend to dive in feet first, head later."

"Better than some lawyers and lawmen I know, who contemplate everything until it's too late to do any good," she snapped.

"I take it that's a dig against me and Jackson," said John. "Though I fancy he's doing a marvelous job as — what is it he does there?"

"He's the deputy sheriff," Nin supplied.

"He'll probably be sheriff next year." John signaled the waiter. "He certainly has the skill for it."

"But not the desire," Nin pronounced.

"Jack is quite happy where he is," she said. "Sheriff Hatfield has a great appreciation for his more procedural methods."

"I imagine this sheriff thinks more like a vigilante than a lawman," John remarked.

Adele put her fork down. "Hatfield is a very decent man."

"So are vigilantes, in their own minds."

"He worked for Wells Fargo as a detective and the San Francisco police before that," Nin pointed out.

"I'll say no more about the matter," John said. "But if he allows you to, well, put your hat in the ring when it comes to small-town crime, I can't say I approve much."

"He doesn't allow or disallow me anything," Adele said in a savage voice, "nor does any man. It's the one thing you never realized about me, John."

"Why shouldn't she be involved in a crime if she can help?" Nin asked.

"Because, Miss Branch, criminal matters are best left to professionals who know the law," he declared. "It is not a toy a child plays with."

Adele felt her temper soar, but the quietness of the restaurant prevented her from losing it. She slowly rose. "Thank you for the lunch, John, but we really must catch our train."

"You say that as if you'd like to run a dagger through *me*," he said sheepishly.

"At this moment, I can't say the idea unappealing." She put on her hat.

He grabbed her wrist. "Look here, Adele, I'm sorry. I'm so used to letting the words tumble out in the courtroom, I'm afraid I use too much impetuousness outside of it."

"More like nastiness than impetuousness," Nin snarled.

"I never did have much subtlety, did I?"

Adele looked at the face with its elongated features, seeing genuine sincerity and anxiousness. "It was good to see you again, John."

"You can always look me up when you're in the city. You know that."

They watched as he strode down the street. Her eyes met Nin's, and they exchanged a knowing look.

# CHAPTER 19

She and Nin arrived at Arrojo in the late afternoon. The gray clouds rolling in as they left the city made their way into town, but there was only a blistery wind and no dampness in the air.

"You go home, dear," Adele said. "I know how trains affect you."

"Are you going home?" Nin questioned.

"I've a few things to do," she said. "Mr. Brethren said he would have the results for me by this afternoon, and I don't think our findings with Mr. Brown can wait until tomorrow."

Her friend hitched her skirt out of the dust, and they went through a particularly dirt-filled area of the train station. "Then I'll come with you."

They went to Adele's house first to fetch the Beaton Roundabout so they could get to the lab before dark. Mr. Brethren looked as if he had been immersed in his chemicals all day. His white coat was stained with bright colors. A half-eaten sandwich and cold cup of coffee sat on the table.

"You won't do your health much good if you don't eat," Adele remarked.

Mr. Brethren laughed and put down his instruments to pick up the sandwich. "You've come just in time. I finished my experiments half an hour ago."

"And?" Adele's eyes peaked.

"Nothing," he said. "A few remnants of some strange plants, of course. Some I don't even know. But certainly nothing remotely like the belladonna leaf."

"So there's no chance Thea's death was caused by the tea." Adele tried not to sound disappointed. "Dora will be happy about that, anyway."

"Unless that repugnant Dr. Rhodes finds anything in Dora's other teas," Nin reminded her.

"This is the one we were concerned about," Adele pointed out. "And the stain in the teacup?"

"Nothing there either," said the man. "I spent several hours trying to get even the tiniest sample."

"At least there's one comfort," Adele said. "If you couldn't get a sample, neither will Dr. Rhodes. So the police have nothing if they can't connect the belladonna in the vial you sent Theo with the stain in the cup."

"The vial?" Lom stared at her.

"You sent Theo belladonna for the raccoons," Adele reminded him. "Mona saw the package arrive at the house. The police found the vial hidden in Theo's desk."

"Good God!" The man stumbled back against the counter. "I forgot about that. That's why they arrested Theo?" Adele nodded. "Perhaps I have something for you after all." He flew to the desk and shifted some papers. "My notes, my notes — yes, here we are. Miss Gossling, I told you I couldn't test the stain, but I can tell you there is something off with it."

"Off?"

"A discoloration," he said. "Granted, that might be due to the combination of herbs in the tea."

"Go on," she said.

"The substance I gave Theo wouldn't leave that sort of discoloration."

"Are you sure?" Her heart leapt.

"I'll check with McCabe, who knows more about these things than I do. But I'm fairly certain."

"Then there is doubt the belladonna you gave Theo will match the stain even if it could be tested," Adele concluded.

"He didn't do it, then," said Nin, "unless he found something like belladonna and used that."

Lom squared his shoulders. "We all know he didn't, Miss Branch."

"Of course he didn't," Adele said with distraction. "Now there's a chance the police will believe it too." She thought about the blond woman.

"I suspect they won't be happy about it," Lom said as he gathered the tea things into a box. "I've heard the police like it when they find who they're looking for quickly and stick with it even in the face of contradictory evidence."

"Sheriff Hatfield isn't like that," Adele insisted.

"I hope you're right, Miss Gossling." The young man handed her the box. "I'm prepared to swear to my findings in court if necessary. You may tell that to the sheriff."

Adele smiled. "Thank you, Mr. Brethren. You're a good, loyal friend."

"Theo is a good man," said Lom with feeling. "The best of men, I would say."

When they arrived at the Arrojo police station, it was filled with women, an unusual state of affairs. Lady Augusta, the sheriff's formidable mother, was there with Rowena, her companion, at her side. Rebecca was in the interview room with the door closed. Louella Fourier, one of the lesser hens of Mrs. Faderman's flock, paced up and down, slapping her gloves against her palm.

Without a word, Adele plunked down on her brother's desk

the box Mr. Brethren had given her. She steeled herself for the reprimands she expected.

But Jackson only smiled grimly and crossed his long arms. "Sheriff," he said quietly.

A sudden silence entered the room. It was as if everyone stopped breathing, waiting in dread for what the six-foot, large-boned sheriff would do. He leaned his head back, his pleasant countenance growing stony. Adele felt her heart beating faster, and she struggled to explain.

But Lady Augusta came to her rescue. "Horatio!" She gave the side of his boot a hard tap. "Don't be a bully. If the young lady took it, she had a good reason, and you know it."

"She always has a good reason," Jackson mumbled.

"Such as proving someone innocent," Nin said.

"And trying to make the police look foolish," he growled.

"Both are equally worthy intentions," Nin snapped back.

"I'm not trying to make anyone look foolish," Adele said sharply. "I'm trying to serve justice as much as you are, Jack."

"Except you have no call to do so," Hatfield said in his quiet voice. He threw his head back. "Edison!"

"Sir!" The young man moved tentatively.

"How did Miss Gossling get hold of this evidence?"

"Don't you dare blame that poor young man!" Adele said.

"I ceased blaming that 'poor young man' since you got evidence out of him for the Blackstone case," the sheriff retorted.

"It's stealing, Del," Jackson said. "I hope the sheriff chastises you."

Adele did not miss Mrs. Fourier's interested gaze. She remembered not only that the woman snapped at every opportunity for gossip, but that she was also a member of the town council.

She spoke in a lighter tone, "As it happens, I had a right to view this evidence."

"A right!" her brother started, but the sheriff held up his hand.

"Rebecca hired me to prove Theo innocent," said Adele. "As his lawyer, she has a right to see evidence."

"And you took that right by proxy, is that it?" Hatfield asked dryly. "If Miss Gold wanted to see evidence, she should have gotten permission from the proper authorities."

"You know lawyers have no time for such nonsense, Horatio," Lady Augusta snapped.

"The teacup was already examined, Sheriff," Adele added. "You can hardly call it stealing"

"You're so sure you have your man, remember?" Nin eyed him.

The sheriff's gaze turned on Mrs. Fourier. "I'll make sure your husband has the permit by the end of the day, ma'am. Thank you for your patience." He rose, holding out his hand.

"I could wait a little more until —"

"I wouldn't want you to waste your time, ma'am," he said with a smile. "A police station isn't a very pleasant place for a woman."

"You seem to have your share of female company, Sheriff," Mrs. Fourier said, throwing an arch glance at Adele.

"That is not my doing, ma'am. Good day." He bowed.

"Good day." She reluctantly put on her gloves and arranged her handbag before leaving Adele noticed she lingered a little, as if waiting for the conversation to continue, but when all remained silent, she sauntered down the street.

"I hope she won't make trouble for you," Adele said.

"I'm not worried about her wagging tongue," Hatfield said.

"It's the more devious females we're concerned with," Jackson said in a harsh tone. "You see what you've done, Del."

"Let your sister alone, Jackson." Lady Augusta spoke with authority. "It's hardly her fault Mrs. Fourier is a shameless busybody."

"You should have thrown her out, Sheriff," Nin piped up.

Hatfield gave one of his hearty laughs, releasing the tension in the room. "That would hardly go over well with the council, Miss

Branch, tempting as it is." He eyed Adele. "So you've worked your witchcraft on my assistant deputy again and took out evidence, eh?"

Edison blushed and trailed back to his filing.

"She just told you she had a right to it," Nin snapped.

"Talk about shameless busybodies," Jackson mumbled.

"I may be a busybody, Jack, but my intentions are honorable," Adele said in a cold voice.

"She saved a young man from the noose, didn't she?" Nin insisted. "And she proved a schoolteacher wasn't what you thought she was."

"Indeed," Hatfield agreed. "So your lawyer friend hired you as a detective, eh? Well, well."

"You can ask her yourself." Adele glanced at the interview room. The woman caught her eye, smiled, and came out.

"I understand, Miss Gold, you've asked Adele to help prove Mr. Marsh innocent?" the sheriff inquired.

She nodded. "It was the only way I could think of to make you see Theo didn't do it."

"Are you aware her tactics are unorthodox, to say the least?"

"They're downright criminal," Jack growled.

"I'm sure you were sometimes forced to perform acts that skirted the law with the Anspaches, Deputy Jackson," said the sheriff in a severe tone. This made his deputy press his lips together.

"Sheriff, if Adele did anything she shouldn't have, it was to help me," said the lawyer. "I take full responsibility."

"Don't worry, dear," Adele said kindly, pressing her hand. "Jack is exaggerating."

"Perhaps I ought to think seriously of putting you on the payroll as a consultant," Hatfield said in an amused tone. "That would at least show the council your antics are worth something."

"Fiddlesticks," Adele growled, and the sheriff laughed.

"I imagine you have something to report to us about these." He tapped the teacup with the edge of his pencil.

"I should think you would be grateful for any help, Horatio," said his mother severely, putting down the plain cup in which Edison made coffee, not without a distasteful look on her face.

"I am grateful, Ma," he said. "It's the council that isn't."

"You won't be very grateful now," Nin said. "We found Theo is innocent."

"Thank God!" Rebecca breathed.

"Well, there is a definite doubt in his guilt," Adele said. She told them about Mr. Brethren's tests on Dora's tea and on the teacup. "He couldn't test the stain," she concluded, "but he could say for certain it contained an anomaly that wouldn't be there if the stain was made by the belladonna he gave Theo. He's willing to testify to that."

"It does seem as if your theory has fallen through the chute, as they say, Horatio," Lady Augusta said.

"It was the district attorney's theory, Ma," Hatfield said. "I'll send someone over right away to collect Mr. Brethren's findings and enter them into evidence." He quickly dispatched one of the assistant deputies just sauntering in.

"Then you can let my client go," Rebecca said. "Now the evidence is even more circumstantial than before."

"I'll have to talk to the district attorney, of course," the sheriff said. "But I imagine he won't have any objections once he examines the new evidence."

Adele leaned across the desk. "You could release him on his honor, couldn't you, Sheriff?"

"That's at my discretion," Hatfield admitted.

"I don't think it wise, sir." Jackson jumped up.

The sheriff eyed him. "I doubt Mr. Marsh is going to run away, Jackson."

"It's a matter of protocol," his deputy argued. "Suppose we

caught a stranger in town with evidence that he knived a farmer. Would you let him out of jail on his honor?"

"Probably not," the sheriff admitted.

"This is entirely different," Rebecca said. "Theo is no vagabond wandering the rails. He's a respectable businessman whose family contributed more than their share to Rosa Gris."

"Then let the authorities in Rosa Gris decide," Jackson insisted.

Sheriff Hatfield cleared his throat loudly. "The Rosa Gris police have put this case under our authority, Jackson. I see no harm in releasing Mr. Marsh as long as I have his lawyer's assurance he remains within county limits."

"Naturally he will, Sheriff," Rebecca promised.

Adele studied her for a moment. It was clear the ordeal had taken its toll on her, as she was thinner and her skin drawn and pale. Dark rims of anxiety stood under her eyes. She knew the sheriff saw it too, as his harsh look left his face, and his features softened.

He produced a ring of keys from a locked drawer in his desk. "Edison!" The young man, pecking away at the typewriter, ceased to his supervisor's call. "Release Mr. Marsh from his cell." He threw the keys at him. "Perhaps you'd like to take him home, Miss Gold?"

Rebecca's eyes were damp as she pressed her lips together. The gratitude on her face was clear as she followed Edison into the hallway.

Lady Augusta reached for her son's hand. "That was very decent of you, Horatio."

"You know I never interfere with young love, Ma," he remarked.

"Hardly young," Nin said. "He's past forty."

The sheriff gave her a short, withering look. "Love makes one young, Miss Branch."

"You mean being sweet on someone makes one feel younger," she corrected. "I wouldn't know about that, Sheriff."

"Perhaps someday you will," he advised.

Nin turned red and tapped the wooden desk with the edge of her knuckles.

"This puts a damper on our case, Sheriff," Jackson said. "Not that I don't like Mr. Marsh, but we're back where we started."

"Perhaps what we found in the city will help you," said Adele.

"You didn't see Dr. Blessings, surely," Sheriff Hatfield said.

"I would hardly have a reason for that," Adele said, "though he's been a marvelous help in the past."

"Who was a marvelous help now?"

"Mr. Josiah Brown & Sons," Adele said.

"Except there are no sons," Nin said. "The pompous ass only believes he'll make more money if people think there are."

Jackson flinched. "Please, Miss Branch."

"I wasn't being profane, Mr. Gossling," she insisted. "It happens to be a very accurate description of the man."

The stern look left Jackson's face, and he broke into laughter. "I confess, it is rather descriptive of the man I saw."

"What reason would you have for seeing him?" asked the sheriff. "Your brother already spoke with Mr. Brown."

"I suppose you didn't notice something else missing from the evidence box," Adele said.

"Is there something else missing?" Hatfield's eyebrow went up.

Adele sheepishly took out the handkerchief with the nib. "I had good reason to borrow this too."

"I can't wait to hear it," the sheriff said.

"My business, of course," she said. "I do sell such things, and I rather took a liking to it. I wanted a few samples from Mr. Brown."

"Such tales aren't worthy even of your imagination, Del," Jackson growled.

Without a word, Nin took Adele's bag and poured out the contents on the sheriff's desk. The nibs Adele had bought from Mr. Brown rolled to the floor.

"You needn't have been so illustrative, Miss Branch," Jackson said.

"You all but accused your sister of lying, Deputy," Lady Augusta said in a haughty tone. "I believe you owe her an apology."

Jackson gave Adele a gentle kiss. "My humblest apologies, dear sister."

"It was nothing I didn't expect," she said in a breezy tone. "That's why I accepted Mr. Brown's offer to let me buy a few."

"What did Mr. Brown have to say about the nib we didn't already know?" Hatfield asked.

"Mr. Marsh came in to buy some ink wells not long before Thea's death. One of the clerks remembered."

"But no spoon-tipped nibs?" Jackson asked.

"No spoon-tipped nibs."

"However?" Sheriff Hatfield eyed her. "I'm assuming there is a 'however.'"

"However," she emphasized, "someone else did."

"Eh?"

"Theo's wife!" Nin burst out.

The expression on both the men's faces gave Adele satisfaction. The sheriff grasped the handles of his chair, and Jackson leaned hard against his desk.

Her brother was the first to speak. "Mr. Marsh has no wife."

"We're well aware of that, Jack," Adele said dryly.

"Mr. Brown made a mistake," Sheriff Hatfield concluded.

"It's hardly something a man would mistake," Lady Augusta said with a small smile.

"Nevertheless, Ma," said Hatfield, "I hardly think he wouldn't know Mr. Marsh is a bachelor. He's known the family for years."

"He wasn't the one who told us," Adele said. "One of his clerks did."

"He was quite firm about it," Nin added.

The sheriff's hands folded on his stomach. "Tell us exactly what he said, Adele."

"A woman bought the same kind of nibs as the one we found," Adele reported. "She said specifically she was buying them for Theo."

"What did she look like?" her brother asked.

"She wore a large, broad green hat with a veil, and she was tall and stiff, the young man said."

"She had yellow hair," Nin added.

"Yellow hair?" Hatfield raised his eyebrow.

"A disguise, no doubt," his mother remarked.

"I should say so, Ma." The sheriff snorted. "I wonder why the young man didn't say anything about this when Jackson visited the shop."

"I didn't speak to the clerks, sir," said his deputy. "I assumed the Marshes were important customers, so Mr. Brown dealt with them himself."

"That's hardly like you, Mr. Gossling," Nin said. "You're always thorough to a fault."

"To a fault, perhaps, but not always when I ought to be." He looked genuinely embarrassed, slapping his hand on the desk. "I deserve to be called out, sir."

"You only did as you were told, Deputy," said the sheriff. "I'm the one who ought to have thought about it." He glanced at Adele. "It's a good thing we have our police consultant to correct us."

Adele hid her smile. "Jack's not to blame, Sheriff. I'm not sure the clerk would have spoken in front of him. You know how conservative people are with the police."

"And no doubt you gave him one of your winning looks to loosen his tongue." Her brother couldn't hide the grin on his face.

"This adds a new problem to the case, doesn't it, Horatio?"

Lady Augusta remarked. "Wouldn't you say, Rowena?" She glanced at her companion.

"Problems sprout up like wild mushrooms, ma'am," Rowena answered with her usual eccentric associations.

"Mr. Marsh might have had an accomplice," Jackson suggested.

"Do you really believe that, Jack?" Adele asked. "Does he look like the sort who would use an accomplice to kill his own mother?"

"No," her brother admitted. "Neither does he look the type to instruct an accomplice to wear a blond wig with a green hat."

"Rather obvious," Nin agreed.

"Perhaps a lady friend?" The sheriff coughed at the suggestion. All the ladies in the room, including Rowena, looked amused at his delicacy.

"We thought of that," Adele said. "Mr. Brethren told us Theo was once engaged."

"I rather think the man incapable of having a mistress, much less sending her to buy something for him in disguise," Lady Augusta remarked.

"The woman may have gone there on her own accord," Hatfield pointed out.

"To what purpose?" asked Jackson. "Why buy something for someone else and make it clear you're doing so?"

"Perhaps someone who knew he might be incriminated in a crime later on," Adele suggested.

He snorted. "You have a suspicious mind, Del."

"It seems unlikely," the sheriff concluded, "but it's clear there *was* a reason this woman bought the nibs in Mr. Marsh's name. If she wasn't working alone, she must have been instructed by someone else."

"Someone who wanted to do Theo harm?" Adele asked.

"Or perhaps just wanted to do him a favor," he said.

"Then why did Theo say he never saw the nibs in his life?"

Nin asked. "If she was going to buy them as a gift, she would have given them to him."

"Excellent point," said the sheriff.

The hallway door opened, and Edison emerged, throwing the keys from one hand to the other with a clatter until a seething look from Lady Augusta made him stop. Rebecca was holding Theo's arm. The man looked worn, his eyes sinking into his face. Adele saw the sharp look passing between Hatfield and her brother as Rebecca led the man to a chair.

"Am I no longer under suspicion?" Theo seemed to recover from the surprise of seeing the outside world.

"I'm not sure I would say that, Mr. Marsh," said Hatfield. His mother gave him a slap on his boots. "It's still up to the district attorney. But in my eyes, you had nothing to do with your mother's death."

The man almost doubled over. "Thank God!" He remained silent for a moment. "You must find out who did it, Sheriff!"

"That's what we intend to do, sir," said Jackson.

"We hope you can shed some light on new information we've just received," Hatfield continued. "Do you still insist you didn't buy this?" He held up the spoon-tipped nib.

"Do the people at Josiah Brown & Sons say I did?" He sat up in the chair. "Is that what you're trying to get at?"

"On the contrary," said Adele, "they say the last time you were there, you bought ink and pencils."

"And successfully avoided wasting money on an awful-looking paperweight," Nin added.

This made the man smile. "It was rather hideous, wasn't it?" Then, his eyes became alert. "You've been to see Mr. Brown?"

"I asked Adele to help us, Theo," said Rebecca. "If it wasn't for her, you wouldn't be out right now."

"I'm very grateful, Miss Gossling," said the man, "though I shudder to think of you being involved. Murder is a dirty business, isn't it?" His eyes wandered toward Jackson.

"Indeed it is," he said. "But my sister has a mind of her own."

"Lucky thing," Nin snapped.

The sheriff leaned forward. "We've now been told someone purchased the same fountain pen nibs in your name."

"What?" The man jumped. "That's madness!"

"No," said Adele, "it's clever planning."

"Perhaps not so clever, Del," her brother pointed out, "considering the lady's appearance."

"Lady? What lady?" Theo looked around the room.

"We're hoping you could tell us," said the sheriff. "A tall lady with yellow hair." He glanced at Adele. "That's the gist of it, isn't it?" She nodded.

"I know no one who fits that description," said Theo.

There was a moment of silence in the room. "We understand you were once engaged."

"To a Miss Thelma Bright." Theo nodded. "I haven't seen her in years!"

"Miss Bright is now Mrs. Langley of Twin Oaks, Ohio," Rebecca said. "Her husband is the manager of a bank, and she has four children."

They all stared at her. "How the devil did you know that, Becca?" Theo asked.

"It's a lawyer's business to know such things," Jackson said.

Rebecca whirled around. "I realize people think we're unscrupulous, Deputy. But there are many of us who are genuine and forthright."

"Defending criminals isn't exactly a recipe for sincerity," Jackson mumbled, "except, perhaps, the sincere illusion of doing anything for a client."

Adele stared at him. He spoke in the tone of bitterness she knew well, and she had no doubt he was thinking of their father.

"I do *not* defend criminals, Deputy," she said. "Theo is not a criminal."

In a quiet voice, Hatfield said, "Anyone accused of a crime

must be proven guilty, Jackson. You know that as well as I do. Until they are, they have a right to a defense just like anyone else."

Adele knew her brother's sense of righteousness was deeply wounded, as he put on his hat and excused himself.

"I apologize for my brother," she said. "He never approved of my father's work."

"I had a feeling that's who he was thinking about." Theo nodded.

"His views are harsh, but there is truth in them, grain by grain," Nin said in a wistful tone. Adele looked at her sharply.

Theo turned to the sheriff. "I realize there were times I didn't tell the truth," he said. "But I'm telling the truth now. I know of no woman who fits that description, and those I do know have no idea I even shop at Josiah Brown & Sons. It's not exactly something that would come up in conversation with them."

"Even your secretary at the mill?" Jackson asked.

"My secretary knows, but she would never purchase anything without my approval." He rose. "May I go now?"

"I think the man has earned his freedom, Horatio, don't you?" Lady Augusta eyed her son.

"By all means, Ma," said the sheriff. "I wish you Godspeed."

Theo bowed and, although he held on to Rebecca's arm, propelled himself out of the station much more steadily than he had come in.

"Edison!" The young man stared with attention. "Go and tell Miss Leslie she may open her shop. And have Assistant Deputy Dooland take the teas back. If he hasn't ruined them, that is." The last made Edison chuckle as he scurried away.

Adele and Nin left the station with Lady Augusta and Rowena. Adele could hear Hatfield mumbling under his breath, "Question marks, question marks."

$\mathcal{A}$s Lady Augusta and her companion headed home, and Adele and Nin turned toward their shops, Adele was surprised to see Rebecca and Theo waiting for them. The dark circles that had been so prevalent indoors were now less marked on the man's face.

Theo cast his grateful eye on Adele and Nin. "You've been brave on my behalf, and I'd like to invite you to tea, if you have the time."

"We do indeed." Adele took Nin's arm. "Even brave hearts must be nourished."

They spoke of lighter subjects as they made their way to the Marsh house.

"I'm sure everyone will be glad to see you back," Adele said with a smile.

"They'll all know you're exonerated," Rebecca assured him.

"And what then?" Theo asked softly. "The question remains: Who killed Mother?"

"The police will find out," Nin said. "They always do."

Mr. Stern was both surprised and pleased when he saw the wagon pull up. The hoe in his hands fell against the hard ground with a clatter. Theo smiled at him as he climbed off the wagon.

"I've been released, Harold," Theo said. "The police believe I had nothing to do with my mother's death."

"Naturally, sir, I'm pleased, though we never believed it." The warm sincerity in his voice put a lump in Adele's throat. "The missus will be pleased too."

Mrs. Stern's hard features slackened with emotion, and she actually raised her arms as if to put them around Theo in a maternal way, but stopped as if realizing her place. "It's good to have you home, sir!" Her voice was as enthusiastic as Adele had ever heard.

"Thank you, Ella." His face and smile softened. "I'm glad to be home."

"I can imagine, sir," she said. "I'd have roasted some pork chops for you if I'd known." She turned, and Adele realized she was brushing away tears.

"You know I don't like to put you out," Theo said. "I'm not very hungry."

"Just exhausted." Rebecca peered at him. "You ought to go rest, Theo."

"I have guests," he reminded her. "Ella, please bring tea. Or do you prefer coffee?" He glanced at Adele and Nin.

"Under the circumstances, coffee," Adele said.

"The stronger the better," Nin added.

"Yes, it's certainly been that kind of day." He let go of Rebecca's arm and started toward the parlor, but each step looked a struggle for him.

"Theo, you *must* go rest," Rebecca insisted.

He glanced over his shoulder with a grimace. "Is that a lawyer's order?"

"It's a request from a friend," she said.

"You've always been a good friend, Becca." He held out his hand. "Ever since we were children. I'm not much of a man —"

"Nonsense!" The lawyer's forehead wrinkled.

"I know what I am," he said. "My father reminded me of it often enough. But since mother died, I'm beginning to understand things."

"When one dies, they leave the shadow of their love and hate behind," Nin murmured.

"Indeed they do, Miss Branch," he said. "It's the duty of those of us left to shed light on them."

"I think you ought to listen to your lawyer," Adele said kindly. "We can take care of ourselves."

Theo smiled. "Three women can take care of themselves much better than any man can take care of them."

"Perhaps not any man." Rebecca's blue eyes dampened.

The study door slid open, and Mona came out, preoccupied with some letters in her hand. When she saw her brother standing at the parlor door, she dropped the letters. Her mouth opened, looking like a key hole with its slightly twisted shape.

"Theo's home, Mona!" Rebecca said.

"Yes." The woman recovered herself as she picked up the envelopes. "Yes, I can see that."

"Thanks to Becca and Miss Gossling, the police let me go," he said.

"You ought to call me Adele," she said, smiling. "We're all friends, remember?"

"Adele," he said with a shy smile.

"The police would have realized their mistake eventually," Adele insisted. "I just helped them see it sooner."

"I'm glad I didn't have to sit in a jail cell until they came to their senses." Theo's eyes closed for a moment as he leaned into the door frame.

"Theo was just going to his room," Rebecca said. "Don't you think he looks exhausted?" She glanced at Mona.

"Yes, I expect he is," said his sister. "You really ought to go up, Theo. I'll take care of our guests."

"That's good of you, Mona. I'm done in," he admitted. He turned to Adele and Nin, carving out a tired smile. "Thank you again. It seems so paltry to say it —"

"We work toward the truth, Mr. Marsh," Adele said. "No one need thank us for that."

"Call me Theo, of course." He started up the stairs, taking each step as if it were heavier than the last.

"Poor Theo." Mona sighed. "He hasn't the stamina to withstand such ordeals."

"He wouldn't have had to go through such an ordeal if it hadn't been for you," Rebecca said after Mrs. Stern had set the coffee down and left.

"Why, whatever do you mean?" the other woman asked.

"Don't pretend, Mona." Her voice was choppy. "The police wouldn't even have considered Theo a suspect if you hadn't put the idea into their heads."

"That's not fair, Rebecca," Adele said quickly. "They have to look at everyone, and beneficiaries are always on the list."

Rebecca pushed away the coffee Mona put in front of her. "Mona made up that ridiculous story of Theo knowing about the will —"

"I did not make it up!" Mona snapped. "You admitted you had a discussion about it."

"We had a discussion about your mother's assets, not her will!" Rebecca snarled.

"It amounts to the same thing, doesn't it?" Mona slid the bowl of sugar cubes toward her.

"Theo would have been the number one suspect anyway once they heard about the will," Nin pointed out.

"I'm afraid that's true, Rebecca," Adele said gently.

"Anyway, it doesn't matter what I said, does it?" Mona asked. "They released Theo so quickly."

"Because he had nothing to do with your mother's death," Rebecca insisted.

"I never said he did," said Mona. "I thought the police don't let someone out of jail so easily. Of course, I don't know the details."

"Come out with it, Mona." The lawyer faced her squarely. "You always imply, but you never just tell the truth straight out."

"I'm afraid Adele might be offended."

"Not if it's the truth," Adele said.

"All right, then." Mona folded her handkerchief carefully into four. "I was thinking it's a lucky thing Theo's lawyer has friends who has such good connections with the police."

"You mean Nin and me," Adele said quietly.

"I mean you and Nin." She turned toward the clairvoyant. "I assume we're on a first name basis too?"

"*We* are not," Nin said in a firm tone. "I don't use first names unless it's someone I can truly call a friend." She gave Adele a warm look.

"I thought we were friends," the woman mumbled.

"Friends don't accuse friends of pulling strings where the law is concerned," Nin said sharply.

"That is what you were implying, isn't it?" Adele asked.

"I was speaking plainly." Mona stirred her coffee, the spoon clanking against the sides of the cup. "That's what you wanted, wasn't it, Rebecca?"

"I didn't pull any strings," the lawyer insisted. "I hired Adele as a private detective to find evidence that would clear Theo."

"But Adele isn't a private detective," Mona pointed out. "She's a shop owner."

"I was working as a private detective," Adele said, feeling her anger grow.

"Did Rebecca pay you anything for your services?"

"None of your business," Nin snapped.

"I was working for justice, not money," Adele insisted.

"And if you had found something to prove my brother killed my mother?" Mona asked in a slow tone. "Would you have kept it to yourself, or would you have given it to Rebecca?"

"How dare you even think —" Nin started.

"It's a fair question," Adele said. "I would have given it to Rebecca. Justice goes both ways, Mona."

"I believe you, Adele." Mona leaned back with her hands laced together. "The question is, what would Rebecca have done with that information?"

"You tell me." Adele glared at her.

"No, *you* tell me. Or better yet," Mona turned to the lawyer, "you tell *us*."

Rebecca looked like an arrow shooting right at the target. "I would have given it to the police, of course."

"Even if it meant Theo would hang?" Mona raised an eyebrow. "Who isn't telling the truth straight out now?"

Rebecca rose. "You've always hated me, haven't you, Mona?"

"What a thing to say!" The woman gave a small laugh. "We grew up together."

"Yes, we did," Rebecca said. "But we were never friends. And we never will be."

The woman sighed. "I'm so sorry to hear you say that. I thought we might eventually become more than friends."

"More than friends?"

"Sisters-in-law."

Rebecca's face turned so pale Adele feared the woman might faint. She grabbed her hat. "I'll send a copy of the official release once I get it from the district attorney," she said. "I suggest Theo put it in a safe place."

"I'll see that he does," Mona said. "He wouldn't want to lose that, after all."

Without answering, Rebecca left the parlor.

"I'm sorry you had to witness that," she said. "Rebecca has always been sensitive."

"She has the interest of the entire family at heart," Adele said slowly.

"She's always been devoted to Theo." Mona held out a plate of cake. "I really do admire her fidelity."

"Admire or resent?" Nin asked.

"Perhaps a little of both, Miss Branch." She leaned back. "Tell me, Adele, why did the police release my brother?"

"Because he didn't do it," Nin declared.

"Yes, I know," she said. "But there must have been something more. I don't pretend to know about these things, but I do read the occasional murder mystery."

"Then I'm sure you've come across the term 'inconclusive evidence.'" Adele poured herself another cup of coffee before Mona could reach for the pot.

The gesture seemed to put the woman out. "I don't think I've heard it, no."

"One is innocent until proven guilty," said Adele. "If there is a shadow of a doubt, the police can't convict."

"I don't always understand things," she said.

"I believe you know what I'm saying." Adele eyed her.

"I think I do," said the woman. "You found something that makes the police doubt Theo was involved with my mother's death."

"Yes," said Adele. "Evidence found at the bottom of a teacup. And the tip of a pen."

"Now you're teasing me," Mona said.

Adele smiled. "I assure you I'm not. My brother calls it talking in circles."

"I prefer you don't," the woman declared.

"I asked Mr. Brethren to do some tests on the teacup we found in Thea's room," said Adele.

The woman looked surprised. "The police would do that, wouldn't they?"

"They did, but they didn't know what to look for," she said.

"And you did?"

"Poison," Adele said. "Belladonna, to be exact. The black water you saw."

The woman put her cup down. "And Lom found none?"

"Not exactly," said Adele. "But he did say whatever stained the cup was not what he sent to Theo."

"Well, he would say that, wouldn't he?" Mona looked out at the window. "He's been Theo's friend since boyhood. If he lied about seeing Theo, he might lie about that too."

"He didn't lie," Nin said firmly.

"No, he wouldn't lie, not even to protect Theo," Mona murmured. She looked at Adele. "You said something about the tip of a pen."

"A fountain pen nib," Adele said.

"The one found in Mother's room?" Mona asked, amused. "I thought that was nothing."

"Everything found near a dead body is something," Adele insisted.

The woman flinched. "Please, don't be so direct. Not about Mother."

"I'm sorry." Adele's voice softened. "We discovered your brother didn't buy any nibs at that shop in San Francisco."

Mona nodded. "William took me there once. I got a headache from the smell of ink."

"Yes, Mr. Brown doesn't seem to understand the importance of opening windows," Adele remarked.

"You assume because no one remembers Theo buying nibs that it wasn't his," the woman said. "I suppose that's logical."

"Is it also logical a lady with bright yellow hair would buy them in his name?" Nin eyed her.

Mona pulled the bell cord, and Mrs. Stern appeared. "Ella, please take these things away and bring the sherry. You'll take sherry?"

"A rather strange time of day for sherry," Adele said.

"I feel we all could use it," said the woman. "Speaking of these things is so distressing," She leaned back. "So Theo sent some woman to the shop. Very clever."

"He says he didn't send anyone," Nin insisted.

"You're rather trusting of what my brother says, Miss Branch," said Mona.

"And you're hypocritical," Nin said roughly. "You agree he didn't do it, and yet you're quick to insinuate otherwise."

"I'm insinuating nothing," Mona insisted. "I'm getting interested in the game."

"Game?" Adele stared at her.

"The same game you're playing," she said.

Adele felt a storm in her chest. "I don't play games when people's lives are at stake!"

Mona patted Adele's hand. "I'm sorry you misunderstood me."

"Do you or don't you believe your brother is innocent?"

"As you say, the evidence can't prove he isn't," Mona said.

"But you think he's guilty?" Adele eyed her.

"I'm merely exploring, as you are. It would be rather interesting if it *were* Rebecca who went to that shop, wouldn't it?"

"Rebecca doesn't have yellow hair," Nin reminded her.

"Yes, that's true," said the woman.

"And she denies having been to the shop," Adele added.

"Well, she would, wouldn't she?" Mona asked.

Adele put her hand to her forehead. "The description the clerk gave didn't sound like Rebecca."

"How did he describe her?"

Adele repeated what the clerk had said.

"You know, it sounds rather like Stephanie," said the woman in a wry tone.

"Your sister-in-law?" Adele stared.

"She's not my sister-in-law yet," Mona reminded her. "I don't know she ever will be. Stephanie is rather superstitious. She might feel we're bad luck now."

"She seemed very devoted to your brother," Adele remarked.

"Indeed she is," said Mona. "She's devoted to both of them."

"You think she's in love with Theo too?" Nin asked.

"Women see Theo as a sort of lost puppy," the woman said. "They like to fancy themselves his caretaker because he needs to be taken care of."

"I saw no evidence of anything between them," Adele insisted.

"No, you wouldn't," Mona said. "Stephanie knows, as they say, on what side her bread is buttered. She wants to be a Marsh, but she knows Theo has no interest in her. So she's settled for the next best thing."

"You don't think much of her, do you?" Nin asked.

"Why should I?" A brutal note came into her voice. "She's filling Forrest's head with folly."

"Folly like moving out of this place after they're married?" Adele asked dryly.

"Forrest won't be going anywhere." The woman spoke with such confidence, it made Adele flinch.

She rose. "I'm afraid we must be going, Mona."

"Oh, what a shame," she said. "I was hoping to show Miss Branch my specimen book before you left."

"Your brother mentioned you had something like that," Adele said.

"I took a sample of plants and herbs while I was in India," she said. "I thought Miss Branch would like to see them." She smiled at her. "Perhaps that will make us better acquainted."

Adele could see her friend was anxious to leave. But an idea struck her. "I think you ought to see them, Nin."

"You're invited too, of course." Mona rose.

"I'm not much interested in those things," she admitted. "I'll go upstairs and see if Theo's all right. He looked so worn."

"Mrs. Stern can see to him."

"No, I'd rather do it." Adele headed toward the stairs. "I'm sure he needs a friendly face right now."

Nin gave Adele a pointed gaze, but her face softened when she saw the determined look on her friend's face.

"I'm very interested." Nin quickly seated herself again.

Mona followed her up the stairs. "I keep it locked, of course."

"I can imagine you would," Adele said softly.

She parted ways with Mona in front of Theo's door, waiting until the woman had entered her room to get the book. Then she crept down the stairs again and seized Polly. "Can you tell me where Miss Peeler is?"

"She's in the garden, miss."

Adele threaded her way through several rooms and finally found a pair of French doors to the back of the house. She stepped out to a pleasant veranda, wide and clean, overlooking a small strip of grass with a few plots of flowers. Further off, hills and mountains offered a grand view.

Stephanie sat at the far end reclining in a wicker chair with her head thrown back and her eyes closed. Her skirt was lifted up to her knees, and Adele couldn't help but admire the shapeliness of her legs. She noted the strength in her calves, toned muscles that had clearly seen more than their share of physical labor.

She tried to approach her as quietly as she could. Stephanie's eyes flew open, and she turned her head.

"I didn't want to disturb you," Adele apologized.

"You weren't disturbing me," said the young woman. "I appreciate the company. Miss Gossling, is it?"

"Call me Adele." Adele took a chair next to her. "I was just telling Theo I felt like one of the family."

"I wish you were," said Stephanie in an almost savage voice. "You might offer some excitement."

"I should think a future mother-in-law's death and brother-in-law's arrest would be enough excitement to last a lifetime," Adele said warily.

"Forrest says this murder business is all poppycock." She sniffed. "Thea died of a medical condition and that's that."

"Poison was found in her body," Adele said gently.

"Doctors make mistakes," she said. "I don't think Dr. Brody is very keen. Neither does Forrest. And he doesn't much like that other doctor — the one at the inquest."

"Dr. Rhodes," Adele said. "They didn't make a mistake, Stephanie. It's all scientific nowadays."

"Forrest says this foolishness about Theo being arrested will all be over soon."

"It is over," Adele said. "He came home an hour ago."

Stephanie looked at her with big green eyes. "You see? Forrest was right." She reached nodded toward a pitcher of lemonade and a few glasses. "Would you like some?"

Adele shook her head. "I've just had coffee and some of Mrs. Stern's pound cake."

"With Mona, I gather?" Her eyes became almond-shaped.

"I'm sorry you didn't join us," Adele said. "It might have proved exciting for you."

"Mona never asks me to join anything," said the woman. "If she could wish me away, she would."

"But you have no intention of going away," Adele said.

She gave her a meaningful look. "I have every intention of going away. But I'm taking Forrest with me, if I can manage it."

"If you can manage it?"

"I mean if I can convince him it's the best thing for him."

Adele sat down. "I think you meant if you can get him away from his sister's influence."

Stephanie looked at the mountains in the distance.

"Mona considers them to be in an alliance, doesn't she?" Adele asked.

"Us against them." Stephanie nodded. "She won't let go of him!"

"He has you now." Adele smiled.

"If only he would listen to me!" She sighed. "I try to be agreeable."

"Is that why you always defer to what Forrest thinks?" Adele eyed her.

The girl stiffened. "He's more worldly than I am."

Adele gave a small smile. "I realize that." She followed the woman's eyes. "Theo will be able to get back to his garden now."

"Such a waste of time," Stephanie said. "What is there a gardener for?"

"You don't admire him for taking an interest in it?" Adele asked.

"I don't find him amusing at all," she said. "Always talking about beams and saws and things."

"I rather thought most women found him appealing." Adele watched the girl carefully.

Stephanie shrugged. "Perhaps some do, but I prefer Forrest."

Adele crossed her legs. "I'm surprised he never married."

"There's no surprise in that," Stephanie snorted. "Thea held on to him like a blind woman holds on to a stick."

"Nevertheless," Adele mused, "there must have been some lady he was serious about. Or perhaps not so serious about."

The young woman smiled. "Forrest told me there was a woman who took tickets at a burlesque show in San Francisco that he took him to meet once. Not that Forrest was ever interested in that sort of thing."

"I'm sure he wouldn't be," Adele said dryly.

"And a telephone operator at the mill he used to lunch with once in a while," the girl continued. "His father put a stop to that, naturally."

"Naturally," Adele mumbled.

"And some scientific woman, a friend of Lom's," Stephanie continued.

"Miss Bright." Adele nodded.

"His mother put a stop to that one. I can't think of anyone else."

"Did Forrest ever mention anyone with bright yellow hair?"

"Yellow hair?" The young lady laughed. "Goodness, I can't imagine Theo with a blond lady!"

"Neither can I," Adele admitted. "But men sometimes do get eccentric as they age."

"It sounds indecent," Stephanie declared.

"But amusing," Adele put in.

"Oh, it would be if it were true," she said.

"Then you don't think Theo might have a lady friend no one knows about?"

"Not him." She shook her head. "He's not the one."

"But someone else is?" Adele's ears perked.

"It's common knowledge in Rosa Gris." The girl waved away a fly. "But you don't live in Rosa Gris, do you?"

"No, but I like to hear what's going on," Adele said.

"It's William, of course."

"Is it?" Adele tried not to sound surprised. "Gossips always exaggerate."

"No, this rumor is true," she said. "I saw them."

"Oh?"

"I have several friends who work at Garret's," she said. "Do you know it?"

Adele nodded. "That restaurant near the railway station. That's where you saw them?"

Stephanie nodded. "She's not a young thing, I must say," she remarked. "I rather thought men always choose women younger than their wives."

"Do you know who she is?"

"Not someone from the people the family knows, but then, one would expect that," she said.

"Do you think his wife knows?"

She fiddled with the lace on her skirt. "I think so. She's always rather cold to him. And, well, I was shopping in town once and saw Mona coming out of the restaurant." She gave Adele a knowing look. "It's not the sort of place she would dine, if you know what I mean."

Adele nodded.

"Not that I blame him." Stephanie shrugged. "Mona is rather a salty fish."

"What does Forrest say?" Adele asked.

"He doesn't like it," she said. "But he lets things be."

"He prefers to be agreeable," said Adele.

Stephanie smiled. "You remembered." She looked at the mountains. "He likes William. He's fine at his work, and his advice is always sound."

"You make it sound as if Mona's brothers like William more than Mona does," Adele said dryly.

The young woman didn't seem to notice. "Forrest is going to stand up to her."

"His sister?"

"He promised me."

"I'm sure he will," Adele said gently. "There's nothing to stop you from leaving now."

"That's the devil of it," said Stephanie, twisting a lock of hair with one long finger. "Forrest thinks there's no need to leave now."

"Because the demon in his life is gone now that his mother is dead," Adele guessed. "But we know it isn't." She pressed the girl's hand. "May I offer some advice?"

She glared at her. "You sound like Mona. She's always giving me advice."

"Mine is different," Adele said. "I imagine Mona's advice is more in her interest. Mine is in yours."

The girl's face softened. "I should be glad to hear it."

"Tell Forrest you won't marry him if he stays here. You stand up to *him*."

The woman's white face became pasty. "You think he's in danger? That whoever killed Thea will kill him?"

"Danger isn't always death," Adele murmured. "One's peace of mind may be in danger from lingerings of the past."

She left Stephanie sitting in the sun as she made her way back to the parlor. Mona was huddled close to Nin, her eyes glowing and her hands moving rapidly as she explained something. Nin sat back silent, her face stony.

Adele cleared her throat loudly. "I'm sorry to interrupt."

Her friend jumped up, looking relieved. "We're leaving, aren't we?"

Mona, clearly offended, slammed the book shut. "I'm so sorry to have kept you from your business."

"We very much appreciate your hospitality," Adele tried to sound kind. "I hope we can come again sometime."

"I'm afraid not for a while," Mona said. "Not to see me, anyway."

"Oh?" Adele put on her gloves.

"I'll be going into the city. Tomorrow."

"To get away from all the black?" Nin glanced at the heavy drapes over the parlor windows.

"To get away from a lot of things, Miss Branch," Mona said in a wistful voice. "At least for a time."

"Then you'll be back to take your place as mistress of the house?" Adele asked as she took her friend's arm.

"Of course I didn't mean what I said about the house," Mona insisted. "I should be glad to have something to do."

"I'm sorry I missed the talk about your plants," Adele said. "It sounds rather fascinating." She eyed her friend, whose expression remained impassive.

"We were just airing our views about the subject," Mona said, smiling at Nin. "No offense, I hope."

"None taken," Nin mumbled.

"I hope you amused yourself," Mona said.

"As a matter of fact, I was talking to Stephanie," she said. "I regret she didn't join us."

"I don't," Mona said abruptly. "She has nothing to contribute to any conversation."

"I found my chat with her very interesting," Adele said. "Very — amusing." She rolled her eyes at the last word.

Mona laughed. "Stephanie will learn one day that life can't always be amusing." She held the door open for them. "Would you like me to bring a message to any of your friends while I'm in the city?"

"That won't be necessary," Adele said. "I see them quite often."

"Then perhaps we shall run into one another there," said the woman. "San Francisco isn't quite so big, you know."

"You'll be staying for long?" Adele asked.

"A few months at least."

"It will be a long way for your husband to go for work every morning," Nin remarked.

"William won't be coming with me," said the woman in a firm tone. "Sometimes a woman wants time to herself."

"Indeed she does," Adele said, pressing her hand.

"If you'd like to borrow the book, let me know," Mona said to Nin, putting her arm around her.

"I won't," said Nin, slipping away and clutching Adele's arm.

"I imagine Rebecca left in your wagon, so I'll get Harold to drive you back to Arrojo."

"That's very kind of you." Adele smiled.

In the back of the Marsh carriage, Adele remarked, "You don't look as if you enjoyed yourself,"

"Sickening!"

"What was?"

"That book of hers." Nin leaned back. "All science, no soul. She and Mr. Brethren would get along just fine."

Adele laughed. "What were you disagreeing about?"

"She thinks dangerous plants are the fault of the plant, not the user." Nin sniffed. "I can see why her brother said she had unnatural ambitions."

"Exactly the opposite of what you believe." Adele nodded. "Potency is in the hands of the one who uses it, not in the plant on its own."

"One must take responsibility for how one treats Sister Nature," Nin declared.

They were silent all the way back to Arrojo.

dele, half asleep, heard a ding-dong vibrating in her ears, the distant chimes offering a pleasant morning knell. She opened her eyes to the mauve and peach room and sat up, realizing she had been dreaming of her old room in their San Francisco house with the church bells ringing a block away. But she was no longer in the city, and bells in Arrojo could only mean the telephone.

She threw open her bedroom door to hear Tomas' sleepy voice answer. She peered over the banister. "Who is it, Tomas?"

"For the master, señorita."

Adele gritted her teeth. Ever since Jackson came to live with her, Tomas referred to him as "the master," even though he knew perfectly well the house belonged to her. "But who is it?" she persevered.

"Police, I think," he said.

"Police!"

"Sí."

"I'll tell him," she said.

"Sí." He bowed and scurried to the kitchen where he was helping Ruth with breakfast.

Jackson was wide awake and dressed except for his vest and coat. "It must be urgent to call at this hour."

Adele lingered at the top of the stairs. She heard a few grunts and "I see." When her brother returned to his room, his step was clearly more thoughtful and labored.

"Who was it, Jack?"

"Edison," he said. "He was delivering a message from the sheriff." He took hold of her shoulders. "Theo's dead, Del."

"Dead!" She felt her head grow heavy. "That's impossible. We just saw him yesterday."

"He's dead."

"What — how?" Adele leaned against his shoulder.

"Edison didn't know the details," he said. "Hatfield is at the Marshes' right now and wants me to come."

"I'll come too," Adele insisted. "The family will need me." Her hands grew cold. "I don't know how Rebecca will take this."

"Edison said Hatfield asked me to break the news to her." He shifted with discomfort.

"And you don't want to," Adele guessed, laying her hand on her brother's shoulder.

He sniffed. "It's my duty."

She remembered when they had to tell their Aunt Belle their father was dead. It was the first time she had realized that, as understanding as Jackson was, there was nothing more frightening to him than participating in someone else's distress.

"You go to the Marshes'." She took his hand. "Nin and I will tell Rebecca."

"It's my duty —"

"It's your duty to find out what happened," Adele insisted. "You can do more good to Rebecca by going to the house."

"It's a terrible burden on you." He pressed her hand to his face.

"I'm sure she would rather hear it from us than the police." Adele did not add that sobbing females were as common to her as leaves falling from a tree.

"Just one thing, Del," he said. "Edison said Hatfield doesn't want Rebecca coming to the house just now."

"She's a very sensible woman," Adele objected. "She's not going to make a scene. And she's the family lawyer, so she has a right to be there."

"She was Theo's lawyer," Jackson corrected. "Hatfield feels she's too — involved."

Adele shot him a look. "Because of how she felt about him?"

"She might end up impeding the investigation without meaning to," he said gently.

"Why shouldn't she be involved when the man she loved is dead?"

"All the same," he headed toward his room, "Hatfield doesn't want her there just now. It's better you convince her not to go than have her turned away by a police officer at the door."

Adele stared. "You really think Hatfield would go that far?"

"You know when the sheriff says something, he means it." Jackson disappeared into his room, closing the door.

Adele dressed quickly. Her hands shook as she did the buttons on her boots, pinching her fingers more than once.

Ruth tried to push buttered toast into their hands, but both she and Jackson were too distracted to notice. He took the wagon, dropping her off in front of Nin's shop.

Adele rushed in, finding her friend at a small table with a brass bowl in front of her. Adele smelled rosemary burning. Her friend looked grave.

Adele caught her breath. "You know, don't you?"

Nin nodded. "Mona sent word to me this morning."

"You're her new friend," Adele said.

Nin gave her a wary glance. "She's no friend of mine."

"Did she ask you to burn rosemary for her brother?" Adele asked.

"She didn't ask me," Nin said. "It's simply the right thing to do." Her voice sounded sad.

"If you know, I suspect Rebecca does too."

"She doesn't know," Nin said. "She's no friend of Mona's either."

"I promised Jack we would tell her." Adele plucked Nin's hat from the coat rack.

"Shouldn't the police do that?" Nin rose.

"Hatfield asked Jack to do it," Adele said.

Nin put on her hat. "And your brother asked you to do it because he's afraid of wailing women."

"I volunteered," Adele insisted as they set off. "His heart is too soft for it, Nin."

"You mean his manliness is too fragile," her friend snorted.

"Women have more tact anyway," she said. "Hatfield doesn't want Rebecca at the Marsh house."

"He doesn't want to contend with a hysterical woman either," Nin growled. "Men!"

Rebecca was in her office, looking sharp in a gray suit and white blouse. Adele guessed she was going to court, as there were papers piled on her desk.

"I'm running late," she said as they walked in. "My first hearing. A woman in Vargas who just inherited her father's estate —" She stopped fiddling with her leather bag and stared at them.

Nin quietly closed the door.

Rebecca looked from one to the other, papers in hand. "You both look so gloomy."

"Rebecca," Adele began, "something's happened to Theo."

The way the lawyer dropped the papers in her hands on the floor made Adele flinch. She had delivered death news to many women in her work with the settlement houses. But those women were used to tragedy. Rebecca looked ready to bend like a willow.

Adele glanced over her shoulder at Nin, who turned toward the window.

"Something rather terrible, dear." She took Rebecca's hand.

The willowy pose turned into a plate of armor. "I'm not weak, Adele."

"I'm afraid he's dead, Rebecca." Adele let the words slip out in a soft tone.

The silence that followed seemed to last for hours. Creaking wheels, chattering voices of people passing, and horses hoofs sounded far off.

Rebecca stumbled a little bit, holding on to the edge of the desk, until she reached a chair and dropped into it. Her face showed horror and shock. "He just got out of jail!"

"I know, dear," Adele said. "Hatfield sent word this morning."

"Dead." The woman's hands began to shake.

Adele motioned Nin toward a cabinet in the corner. Nin found a bottle and a glass. She placed it in Rebecca's hands. The girl held on to it, her eyes frozen.

"Shall I make tea?" Nin asked in a soft voice. Adele shook her head.

The lawyer managed a few sips. "I keep that for clients," she said ruefully. "I never dreamed I would need it myself."

"He was a good man, Rebecca," Adele said, "and a good friend to all of us."

She reached for Adele's hand. "He was more than that to me. I suppose you know I was in love with him. I loved him since we were children."

"We all knew," Nin said.

Rebecca peered at her with a slight shake of her head. "I've never been good at hiding my feelings."

"One can't hide one's feelings all the time," Adele said.

"You mean women can't," Rebecca said with a short laugh. "My father always told me, 'Act like a woman.' If he were here, he would reprimand me for not bursting into tears." She suddenly gave Adele a terrified look. "Why am I not bursting into tears?"

"You will," Nin said. "Later."

"Yes, I suppose you're right," Rebecca said. "If there's one thing about lawyers, we know the proper time and place for everything." She drank the rest of the brandy. "Perhaps here isn't the time or place for me."

"What do you mean, dear?"

"I never should have come back," she said. "A senior lawyer in Chicago told me I would find demons. He was right."

"Nonsense!" Nin snarled.

"Oh, not your sort of demons, Miss Branch," Rebecca said. "My own."

"Real or imagined?" Adele eyed her.

"Both, perhaps." She pressed her hands on the edge of the desk. "I ought to go back there. At least it's a clean slate for me. I could work as a clerk again. I was quite good at fussing with papers." She gave a small laugh and glanced down at the pages still on her desk.

"If you go," Adele asked slowly, "how will you do justice to your friends?"

"My friends?" The woman stared.

"Theo and his mother," Adele said. "They were your friends as well as your clients."

"That's true." Rebecca nodded.

"Do you think they'll rest in peace until the mystery is solved?" Adele asked. "Do you think you will?"

Rebecca stared at a crack on the flooring. "You think Theo didn't die a natural death, just like his mother."

"We don't know that," Nin said quickly.

"But you suspect it?" She gave Adele a hard look. When Adele didn't answer, she took hold of her wrist. "You think he was murdered!"

"Don't you?" Adele gave her an even look.

The woman bit her lip. "But who? How? Why?"

"Those are the sheriff's question marks," Adele said. "Now he has two mysteries to solve instead of one."

Rebecca rose, dusting off her jacket with resolve. "Let me send word to my client, and we can be on our way."

"On our way?" asked Adele, biting her lip.

"To the Marshes', of course."

"The sheriff doesn't want you there," Nin said briskly.

"He doesn't want any of us there," Adele corrected. "Not yet."

Rebecca stiffened. "He thinks I'll throw a fit."

"The police like to have the initial investigation of the crime scene to themselves. Hatfield does, at least."

"But how are we to know what happened?"

"We'll go to the station at lunchtime," Adele said. "Jack should be back by then, even if the sheriff isn't. He'll be able to tell us some details."

"And you'll pump him for the rest," Nin added.

Adele gave a small smile. "I've been doing that since we were children. I'm sure we'll know all there is to know by the time lunch is over."

"I would prefer —"

Adele patted her arm. "You have your work to do," she said. "Don't be late."

They parted ways, and as she and Nin returned to their shops, Adele saw Mrs. Faderman waiting and tapping her foot, with Mrs. Lynn hanging on with worried eyes.

"Oh, lord, what does she want?" she muttered.

Nin's hand pressed firmly in Adele's arm as if determined not to leave her.

"Good morning, Mrs. Faderman." She tried to make her voice as cheerful as possible. "Come to see the new stationery?"

"I most certainly have not," the woman said. "I've come to have a word with you, Miss Gossling." Her pince-nez was on the edge of her nose, and the arch expression emphasized her sharp features. She gave Nin a meaningful look, but if Nin understood the hint to go away, she ignored it and remained where she was.

"The new Starry Night paperweights, then?" Adele unlocked

the door, taking her time. "I told you about them last week, remember?"

"I am not here for paperweights or stationery," the woman growled.

"You're here to scold." Nin sat on the stool she usually frequented when she visited Adele.

"You may go now, Miss Branch," said Mrs. Faderman. "This doesn't concern you."

"This is my shop," Adele said sharply. "I think I still have the right to decide who goes and who stays."

This made Mrs. Faderman drop her pince-nez. "I dislike having the same conversation twice, Miss Gossling. But we always seem to be talking in circles."

"What circle have you come to talk about this time?" Adele eyed her.

"Your liberties with the police."

"I could hardly call it liberties, Mrs. Faderman." Adele straightened a desk set display. "My brother naturally can't help mentioning his work at home."

"I'm not referring to that," said the woman. "If it were only after-dinner conversation, that would be a different matter."

"Your skirts are too ruffled to be a preacher, Mrs. Faderman," Nin said in a sweet voice. Adele had to turn away to hide her smile.

"I do not preach, Miss Branch," the woman barked. "I offer advice based on what is best for the community."

"You always have the community in mind, don't you, Mrs. Faderman?" Adele asked in a wary tone.

"I realize the New Woman allows herself an independence far beyond her comprehension and good taste," Mrs. Faderman continued. "Perhaps it's the direction the world is going now."

"Well!" Adele put her hand on her hip. "That's quite a different tune from the one you were singing when I first came to town."

"I'm not one of those curmudgeons who resists progress, Miss

Gossling, but I speak up when I don't approve of certain things." The pince-nez went back on. "This is one of them."

"One you don't resist or one you don't approve?" Nin asked.

"I think you know, Miss Branch." The woman sniffed. "You know how I felt about your involvement with the Blackstones, Miss Gossling."

"When a young woman shows up dead in my garden, I can hardly ignore it," Adele snapped.

"And poor Miss Millie Gibb?"

"Poor Millie!" Nin spit out. "That woman —"

"Yes, well, we'll dispense with that," Mrs. Faderman said quickly. "You made a promise to the council that you would no longer involve yourself in such matters."

Adele stared. "I don't recall making any such promise."

"Not formally, naturally," said the woman. "But since that unfortunate occurrence with Miss Gibb, you've kept your nose out of police business, and you've been all the wiser for it."

"One can hardly keep one's nose clean when there is nothing to dirty it," Adele pointed out.

"I'll admit, Miss Gossling, I had my doubts about you when you first came to Arrojo."

"Roaring down Bridge Street in that dangerous automobile of mine?" Adele said with amusement. "I believe that's how you phrased it."

"If you wish to put it that way," said Mrs. Faderman. "But you've made your contribution to the community, and for that, we are all grateful."

"You should be." Nin cocked her head. "She contributed the deputy sheriff."

"That's beside the point, Miss Branch," said the woman. "It has come to my attention there were certain objects in your possession relating to the death of Theodora Marsh."

"They weren't in her possession," Nin defended. "The deputy assistant let her borrow them."

"Yes, we know all about Mr. Edison and his confused mind," said the woman.

"He wasn't confused when you ordered him to close Dora's shop," Adele said dryly.

"I was told you removed important evidence for your own purposes," Mrs. Faderman continued. "I find that to be going beyond an uncommon interest in crime."

"Especially for a woman?" Nin eyed her.

"For anyone," the woman said emphatically.

"I had a right to those things, Mrs. Faderman," Adele explained. "Miss Gold, Theo's lawyer, asked me to find out anything that might clear him."

"She hired Adele as a private detective," Nin added before Adele could stop her.

"Private detective!" The blood drained from the woman's face. "That is going too far, Miss Gossling."

"What is?"

"You offering your services in a profession you know nothing about. It's not only irregular, it's dangerous!"

"I assure you, Mrs. Faderman, I was in no danger," Adele said.

"I meant dangerous for others," said the woman. "Suppose you should give the police wrong information? You might incriminate the very person you're trying to help."

"You old crow!" Nin shouted. "How dare you make an accusation like that!"

"It's not an accusation, Miss Branch," said Mrs. Faderman in a calm voice. "I'm merely raising a point."

"I would never do such a thing," Adele lamented.

"I can't stop you from dabbling in crime on a personal level," Mrs. Faderman said, "but I can do something about using the police to prop yourself up in this new profession."

"I'm not going into any new profession, ma'am," Adele assured her. "Miss Gold wanted to hire me, it's true, but I accepted no money."

"But you did investigate the Marsh case and take out evidence?" the woman challenged.

"And set a man free."

"Who is now dead." Mrs. Faderman crossed her arms over her chest.

Adele's blood went cold. "Are you implying I had something to do with his death?"

"I'm sure I don't know, Miss Gossling," said the woman. "But I shall have a strong word to say to the sheriff about your taking license with police evidence."

Adele grabbed her arm. "Please don't do that, ma'am. He knew nothing about it."

"I was told he was rather amused by the entire thing," Mrs. Faderman said stiffly.

"Who is this chatterbox who told you all this?" Nin eyed her.

"That hardly matters, Miss Branch," she said. "I hope we can expect better conduct from you in the future, Miss Gossling."

"Or you'll do what?" Nin rose. "Gather a posse of society ladies to run her out of town? Call in the militia?"

Although Nin was a small woman, her cat-like grace and elongated features made her look menacing. Mrs. Faderman pressed her lips together.

"I don't make threats, Miss Branch, as you know," she said. "Neither do I run people out of town. No matter how dangerous their knowledge of certain elements may be." Her gaze lingered a moment before she turned on her heels and walked out of the shop.

"The shrew!" Nin exploded. "You know who she was talking about?"

"Your mother," Adele said quietly.

"She would have loved to chase Mama across the county line," said Nin. "She was the one who started the rumors about Mama being a witch." She pouted. "I bet I know who that chatterbox was."

"Mrs. Fourier," Adele said. "She *would* have to be there when we came in."

"You know what *fou* means in French, don't you?" Nin arched her eyebrow. "The woman is crazy, and Mrs. Faderman is a fool to believe her."

"And if she's right, Nin?" Adele felt weak. "If someone got wind of what we were doing and killed Theo because of it?"

"That's hogwash, and you know it." Her friend put her arms around her. "If someone wanted the evidence hushed up, they would have gotten rid of it long before the police found it."

"Perhaps you're right," Adele said in a small voice.

# CHAPTER 22

*A*dele went through the morning with the weight of Theo's death growing on her heart. A few customers anxious to see the new stock came in, and she helped them without knowing what she was doing. Even when Mrs. Shaffer, a relative newcomer to town but an old friend of Mrs. Jessel's, enthusiastically bought four boxes of stationery, marveling at the shop's elegance and praising Adele as one of the "up and coming businesswomen, and about blessed time too," Adele could hardly relish the praise.

At noon, she shut up her shop and collected Nin and together, they went down to the station. Rebecca was sitting on the wooden bench outside, her body rigid. "I don't think the police will want to see me," the lawyer mumbled.

"If you make it clear you won't burst into tears all over their reports, they will," Nin remarked.

Rebecca glanced at her and even Adele felt her friend may have taken her bluntness too far. Nin hunched inside the large shawl. "I didn't mean that."

"I know what you mean." The lawyer gave her a small smile. "I won't shed a tear."

They entered the station where the scent of chicken soup filled the small space. Edison rose abruptly. "They're not here, Miss Gossling."

"Are they still at the Marsh house, Assistant Deputy?"

"Well —" He glanced at Rebecca.

"Miss Gold *was* the dead man's lawyer," Nin snapped. "You best tell us where we can find the sheriff and be quick about it."

The young man flinched. "They're at the sheriff's."

"You mean they're lunching with Lady Augusta?" Adele asked. The young man nodded.

"Then we shall lunch there too." Nin took Adele's arm.

Rowena let them in with her usual briskness. Jackson looked uneasy as he put down his fork. Sheriff Hatfield rose and with a kind look in his eyes, said, "I'm very sorry, Miss Gold."

"He was a good friend," Rebecca lamented. Adele could see she was holding back tears.

"He was a very kind man," Lady Augusta said with equal warmth. "Rowena, three more places."

"I'm not hungry," Rebecca said.

"Hungry or not, young lady, you'll eat," the woman ordered with all the aristocracy of her name. "I won't have fainting females on my doorstep."

"No weeping ones?" Rebecca asked, glancing at the lawmen.

"It's a good thing we have a woman to do a man's job," Hatfield said, glaring at Jackson.

"Sometimes it takes a woman to do any job, man's or otherwise," Lady Augusta said dryly.

"You're right, as always, Ma," said the sheriff, kissing her cheek.

Rebecca picked up the soup spoon but lingered over the bowl put in front of her. "Sheriff, we came to find out about Theo."

"As a friend or lawyer?" Jackson asked.

Adele shot her brother a look. "Does it matter, Jack?"

Lady Augusta tapped the edge of her son's shoe. "Horatio! Tell the lady what she wants to know."

"I intend to, Ma," he assured her. "I'm sorry I had to prohibit you from the house this morning, Miss Gold. I know you understand."

"I understand." Rebecca nodded. "I'm impressed by your modern methods, Sheriff. Even in Chicago, the police weren't as strict about disallowing people on the premises of a murder scene."

"I learned during my time on the waterfront that it's far too easy to mess about with evidence when one doesn't even know what one is looking for," he said.

"You're prepared to tell us what you found?" Adele asked. "You're always forthright, Sheriff. Unlike some lawmen I could name." She shot her brother a look.

"Lawmen keep information back to avoid meddling and interfering from some sisters I could name," he shot back.

Rebecca leaned forward. "How did Theo die?"

Hatfield tore a slice of bread in half and buttered it before answering, "He committed suicide."

"Suicide!" Rebecca clenched her fists.

"What makes you believe it was suicide, Sheriff?" Adele asked in a calm voice.

"He left a note," Hatfield said.

"I want to see that note," Rebecca said in a harsh tone.

"We don't have it here, Miss Gold," Jackson said.

"She has a right to see it, Jackson," said Hatfield. "If you come to the station with us after lunch, we'll be glad to show it to you."

"Is that all the evidence you have?" Adele eyed him.

"Isn't it enough, Del?" Jackson put down his fork. "When a man writes a note saying he's going to kill himself and is found dead, one is apt to believe him."

"Tell me all the details, Sheriff," Rebecca insisted.

"Mr. Marsh told Mrs. Stern he wished to have his meals sent to his room on a tray," Hatfield began.

"Very understandable," Lady Augusta said. "Those jail cells are hardly agreeable. You really ought to get some new blankets, Horatio."

"I already put in a request with the county, Ma," her son said. "A breakfast tray was sent up to him this morning at seven o'clock."

"Who brought it to him?" Adele asked.

"Polly, of course."

Rebecca raised her eyebrows. "Are you assuming or did you verify this?"

"Some details are more important than others, Miss Gold," Jackson said in a hard tone. "Policemen must pick and choose what to examine first. They may go back later if they need to, once they know more what they're looking for."

"And once everyone has forgotten them," Nin mumbled.

"We do our best, Miss Branch," Jackson snapped. "It's why we keep a crime scene under lock and key as long as we need to."

"As it happens," Hatfield said in a patient tone, "Mrs. Bridge herself sent Polly up with the tray. Polly told us she knocked three times on Mr. Marsh's door and, when he didn't answer, left it outside."

"Go on," Rebecca said, her eyes wide.

"A few hours later, Mr. Bridge passed by the door and noticed the tray still there," Jackson said. "He knocked on the door but there was no answer. When he found it locked, he called Mr. Marsh — the younger one — and they broke it down and found — found him."

Rebecca let out a soft cry and covered her face with her hands. Lady Augusta put her arm around her shoulder. "Rowena, pour the lady a brandy."

"I don't need it."

"When my mother tells you to do something, Miss Gold, it's best not to argue," Hatfield said with a small smile.

"Only because I've lived long enough to know what's best," Lady Augusta insisted. Rowena brought the brandy, and Rebecca drank it reluctantly.

"Where were the others?" Adele asked. "The rest of the family, I mean?"

"Mrs. Bridge was away," said Hatfield. "She left to stay with friends in San Francisco. Mr. Forrest Marsh's fiancée was in the house, of course."

"And nobody heard anything?" Adele asked. "No shot, no cry, nothing?"

"Mr. Marsh didn't die that way," Jackson said.

"How did he die, then?" Rebecca asked. "Please, Sheriff, I must know."

"Dr. Rhodes thinks he died of some plant poisoning."

"Like Thea." Rebecca sank in her chair. With a signal from Lady Augusta, Rowena poured another brandy.

"He thinks it might have been the one Mr. Marsh got from his chemist friend," Hatfield said.

"But that's impossible!" Rebecca looked up. "The police confiscated the extract Lom gave Theo."

"He might have gotten more," Jackson pointed out. "He may even have stolen it."

"In order to commit suicide?" Rebecca scoffed.

"When people are desperate, Miss Gold, they reach for the first thing they can think of," Hatfield said. "The belladonna extract would be on Mr. Marsh's mind because of the investigation into his mother's death. It would only be natural —"

"None of this is natural, Horatio," said his mother in a incredulous tone.

"Yes, Ma," he said, a little weakly.

"Dr. Rhodes is only guessing," Adele reminded her friend, pressing her hand.

"He's doing an autopsy now," Jackson said. "We'll know for sure this afternoon."

Clanking dishes signaled the end of the meal. In her brisk, grated voice, Lady Augusta suggested they retire to the parlor for coffee.

"I can't believe any of this," Rebecca lamented as she took the chair next to her hostess.

"Mr. Marsh went through quite an ordeal the past few weeks, Miss Gold," Jackson said, his tone gentle. "His mother dying so suddenly, the question of her death, being in jail. It's enough to break any man's spirit, even a strong-minded one like Mr. Marsh."

"You don't understand, Deputy." She grasped her handkerchief with both hands. "We had a long conversation yesterday after he returned home. He was in the best of spirits. He told me he was really going to begin again. This experience taught him that holding back one's life only leads to misery."

"He was miserable most of his life," Nin murmured.

"You can't know that, Miss Branch," Jackson said sharply.

"I have ways of knowing things, Mr. Gossling," she snapped.

"You're not far off, Miss Branch," said the lawyer. "He was never really happy. I don't think I saw him smile once, a true smile, that is, since I came back. But he was smiling yesterday." Her eyes filled with tears. "He was like a little boy telling me of his plans for the mill. He was going to take time off to travel, and then find himself a place in the city."

"Away from lingerings of the past," Adele echoed, remembering her conversation with Stephanie.

"Yes, that's it exactly." Rebecca wiped her eyes and looked squarely at the sheriff. "Does that sound like a man who's going to commit suicide?"

"One can never tell what's on a man's mind," Jackson pointed out.

"I could with Theo, Deputy," she insisted. "He wanted to

expand the lumber mill. He wanted to be involved in helping build low-cost housing so people could have their own homes. He said one's own home is the most grounding thing a person can have."

"I wonder how his brother would have felt about that," Hatfield mused, digging into the coconut cream pie put in front of him with relish.

"He would hardly have much of a say." Rebecca sniffed.

"And Mr. Bridge?" Adele asked.

Rebecca stared at her. "What about Mr. Bridge?"

"According to the terms of Thea's will, he's now part owner of the mill."

Rebecca dropped her spoon. "I never thought of that!"

"It's what he's wanted all along?" Adele suggested.

"Who says he wanted it?" Rebecca stared at her.

"He might be pushed to want it," Nin said.

"By whom, Miss Branch?" Jackson glanced at her.

"Mona always wanted to be a part of the mill, didn't she?" Nin sniffed. "That's what the ladies said."

"Gossips!" he grumbled.

"Sometimes there's a grain of truth in Mrs. Faderman's babble, Jackson," Lady Augusta pointed out.

"Playing the businesswoman appealed to her," Nin added.

"Unnatural ambitions," Adele echoed. "If she couldn't be part of it, having a husband who owns half the shares might be the next best thing."

"Businesswoman by proxy?" Hatfield couldn't hold back a grin.

"Women do it all the time, Horatio," his mother snapped. "Smart men know when to listen to their wives."

"As smart sons know how to listen to their mothers, Ma," said her son. She rewarded him with a pat on the hand.

"I can't picture William killing his wife's mother and brother just to be a partner in a company." Rebecca shook her head.

"Perhaps Mona knew nothing about it," Nin pointed out. "For all her fancy talk, she isn't very bright."

"I suppose you're going to suggest it was Mona who dressed up in the veiled hat and blond wig and bought the nibs?" Jackson questioned, half-smiling at his sister.

"Not Mona, no," said Adele. "Someone else might have."

"Who?" Hatfield leaned forward.

Adele put her coffee cup down. "I never told you about the interesting conversation I had with Miss Peeler, did I?"

"Stephanie?" Rebecca stared at her. "What in the world would you want to speak to her about?"

"There was an insinuation she had some affection for Theo," Adele said.

"That's bunk," Rebecca scoffed. "She's devoted to Forrest."

"Indeed she is," said Adele. "She repeats almost everything he says. And yet, she's bright in her own way. She's picked up on things from life's heavy blows."

"Yes, I've always liked her for that," Rebecca admitted.

"She insisted that William has a mistress."

"Del, really!" Jackson flinched, glancing at Lady Augusta.

"You needn't worry about me, young man," said the woman. "I've seen and heard things you would blush to know."

As if at the mere thought, his face turned red, making Hatfield laugh outright.

"Such things happen all the time, dear brother," Adele said. "I've known several ladies who had quite prominent politicians wrapped around their little fingers."

"Is that what's going on here?" Hatfield asked. "A lady involved with a prominent — or soon-to-be prominent — businessman?"

"I don't know," said Adele. "Stephanie couldn't tell me much about the lady. She only said she'd seen them at the restaurant by the railroad station in Rosa Gris."

"She could be a waitress there," Jackson pointed out.

"Perhaps we ought to reserve judgment until we know whether it's true or not," Lady Augusta said. "Rumors can be vicious among family members, especially if they're not very close."

"Even if the rumor is true, Ma," said Hatfield, "it's hardly our business."

"It's good to see there are some things the police don't consider their business," Nin muttered.

"It might be police business if the lady was involved in some kind of illegal activity," Adele pointed out.

"I don't follow." Rebecca played with the edge of a cushion.

"Perhaps she knew what William had in mind and decided to help him," said Adele. "It's possible she did go to that stationery shop in a disguise."

"Why would she do that?" Jackson asked.

"To incriminate Theo, of course," said Adele. "The clerk at the shop said the woman told him she was Theo's wife."

"Theo's wife!" Rebecca looked stunned.

"She made herself conspicuous with that wig and veil," Adele continued, "so they would remember her when the nib was found near Thea's body."

"A clever plan," Hatfield admitted, "if it's true."

"We have one way of finding out, sir," said Jackson.

The sheriff rose. "Mr. Bridge might be worth questioning. In the most delicate way, of course."

Lady Augusta smiled. "I have no doubt if delicacy and tact are necessary, you shall use them more admirably than any man with a badge, Horatio."

"You're too kind, Ma," he said, giving her hand a few affectionate pats.

~~~~~

Rebecca asked Adele and Nin to accompany her back to the police station to see Theo's suicide note. Adele accepted, but Nin
~~~~~

declined, as a few ladies had made appointments for herbal consultations that afternoon.

When they entered the station, only one assistant deputy was there. The young man, named Carson, looked like a scraggly dog rescued from a back alley and had a tendency to mumble rather than speak. He had a fondness for the sheriff's chair, and he was spinning himself around when they entered.

"Carson!"

The young man became rattled as he leapt up, sending the chair flying across the room.

"Where's Edison?" Hatfield asked.

"Stepped out, sir," said the young man.

"Stepped out?" The sherrif gave him an incredulous look.

"Called away, Sheriff," said Assistant Deputy Carson in a meek voice.

"Leaving you to uphold law and order by yourself?" Sheriff Hatfield clicked his tongue with exaggerated pity. For the first time that day, Rebecca smiled.

"Well, sir, it isn't as if there's much to uphold," the assistant deputy mumbled.

"You never can tell, lad," said the sheriff as he retrieved his chair and indicated a bench for Adele and Rebecca. "Many a Wells Fargo driver made the same observation when I rode alongside them, only to find themselves facing the barrel of a gun along the way."

"How exciting!" The young man's eyes glowed.

Jackson gave him a wary look. "If you find it so exciting, Carson, I'll be glad to take you on our next shootout."

The young man quivered, and Jackson led him by the scruff of the neck into the file room.

Hatfield shook his head. "These lads read too many adventure novels."

"I wonder why you gave up being a Wells Fargo detective,"

Adele lamented. "It certainly must have been more exciting than being sheriff of a sleepy town like this."

"There are times in a man's life when adventure is not the only consideration, Adele," said Hatfield in a rueful tone, digging through the papers on his desk.

"I'm sorry," she said softly. "I forgot about your mother."

"Ma takes better care of me than I do her," he insisted. He unfolded a piece of paper, glanced at it, and handed it to Rebecca. "This is what you wanted, Miss Gold."

Adele studied Rebecca's face as she read the note. What began as an expression of anxiousness eased with relief.

"I'm sorry to tell you, Sheriff," said the lawyer, laying the letter at the edge of the desk, "that if this note is the only thing you have to prove Theo committed suicide, your assumptions are false."

"Eh?" Hatfield raised an eyebrow.

"May I read it?" asked Adele.

At the sheriff's nod, she picked up the letter. It was type-written on clean white paper and was quite short:

*My time has come. I must go to my mother. The world is too much for me without her. I'm sorry. Theo.*

"It hardly sounds like something he would write," Adele agreed.

"Theo wrote like a carpenter hitting a nail," Rebecca said. "He was hard and direct. Always tactful, of course, but direct. Language such as 'my time has come' and 'the world is too much for me' isn't him at all."

"One is apt to get philosophical when one is about to end one's life," Jackson mumbled.

"It's typed and not signed," Adele pointed out. "Anyone could have written it."

"You mean someone killed Theo and typed the note to make it look like suicide?" Jackson snorted. "You really are taking too much from those detective novels, Del."

"I don't read detective novels, and you know it," she snapped.

"If Theo had intended to leave a note," Rebecca said, "he wouldn't have typed it."

"He was a businessman," Jackson said. "I'm sure he used typewriters quite a bit in his work."

"*He* did not, Deputy," said Rebecca emphatically. "His secretary did. He never touched the machine."

"I can't say I blame him," Hatfield said dryly. "I'm rather glad Edison is so attached to ours."

Adele rose, packing and slapping her gloves against her hands. "I've sold one or two typewriters, Sheriff. They're complicated machines to learn."

"Indeed," said Hatfield, "not to mention they make an infernal racket." He gave the Underwood sitting on Edison's desk a menacing look.

"Did Theo know how to type?" Adele asked.

Rebecca shook her head. "He hated them as much as the sheriff. He told me he tried to type a letter once when his secretary was away, and he was all thumbs."

"All thumbs," Adele repeated. "So it would have taken him a long time to type even a short note."

"What's your point, Del?" Jackson asked.

"Why would a man who was going to commit suicide spend time and effort typing a note he could have written by hand in a few minutes?" she questioned.

"And a vague and cold note at that," Rebecca added. "If Theo really were going to kill himself and wanted people to know it, he would have addressed his letter to someone. Me, perhaps." She said the last in a soft tone.

"It would have been a personal note," Adele agreed.

The sheriff folded his hands in his lap. "Perhaps you have a point there, Adele."

"We can have the type analyzed," Jackson suggested. "See if it has any quirks matching one of the typewriters at the mill."

"You're fishing without a net, Deputy," Rebecca remarked.

"Perhaps we are, Miss Gold," said Hatfield. "Police work is about casting the net and seeing what comes up to the surface. Sometimes what we find may surprise you."

"The sheriff ought to know," Adele added, smiling. "He was once captain of a fishing boat."

The man did not answer, but there was a discernible blush on his face.

# CHAPTER 23

The two women left the station and took their time strolling down Bridge Street, discussing the note. Rebecca had completely recovered and was determined to prove the death of the man she had loved was not by his own hand.

"What do you propose to do?" She asked when they reached her office. "I assume you're not going to let sleeping dogs lie."

"No indeed," said Adele. "I'm not entirely satisfied with what the sheriff told us about their search of Theo's room. It's too neat and tidy, just like the evidence in Thea's death."

"The police may have stopped being thorough once they found that note," Rebecca agreed.

"I wish Nin and I could get in there." Adele sighed.

Rebecca unlocked her office door, the wind blowing the tulle on her hat like the wings of a bird. "Do you really think it would help if you could get into Theo's room?"

"It's worth a try," Adele said.

"Perhaps I can do something." She motioned Adele into her office and, taking a sheet of stationery, scribbled a note, signed and stamped it. "Show this to the family when you go to the Marsh house."

"What's it about?" Adele asked.

"Before he — Theo wanted my legal advice on some of his new business ideas. I prepared some papers for him to look over and sign. I never got those papers back."

Adele's eyes brightened.

"I'll be away all day tomorrow," the woman continued. "I need those papers, especially with Theo — gone." She faltered.

"So you're authorizing Nin and me to get them for you." Adele said. "How clever you are, Rebecca."

"Sometimes cleverness comes from the good side of the law." Rebecca smiled a little. "You'll tell me what you find, won't you?"

"Of course." Adele pressed her hand. "Thank you."

"It's for Theo's sake," said the woman, tears in her eyes.

"We'll work for Theo's sake and for Thea's too," Adele promised.

~~~~~

The next morning was strangely misty, reminding Adele of the thick gray fog carpeting the city before the sun had a chance to warm it. She and Jackson were forced to have their breakfast in the dining room instead of the back porch which they both preferred.

As Jackson dug his spoon into a grapefruit half, Nin entered, fully dressed in impressive shades of yellow and gold.

"Good morning, Nin." Adele motioned for Tomas to bring another coffee cup. The man tentatively set it down, eyeing Nin as he retreated near the wall.

"You intimidate the men in my house," Adele said with a smile.

Nin glared at Tomas, who ducked his head. Jackson seemed equally put out as he buried his nose in the *Arrojo Courier*.

"We were just talking about you," Adele said, pouring her coffee. "Jack was saying even you can't predict the future."

"I never try," Nin insisted. "That's for charlatans."
~~~~~

"It was an off-hand remark," Jackson mumbled. "I meant no offense."

"You never do," Nin said, "but your tongue always manages to slip in an insult."

He gave her a wary look and returned to his paper.

Adele finished her breakfast, and they left, armed with the note Rebecca had given them. They found the Marsh house more forlorn than after Thea's death. Polly answered the door, her handkerchief crumpled in her hand.

"It ain't right," she lamented. "It ain't right."

Adele put her arm around her shoulders. "We're all trying to find out what happened."

"No, miss, not that," said the woman. "Oh, that ain't right neither, but for ladies to be fighting like cats, and Mrs. Bridge gone, and all —"

"Who's fighting?" Adele asked.

"Mrs. Stern and that nurse," she said between sniffs. "At it just like always."

"You mean Nurse Pegg." Adele handed her the parasol and gloves.

"Ain't no one to stop them," said the girl. "Miss Peeler won't come down, Mr. Marsh and Mr. Bridge at the mill, and Mr. Stern —" her expression turned snide, "well, *he* just slinks away like a possum. Afraid of his wife if he so much as dares to hint he's taking the nurse's side."

"All they need is a diversion," Adele said briskly. "They're in the kitchen?"

"Yes, Miss."

Adele took Nin's hand and they marched down the stairs to the more hidden area of the house where the servants lived and worked. They heard the growling voice of the housekeeper against the high-pitched tone the nurse used.

"I thought she went away," Nin said in a low voice.

Adele pressed her hand as they crept down the hallway.

"A greedy old bat, that's what you are!" Mrs. Stern shouted. "Coming here making demands for that painting when we're still mourning Mr. Marsh."

"I'm sorry about Mr. Marsh, truly I am —"

"You're not the least bit sorry about anything or anyone!"

Adele was surprised to hear genuine tears in Mrs. Stern's voice. She realized how fond the woman had been of Theo.

"How dare you accuse me —" Nurse Pegg's voice rose.

"Good morning, ladies!" Adele said as she and Nin entered the kitchen.

The two women were alone. A kettle was smoking on the stove.

"You mustn't let your coffee spoil," she said cheerfully as she turned off the gas.

"Oh, Miss Gossling!" Mrs. Stern collapsed in tears. "Please tell this woman to get out of my sight."

"I never wanted to be in your sight," Nurse Pegg growled. "I've never had anything to do with you."

"No, you just thought yourself above us because you were with Mrs. Bridge in India!" Mrs. Stern shouted.

"I never thought myself anything of the kind and you know it!"

"You had privileges," Mrs. Stern continued.

"What I had or didn't have is no concern of yours," Nurse Pegg insisted. "I've come for what was promised me and that's all."

"How you persuaded Mrs. Marsh to leave you that much, I don't care to imagine." Mrs. Stern sniffed.

"If you tell me where the picture is, Mrs. Stern, I shall leave here and never come back," said the nurse. "I won't have to be in your sight ever again."

"You're not taking a thing out of this house until I that lady lawyer says so," Mrs. Stern said. "The very idea of coming here and —"

"I didn't expect to find another dead body in this house, did I?" Nurse Pegg snarled. "Worst case of death mania I've ever seen."

"Death mania!"

"As a rule, I don't believe in curses," said Nurse Pegg. "But in the case of the Marshes, I shouldn't wonder —"

The housekeeper flew to her but Adele and Nin managed to hold her back.

"Mrs. Stern, I think it best if you go lie down," Adele said.

"I can't, miss," she said. "All the work to do —"

"A half hour's rest won't keep you from your work for too long," she argued. "Polly can see to anyone who comes in."

"The family needs me," Mrs. Stern protested, though her voice was weaker.

"We'll call you if they need you," Nin promised.

The woman blinked. "I suppose you're right, miss." As Adele and Nin led her to the door, she whispered, "Don't let that woman take the picture out of this house, miss, not until Miss Gold says so. It's not right."

"Yes," Adele said. "There's a lot that isn't right at the moment. Miss Branch will see you to your room."

Her friend treated Mrs. Stern with such delicacy the woman was completely calm as they left the kitchen.

Nurse Pegg collapsed in the chair. "That woman is truly a monster!"

"You did choose an inopportune time to collect on the will," Adele said gently.

"I've been in Los Angeles for the past three weeks," said the nurse. "I had no idea Mr. Marsh was dead."

"I'm surprised Mona didn't tell you," Adele said, "since you were her nurse in India."

"Mrs. Bridge and I weren't as chummy as Mrs. Stern seems to think," the woman stiffened. "I had a duty to perform, just as I had with her mother."

"You preformed it admirably, I'm sure," Adele complimented, "though I find it hard to imagine Mona needing a nurse."

"There were some extenuating circumstances, you understand," said Nurse Pegg.

"The climate, I should imagine," Adele said. "Tea or coffee?"

"What? Oh! Very generous of you. That woman wouldn't even offer me a cup of hemlock," she snorted. "Tea will do. Thank you, Miss Gossling. You're terribly kind."

Adele made the tea slowly. "I've always wanted to see India."

"It's certainly an experience."

"You didn't enjoy it," Adele guessed as she set the tea in front of her.

"Frankly, no," said Nurse Pegg. "I'm an Iowa farm girl, born and bred. I don't like traveling abroad."

"But Mona does," said Adele. "I understand she's quite fond of it."

"Yes, she did enjoy some things in India," said the woman. "She would have enjoyed others if —"

"If?" Adele persisted.

"Shall we say, her nerves had been steadier."

"Oh, I see," Adele said. "Well, her father died not long before they left, didn't he?"

"Yes, a year or so."

"I should think that would leave any woman melancholy," Adele said.

"Grief is not the same as melancholia, Miss Gossling," said the woman with authority. "One does not sink into the hole with grief. At least, not for long."

"Not physically, perhaps," Adele said, "but one finds it difficult to forget nonetheless." Her heart ached at that moment, remembering her own father.

"One can if one has healthy pursuits to occupy one's mind," said Nurse Pegg.

"And Mona didn't have those pursuits."

The woman was quiet for a moment, sipping her tea. "She had pursuits all right."

Adele inched forward in her chair. "Unhealthy ones?"

"That's a matter of context, Miss Gossling."

"How do you mean?"

"If the Bridges had been in America, Mona's interests would have been discouraged," said Nurse Pegg. "But in India —"

"Are you referring to her interest in exotic plant life?" Adele ventured.

"Oh, you know about it!" The woman looked surprised.

"Her brother told us," she said, "before he died."

"I see." The nurse's voice softened.

"Mona told us herself," she said. "You see, my friend —" she motioned toward Nin who had just entered the kitchen, "— has the same interest."

"I have every respect for a common interest in plants," said Nurse Pegg. "They have many vital medical benefits if one knows how to use them properly."

"I know how to use them properly," Nin snapped.

"I wasn't implying you didn't, miss," said the nurse. "I've heard good things about you from a few people. You're the daughter of Atha Branch, aren't you?"

Taken aback by this homage, Nin looked away.

"Mona's interest in plants isn't common," Adele agreed.

"It's entirely irregular," said the woman, "following those native women into the depths of the forests like that. And she attended medicine men in their rituals." The woman shuddered. "Once she persuaded me to come with her."

Adele studied the darkened look on the woman's face. "That frightened you, didn't it?"

For the first time, she saw a genuine look of pain cross the woman's face. "I tried speaking to Mr. Bridge, but he thought it was good she was taking an interest in life again."

"Because her life had stopped after the loss," Nin murmured.

"Loss?" Adele glanced at the nurse.

"I'm not at liberty to say anything about that." The woman looked at her watch. "Oh, dear, I'll be late for my train!"

"Back to Los Angeles?" Adele asked.

Nurse Pegg nodded. "I've a position at a children's hospital there. Rather a nice change." She smiled. "I like children. It's very sad to see them sick and, well, parents mean well, but sometimes they do more harm than good."

"I'm sure you do them good," Adele said as she and Nin followed the woman upstairs.

"I don't suppose Mr. Stern will drive me to the station," she said. "Afraid of his wife, I'm sure."

"Leave it to me," Adele reassured her. And, indeed, she convinced Mr. Stern to bring out the carriage, and he was civil enough to help Nurse Pegg into the back seat.

"Now is our chance." Adele pulled her friend into the house. "Mrs. Stern and Stephanie are in their rooms and Polly's at her work so we can go where we like."

"We don't need a lawyer's letter," Nin agreed.

They went quietly up the stairs and found Theo's room. Just as Adele predicted, Hatfield left no assistant deputy to guard it. The place was eerily tidy as Adele expected, remembering Theo's immaculate habits.

"We have the papers, anyway," Adele remarked as she produced a folder with Rebecca Gold, Attorney at Law on it from the desk in the corner. She examined them. "It looks like he had time to sign everything. He must have been excited about it. Look at how wavy his handwriting is."

"No typewriter," Nin observed. "That doesn't mean he didn't type the note elsewhere, though."

"And bring it home so he could kill himself here?" Adele asked. "I don't think that's very likely." Her eyes fell on the desk. "The blotter is clean. Odd, considering how unsteady his hand was signing these documents." She glanced around the desk.

"What strange ink. I don't think I've ever seen such a color." Her stationer's interest got the better of her and she reached for the bottle.

Her friend grabbed her wrist. "Don't touch it!"

Adele backed away. The bottle suddenly seemed menacing, like a bottle of blood.

Nin dropped down into a chair, her limbs rigid and her eyes wide.

"Are you all right, dear?" Adele peered at her friend.

"Yes, yes," she said. "I feel bitterness here. Bitterness of years seeping out like some poisonous gas."

"There is a smell of gas in here," Adele said, opening a window. "Perhaps Theo died that way."

"No, it wasn't gas," said Nin. "And the bitterness wasn't his either. It wasn't his!"

She gently led her out. "Hatfield and Jack were right when they said there was nothing disturbed in the room. We would have noticed it right away. Theo was a well-ordered man."

"In all things, not just his room," Nin agreed.

Adele nodded. "Remember how he was after his mother died? Every time he lost his equilibrium, he hid his face in his hands, as if he were trying to force the tears back. He wouldn't take them away until he regained his composure."

"That bottle," Nin's face became distorted. "We must get rid of it!"

Adele took two of Theo's handkerchiefs from the pile on the bureau and wrapped the bottle, putting it in her bag. "There now. No one will touch it."

The anxious look left Nin's face. "I don't know what came over me."

"I felt it too," said Adele. "There's something sinister about it."

Adele's eyes fell upon the door just to the left of the stairway. She tried the doorknob. It opened easily. "Mona's room."

"What of it?"

"Nothing," Adele said. "But it does make me curious."

"You're never curious unless you have a reason," her friend countered.

The room looked like nothing Adele had ever seen. Gone were fussy carpets, oversized chairs, and heavy drapes. The floor was made of brick and the furnishings were thinly covered with afghans with elaborate arabesque patterns. A large four-poster bed draped with red and gold stood in the center of the room, and small tables with bell-shaped lamps filled the wide space. Two windows were framed with arches and heavy drapes, reminding her of a cathedral.

Nin spoke before she did. "She thinks she's living in India again!"

"Mona appreciates all its beauties, including its architecture," Adele remarked.

"It's fantastic," Nin said, shivering.

"I think it's rather lovely," Adele said. "Different." She examined the two bureaus against the wall. "Both locked."

"She's had too much interference in her life," Nin said.

Adele looked at the bookcase. "She seems to have read a great deal about India."

"Before she left," Nin suggested.

"She kept the books even after she returned," Adele remarked. "They bring back memories for her, I suppose." She peered at the titles on the spines. "Some of these look quite academic for a woman who keeps insisting she had no education." She yanked a book of the bottom shelf, a few others tumbling to the floor. "Nin! Look at this."

Her friend joined her and together they read the cover: *Marvels of Plant Life in the Subcontinent.*

"I wouldn't consider that strange," Nin pointed out. "She has an entire book of specimens."

Adele looked through the page, which were very old and fragile. She studied the drawings and the Latin names. A slip of paper fell out and she picked it up to put it back. Then, she stiffened. *Atropa acuminata.*

"Nin, have you ever heard of this plant?" She showed her the paper.

Her friend shook her head. "I've heard of atropa, of course. A nightshade."

"Like the atropa belladonna," Adele said. "Lom told us."

"Yes, it's from the same family," said Nin.

Adele went through the book carefully and found the page with the name. The drawing showed a plant with flat leaves, bell-shaped flowers, and large berries.

"Do you think it's the same thing as the atropa belladonna?" Adele asked.

Her friend's eyes were so wide they looked nearly burst through her slim face. She was staring at the drawing as if it were going to eat her alive. She fell back against the bed. Adele rushed to her, afraid Nin was in a swoon, but she was only breathless. As she led her out of the room, she realized she had the answer to her question.

# CHAPTER 24

She arrived home late that night, as she took Nin back to her flat above her shop and stayed with her until she was tranquil again. Her friend kept lamenting her apologies but Adele waved them away.

It was past the dinner hour and both the men in the house were agitated. Tomas immediately brought her a tray of food that could have fed a family and the severe look in his eyes made her ready to eat the entire thing. Jackson stayed in the parlor while she ate but she could hear every move he made, from knocking tobacco in his pipe to shaking his paper. The sharp movements always indicated great annoyance.

She slipped into the parlor with a cup of coffee in her hand and sat down in her usual place on the couch next to the basket of lacework she never seemed to finish, peering at him. His handsome features were shaped like the statuette of Abraham Lincoln that once sat on a shelf in her father's study. She almost let out a laugh at how the lines in his cheekbones and jaw matched the stoic Lincoln. But she knew her brother would not find it amusing.

"I wasn't late from carelessness, Jack," she began.

"You were the one who insisted we have that telephone installed," he said with a sniff. "I've hardly seen you use it."

"I don't propose to call every time I'm late for dinner." She barked.

"If it wasn't carelessness, what was it, then?"

"Nin," she said. "She wasn't feeling well after we left the Marsh house."

"The Marsh house!" He threw his paper aside. "Why am I not surprised?"

"Because they called and told you we were there," Adele guessed.

"They had no need to," he said. "I suspected you wouldn't be able to keep away when we told you about Theo."

"You must admit, Jack, you and Hatfield didn't exactly do a thorough job," Adele ventured.

"Thorough job!" He snatched up his pipe. "The man committed suicide."

"Or so you thought," she reminded him. "I think it's safe to say suicide is highly unlikely now."

"Are you the judge and jury?" her brother asked in a snide tone.

"I'm not trying to be." Adele took his hand. "Look, Jack, we came across some very odd things in that house."

He eyed her. "I'm assuming you're not going to withhold evidence from the police this time?"

"Have I ever?" she snapped back.

Adele could almost feel Tomas holding his breath, making prayers for peace between brother and sister.

When Jackson spoke, his matter was warmer. "No, but you've delayed them often enough."

"I'm not delaying now," Adele said. "We found this in Theo's room." She extracted the bottle of ink. "Nin advised being very careful. She thinks it might be deadly."

"A bottle of ink?"

"If it is indeed ink," Adele said. "I rather think it's what killed Theo."

"You mean poison ink?"

"Or poison something else," she said. "I'm giving it to you to take to Dr. Rhodes for testing. Or perhaps Mr. Brethren would be better. I have a feeling he'll be more forthright and less self-centered."

He motioned for Tomas to bring him a small box from the kitchen and carefully laid the wrapped ink bottle inside it.

"We also looked in Mona's room," she said.

Jackson glared. "Even the police don't go poking their noses into someone's room unless they have a warrant."

"Nin and I are not the police," she retorted. "We had permission from Stephanie. Well, almost." She leaned forward. "You walk into her room and it feels like you're in India, Jack."

"That's hardly surprising," said her brother. "She and her husband spent many years there."

"One would think she would want to forget a place associated with tragedy."

Jackson put down his coffee cup. "What are you talking about? What tragedy?"

"No one seems to know," Adele said. "At least, no one I talked to."

He rose. "Well, well. Now I've something else to ask Mr. Bridge."

"You're going to see him?" Adele glanced at him.

"Hatfield is sending me to the mill to speak with him," said Jackson. "After what you told us about him, he thinks it's worth questioning him." He folded the paper carefully and threw it away in the trash, earning a grin from Tomas. "I'm almost afraid to ask what your plans are for the day."

"I have a business, Jack," Adele reminded him.

"You can't believe I think for a moment that's the only thing on your mind."

"Shall we say, I might satisfy a curiosity?" Adele asked.

He grumbled. "Circle talk." But he knew better than to ask questions.

~~~~~

Adele collected her friend the next morning. "We're going to see Rebecca."

"What for?"

"To get a look at a will," Adele said.

"Thea's will?" Nin locked her front door.

"No, dear," said Adele. "The husband's, not the wife's."

Her friend gave her a questioning look.

"The missing link to these deaths lies with Gregory Marsh's will, I think," Adele said. "It's a feeling."

"One ought never to ignore a feeling," Nin agreed.

They reached Rebecca's office just as she was putting up the OPEN sign.

"You look well recovered from yesterday," Adele said, pressing her hand.

"I suppose so," said her friend. Adele could see she was still a little wan, but her voice was more assured. "Did you find anything in Theo's room?"

"A bottle of poisoned ink!" Nin shivered.

"We don't know that yet," Adele reminded her, "but it did seem out of place. I gave it to Jack this morning so the police can examine it."

"Do you mean to tell me Theo was poisoned with ink?" Rebecca stared at her.

"It's possible." Adele hung her parasol on the back of a chair.

"Incredible!" Rebecca leaned against her desk. "Why on earth would someone want to poison him?"

"Because they're next in line when he dies," Nin said. "It happens all the time."

"Please, Miss Branch." The lawyer flinched.
~~~~~

"Nevertheless, wills seem to be important to the Marshes," Adele remarked.

"They are in most families of considerable means," said Rebecca. "I've seen it too often. Battles, fights, relationships ruined." She sighed. "Sometimes I wish all families had only one child."

"It would make things much simpler." Adele smiled. "We were thinking if we could see Gregory Marsh's will, it might shed some light on a few things."

"What light could a will drawn up twenty-two years ago shed?" Rebecca asked.

"It gives us a family history." Adele stood her ground.

The woman's hands fell into her lap. "Yes, I suppose you're right."

"And it may prevent future family deaths," Adele said softly. "That's our main concern now."

Rebecca stared at her. "Do you really think that's likely?"

"I don't know," Adele said. "We're merely exploring possibilities."

"Do you have the will?" Nin asked.

"I didn't draw it up, of course," said Rebecca. "I wasn't even here when Gregory died. I've a copy of it, though. Thea gave it to me."

"May we see it?" Adele asked.

The woman didn't hesitate as she had with Thea's will. She ambled over to the filing cabinet and pulled the "M" file, handing it to Adele.

The language of the will was closely adherent to the sort of stiff, technical wording Adele heard from her father when he told her about his cases. Nin, reading over her shoulder, quickly gave up. Adele, well trained in legal language, could decipher the main points.

"Rather wooden, isn't it?" she remarked as she folded it up and handed it to Rebecca.

Rebecca smiled. "Lightfoot & Waverly Law are that way. Never a word out of place."

"Nor a word to implicate wrongdoing on their part," Adele said. "It's a good thing I'm a lawyer's daughter." She crossed her legs. "So Marsh Lumber Mill really belonged to Thea upon his death."

Rebecca nodded. "It was rather a surprise, considering Gregory's opinion of women and business," she said. "Those were Thea's words, not mine."

"I'm sure he knew she would leave it in the hands of her son," Adele pointed out.

"So she did," said Rebecca.

"She trusted Theo completely," Adele guessed.

"And he did right by her," Rebecca insisted. "I only hope Forrest and William will continue now that Theo —" She bit her lip, tears welling in her eyes.

Adele pressed her hand. "I can see why Mona was upset when the will was read."

"Yes, she was upset," Rebecca said.

"'The business goes to Theodora Marsh and, upon her death, Theodore Marsh and Forrest Marsh.' No mention of Mona at all."

"Mona received a generous dowry when her father died."

"I see no mention of that either."

"It was Thea's doing," Rebecca admitted. "Gregory spoke to her about it when Mona turned eighteen but with one thing and another, he never set it up properly."

"So it was Mona's mother who gave her the dowry?" Adele asked.

"Tyrants always hold all the cards until the very end," Nin said sourly.

Rebecca sighed. "I wouldn't have put it that way, but I suppose you're right."

"Mona really got nothing from the will." Adele rose and wandered to the front windows. The street was busy with the shopping hour at its peak. A pallor of gray seeped into the sky but there was no threat of rain.

"Gregory didn't feel an unmarried woman needed material things," said Rebecca.

"Not even mementoes, it seems." Adele pressed her hand to her chest where underneath was buried the gold magnifying glass her father left her.

"Gregory wasn't a sentimental man," Rebecca remarked. "I don't think Mona wanted mementoes."

Adele returned to her chair. "She wanted something much more tangible."

Rebecca put away her purse. "You know about the lawsuit, then."

"Lawsuit?" Adele threw a glance at Nin. "We heard nothing of a lawsuit."

Rebecca rubbed at a smudge of ink on her desk. "It wasn't a very pleasant experience for Theo or the rest of the family."

"What happened?"

Rebecca shrugged. "I never asked Thea about the details, but I understood Mona took the family to court. Well, she took her and Theo to court. Forrest was just a boy."

"I admire her gumption," Adele said.

Rebecca stared at her. "You can't be serious, Adele."

"It takes gumption for a woman to demand what is rightfully hers," Adele insisted.

"She tried to break the will," Rebecca said. "That I do know. I've been to enough court cases to know when someone tries to break a will, it leaves a bitter air in the family no one can overlook."

"They've hated one another from the beginning," Nin said.

"That's not true, Miss Branch," Rebecca insisted. "I remember how pleasant it was going to play in the house. Gregory wasn't there and it was like a holiday. Thea was very different then. She used to play chase with us in the garden. And Mona and Theo talked as if they were best friends."

"Then the monster of tyranny took over," Adele said.

"It always does when it comes from the grave." Nin sighed.

Rather than head back to the stationery shop, Adele turned to the road that led into the prominent residences of Arrojo.

Nin followed her. "You feel sorry for her, don't you?"

"Who?"

"Mona Bridge," she said.

"Don't you?" Adele asked. "She was treated badly by her father. If a father can't believe in his daughter's right to live her own life, everything follows."

"Even her own sense of justice," Nin murmured.

Adele took her friend's arm. "We must know what that lawsuit was about and what happened. I feel it might be important."

"How can a lawsuit twenty years ago be a motive for murder now?" Nin eyed her.

"I don't know that it is," Adele said. "I just feel it's important."

"Where do we go to find out?"

"To the highest source of information about this town," Adele declared.

"Not Mrs. Faderman." Nin winced.

Adele smiled. "We go one better."

They arrived at Mrs. Lynn's house just as the early afternoon set in. Mrs. Lynn lived in a large house like the other ladies but hers looked more modest and inviting. The woman sat with her lunch on the veranda, a table set for four but the other three places cleared. Her small, wrinkled face lit up when she saw them, and she waved, turning to say a few words to the maid, who disappeared inside the house.

"How kind of you!" She gestured to the table. "Everyone ate their lunch and left me as if a bear were chasing them!" Her three children were, Adele knew, the sort eager to get in with the activities taken up by Vanessa and Percy Faderman and their crowd so Adele imagined they had rushed out to some social activity.

"They oughtn't to leave you alone in this weather," Nin said kindly as she pulled the shawl half fallen on the chair over the woman's shoulders. The breeze was picking up as it usually did at that hour, raking through her loose hair.

"Amanda takes very good care of me." She smiled. And indeed, the maid who had gone into the house came out with two coffee cups and a sweater hanging over her arm which she gladly handed to Nin.

"It's lucky we decided to visit," Adele said.

"It's good to have visitors when there's been a tragedy," said the woman in a small voice. "We've just heard about Mr. Marsh. Terrible!"

"Mrs. Faderman is already gathering the ladies, I expect," Adele said.

"It's none of her business," Nin growled.

"She only has the town's interests at heart, Miss Branch, truly," said Mrs. Lynn. "It's always been Irene's way to bring things out into the open. She can't help it if other ladies gossip."

Adele hid a smile. "No, she can't. Some things ought to be brought out into the open."

"Just like the last time," Mrs Lynn lamented, the shawl rolling off her thin shoulders.

"You said that before, Mrs. Lynn."

"Did I?"

"At the inquest for Thea Marsh's death." Adele leaned forward and took the woman's hands. "You were referring to Mona's lawsuit, weren't you?"

"Oh, that's all forgotten now," the woman insisted.

"Mrs. Cricket thought it might be instructive for us to know about it," Nin reminded her. "She said so."

"Gregory ought to have been more considerate!"

"I agree," said Adele. "We've seen his will."

"Oh!"

"It's all right," Nin assured her. "Miss Gold showed it to us."

"Mr. Marsh's lawyer," Adele supplied when the older woman looked confused.

"Yes, such a bright young lady, isn't she?" She sighed.

"I'm sure it was no surprise at the time," Adele said.

"Oh, we all knew Theo would get the business," said Mrs. Lynn. "Thea knew so little about it and Forrest was so young."

"And Mona?" Adele asked.

"Well, she was a lady," Mrs. Lynn said. "One would hardly expect —"

"Yes, in those times, one would hardly expect." Adele nodded. "What Mrs. Cricket said was true, wasn't it?"

"I can't remember what Belinda said." The woman blinked.

Adele patted her arm. "Young ladies aren't so fragile these days, you know, Mrs. Lynn."

"It was all so unpleasant!" She squirmed in her chair.

"The past isn't as unpleasant when it's in the past," Nin said.

"But will it stay in the past? That's the question, Miss Branch."

"If we can manage it, we will," Adele promised. "Won't you tell us what happened?"

"Goodness, can it really matter now?" the woman lamented.

"Remember there were suspicious circumstances surrounding Thea's death," Adele persisted. "We still don't know what happened."

"Oh, but you don't think —" The woman jumped.

"I don't think anything, Mrs. Lynn," Adele said. "But the family history might be important."

The woman sighed. "Well, I suppose you'll find it out anyway. It was in all the local papers at the time."

"Including the *Arrojo Courier*?" Adele asked.

The woman nodded. "I don't know much about it, but it had something to do with the will. I remember Mona saying something about 'fair division of assets' or something rather official-sounding."

"The rumors must have been flying for weeks," Nin said.

"Oh, they were," said Mrs. Lynn. "Not that the papers were any help. Miss Grace's brothers were running the *Arrojo Courier* then." She flinched, for it was well known Missy Grace's brothers believed in the then-new practice of yellow journalism.

"I gather Mona was contesting the will," Adele probed. "From what she told you all at Mrs. Leighton's engagement party, she wanted something to do with the business."

"She wanted to be a part of it," said Mrs. Lynn. "Own shares, I think."

"So she took Thea to court," Adele said.

"She took all of them to court," said Mrs. Lynn, her face paling. "Not Forrest, of course, he was too young."

"They weren't happy, I should imagine," Adele said.

"They weren't angry either."

"Indeed?"

"They were grieving Gregory's loss, you see," she said. "He was so — well, the head of the family. When the head of the family is gone, a family becomes like a boat sailing on an aimless voyage." She slipped a handkerchief out of her pocket and dabbed her eyes. "I know."

"Yes," Adele said softly. "I know too." She thought of the aimlessness that had pursued her and her brother when her father died.

"The judge ruled in their favor?" Nin asked.

"The newspapers said he threw the case out of court," Mrs. Lynn said. "He said it was a disgrace to even bring it to his attention. How he chided Mona for being an ungrateful daughter. The poor dear." Suddenly, her hands grasped the arms of the wicker chair and she slid to the edge of her seat.

"Are you all right, dear?" Adele glanced at the maid, who

appeared in the doorway, and the woman, taking the cue, brought a glass of water to the table. "Here, drink this."

"I was only thinking —"

"Yes?"

She looked at Adele with wide eyes. "Do you think that's why she married William? It must have been!"

Adele realized Mrs. Lynn's hazy mind was following its own path, and she went on with a cautious tone, "I really can't say."

"She married William right after that," the woman continued. "Such a nice young man, he was. Always chasing her about. Said he would marry her even if she didn't have a penny. That's love for sure."

"Yes, that's love." Adele thought of the couple she witnessed the first day at Marsh house and the way Mona had drawn back from her husband's comforting arm. "Perhaps she married him because he was going to India."

"She wanted to get away." Nin nodded, her voice distant, as it became sometimes when she was speaking from her visions. "The disappointment and pain were too much for her."

"She was terribly hurt," said Mrs. Lynn. "Not that she ever said anything." The woman looked confused. "She never said anything about anything after she lost the lawsuit."

"The failure silenced whatever little voice she had," Adele murmured. She thought about the women she had grown up with and how lively some had been only to become complacent and quiet when they realized their pluck had no place in their future as a lady. "She must have been anxious to get away from here."

"They went to India right away," Mrs. Lynn said. "He wasn't to go until October but they got married in March dead went. It all makes sense now." She looked at Adele. "We thought it was so sudden at the time. Only a few days after, the paper said Mona had come to her senses and was now Mrs. William Bridge."

"I'm sure it was best thing for Mona," Adele said kindly, "given her bitter disappointment."

"Yes," Nin echoed. "The best thing for both of them."

"She ought to have gotten the house," Mrs. Lynn insisted. "Thea didn't need it. She could have moved to a smaller place. She didn't give many parties or soirees or things of that nature. Gregory hated social life. He did what he had to do for his business and that's all."

"She had to keep the house," Adele murmured. "For the others."

"She succeeded in keeping Theo from marrying," Nin remarked.

"He was always a mother's son," Mrs. Lynn agreed. "I suppose when Miss Gold went east — oh, I beg your pardon!" She put her hand over her mouth.

"It's alright, Mrs. Lynn," Adele said with a small smile.

"We know about Rebecca being sweet on him," Nin added.

"I suppose he felt he had enough on his shoulders without a wife," Mrs. Lynn said. "Everyone expected the mill to prosper in his hands."

"It was a big responsibility," Adele mused. "Gregory Marsh had it all planned for his children: Theo and Forrest in the business, Mona in marriage."

"I don't think he had much regard for her headstrong ways," the older woman agreed.

"Men are afraid of headstrong women," Nin snorted. "They know how to fight back."

"They didn't fight back then, Miss Branch," said Mrs. Lynn. "The papers said —" She stopped, paying with the fringes on the shawl that had slipped down her shoulders again.

"What did they say?" Adele asked.

"They said the lawsuit couldn't possibly have been Mona's idea," said the woman.

"You mean someone else was pulling the strings?" Nin asked.

"If you want to put it that way, dear," said Mrs. Lynn.

"William Bridge," Adele guessed.

"But it couldn't have been!" The woman's forehead wrinkled. "He was such a nice young man."

"Even nice young men have ambitions," Adele said softly.

"I suppose that's true," Mrs. Lynn admitted. "William came from, well, not very bright prospects."

"I find it hard to believe Mona would be influenced by anyone," Adele said.

"Young ladies were very influenced back then, Miss Gossling." The woman sighed. "Not like today when you do what you like. Oh, I think it's grand!"

The sparkle in her eye when she said this made both Adele and Nin laugh.

# CHAPTER 25

In the morning, Adele didn't go to her shop right away. She waited in the short line crowding Rutledge Bakery, the scent of yeast and sugar making her head spin. She bought sweet buns and oatmeal cookies and struggled with the doorknob of the office of the *Arrojo Courier* as she balanced the bags in her hands so as not to crush the buns.

Missy Grace had taken an assistant that summer, a rather harried girl of fifteen by the name of Carla with horse-like features and a dim-witted sense of the world. The girl had her back to the door and didn't pay much attention to the fiddling and creaking going on behind her until Adele was inside the office. Missy came out of the back room, looking rather undone as usual with pins slipping out of her hair, ink on her sleeves, and her shirtwaist collar shifted a little more to one side.

She rushed to help Adele, crooning over the buns. "I haven't had breakfast yet. I was going to send Carla out for something." She glared at the girl who was now all attention, her lips in a small "O" like a fish.

"Wrestling with the evening edition, no doubt." Adele smiled as she found an empty chair in the cluttered office.

"A very thin edition," Missy admitted. "Not much going on after yesterday's splash about Theodore Marsh's death."

"The family is in mourning," Adele reminded her.

"There is still a murder case attached to it." Missy leaned forward. "Anything for this evening's paper?"

"Not in front of the child," Adele said dryly. Carla drew back with the petulant glance of her age.

"Carla, will you please go in the back and reset the type?" Missy asked in a tone of tried patience. "We don't want to risk printing the same paper twice this afternoon."

"You wouldn't do that, Miss Grace," said the girl.

Missy smiled. "Sometimes I wonder if I don't leave my head in the printing press. Go do it, please."

The girl saluted and disappeared.

"She is loyal," Adele admitted.

"But not the brightest porch light on the block, as my mother would say," Missy said. "Well?"

"I expect if you go down to the station and catch Hatfield in one of his good moods, he might tell you about a certain bottle of ink we found in Theo's room," Adele said. "I can't say more than that."

"Splendid!" Missy's eyes brightened.

Adele leaned against her parasol. "And now, Missy, you might do something for me."

"I'm always at your disposal." Missy bowed. "We ladies of commerce must support one another."

"This isn't about business," Adele said. "It's about the law."

"Oh?"

"A lawsuit, to be more exact. One that occurred twenty or so years ago."

"In Arrojo?" Missy raised her eyebrows. "The town that prides itself on its clean-minded citizens?"

Adele smiled. "And one brought on by a woman, no less."

Missy leaned against one of the empty desks in the office. "It does sound familiar."

"You would have been a child at the time."

"So would you," she countered. "Why this interest?"

"It was the Mona Marsh lawsuit," Adele said shortly.

Missy's eyes widened. "Good Lord! Why didn't I think of it before? I ought to have, with all the flying tongues going about."

"Gossip is easily forgotten in this town," Adele said dryly.

"You're welcome to the archives, of course," said the newspaperwoman. "I remember my father and mother speaking of it at the time. Dad must have published something about it in the *Courier*."

"I would rather think it was more in your brothers' line than his," Adele remarked.

"They wanted to dredge it up again when Mona and her husband came back from India, as a matter of fact."

"And your father wouldn't let them so they didn't," Adele said with a nod of approval.

"I won't bring it up either," said Missy in a firm voice. "Unless, of course, it has something to do with the recent deaths."

"I don't know that it does," Adele said. "Say it's merely my own personal curiosity."

"Well, then, you must take your own personal curiosity down to the archive room." Missy smiled and fingered the brown paper bags. "While I shall indulge in my little feast, and Carla will clank away at the printing press, probably losing a few of the letters in the bargain."

Adele laughed and waved as she descended the stairway to the room underneath the office. Missy's father had been a prudent man and kept copies of all the newspapers the *Courier* had ever printed in neat boxes with tight lids marked with the dates. So it was easy for her to find the boxes from 1882, the year of Gregory Marsh's death.

She found no mention of the lawsuit there but then realized it must have appeared the following year and, sure enough, she found what she was looking for. The papers themselves were gray and the print smudged but she was able to make out portions that began with Mona's "rather startling" announcement at the engagement party of Renee Coldwell and Seamus Leighton about "taking her place at the Marsh Lumber Mill" in the wake of her father Gregory Marsh's death and his "broad-minded view of family obligation." Adele marveled at how accurate Mrs. Lynn's memory had been regarding Mona's exact words.

In the next edition of the paper, the story took center stage:

*Miss Mona Marsh, daughter of the late Gregory Marsh of Rosa Gris, has filed a lawsuit against her mother Theodora Marsh to break the will of the late Gregory Marsh which leaves the Marsh Lumber Mill entirely to her mother. Miss Marsh stated she had a right as the second child in the Marsh family to a third of the family business. "I am only out for my share," she stated. "I have no ill will against my mother or my brothers." The trial will take place on the twentieth of September.*

Adele sifted through the newspapers dated that year in late September but was surprised to find only a few words about the trial, as if Christopher Grace, Missy's father, lost interest in it or perhaps his readers decided a young woman's attempt to gain access to the family business was less than salacious news. She caught a few items here and there and one insinuated "Perhaps Miss Marsh's sudden interest in the Marsh Lumber Mill has to do with the attentions of Mr. William Bridge." Beyond this, there was nothing of the trial details.

It was only in an early October edition that Adele found the Marsh trial mentioned one more time:

*After two weeks of battling the courts, Gregory Marsh of Marsh Lumber Mill can finally rest in peace. Judge Frederick Corland ruled Miss Mona Marsh's case had no merit, and the idea that a young lady of her age and rank should "bring forth such a sordid lawsuit" was nothing short of "disgraceful and indecent." He advised Miss Marsh to "count her blessings and take her place in society as every young lady should." Miss Marsh refused to comment as she left the courthouse, but it seems she has taken Judge Corland's advice to heart. Later that same day, this editor was told of the engagement of Miss Mona Marsh to Mr. William Bridge.*

Adele crushed the paper to her chest, inhaling the faint smell of ink. She envisioned Mona's face as the judge delivered his sanctimonious speech and the snickering throughout the courtroom. She pictured a desperate young woman, her hopes shattered, accepting a proposal of marriage as the only means of regaining her dignity.

Missy appeared on the stairs, brushing a hanging cobweb out of her face. "Remind me to send that assistant of mine down with a broom."

"This place could use a good dusting." Adele smiled as she closed the box and shoved it back into its corner.

Missy watched her. "I take it from the angry look on your face you found what you were looking for."

"Your father might not have been sensational," Adele said sharply, "but he had little sympathy for Mona nonetheless."

"If you mean he wasn't entirely an objective reporter, you're right," Missy admitted.

Adele followed her up the stairs with her arm around the woman's shoulders. "I'm sorry. It was rude of me to speak about your father like that."

"But true nonetheless," said Missy. "What did you find out about the lawsuit?"

"The judge called her disgraceful and indecent," Adele said in a bitter tone.

"No doubt Dad agreed with him," Missy guessed.

"I don't know about that," Adele said.

"I do." Her friend grimaced. "I don't have to read what he wrote to know that."

"I realize it was twenty years ago." Adele sighed. "It's unfair just the same."

"Perhaps it would have been better if he had erred on the side of sensationalism like my brothers wanted him to," Missy remarked. "People can disregard sensationalism. Serious editorials are different."

"If I were in her shoes, I wouldn't forgive and forget very easily," Adele murmured. "Yet I wonder how far she would go."

"You mean with the lawsuit?" Missy studied her.

Adele smiled. "Thank you for letting me see these."

She went to her shop, but her mind was absorbed with what she had read. Nin slipped in with a cup of tea which eased a little of the sadness in Adele's heart.

"Nin," she said, "we need to make a call."

"To whom?" asked her friend.

"The Marsh family," she said.

"I don't quite follow."

"Mrs. Jessel came in to buy some envelopes and told me Mona returned from San Francisco." She put on her hat. "I think we ought to go and see her."

"You mean throw accusations at her?" Nin looked at her shrewdly.

"Nothing of the kind," Adele insisted. "We're going to console her for the loss of her brother."

They reached the house as the sun was starting to set. She and Nin found Mona sitting alone in the parlor doing lacework. Her bony figure looked sharp against the black dress with white highlighting the sleeves and collar. Her face looked haggard but composed.

"It's kind of you to come," she said with a wan smile.

"It's good you're here," Adele remarked as she settled on the couch. Nin chose a backless chair nearby instead of the floor. "I'm sure your brother appreciates it."

"It was so — unexpected," Mona said.

"Where's your sister-in-law?" Nin asked. "Still sleeping?"

Mona's voice took on a slight edge. "I have no idea where Stephanie is or what she's doing."

"You must be rather lonely here," Adele said.

"I'm used to it," said the woman. "I've been used to it for most of my life."

"Not in India, I imagine," said Adele. "I've heard the cities are quite crowded there, and it's not uncommon to have people attending you."

"If you mean servants, we couldn't afford it," she said. "We did have a few women come in for a short time. I was ill, you see."

"I'm sorry to hear that." Adele accepted the coffee Mrs. Stern handed her.

"I take it neither of you have ever been there?" Mona asked.

"Regrettably, I've done very little traveling," said Adele.

"I prefer my feet firmly planted in places I know," Nin declared.

Mona gave a rueful look. "When one is used to locked doors, Miss Branch, one relishes the chance to explore places where no doors are locked."

"Is that why you married your husband?" Nin asked in her brutally honest way, "because he was going to India?"

Mona went back to her needlework, a dispassionate look on her face. "William was very attentive. Other men were too in those days, but for the wrong reasons."

"He loves you," Adele said softly.

"I suppose he did," she said.

"And he helped you through a difficult time," she added.

"Difficult time?" The woman blinked.

"I was referring to the lawsuit," Adele said.

"Oh, yes." The woman's hands hesitated on the needles. "I almost forgot about that."

"Forgot about taking your mother to court?" Nin eyed her.

"I never saw it that way, Miss Branch," Mona said. "I was trying to get what I thought was rightfully mine."

"And it was rightfully yours," Adele said in a firm voice, "even if it wasn't what your father wished."

Mona blinked. "I'm surprised you know so much about it, Adele."

"She looked at the newspapers," Nin said.

The woman's face grew red. "What you must think of me!"

"I didn't read the yellow journalists," Adele assured her. "I only read the *Arrojo Courier*."

"I made a mistake," the woman said shortly.

"I don't think you made a mistake," Adele insisted.

"Call it fighting a losing battle, then." Her voice grew ragged. "I had ideas then. I have since learned my lesson."

The woman did not look at her but kept her eyes on the lace. Her hands moved sharply, jerking the needle around as they created the lace pattern. Adele watched the points of the small stars emerge, perfectly shaped.

"I've upset you," Adele said softly. "I'm sorry."

A small smile spread on her lips, her eyes piercing. "You were only trying to make conversation."

"The situation with the mill will change now," Adele ventured.

"You mean because my brother is dead, I might get my chance?" Mona gave her a crooked smile. "Whatever thoughts I had about that have been dead for some time. I shall be quite content to be the Marsh house chatelaine."

"You've already begun to change a few things," Adele observed, looking around. Some of the furniture had been taken out, and a few more modern paintings were on the wall. She also noted there were no black mourning curtains and curtains were drawn with the windows open.

"Theo would have thought it inappropriate," Mona said ruefully. "He would have liked things to be just as they were since my father lived here. But things must change, mustn't they?"

"If they're agreeable changes, they must." Adele felt alarm at the sudden desperate tone in the woman's voice.

"Theo was rather finicky, wasn't he?" Nin asked.

To Adele's surprise, Mona threw her head back and laughed. It was the first time she had seen real mirth in the woman's face. The tightly drawn face, when slackened, revealed a pretty countenance. Adele could see what Mrs. Lynn meant when she said Mona had been so alive in her youth.

"My friend sometimes has a bold way of putting things," she said, though she didn't feel apologetic about it.

"I don't think Mona is offended," Nin protested. "Are you?"

"Quite the contrary," said the woman, "I admire people who can speak their minds without worrying about what others think."

Nin became embarrassed as she usually did when people complimented her. She blushed furiously and looked away.

"He was a little painstaking, but always kind and thoughtful," Adele said gently.

"Yes, he was," said Mona. "I don't want you to think I didn't love my brother. I know what he went through with my father's tyranny and my mother's suffocation. I know exactly what he went through."

"None of you had it easy," Adele remarked.

"You're very understanding." The woman patted her hand. "I don't blame him because we had to form alliances."

"Us against them," Adele murmured. "Forrest told us about that."

"I suppose all families form alliances," Mona mused.

"Theo ought to have married Rebecca," Nin declared. "It would have broken the chain."

"Rebecca was always a dear," Mona said. "I don't know what we would have done without her."

Nin leaned toward Adele and said in a harsh whisper, "She's lying!"

Adele's respect for her friend's sudden instincts deepened. "Forgive me for saying so, but it doesn't seem as if she feels the same way."

"You mean the scene when Theo came home?" Mona asked. "That was my fault. I was surprised to see him home, even shocked. I don't take surprises very well, and I lash out at those who don't deserve it."

"You ought to apologize to her," Nin said.

"I shall at the first opportunity," the woman promised. "She's coming tomorrow to see if she can find anything among Theo's papers. I'll mend my broken fence with her then."

"Very admirable of you." Adele fingered the cookie crumbs in her saucer.

"I'm very glad now Mother took her on as her lawyer."

"What do you mean, 'now'?" Adele asked.

Mona went back to her lacework, her head bent as she spoke so her voice was almost muffed. "You must understand my mother had very conventional ideas. It was a shock to all of us when she announced a woman was taking care of her legal affairs."

"I wouldn't think it would be so surprising," Adele said. "Rebecca told us she had been a family friend for a long time."

"She was *my* friend, really," Mona said in a pointed voice. "The only one I ever had."

"That wasn't what she told us," Nin said.

"She was the only real friend I had," the woman repeated.

"Rebecca is a fine lawyer," Adele insisted.

"Oh, yes!" Mona put down her lacework. "I know how hard she studied. When we were in school, I used to invite her with us to picnics and things, but she was always too busy with her studies."

"I can't quite imagine Rebecca being very keen on social activities," Adele remarked. "She struck me as a rather serious person."

"A little too serious," Mona agreed. "I suppose every woman has her preoccupation."

"You had yours in India, we heard," Adele said, crossing her legs. "The forest interested you very deeply."

A cold look appeared in the woman's eyes. "I've always been interested in plant life, Adele. So was Theo."

"Yes, he told us," said Adele.

"I can imagine what he told you." Her voice rose a little. "He thought I was mad!"

"He did say he was rather surprised when he visited you in Bangor."

"He said you showed unnatural ambitions," Nin said.

The lacework slipped from her lap. "He said that?"

"His words sounded like they came from someone else," Adele said quickly. "Your father, perhaps, used that term when speaking of women with interests he felt were inappropriate for them."

"Yes, now that I think of it, Father did speak about women in that way." She bent down to pick up the lacework and it slipped from her fingers. She tried to grab it one more time but it escaped her again. Adele picked it up, handing it to her.

"He did say your interest in plant life was a little unusual," Adele continued.

"I don't see why," she snapped. "His interest in the plant life never disturbed anyone."

"Men's interests rarely do," Nin said, "because they belong to men."

"You're so right, Miss Branch," Mona said.

"Your interest in plant life was quite different from his, wasn't it?" Adele asked.

"How do you mean?"

"You seem as taken by exotic plant life as your mother was with her exotic teas."

"That was different," she insisted. "Mother never traveled because my father didn't like it."

"Yes, she told me," Adele said.

"I suppose she thought she could experience another place in a teacup," Mona lamented.

"One can get much out of a teacup," Nin insisted.

"If one knows how," Mona agreed, "like you and I. We both respect the potency of plants, like the sage women." She smiled.

"So many sage women are mistaken for witches," Nin murmured. A shadow fell over her face.

"But we don't care what others think of us, do we?" She touched Nin's hand. "I'll come by your shop sometime and we can exchange knowledge."

Nin smiled, but it was clear to Adele the smile was forced.

$\mathcal{A}$dele could hardly wait to tell her brother about her visit the next morning, but he took his time coming to breakfast.

"You were up late last night," she observed, pouring him coffee.

"I had reports to file," he said. "Murder creates a lot of paperwork."

"I'm sure the Marshes didn't intend to make so much work for the police," Adele said dryly.

"Hatfield and I paid Mr. Bridge a visit at the mill yesterday."

Adele glanced at him. "Did you indeed?"

He eyed her. "I'll tell you what we found if you tell me what you and Miss Branch found in Mrs. Bridge's room other than the ink."

"How on earth did you know we found something else?" She stopped eating.

"There isn't much we don't know about, dear sister," Jackson said.

"You mean you have your spies!" Adele dropped her fork.

"When a man has a sister always nosing about —"

"We were not nosing about," Adele said crossly. "We were looking for evidence."

"And you found it."

"All right. Yes, we did." She told him about the book in Mona's room.

"That's hardly evidence, Del," he said as he finished off the last of the toast.

"A book marked with the same poisonous plant that killed Thea?" Adele gave him an incredulous look. "You don't find that significant?"

"You said yourself they're not the same," Jackson pointed out. "The one in the book has a different name than the one Mr. Brethren gave Theo."

"Nin said they're the same family."

"Perhaps," he said. "It might all be a coincidence. It wouldn't be unusual for someone write down the name of something they're particularly interested in on a slip of paper to remind themselves to look into it further."

"Everyone admits Mona's interest in plants is bizarre," Adele insisted. "Theo said it, and so did Nurse Pegg."

Jackson put down his coffee cup. "So you know Theodora Marsh's nurse was also Mrs. Bridge's?"

Adele nodded. "Apparently Mona had some sort of trouble in India and needed one."

"Yes, we know all about that," said Jackson.

She stared at him. "Do you?"

"Mr. Bridge was quite forthright about his marriage," he said. "He and his wife have been estranged for some time."

"I'm not sure I blame him," Adele remarked. "Mona didn't seem quite the affectionate type. Though she does all the right things."

"I don't follow," her brother said.

"No, you wouldn't," she said softly. "I've seen it dozens of times. Women who fight their own natures to keep their place in marriage and society, making everything look pretty on the outside when they're torn apart on the inside."

"Patmore's 'Angel In The House,'" Jackson suggested.

She frowned. "I always hated that poem."

"Mother liked it," he said quietly. "She must have read it to me a dozen times."

"I'm lucky she never read it to me," Adele said roughly. "I would have thrown it into the fire."

Her brother laughed.

"What did William say was wrong with his wife?" Adele asked.

"Didn't Nurse Pegg tell you?"

"She was not at liberty to say." Adele couldn't hide her annoyance.

"She knows her job." Jackson nodded. "The Bridges had a child not long after they arrived in India, a little boy, but the child died."

"Oh, how horrible!" Adele shuddered.

"Some kind of fever, I believe. Mr. Bridge said they never found out what it was."

"That would make any woman sink into melancholia," Adele said.

Jackson folded the linen napkin. "That wasn't why she needed a nurse."

"Oh?"

"According to Mr. Bridge, the birth of the child set her on the downward spiral, not his death. She could hardly get out of bed and was very agitated when she did so. He got so worried he sent for an American nurse."

"It must have been very difficult for him," she said softly.

"After the child was born, his wife was more interested in leaving the nanny to care for him than she was having the nurse care for her," he remarked.

"How old was the child when he died?"

"Two years and four months," Jackson said. "Mr. Bridge remembered exactly."

"Naturally, he would," Adele said softly.

"He said Mrs. Bridge was relieved."

"Men always see what they want to see when a woman doesn't behave as they think she should," Adele growled.

"He said she was almost light-hearted after it, Del," he defended. "One can hardly mistake that."

"I assume it was then he began seeing other women?" She eyed him. "He did see other women, didn't he?"

"I told you he was forthright," Jackson said. "He admits to seeing a woman named Dorothy Reynolds — he calls her Dot — for over a year now."

"He defended himself, no doubt," Adele snarled.

"He didn't defend anything, Del," he insisted. "Try to see it from his point of view. A woman he adored marries him to compensate for a disappointment —"

"You mean losing a lawsuit that might have made him one-third owner of Marsh Lumber Mill," Adele said.

"You know about that too?" He stared at her.

"I read the newspaper accounts of the trial, and Nin and I spoke to Mrs. Lynn."

"He said he never had any interest in the mill," Jackson insisted.

"*He* said?"

"He was sincere, Del. He never even wanted the management position he has now, but Mona wanted him to take it, so he did. He thought it would be a new start for them."

"You're rather sympathetic, aren't you?" Adele eyed him.

"Just as you're sympathetic to Mrs. Bridge," he countered. "I can imagine your reaction when you read about her losing the lawsuit."

She could not deny this. "William has no ambition even now that he is co-owner of the mill?"

"His ambition was always to seek adventure," said Jackson. "That's why he took the position in India. He wanted to see something of the world. He thought Mona would be as enthusiastic as he was. She was, it seems, much more adventurous in her youth."

"But a man must cease to be a nomad and establish roots sometime," Adele argued, "especially when he has a wife and child."

"There was no child," he pointed out. "The poor boy died."

She sighed. "And now I'm supposed to feel sorry for him because he's carrying on with another woman?"

"They're not carrying on," said her brother severely. "He loves her."

"Loves her!"

Jackson leaned forward. "You weren't there, Del. The way he spoke of her with such tenderness and respect. He wants to marry her, but he's been waiting for the right moment."

"Is there a right moment to tell a woman you've been married to for twenty years that you're throwing her aside for someone else?" Adele asked softly. "I assume Miss Reynolds is younger than Mona."

"Not necessarily," Jackson said. "She owns the Garret."

"The railroad restaurant in Rosa Gris?"

"She's nothing to do with the railroad," he said. "She's only located near there."

Adele put down her coffee cup. "Now with both Thea and Theo gone, he's in a position to leave his wife with a nice sum of money."

"He insisted it would be at least a few years before he would even think about broaching the subject with Mona," Jackson argued. "He's a good man, Del. He wants to make sure his wife is settled before he leaves. He thinks she'll be happier without him."

"Perhaps she will be," Adele said. "But maybe Miss Reynolds can't wait that long."

"Del, really." He gave her a disapproving look.

"She might have been the yellow-haired woman at Josiah Brown & Sons, Jack."

"He insisted he never set foot in the place. He didn't even know the address," said Jackson. "He said the description of the woman didn't match Miss Reynolds, though we can't take much stock in that, since we suspect she was disguised."

"Did you check this?" Adele asked.

He gave her a wary look. "Certainly we did. Mr. Brown confirms Mr. Bridge never entered his shop."

"And what did his clerks say?"

"I assume he was speaking for his clerks as well."

"Yes, he would," Adele grumbled.

"Hatfield sent a photo of Mr. Bridge to a friend of his with the San Francisco police to check on it further," said Jackson. "But I don't imagine he'll find anything."

Adele laid her napkin on the table, the signal for Tomas to clear the breakfast away. "So that's that?"

"Not quite," said Jackson. "We're going to the railroad station this morning to speak with Miss Reynolds. We had a time getting her address from Mr. Bridge. Didn't want to involve her, but when we pointed out it might help with our investigation, he gave in."

"How very commendable," Adele said dryly.

"I should think you would find the woman to your liking," Jackson remarked. "The owner of a restaurant and likely as independent-minded as you."

"Garret's," Adele murmured. "That's where Stephanie told me she saw William with another woman."

"Indeed?" He was all attention.

"She also said she thinks she saw Mona at the restaurant one time."

"That could be wishful thinking," Jackson said with a little amusement. "I gathered Miss Peeler and Mrs. Bridge don't exactly get along. We shall certainly ask Miss Reynolds about that when we see her." He rose, putting on the jacket he had thrown over the back of his chair.

"I'd like to come too," Adele said.

He stared at her. "You've already made clear your strong views on the woman."

"Then it's just as well I get her side of the story," Adele said lightly.

"Del —"

"I shall remind you, dear brother, my presence interviewing ladies in the past has made them more comfortable during their police grilling."

"We do not grill anybody," Jackson objected. "We ask the questions to get the information we need."

"Very judiciously stated." Adele grabbed her jacket as well. "The fact remains, Nin and I can ease the mind of a lady who isn't used to being questioned by the police, and we're as discreet as church mice."

"Discreet," he scoffed.

"Well?" She looked at him.

"Naturally, it's not for me to say," he said. "The sheriff makes those decisions."

"Then I am at liberty to ask him?"

"You are always at liberty to do what you like, Del," said her brother with a sigh.

Adele smiled and plucked her parasol out of the stand.

~~~~~

As she anticipated, Hatfield had no objection to either her or Nin coming with them to speak with Miss Reynolds, especially after he heard her report about their visit to the Marsh house. When they reached Rosa Gris, they stopped off at the university and gave Mr. Brethren the bottle of ink Adele found in Theo's room with strict instructions as to the possible danger of its
~~~~~

contents. Adele saw her friend give a heaving sigh when the bottle was safely put in a glass container.

"If it is belladonna, I wonder where the killer got hold of it," Adele lamented.

"It's fairly common in the forests here," Nin said as they walked toward the railroad station arm in arm. "If one knows what to look for."

"It seems so vile," Adele said.

"It is," said Nin. "This entire case has been vile in such a strange way." Adele felt her friend's hand digging into her arm.

Garret's opened in California along the Southern Pacific Railroad line as a rival to the Harvey restaurants, and its local reputation was as immense. It had a special section for ladies who were traveling without male companionship and needed refreshment, which made it popular among the female sex. Adele had been there several times, mostly in cities closer to San Francisco. She once persuaded Nin to accompany her on one of their excursions to San Francisco, but Nin found the squeaky atmosphere and attentiveness of the waitresses annoying.

The moment they entered, a balding man with a mustache darted forward, a linen napkin draped over his arm. "Table for four?" he asked in a trilling, refined voice. "Section six, near the window?" He nodded toward the far end of the room.

"We're not customers," said Hatfield, producing his badge.

The man eased into gruff language. "Our girls ain't never had any trouble with the police."

"What makes you think we're here because of trouble with one of your girls?" Jackson eyed him.

"They ain't my girls, praise be," said the man. "It stands to reason."

"I should say it would stand to reason more we would be after one of the boys." Adele glanced at the busboys shuffling around the tables.

"Not when cops bring ladies," the man growled.

"As a matter of fact, we're here to see the owner," said Hatfield. "Miss Dorothy Reynolds."

"You'll have to speak to the manager," said the young man, flicking his head toward a pair of frosted glass doors.

"I don't wish to speak to the manager," Hatfield said in an equally rough tone. "I wish to speak to Miss Reynolds."

"Manager's office is just through those doors." The young man teetered away to tend to a couple just finishing their meal.

"Impudence!" Jackson snarled.

"He was probably warned by the manager to suspect every lawman that comes through the doors," said Hatfield, almost good-naturedly. "Let's go repeat our story to this manager."

The manager, Mr. Nyman, was more amiable than his employee. "I don't see how Dot can help you, Sheriff, but I'm more than happy to answer any questions."

"That's kind of you, sir," said Hatfield briskly, "but we particularly need to speak with Miss Reynolds."

"Well, I don't know about that." The man pondered. "I don't know as she would like it."

"That's for her to decide, don't you think, Mr. Nyman?" Adele said.

"As manager, miss," said the man, hooking his thumbs into his overalls, "it's my duty to keep any nuisance from her."

"I realize the police are a nuisance," Hatfield said with irony, "but they are necessary when a crime has been committed."

"A crime?" The man paled slightly. "Here at Garret's?"

"That's our business, sir," Jackson said, meeting the man's gaze. "If you'll kindly let Miss Reynolds know we're here, it would avoid having us search for her."

The man flinched. "That won't be necessary, Deputy. You can wait in the meeting room across the hall."

"Much obliged, sir," Hatfield mumbled.

"You won't take up too much of her time, will you, Sheriff? It's peak train hour, and we're a little short-handed. Dot helps out when there is need." The wrinkle of his face clearly showed his distaste for this liberal approach.

"Very sensible of her," Adele said, nodding with approval.

The man looked at her with the eyes of a fish. "I wasn't implying she shouldn't, young lady."

"It's too bad you don't take her example," Nin murmured. Even Jackson had a hard time biting back a smile.

Miss Reynolds turned out to be a pert strawberry blond with a long neck and delicate voice. Adele had to admit she could see how she might attract a man like William after Mona's acidity and frostiness.

"Will said you would be coming by." She sat upright with her hands folded on the table. "He said I wasn't to hide anything. I wouldn't anyway."

"I'm sure you wouldn't," Adele said, smiling. As was usual with female interviews, the sheriff let her take the lead. "You're rather young for a restaurant owner, Miss Reynolds."

"And you're rather young for a stationery shop owner, Miss Gossling," the woman countered. "Will told me about you."

Adele grimaced. "I suppose I deserve that."

"My parents left me the building," she said. "I live upstairs, but downstairs was going to rot, so I made it into a restaurant for train people. I needed the money."

"I understand," Adele said. "You've made quite a success of it."

"Women are much more level-headed when it comes to business if they're willing to learn," said Miss Reynolds with a smile. "As I'm sure you know."

Adele nodded. "We won't be coy with one another, business-woman to businesswoman."

"I would prefer we not be."

Adele leaned forward. "You're in love with Mr. Bridge, aren't you?"

"We're going to be married," the woman's eyes glowed, "as soon as it's appropriate, of course."

"You'll wait an awful long time," Nin remarked.

"I'm patient, Miss Branch," said the woman. "I knew what I was getting into when I met Will."

"When was that?" Adele asked.

"Four years ago," she said.

"Mr. Bridge told my brother you and he have been — involved — for a year," Adele said.

"He's an honorable man," the woman insisted. "Don't you think an honorable man has a right to be happy?"

"Everyone has a right to be happy," Nin said, "but not to stomp on someone else's heart to do it."

"His wife has no heart," said Miss Reynolds with a growl. "She's like a marionette, letting everyone else pull the strings."

"You don't have much sympathy for her," Adele remarked.

"Will told me all about her," said the woman in a stubborn tone. "A woman can guess things about another woman just by stories she hears about her."

"Yes, sometimes," Adele admitted. "If the stories are genuine and not colored by the man's perception."

"I know what you're trying to say," said Miss Reynolds. "You think Will is bitter toward Mona, so he presents her in the worst possible light. It's not true. He has nothing but pity for her."

"Pity!" Nin growled.

"Fighting her family in the way she did," said the woman. "Being driven to it. That must have been awful."

"Then you do have sympathy for her." Adele raised an eyebrow.

"I have sympathy for her plight," said the woman. "That's a very different thing, Miss Gossling. I don't have sympathy for how she married Will just to get away from her family. They lost a child, you know, in India."

"Yes, we know," said Nin.

"Do you also know when they told her the child was dead, she let out a loud, long breath. Like she was relieved!" Miss Reynolds shivered. "Imagine being married to a woman like that."

"There might have been extenuating circumstances," Adele said, thinking of what Nurse Pegg had said.

"I keep telling Will she'll do the same when he leaves," said the woman. "He's worried she'll crumble, but she won't. She'll put on that tolerant expression of hers and tell everyone it was for the best."

"You talk as if you've met her," Hatfield said.

"No, but I've seen her."

"Eh?" Hatfield's eyebrows perked and Jackson, who had been writing in his pad, stopped and looked up.

"She's come here a few times," said Miss Reynolds.

"With her husband?"

"Oh, no, alone of course," said the woman.

"Do you think she knows about you and him?" Nin leaned forward. Adele pressed her hand.

But the woman was almost eager to answer the question. "I'm sure of it. I'm only here four days a week. She always comes on the days I'm here and sits there." She pointed in the general direction of the dining room. "Right near the entranceway to these offices. You can see the door to my office from there."

"You think she sits there deliberately?" Jackson asked.

"Of course she does," Nin snarled.

"One time, Whitey — that's the young man who seats people — tried to give her a table at the other end of the room, but she refused. She said she'd wait until a table opened near the door. She waited thirty minutes."

"Did she ever try to speak to you?" Jackson asked.

The woman let out a laugh. "Heavens no! She wouldn't dare."

"She knows you would scratch her eyes out," Nin guessed.

"I would be as polite to her as to anyone, Miss Branch," the woman insisted. "But it would ruin her sense of propriety to come out in the open. She's like a picture in a cameo. Always the right profile, never a hair out of place."

"Perhaps you're mistaken, and she doesn't know about you and her husband," Hatfield suggested.

"She knows, Sheriff," the woman insisted. "Will must have told her."

"Why do you think that?" Adele asked.

"Several weeks ago, Will took her to the theater. My sister and I were there. She looked right at the balcony, right where I was sitting. She knew me all right. Will saw it too. He told me during intermission."

"What play was that, Miss Reynolds?" Jackson asked.

"Oh, some Shakespearian thing." She shrugged. "It's more Will's taste than mine. I'm trying to be more cultured for his sake."

"You mean *A Midsummer Night's Dream?*" Adele asked.

"Yes, I believe that was it," she said.

"Are you aware, Miss Reynolds, that was the night Mr. Bridge's mother-in-law died?" Hatfield asked.

"Yes." The young woman leaned back. "Sad thing. Will wasn't exactly fond of her, but he was sorry. He's that way."

"A steady, nice man," Adele remarked, trying not to think about the same man stepping out on his wife.

But Nin was less tactful. "That hardly excuses him for taking a mistress."

"I'm not his mistress, Miss Branch." The woman glared. "I told you, we're going to be married."

"You met Mr. Bridge during the intermission after the second act of that play?" Hatfield asked. "Jackson, when would that have been?"

Jackson consulted his notes. "About nine o'clock, sir."

"Where was his wife at that time?" the sheriff asked.

"She went out for air," Miss Reynolds said. "That's why he was able to get away."

"He left you when the third act began, at —" He glanced at Jackson.

"Nine-fifteen."

"No, he stayed for quite some time." A vague smile appeared on her face. "We always have so much to talk about."

"He wasn't worried his wife would miss him?"

"I don't think he was thinking of that," Miss Reynolds said with a smirk.

"How long did he stay?"

"Oh, I don't know."

"But he was with you that entire time."

"Will told me you think he might have killed his mother-in-law." The woman grunted. "It's ridiculous, of course. He wouldn't hurt anybody. He abhors violence."

"We'd like to know your whereabouts on Thursday, October eighteenth, Miss Reynolds," the sheriff proceeded.

"Heavens, I can hardly remember," she mused. "I don't keep a diary."

"When was the last time you were in San Francisco?" Hatfield asked patiently.

"The last time?" she asked. "I was only in San Francisco once in my life."

"When was that?"

"Months and months ago." She sighed. "Last spring. Will took me to see the conservatory at Golden Gate Park. I do love flowers."

"Did he ask you to go to a shop called Josiah Brown & Sons Stationers?" Adele asked.

"Why should he?" She shrugged. "He takes everything he needs of that kind from his office."

"You've never been there, then?" Jackson asked.

"We didn't do any shopping," she said. "Except we did go to The Emporium. I did so want to see one of those new department stores. He tried to buy me a hat, but I told him I won't take a penny from him until we're married." She lifted her chin. "It's the right thing to do."

"Indeed it is," Adele agreed.

"You were not in the city on October eighteenth?" Hatfield asked.

"Thursday, you said? I wouldn't be anywhere but here." She sat up. "We had a girl out sick that day, and I had to help with the service. You can verify that with Mr. Nyman."

They called in the manager, and he confirmed Miss Reynolds had been in the restaurant from eight o'clock in the morning until seven o'clock that night. When the man left, she asked, "Why are you so interested to know where I was on that day, Sheriff?"

"We believe there was a woman involved in the murder of Mrs. Marsh," he said abruptly.

"And since you suspect Will, you suspect it was me." The woman laughed. "Well, it wasn't me, and it wasn't Will." She leaned back. "If you're looking for a woman, I wouldn't be surprised if it was Mona who had something to do with it."

Jackson eyed her. "That's quite an accusation."

"I wouldn't put it past her to plan something," she said. "Will told me she hated her mother. Waiting for her to die was the way he put it. She's erratic all right. The things I've seen here —"

"Such as?" The sheriff eyed her.

"She's friends with a woman named Barbara who works at the railroad station and comes here often. She's a track operator or something of that nature. Not the sort of person a rich lady like Mona would consort with."

"Consort?" Adele asked.

"The strangest thing is they look like two peas in a pod. It scared Will half to death one day when he saw Barbara here and thought it was Mona."

"What would this Barbara have to do with it?" Jackson asked.

"I'm not the police," the woman shrugged, "but Mona once

made quite a fuss over Barbara with the waitress, and they're as thick as thieves every time they meet. Who knows what a woman with an evil mind will do?"

"Yes," Adele murmured. "An evil-minded woman is unpredictable."

At the railroad station, they were directed to shacks behind the tracks where workers gathered between shifts. Men with the overalls and coal-smudged faces leered at her and Nin, regarding the view of ladies' skirts a treat. Nin sneered back at them but, unlike the gentlemen who often ogled her in the street, they did not turn away. They laughed heartily, and one even offered her a cup of coffee from his thermos.

Adele spotted Mrs. Barbara Downing at a distance. She was a crusted, middle-aged woman with a man's figure underneath the same heavy coat and overalls worn by her coworkers. The growling expression on her face would have scared away a stray dog. In spite of this, Adele was struck by how much her features reminded her of Mona's. They did not look exactly alike, but there were enough similarities so she could understand how one could be mistaken for the other.

She motioned the lawmen behind one of the huts. "Sheriff, I think you ought to let Nin and me talk to her alone."

"Don't play policewoman, Del," her brother hissed.

"I know women like her," Adele insisted. "If you flash your badge, you'll never get a word out of her."

"We won't flash our badges, then," Jackson said.

"You won't have to," Nin said. "You have 'police' written all over you, Mr. Gossling."

"I'm not ashamed of what I do, Miss Branch," he growled.

"She's probably seen the law from the other side," Adele said, "not for herself, maybe, but for friends or relations. That sort of woman doesn't forget."

"It's preposterous, Sheriff."

"Not so preposterous, Jackson," said Hatfield. "I've seen women like her as well on the waterfront. Your sister is right. Their lips lock as tight as a safe when the law's about." He leaned against the wall of the hut. "I trust you to get the information we want."

"You trust my sister too much, Sheriff," Jackson grumbled. His superior shot him a look.

Adele and Nin made their way, avoiding mounds of dust, to the woman. "Miss Downing?"

"Mrs." The woman eyed them, a sandwich poised in her hand. "Who're you?"

"A friend said you could help me," she said.

"I don't help no one. Go away!"

"I lost a valuable handkerchief on the train," she said. "It flew out the window, and my friend told me you know these lines well. I was hoping you could take me down the track and help me find it."

"Handkerchief!" the woman scoffed. "Pretty lace thing with gold embroidery, I'll bet. Cost twenty dollars a rag, maybe?"

"You needn't be so rude," Nin snapped.

"I got a right to be rude," the woman snapped back. "I ain't got time for fluttering ladies."

"The handkerchief was white with a black border and the letters *O. G.* embroidered on it," Adele said. "It belonged to my father."

"Oh, ho, sentimental, are you?" The woman closed one eye.

"Tailing the tracks in those nice shiny boots of yours just for that?"

"What of it?" Nin growled. Adele pressed her hand.

"My father was a criminal lawyer," she said, "the best in San Francisco."

The woman's face immediately softened. "Got them that did a bad thing off so they could start over, eh?"

"Something like that," Adele said. "His name was Otis Gossling. Maybe you've heard of him." She eyed her.

The woman looked down, kicking a small rock near her feet. "Heard the name. My husband wanted him badly, but we had to go with a lad who could hardly get his britches up."

"I'm sorry," Adele said softly. "No one told you, I suppose, my father didn't always take those who paid him the highest."

"I'll bet!" The woman glared at her.

"If she says he didn't, he didn't," Nin growled.

"He helped Large Louis." Adele saw the woman's face dawn with recognition. "And Steven Crow. I see you know the names."

"Know them too well," she said. "Worked with my husband, then signed some bad checks. Did a bad thing, but they had hungry mouths to feed. Gone straight now."

"My father got them off," Adele said.

The woman chewed on her sandwich, staring into the distant hills beyond the tracks. She was silent for quite some time. Adele could feel Nin fidgeting beside her, and once, her friend leaned toward her as if wanting to whisper something, but Adele pressed her hand to be silent.

Mrs. Downing finished her lunch and balled up the wrapper, throwing it in the dry grass. "Them boys never had a dime to rub together, so I reckon you're telling the truth. I also reckon you ain't come here in them fancy clothes to find a handkerchief."

Adele smiled. "I should have known a woman like you wouldn't believe my story."

"Suppose you tell me what you did come for," said Mrs.

Downing. She covered her eyes and glanced over her shoulder. "Manager's looking this way."

"We'll go along the track, and if he asks, I'll explain to him how you're helping me," Adele said, taking the woman's arm.

Mrs. Downing extracted a grin on her coal-dusted lips. "You're all right, Miss Gossling."

"My friend, Miss Branch," Adele said, nodding toward Nin.

They began walking, moving out of sight of the huts and the manager's keen eye.

"You know Mrs. Mona Bridge?" asked Adele.

"Know the name," she said. "Right nice lady."

"Where did you meet her?"

"Down at Garret's. Railroad people get a discount there, or I wouldn't be able to afford it." She seemed almost proud of her poverty. "One day she comes up to me and says, 'We look like twins.' Well, I guess we do at that." The woman cackled.

"You got to be friends?" Nin asked.

"Well, don't know as I would put it that way. But someone looks like you, you can't help but be curious about them. She asked me lots of questions, bought me lunch now and then. Can't refuse someone buying you a meal."

"As you shouldn't," Adele agreed.

"Spilled my coffee one day — them tables are so rickety — and she made a big fuss over it to the manager. He ended up footing the bill for lunch, and she gave me the money. Real class." Mrs. Downing whistled.

"And she took you to the theater," Adele said quietly.

"Oh, so you know about that?" The woman eyed her. "You a friend of Mona's?"

"We both are," Adele said. "Miss Branch shares some common interests with her."

"You mean them strange flowers and such she showed me in her book?" The woman narrowed her eyes. "Got what amounts to a bug over those."

"I don't," Nin said shortly.

"Thing is, it was all for the good of the marriage," said the woman. "I believe heartily in the married state." Her eyes fell to Adele's ringless fingers.

"Yes, that's what she told us," Adele said, playing along.

"It weren't no harm either," she said. "I got to wear some fine clothes for one evening. Got to keep them too." She grinned.

"Mona didn't tell us exactly what happened," Nin ventured. "We've been curious."

"Well, it weren't much, really," she said. "Just used the fact that we look alike, you might say. That waitress been stepping out with Mr. Bridge. You know that?" Adele nodded. "She thought if she could talk to the girl, quiet-like, in an elegant place, she could reason with her to leave her husband alone." The woman sighed. "Some husbands just take a wrong turn, but they're sorry for it afterward."

"I doubt it," Nin mumbled.

"She told me to wait out the door of the theater until the bell rang twice."

"Second act intermission," Adele explained to Nin.

"She came out, and we exchanged clothes. She wore my Sunday clothes, and I wore her fancy dress. Then I went back to the play instead of her."

"When did you go back?"

"Just after the play started up again. She said with the lights out, no one, including her husband, would notice."

"And what was she going to do?" Adele asked.

"Go up to the balcony — that's where the woman was — and have a talk with her, woman to woman." Mrs. Downing picked at the dirt under her nails. "She was sure the girl would listen to reason."

"How long was she gone?" Adele asked.

"'I ain't got no watch." She sniffed. "She was gone a long time, though."

"How did you arrange it between you?"

"Gave me a sign from the door, and I slipped out while she slipped back in. Easy as pie." The woman grinned. "She gave me the dress later on. Said it looked better on me than on her."

"So you have both dresses?" Adele glanced at Nin.

The woma nodded, blinking into the sunlight. "I hope she got what she wanted from that woman. Nice woman, at least, I think she was. Had her a few times at the restaurant."

Adele took both her hands. "Mrs. Downing —"

"Call me Barbara." The woman smiled. "Daughter of Otis Gossling's all right in my book."

"You've been honest with us," Adele said. "I'll be honest with you. We think Mona used you."

"Used me?" The woman stared.

"Your resemblance to her," Nin corrected.

"We'd like to see the clothes you wore that night," Adele said. "You said you still had them."

"In my room." The woman looked uneasy. "You ain't trying to tell me she did something bad to this woman. Why, I saw her at the restaurant just the other day."

"Not to Miss Reynolds," Adele said. "She may have done something very bad to someone else."

The ragged features slackened with fear. "You mean a crime?"

"Maybe."

"Me involved in a crime?" The woman's eyes showed true terror. "That can't be! Mona's the nicest lady I ever met."

Nin's earlier hostility toward Mrs. Downing was gone, and she put her arm around her shoulders. "You won't be arrested. You didn't know."

"Me involved in a crime!" the woman whispered.

"You'll help us, won't you?" Adele asked.

"Sure I'll help you," the woman said in a growling voice. "Ain't no one getting me mixed up in any crime!"

"Will you take us to your room and show us the clothes?"

Adele asked. "We've brought the police with us." At the woman's fierce look, she reassured her with, "The deputy is my brother, and the sheriff is a very reasonable man."

"I guess you need the law right about now," the woman admitted.

They returned to the shacks where Sheriff Hatfield and Jackson were speaking with the manager who had eyed them earlier. Adele took the lawmen aside and gave them a brief explanation of what they had discovered.

Hatfield returned, saying in his authoritative voice, "Mr. Anderson, I must borrow your employee for a little while. It's a matter of police business and very urgent."

"It ain't my fault, Mr. Anderson," Mrs. Downing said in a quivering voice.

"Mrs. Downing is trying to help us, sir," Jackson added. "She's not in any trouble."

"I'm not one to step in where the law is concerned," said the man in a brisk tone. "Mrs. Downing is at your disposal, Sheriff."

Barbara's apartment was near the station in a building that looked as if it had seen better days. But the small place was clean and almost homey with old rugs and photographs of a young, happy couple which Adele guessed were Barbara and her husband.

The woman went into the bedroom and emerged a few moments later carrying a lavish green and white dress on a hanger. "Real pearl buttons," said the woman softly. "I ain't never had pearls before. Ralph — my husband — promised to buy me some one of them days, but he didn't get the chance." She blinked back tears.

Hatfield took the dress gently by the hanger and laid it across the couch. "We'd like to see everything from that night, Mrs. Downing, including the clothes you came in. Shoes and jewelry too, if you please."

The woman's face reddened. "I got no fancy things. Just my calico Sunday dress. Made it myself."

"I'm sure it's beautiful," Adele said. This made the woman smile.

"You'll be careful, won't you?" she asked, looking from the sheriff to Jackson.

"We'll be very careful," Jackson assured her.

She examined his immaculate figure and grinned. "Of course you will. You're Otis Gossling's son, ain't you?"

"Yes, ma'am," he said.

"Wouldn't expect anything else." She nodded and retreated to the bedroom again.

Jackson glanced at his sister, who murmured, "I'll tell you later."

The woman returned with the calico dress and plain shoes. True to their word, Hatfield and Jackson examined the dress with delicate hands.

"Has it been washed?" Jackson asked.

"Well, I ain't had the time." She blushed again.

"Very fortunate for us, ma'am," he said respectfully.

"It's very useful when people don't wash away evidence," Hatfield agreed.

"Evidence?" The woman squinted.

He showed her black powder marks in the folds of the dress.

To Adele's surprise, the woman blushed. "Guess that's my fault. Always getting coal dust on everything." She looked down at her rough clothes.

"Then they aren't from a fireplace?" Jackson asked.

"No fire around here, Deputy," she said. "I complain to the landlord all the time, but of course he don't care."

Hatfield picked up the shoes and turned them over. "Flower petals," he remarked, peeling one off the sole of the left shoe.

"They're daisies, sir!" Jackson stared at his superior.

"Must've passed the flower seller or something." Mrs.

Downing shrugged. "Always letting them daisies drop all over the place.

"Sheriff," Adele took out her magnifying glass, "I think there's something else on the shoes." She took the right shoe and turned it on its side. "Purple stains. They're almost black."

All at once, there was a scream and they all jumped. Nin had a wild look in her eye. "Don't touch it, for God's sake!"

"Honey, some spook's sure got hold of you." Mrs. Downing looked genuinely alarmed.

Nin began to shiver, and she looked as if she were ready to collapse. Adele rushed to her as the sheriff ordered brandy. Mrs. Downing produced a masculine-looking snifter glas, and they managed to get Nin to drink some of it.

"It's the same," she breathed, "just like in that bottle."

"We'll need to take everything, Mrs. Downing," said the sheriff, nodding to Jackson, who collected the dress and shoes. "We'll return it to you after we're finished, and in much better condition than it is now." This last he said with a wink.

"I see you know a woman's vanity, Sheriff." Mrs. Downing grinned, then turned to Adele. "You sure your friend's all right?"

"I'm all right," Nin insisted. When she stood, she was indeed steady on her feet.

On the street, the sunshine further revived Nin, and she took Adele's arm.

"We're beginning to erase those questions marks, aren't we, Sheriff?" Adele asked.

"It's unfathomable," Jackson lamented.

"Perhaps the picture was clearer than we thought all along," Hatfield said. "We can't be sure until we get everything tested and put the pieces together."

"Dr. Rhodes?" Jackson asked with a groan.

"I like young Brethren's work," the sheriff said. "I happen to know Dr. Rhodes will be in San Francisco for a conference for the next few days. I don't think we need call him back, do you?" There was a twinkle in his eyes.

"It's best to avoid it," Jackson answered in his usual tactful way, but he was smiling as well.

As they drove the wagon to the university, Nin leaned toward her friend. "Why would the evil berry be on Mrs. Downing's dress?"

"Because she and Mona exchanged clothes, and Mona was careless," Adele answered. "I'm sure she thought Mrs. Downing would wash them before anyone suspected anything."

"She must have realized the police might find Mrs. Downing," Nin objected. "The resemblance between them is so strong."

"And coincidental," Adele reminded her. "It was pure accident they discovered it themselves. I suppose she didn't think anyone would consider her interest in Barbara anything more than a look-alike's curiosity, perhaps even compassion for the poor."

"Compassion!" Nin sneered. "A woman who gets excited about deadly herbs has no compassion."

"The excitement came in spite of itself," Adele said, "or else she would have tried to hide it, just as she hides everything else."

Mr. Brethren was coming out of his laboratory just as they entered. "I was coming to see you, Miss Gossling," he said. "I had a call from my friend, Mr. McClure. I asked him to examine the ink bottle you brought me."

"We've another job for him," Sheriff Hatfield said, showing him the shoes.

"I'm sure he'll be happy to help," said Mr Brethren, leading them across a small courtyard. "He's working in his lab today. He's as fascinated by this entire case as I am. Naturally, it's purely a scientific interest with him, whereas with me —" The man stopped.

"It's more personal," Adele finished.

"Yes," said Mr. Brethren. "Very personal."

The laboratory was completely the opposite of Mr.

Brethren's. Glass slides, test tubes, and other scientific equipment were thrown all around the room as if a strong wind had rushed through it. The young man bending over the microscope was, unlike the tidy Mr. Brethren, a true mad scientist with his hair spiked and his clothes wrinkled.

"You were right, Lom!" The young man rushed to his friend. "Atropa acuminada. Gad, if I could get hold of the actual specimen! Not much good in the juice alone." He picked up the ink bottle by the neck with a pair of tongs.

"Then it is belladonna poison?" Adele asked.

"Indian belladonna, they call it," said the young man, eyeing her over his spectacles.

"Indian belladonna!" Nin leaned against the lab counter. "It was in the book!"

"Mona's book." Adele nodded. "I was thinking the same thing."

Lom quickly introduced everyone. "Miss Gossling and Miss Branch are helping to investigate the death of my friend and his mother."

"Could the atropa acuminada kill someone if they used it in ink?" Adele asked.

He looked at her again from the tops of his glasses. Lom whispered something to him. Adele guessed the young man had little faith in the intelligence of women when it came to scientific matters, but what his friend told him apparently eased his mind, as he answered, "Just as toxic as drinking from the bottle itself. It's very lethal, you see. One need only to press one's hand into it and —" Both Adele and Nin shivered.

Hatfield put the shoes on the table. "And this stain here, sir? Is it the same?"

The young man's eyes opened so wide they looked as if they filled his spectacles. "You're the Arrojo sheriff, aren't you?"

"The county sheriff," Jackson said, not without a little pride.

"Yes, yes, I've heard of you," said Mr. McClure. "Martin

Sanders and I shared a flat in medical school. He speaks very highly of you."

"Indeed." Sheriff Hatfield was clearly pleased.

"He said you do what has to be done, no matter how many feathers you ruffle," the young man continued. "Including Old Sniffy."

"Old Sniffy?"

"Rhodes."

This made the sheriff burst out laughing. Jackson frowned, looking down at the table.

The young man got to work with his chemicals and slides. It took him a good half hour but he finally pulled off his spectacles and said, "To answer your question, Sheriff, yes."

"That's conclusive?"

"No test is ever conclusive," the man declared. "We can only go so far."

"More or less conclusive?" Jackson asked impatiently.

"The stain is fresh enough to make that judgment, yes."

"Its poisonous effects are similar to the atropa belladonna?"

"They're related to one anther," the man gurgled.

"Mr. McClure." Adele neared the table. "Can Indian belladonna be cultivated here?"

"What an extraordinary idea!" the man breathed.

"Can it?" she persisted.

"I suppose so, if the soil is moist enough," he said. "Atropa acuminada grows in best in well-shaded areas, but even that isn't a necessity. It's quite resilient."

"Someone would have had to bring it from somewhere like India to here," Jackson said. "It isn't native to our soil."

"Hardly," said the man. "Its sister plant, atropa belladonna, is found in common areas —"

"I told you," Nin whispered to Adele.

"But not this variety," the man finished, glaring at her.

Nin neared the table and stared at the slide. "It came from a hidden garden," she murmured.

"What is the woman blathering about?" Mr. McClure looked at his friend in annoyance.

Adele took her friend's arm. "What hidden garden?"

Nin slowly raised her hand above the tablet. "That's why I fainted," she said, her voice thick. "It was so close."

"The hidden garden?" Adele prompted.

"Theo had his place in the garden," said Nin. "She has hers."

"You mean Mrs. Bridge has her own garden on the grounds, Miss Branch?" Sheriff Hatfield asked.

"Under a shed they no longer use," Nin said.

"So you're telling us she has this poisonous plant growing underneath this shed," Jackson said.

"What an absurd notion," Mr. McClure scoffed with a high-pitched laugh.

This broke Nin's trance. "There are some things one cannot discover through a test tube, Mr. McClure."

"Science and nature," Adele murmured.

They left the university just as the late afternoon was coming to an end. Rosa Gris had less dust than Arrojo but the winds were colder, and Adele grabbed her hat as the rim flipped back with a gust. But the breeze didn't help the sickening feeling in her stomach.

"The Marsh house, sir?" Jackson asked with the wagon reins in his hands.

"Mr. Marland first," said the sheriff, pushing a few stray curls away from his forehead.

"Why do we need the district attorney?" Adele asked.

"We can't demand to see a garden without a warrant, Del," Jackson said, pulling the reins.

The visit to Mr. Marland's house was quick, and they waited in the wagon for what seemed like only ten minutes before Hatfield came out of the squeaky gate, waving the paper in his hand.

"Leave it to Marland to have a judge dining with him." He grinned.

"Lucky for us," Jackson agreed.

"He agrees if the plant we're looking for is in the house, there is no time to waste," he said. "Mrs. Bridge may have gotten rid of it by now."

"It's still there," Nin insisted. "I wouldn't have fainted if it wasn't."

"We rely on your help, Miss Branch," Jackson said. Her friend turned her head away but Adele caught the shy smile on her face.

When they reached the Marsh house, Mona answered the door. "My, quite a party," she remarked as she stood back to let them in.

"You've taken your place as chatelaine, I see," Adele said.

"One must go on with life, Adele," she said.

"Still in black too."

The woman gave her an odd look. "It's the thing to do when a family member dies, isn't it?"

"Theo didn't die, Mrs. Bridge." Jackson eyed her. "We now believe he was killed."

"Killed!" Mona laughed. "That's absurd. Will told me he left a note."

"Indeed he did," the sheriff said, "typed, with no signature."

"You suspect someone?" the woman asked. "I assume that's why you're here."

Adele pulled her gloves off. "Your brother kept you from getting what you wanted, didn't he?"

"Whatever do you mean?"

"I read the accounts of the lawsuit twenty years ago, remember?"

"Those newspapers!" Mona growled.

"Mr. Grace, Missy's father, was more subtle than the rest," Adele continued. "He preferred quoting the source. 'One day, I shall be sitting behind a desk like my brothers and giving orders. I shall be queen where they are now kings.'"

The woman's face turned pale. "Dear God!"

"You said those words on the steps of the courthouse after you lost your lawsuit," Adele said.

"It's true, Mona." William stood at the foot of the stairs. "You did say that. I'll never forget those words. They frightened me."

"I can't imagine why, William." She gave him an even look. "If it hadn't been for those words, Mother never would have given you a job at the mill when we came back."

Sheriff Hatfield held out the warrant. "We've come to search the gardens of this house."

The words sent a shiver through Mona's slim figure. "Search the gardens?"

"What is it, Will?" Forrest emerged from the study.

"They're going to look outside." William nodded toward the police.

"We have a warrant, sir," said Hatfield, handing him the paper.

"What exactly are you looking for, if I may ask?" Mona questioned.

"We keep no secrets, ma'am," Jackson said stiffly. "We're looking for a plant."

She laughed. "Well, you didn't need a warrant for that! Theo crowded the garden with them."

"This is a very special plant," said Adele. "It's called atropa acuminada." She stepped forward. "Commonly known as Indian belladonna."

"My God!" Forrest let the warrant fall from his hands.

"I know what it is, Adele," said the woman in an agitated voice. "I encountered it in the forests. But it doesn't grow here."

"It does in your secret garden," Nin said.

"Secret garden, Miss Branch?" The woman blinked. "I haven't any secret garden, though I must say, you've given me an interesting idea."

"The gardens, sir." Hatfield looked expectedly at Forrest.

"It's a waste of time," Mona said. Adele noticed her words were coming out in a dull tone.

"They have a warrant, Mona," said her brother.

"What a law-abiding citizen you are, dearest," she said with a smile. "All right, then." She stepped aside.

He led them out to the garden. Instead of beginning the search, both the sheriff and Jackson looked expectedly at Nin. She pressed her hands together and closed her eyes.

"What is this?" Mona growled.

"Quiet, Mona," her husband said.

Nin began walking across the garden, her steps slow like a stalking animal. They followed her across the red brick path but then she strayed, moving through the mud toward the shed where the carriages were kept. "There's a wall," she murmured.

"Mr. Marsh," the sheriff turned to Forrest, "are there any unused sheds or huts on the grounds?"

"There's a small hill and a few sheds in the grotto once used for workers' houses when my grandfather kept vineyards in those fields," he said. "They dried up some time ago, so we don't use them anymore."

Nin turned to Mona. "One of you uses them."

"Miss Branch, you truly amaze me," said the woman. "I thought you were a clairvoyant, not one prone to flights of fancy."

"Go on, Nin," Adele said softly.

They made their way down the hill, which was little more than a small mound. There were indeed two structures with small windows. One of them was half torn through, but the other was intact. "There," Nin said, pointing. "Cover your faces before you go in."

Mona rushed to the door. William reached her and quietly took her away. Hatfield glanced at Jackson. They both covered their mouth and nose with their handkerchiefs, tying them around their heads like bandits and advanced to the shed.

When they emerged, Hatfield held violet-black berries, his hands covered with working gloves. He held them out to Nin. She nodded and buried her face in Adele's shoulder.

~~~~~

An hour later, they were all settled in the parlor. Mona played with a handkerchief. William sat rigidly next to his wife. Stephanie had joined them and now huddled next to Forrest, who looked more bewildered than anything else. Rebecca had been called and sat like a stone beside Adele.

"It's in your best interest to tell us everything, Mrs. Bridge," the sheriff began.

"I have no intention of holding anything back," she said.

"You sound almost proud," Adele said.

"How can you understand?" She shot her a look. "You've always done what you pleased. You've never been shackled."

"No, I've never been shackled," Adele said softly.

"For God's sake, Mona, why?" Forrest's voice shook. With a signal from Hatfield, Jackson poured the man a stiff brandy, which he accepted willingly.

"You know I don't give up, dearest," said Mona. "The lawsuit fueled the fire."

"Theo would have eventually given William a third of the business," Forrest insisted.

"I couldn't wait for eventually," said Mona, "and it wouldn't have done any good. He wants to leave me and go away with his waitress."

"She's not a waitress," William said quietly.

"He didn't want it," Mona explained. "I did. For myself. I tried by proxy, I really did." She looked at her husband. "It wasn't enough."

"But killing your mother and Theo!" Rebecca buried her face in her hands.

"It was the only way," she said. "It was always Forrest and I against them. Mother wouldn't give in and neither would Theo. I knew Forrest would, especially after William left. He couldn't run the mill by himself."
~~~~~

"You've led him around like a dog on a leash all his life," Stephanie snarled. "You won't anymore." She took Forrest's hand.

"You killed them both to get them out of the way," Jackson said.

"Not quite, Jack," Adele said. "I don't think Mona intended to kill her brother at first."

"You're very clever, Adele," said the woman. "I knew in the end you would find me out. I had my doubts about the police, but I knew you would."

"Why both of them?" Hatfield asked.

"I saw the will," she explained.

"Mrs. Stern told us you had an argument with your mother that day," Adele said.

"I wanted to know what Mother intended," she said. "I had a right to know."

"It was her will!" William glared at her.

"It was my life!" she snarled. "Of course Mother wouldn't tell me. I had to find out for myself. I saw where she put it after Rebecca brought it to the house, and while she was asleep, I took it."

"Mona!"

"A woman must resort to devious means once in a while." She smiled at Forrest's exclamation. "It was in your best interest too."

"You were the one who knew what was in the will before I read it," Rebecca said.

"Part of it," said Mona. "I hadn't time to read all of it."

"But you read enough," Nin said.

"Enough to know what would happen if Mother died and Theo was — indisposed."

"A rather cold-blooded way of putting it, Mrs. Bridge," Jackson said.

"It's what one must do to get rid of obstacles to one's dreams, Deputy," she said simply. "When the women in India wanted a plant to grow, they burned the weeds and flowers and everything else around it."

"Poison!" Stephanie looked horrified.

"A woman's weapon, they say," Mona remarked, "Growing right in my garden where no one knew about it. Or so I thought." She gave Nin a hard look.

"One cannot hide evil forever," Nin said.

"Is Adele correct in her assumption that you never meant to kill your brother?" Hatfield inquired.

"Only if necessary," she said. "I thought if there was enough to incriminate him, and he was arrested and tried and found guilty —"

"He would be, as you said, no longer an obstacle to your dreams," Jackson said dryly.

Hatfield's mild countenance became dark and thundering. "We don't appreciate criminals using the law for their own ends."

"Not to mention you were clumsy," Nin remarked. "Dressing up in a yellow wig and veil and making a point to let everyone know you were Theo's wife when he didn't have a wife!"

"Yes, that was rather stupid of me," she admitted. "I suppose, like most people committing a crime, I thought too much about it."

"I knew everything was too neat and tidy," Rebecca said.

"Perhaps you'll tell me now, Sheriff." Mona leaned forward. "How did you trace the poison to me?"

"It was rather clever of you to leave it in Theo's room," Adele remarked.

"I knew what was in the vial Lom sent him, of course," said Mona. "I fished it out of the wastepaper basket after he threw it away. It's what gave me the idea for Mother."

"The poison you put in your mother's tea and the one Lom gave your brother weren't the same," said Hatfield.

"What do you mean?" She stared at him.

"Laboratories can tell the differences between plants nowadays, Mrs. Bridge," he said. "Theo's was atropa belladonna, and yours was atropa acuminada. They're similar but not the same."

"You didn't think of that?" Adele studied her.

"No." She began to shake with laughter. "I was so proud of my knowledge of plants!"

"Perhaps you'll tell us the whole story now?" Hatfield prompted.

"Confess, you mean?" Mona said. "I suppose you'll tell me the judge will go easier on me if I do?"

"Perhaps he will, Mona," William said.

"I suspect you know it all anyway." Mona gave the sheriff a shrewd look. "I heard you were very thorough."

"We know about Mrs. Downing," said Hatfield. "We know you changed places with her that night at the theater."

"What on earth are you talking about?" William blinked.

"It might interest you to know, Mr. Bridge, while you were rendezvousing with your soon-to-be fiancée," Jackson said, "your wife was taking advantage of the intermission too. She met a woman who looks almost exactly like her outside the theater and exchanged clothes. You were sitting alongside this woman for part of *A Midsummer Night's Dream*."

"Good Lord!" The man's mouth flew open.

"I'm surprised you're so disturbed, William." His wife gave him a sly look. "I'm sure your mind was on something else. Or someone else."

"And yours was on murder!" he growled.

She gave a small smile. "Do you know how the plan came about? I called at the mill one day looking for you, and they said you'd been out since lunchtime. I knew you were at Garret's visiting that bright-eyed bird of yours. So I went there."

"I do occasionally go out on business," he sneered.

"You weren't there and neither was Miss Reynolds. But Barbara was." A streak of memory came across her face. "It was quite a shock at first. Then I found it amusing. A railroad operator with my face!"

"When did the idea of switching places with her come to you?" Jackson asked.

"Oh, I don't know, the way these things do," she mused. "I bought her lunch — poor woman, she is grossly underpaid. You really ought to tell your progressive friends to put women railroad workers on their agenda, Adele."

"Go on," the sheriff murmured.

"We talked. Then I saw her from the window of a train I took to the city one day, there at the crossroads, changing tracks. And it struck me that could have been *me*. I think that's when it came to me because I had the will on my mind."

Forrest let out a whimper, and Stephanie leaned toward him, whispering in his ear.

The interruption threw Mona off for a moment, and she looked at her younger brother with pity in her eyes. She went on, "I started going to the restaurant as often as I could, when I knew William wouldn't be there. We became friends, Barbara and I. I made a noise about one of the stupid waitresses spilling coffee all over her one day."

"She told us about that," Adele said quietly. "She said you had 'real class.'"

"And so I do." Mona sniffed. "You may not believe this, Adele, but I liked Barbara very much. She had spirit."

"Go on," Jackson said.

"I put it to her one day about switching places at the theater," she said. "I told her I thought my husband was having an affair with a waitress, and I wanted to see if he would meet her at the theater that night. She believed it." She sighed. "Barbara is such a simple soul."

"So you changed clothes with her during the intermission," said Adele, "and while she took your place beside your husband, you went and killed your mother."

The brutal words made the woman flinch. "It was hardly as simple as that. I had to hide in the bushes for a time until the Sterns went to bed, and that silly girl Polly turned off the light."

"How terribly inconsiderate of them," Nin snarled.

"It was all very discreet," Mona continued. "Mother was asleep when I came in. The tea was sitting right there on her table as it always was, piping hot, of course. That gave me time."

"Never drink tea piping hot," Forrest said in a soft voice.

"I'm surprised you didn't make any noise when you spilled the water in the vase," Jackson remarked.

"I didn't spill it, Deputy," she said. "I used it to cool her tea. I wanted her to drink it as soon as possible when she woke up."

Forrest let out a groan and buried his face in is hands.

"It was clean water," Mona said defensively. "I never would have put a drop of dirty water in her tea. I have my standards."

"But you put the belladonna in her tea," Hatfield prompted.

"It took me weeks to get the consistency just right," she said. "I wasted so many berries."

Nin's eyes narrowed, and Adele held her hand.

"They have a rather sour scent," she explained, "but they're sweet. I thought they would go rather nicely with her herbal tea."

"Mona, stop!" William turned away.

"When you put the poison in the tea and cooled it, then what did you do?" Jackson asked.

"The rest is rather routine," she said. "I went back to the theater, gave Barbara the signal we agreed upon and slipped into my seat. William didn't even notice." She gave her husband another sly smile.

"You left the fountain pen nib you knew your brother sometimes used beside your mother's bed," Jackson said.

"I knew it would lead to Mr. Brown and he would tell you about the woman with the blond hair," she said. "I thought you would learn about Theo's engagement to Thelma and put two and two together." She gave Rebecca a sour look. "I should have guessed Rebecca would know exactly what became of her."

"It was all very clear to you, wasn't it?" Adele asked. "Kill your mother and leave enough evidence to hang your brother for her death."

"That was the idea, Adele."

"But it didn't quite work out as you had hoped." Hatfield leaned back, folding his hands in his lap.

"You let Theo go!" she snarled. "That was Rebecca's doing."

"It was our doing," Jackson said sharply.

"How does it feel to know you signed the death warrant of the man you loved when you got him out of jail?" Mona taunted the young lawyer.

"Rebecca had nothing to do with it!" Adele took the woman's hand.

"It was your evil mind," Nin added.

Rebecca hid her face in her hands.

"If the rope wouldn't take him, he had to go another way," Mona said. "It was as simple as that."

"You put poison in the ink bottle," Jackson said.

"He told me himself he had to sign some papers that night before he went to bed," she said. "Theo was always careless with ink and pen. He hated blotters, you know. He used to blot the ink with his handkerchief. One's hands get all over one's handkerchief." Her eyes were almost sparkling. "I thought it was rather ingenious."

"But not altogether." Adele gave her an even look.

Hatfield looked at Jackson. They both rose. "We must ask you to come with us, Mrs. Bridge."

She stood up, straightening her skirt. "I'll just get my hat and gloves."

"I'll get them for you." Stephanie jumped up.

Mona gave her a crooked smile. "I'm not going to run away, you know."

"We would catch you if you tried," Hatfield said.

"I've no doubt you would, Sheriff." She looked at Forrest for a long time. The man's tears had ceased but he was looking down at the carpet, his hands tight in his lap. "We're free now, dearest. William will go away and leave the mill to us. Won't you?" She eyed her husband.

The man walked out of the room without answering.

"It's all ours, Forrest," she said. "Our side won."

Her brother closed his eyes as the police led her out of the room.

# CHAPTER 29

Soon after the Marsh case was closed, Lady Augusta insisted on giving a picnic and Adele volunteered the pleasant back yard of her house. Upon hearing this, Tomas and Ruth insisted on canceling their trip to Ruth's parents in Sacramento, and it looked to be a battle of wills between Jackson and the golden-hearted Tomas until Lady Augusta came to their rescue. She sent Rowena over with picnic baskets of food and shooed the Cordobas back to their own little house on the other side of the garden.

"Ma, you're not feeding the entire police force," Hatfield remarked when he saw the platters.

"Perhaps I ought to," said his mother with a laugh. "Those poor young men you torture with your commanding presence deserve some kind of compensation."

"He's training them to be good lawmen, ma'am," Jackson objected.

"They're good lads," Hatfield said with affection. "Even Edison."

"They helped me a great deal with Mona's case," Rebecca said. "I'm rather surprised she agreed to allow William to hire me."

"It was a feather in your cap, dear," said Lady Augusta.

"I assume that means you're staying in Arrojo." Adele eyed her.

Rebecca looked at her with a smile, silent for a moment. "I'm staying."

"No more demons?" Nin asked.

"The demons are still here," said the lawyer, "but I'm ready to face them now." With a sigh, she added, "I only wish Theo were here to help me."

"You must do it on your own," said Lady Augusta. "I speak from experience. No shadow ever disappears until one shines a light on it, and that one must do alone." A look of pain crossed her face. Her son took her hand and kissed it.

"We'll be glad to call on you for any legal help we need, Miss Gold," Jackson said. "A lawyer's opinion can sometimes be very helpful."

"And sometimes it can get you in trouble, Mr. Gossling," Nin remarked.

"I accept all opinions, Miss Branch," he said, "even when I don't agree with them."

Hatfield laughed. "We'll be looking to Mr. Brethren for help in the future as well."

"Oh?" Adele raised her eyebrows.

"The young man proved to be solid, and his knowledge of organic substances is valuable to us," said the sheriff. "I made that point to the council during yesterday's meeting, and they agreed with me."

"What did Dr. Rhodes say?"

"He's glad to have that burden off his shoulders," said Jackson.

"Not that it was much on *his* shoulders," Nin said. "He pushed it all to Mr. Sanders' shoulders."

"I think Mr. Sanders won't mind now that he'll have his friends working alongside him," said Hatfield. "Mr. Brethren and the odd Mr. McClure."

"That scientist!" Nin growled.

"He was a great help, Miss Branch," Jackson reminded her.

"Test tubes and vials." She spit the words out as she drank from her wine glass.

"Progress is progress," Adele reminded her, "whether we like it or not, dear."

"Science and nature?" Nin smiled.

"To science and nature." Hatfield held up his glass and everyone drank to the toast.

Later, after they retired to the Gossling parlor, Adele sat near the window, looking out at the clean black night. Hatfield wandered over and sat beside her on the window seat.

"Mr. Brethren wasn't the only topic of conversation at the meeting," he began.

"I was wondering when you would say something." She looked at him. "Mrs. Faderman, wasn't it?"

"She was quite upset when she heard about you taking that evidence from the station."

"If Mrs. Fourier had kept her mouth shut —" Adele snarled.

"It would have come out some other way even if she had," the sheriff said.

"I'm sorry you got a verbal beating, Sheriff," she said softly. "You don't deserve it."

"It wasn't all for naught," he said. "Remember I remarked how I ought to make you a police consultant?"

She stared at him. "You were joking, surely."

"I've been thinking it might not be a bad idea," he said. "You've helped us on a number of cases, Adele. The Blackstone case and then Millie Gibb and now this."

"I suppose Mrs. Faderman said I'm going places unbecoming for a lady," she remarked.

"I thankfully forget everything Mrs. Faderman says once I leave those meetings," he said with a grin. "Luckily, the mayor doesn't always agree with her."

"Oh?"

"I put in a request, Adele."

"A request?"

"To employ you as a police consultant," he said. "There's no guarantee the mayor will be amenable to it, but I thought it wouldn't hurt to try."

Adele felt warmth and pride. Without thinking, she threw her arms around the sheriff and kissed him. His lips were warm and dry, and she realized he was returning the kiss. She pulled away quickly and put her face close to the window. "I shouldn't have done that. Silly of me."

When she turned around, she saw the sheriff had gone back to his mother's side. For the rest of the afternoon, she noticed he kept his eyes away from her.

~~~~~

## Author's Note

Hi, reader! I'm so glad you've reached the end of Death At Will (and I'll make it worth your while even more in the following pages, trust me!) I really hope you enjoyed this third book of the Adele Gossling Mysteries.

This book is very much a family murder mystery. I love this cozy mystery trope! I've always been fascinated by family secrets and what lies behind a family mystery. In fact, my entire Waxwood Series, a family saga set in the Gilded Age, was inspired by this idea that families hold on tight to their secrets, and it's the one family member who is the truth-seeker who must persevere in breaking those secrets wide open if the family is to survive for future generations.
~~~~~

. . .

*T*his book was inspired by classic mystery films of family mansion murders that usually follow the same or similar storyline: The wealthy matriarch or patriarch of the family, who isn't the nicest or easiest person to get along with, makes his/her will and the family gathers in the family mansion (usually for a special weekend or holiday), anxious to find out who inherits what. And then the family matriarch or patriarch is killed. Whodunit? Why, one of the family, of course, though sometimes the screenwriter shakes things up by pointing the finger to someone close to the family.

*W*hy are family murder mysteries so intriguing to so many people? Because the family is a crucible in itself. We know so much about our families, or we think we know so much about them. And, yet, there is so much we don't know. Most families, of course, don't have murder embedded in their family tree, but even the strange, little quirk that pops up now and then can make us say, "Whoa, we didn't know that about Uncle Harold!" It's the perfect set-up for a murder mystery because mysteries are about solving a puzzle based on random clues. We often times have random information about someone or something in the family but it takes all our intelligence to solve the mystery, whether they involve a crime or not.

*M*y sister and I once found among our grandmother's things an old postcard addressed to my Great-Aunt Bella, my grandmother's sister whom we never met because she died in childbirth in the early 1930s. What intrigued us was the black-and-white postcard's photo of a kissing couple and the message in French on the back. It was sent to her by some unknown Frenchman in 1920's. We were in college and I was taking French to fulfill the foreign language requirement necessary at the time. I went to my teacher and asked her to translate the message. The message roughly translated into, "The kiss you gave was divine — but it was even more divine to receive it!" All we could find out from our grandmother was that Bella had taken a trip to Paris in the 1920s. Beyond that, we never found out who the man was or what kind of romantic interlude they may have had that prompted him to send her the postcard.

Some mysteries aren't about the family crucible but about a different kind of crucible, like house or a small town. Arrojo is a crucible in itself and the next book of the series is about a mystery that involves the entire town on Labor Day of 1905. If you want ot read an excerpt from Book 4, turn the page!

Happy reading!
Tam

*Can Adele help the police catch a thief before he ruins Labor Day for the whole town?*

For Adele Gossling, Labor Day is about giving voice to progressive reforms such as the eight-hour work day and minimum wage for women. But for business owners in Arrojo, California, Labor Day is about making money. City slickers flock to the country seeking holiday deals they can't get in San Francisco or Sacramento. What better way to celebrate than with bargains and the community picnic?

What they don't know is there's a thief in town. He's already succeeded in getting away with burglarizing business owners in neighboring cities, and the county police can't seem to get their hands on him.

Who is stealing gold trinkets from the shops in Arrojo, California? Is it the dandified Mr. Lyman? The town's junk collector and pariah, Zephyr Brown? or is it someone or something beyond their wildest imagination?

Follow the adventures of epistolary expert and suffragist Adele Gossling and her aura-seeing friend Nin Branch as they embark on an adventure to catch a thief and his unique accomplice.

Pick up this fourth book of the mysteries reviewers have praised as a "great new series" where "characters come alive".

Read on for an excerpt from this book!

Hatfield said, "I'm sure your brother told you about the reports we've received from my friend Sheriff Hill about thefts they've had in Sacramento."

"But that's far away from here."

"Not far enough, Del." Jackson folded the paper on the crease and laid it down. "Last week, we had a few thefts in some of the towns in this county."

"Vargas was the first," Hatfield said. "And yesterday, we received a dispatch from Wells Fargo that Rosa Gris and Blue Springs reported items missing from some of their shops."

"That's ghastly!" Her cup dropped to the table, missing the saucer. Tomas mumbled his dismay in soft Spanish. "No one was hurt, I hope?"

"The thief is only interested in valuables, not people," said Jackson. "There have been no reports of violence."

"Still — it's horrible to think —" She took another slice of toast from the holder, feeling her hand shaking.

Hatfield drew his hand toward the edge of the table between them. Adele's shoulders gave a quick flinch, though she knew the sheriff would never take liberties. But there was something in the man's gaze, his mouth closed but his eyes large and almost innocent, that gave her the feeling of being in a too intimate corner with him just then.

"Perhaps Nin and I should warn the Bridge Street merchants before Monday," she suggested. "From one shop owner to another."

Silence buzzed around her, muting the brilliant blue sky to gray. Even the pair of doves nesting on the gazebo hushed up their morning song.

"We'll be very discreet, of course," she continued, her voice less assured. "We'll ask to speak to them in private."

The sheriff cleared his throat. "I'm afraid you can't do that, Adele."

"Why can't we?"

"Because," Hatfield said, "the town counsel refused to allow it when I suggested it."

"Refused!"

"They want us to keep it quiet, Del," said her brother. "We shouldn't have even told you."

The butter knife slipped from her hand and scraped against her empty plate. Tomas darted forward, mumbling in Spanish, glancing around to see if anything had been broken. "That's perfectly ridiculous! Why, for heaven's sake?"

"They believe it would cause 'unnecessary panic' and 'soil the potential prospects for prosperity in our good town,'" Hatfield grumbled. "Those were Mrs. Faderman's words. They all agreed with her, of course."

"They didn't have much choice," Jackson remarked.

Adele threw down her napkin. "So that's what you meant when you said their behavior borders on negligence! That civic pride of hers has blinded her again!"

"Not to mention made her deaf and dumb," Hatfield said dryly.

Adele rose, pacing the veranda. "Her behavior doesn't border on the negligent, Sheriff. It *is* negligent. Even criminal!"

"Really, Del," her brother mumbled. "Must you always exaggerate?"

"What else would you call it, Jack?" She insisted. "She's prepared to risk what could be a mess of thieves roaming in our midst."

**Adele has gotten around Irene Faderman's tyranical decisions before — will she this time? You're going to have to read the book to find out! Copies are available at your favorite online bookstore here: https://tammayauthor.com/the-mystery-of-the-golden-cat-adele-gossling-mysteries-book-4.**

**How about a little more of the Adele Gossling Mysteries, right here, right now? Read on for how to get hold of my free novella, *The Missing Ruby Necklace*.**

*When a jewel and a girl go missing on New Year's Eve...*

Eleanor McCarthy, a lovely though somewhat flighty debutante, has graced the tiny town of Arrojo, California, with her presence. One of Arrojo's prominent ladies throws a New Year's Eve shindig to introduce her to Arrojo's high society — whatever little of it there is. Naturally, the daughter and son of one of San

Francisco's influential lawyers, Adele and Jackson Gossling, are invited.

But screams replace popping champagne corks when Eleanor's priceless ruby necklace is discovered missing. And soon, so is Eleanor!

In this historical cozy mystery set in the early 20th century, follow Adele Gossling, stationary store owner and amateur sleuth, and her clairvoyant sidekick Nin Branch as they search for a ruby necklace that may or may not have been stolen and a young woman who may or may not have run away.

Want to read an excerpt from this book? I got you covered! Turn the page.

"Coffee!" Miss McCarthy laughed. "Heavens, no! I haven't had my first taste of champagne yet." She flung her hand out to her brother. "Bring me a bottle of champagne, my good man."

"I don't mind," he said.

Before he could saunter out the door, Mrs. Abberton jumped up. "I'll get it."

"I really think we ought to get coffee," Mr. Abberton mumbled.

"She wants champagne," Mrs. Abberton was almost stern. "It's a celebration, after all!" She practically fled from the room.

Adele followed her and caught her arm. She spoke in a soft tone. "Mrs. Abberton, why did Miss McCarthy faint?"

"She just told you, didn't she?" The woman gave a shrill laugh. "Albert said we ought to open some windows, but it was such a windy night, I —"

"It wasn't the windows," said Adele. "Or the corset."

"Of course it was!" The woman examined some bottles on the floor. "I never could read these labels."

"You were staring at Miss McCarthy as if something that wasn't there."

"What an imagination you have, dear." The woman said.

"Miss McCarthy had her hands on her throat when she fell," Adele continued. "You kept looking at her throat."

"Nonsense," the woman hissed.

"Miss McCarthy wasn't wearing her ruby necklace," Adele declared.

Mrs. Abberton tore through a row of bottles lying on a table. One rolled onto the floor with a crack and the bubbly drink spilled across the marble. She sunk into one of the chairs. "You're too observant, Miss Gossling."

"You saw it too."

"Just before the lights went out," she said. "But Eleanor is one of those girls who gets easily flustered with her jewelry. She says it weighs her down."

"If that's true, why were you so alarmed just now?" Adele said.

"I wasn't," the woman insisted. "She locks that necklace in a box. Albert tried to persuade her to put it in our safe at the finance company, but she refused."

"That's rather unusual," Adele said.

"Eleanor's a lovely girl, but rather flighty," The woman said in a harsh tone. "I expect Celestine spoils her."

"If the necklace is missing, there might be a theft involved," Adele suggested.


**Jewelry goes missing all the time. But does that mean theft? And why is Mrs. Abberton so nervous?**

**How can you get your hands on a copy of *The Missing Ruby Necklace*, not available in any bookstore? Simple. Go to this link:       https://landing.mailerlite.com/webforms/landing/ l2u0c3. What else will you get when you get this novella? How about fun facts about women in history and true crime classic mysteries, which are just as fascinating, if not more so, as contemporary true crimes?**

# ABOUT THE AUTHOR

As soon as Tam May started her first novel at the age of fourteen, writing became her voice. She writes engaging, fun-to-solve cozy mysteries set in the past. Her mysteries empower readers with a sense of "justice is done" for women, both dead and alive. Her fiction is set in the San Francisco Bay Area because she adores sourdough bread, Ghirardelli chocolate, and San Francisco history.

Tam is the author of the Adele Gossling Mysteries which take place in the early 20th century and feature sassy suffragist and epistolary expert Adele Gossling whose talent for solving crimes doesn't sit well with her town's Victorian ideas about women's place in life.

Tam has also written historical fiction about women defying the emotional and psychological confinements of their era. Her post-World War II short story collection, *Lessons From My Mother's Life,* debuted at #1 in its category on Amazon, and the first book of her Gilded Age family saga, the Waxwood Series, *The Specter*, is in the top 20 in several categories and is available for free.

Although Tam left her heart in San Francisco, she lives in Texas because it's cheaper. When she's not writing, she's devouring everything classic (books, films, art, music) and concocting yummy vegetarian dishes in her kitchen.

**Tam May can be reached at:**
WEBSITE: http://tammayauthor.com/
EMAIL: tammay70@tammayauthor.com
FACEBOOK: https://www.facebook.com/tammayauthor
INSTAGRAM: https://www.instagram.com/tammayauthor/
PINTEREST: https://www.pinterest.com/tammayauthor/